PRAISE FOR

The Diagnosis of Love

"Maggie Leffler's is a fresh and welcome new voice. She's wise and funny, and *The Diagnosis of Love* went straight to my heart."
—Hilma Wolitzer, author of *The Doctor's Daughter* and *Summer Reading*

"This novel celebrates the support system that family and friends can offer in difficult times. Leffler . . . writes with warmth and confidence about new beginnings." —*Booklist*

"A young doctor learns the true meaning of 'physician, heal thyself' in Leffler's inspiring debut. . . . Leffler, a practicing physician, infuses Holly's spiritual search with liberal doses of humor, exquisite insight and rich details about the U.K. medical profession."
—*Publishers Weekly* (starred review)

"I loved this book and loved its voice. How often is one both charmed and intrigued on page one and ever onward? Maggie Leffler's writing accomplishes that thing I enjoy the most: lively storytelling that is in equal parts wryly witty and touching."
—Elinor Lipman, author of *My Latest Grievance, The Pursuit of Alice Thrift,* and *Then She Found Me*

"It is often rare to really have such a character spin an electric force on a reader but Maggie Leffler makes this idea tale so vivid and believable that one can almost experience the same sensations that Holly encounters. At times heartbreaking, and others filled with a touch of humor, *The Diagnosis of Love* . . . [is a] remarkable tale." —coffeetimeromance.com

"In *The Diagnosis of Love* we take a highly entertaining, hilarious journey alongside a young physician, Holly Campbell, as she faces her fear of life, love, and her mother's past. . . . A vividly written story that pulls you in from the first page and doesn't let go until the end."
—Doris Iarovici, M.D., author of *American Dreaming and Other Stories*

ALSO BY MAGGIE LEFFLER

The Diagnosis of Love

THE
Goodbye
Cousins

MAGGIE LEFFLER

BANTAM BOOKS

A Bantam Books Trade Paperback Original

Published in the United States by Bantam Books, an imprint of
The Random House Publishing Group, a division of Random House, Inc., New York.

BANTAM BOOKS and the rooster colophon are registered
trademarks of Random House, Inc.

Grateful acknowledgment is given for permission to reprint an excerpt of
W. D. Snodgrass's "Heart's Needle" from *Not for Specialists: New and Selected Poems*.
Copyright © 1959, 2006 by W. D. Snodgrass. Reprinted with permission
of the BOA Editions, Ltd., www.boaeditions.org.

Library of Congress Cataloging-in-Publication Data

Leffler, Maggie.
The goodbye cousins / Maggie Leffler.
p.   cm.
ISBN 978-0-385-34047-2
eBook ISBN 978-0-553-90661-5
1. Cousins—Fiction.   2. Family secrets—Fiction.   I. Title.
PS3612.E3497G66 2009
813'.6—dc22   2009009863

Printed in the United States of America

www.bantamdell.com

BVG 9 8 7 6 5 4 3 2

Book design: Ginger Legato

For my father,
DR. ALLAN T. LEFFLER II,
a true, gentle man.
We miss you here.

Failing to fetch me at first keep encouraged,
Missing me one place search another,
I stop somewhere waiting for you.

—WALT WHITMAN, *Song of Myself*

Prologue

or

SEVEN MISCONCEPTIONS YOUR BIOLOGICAL FATHER MAY HAVE HAD ABOUT ME

1. That I remember the day we met. It happened in Amsterdam, at a coffee shop, when I waited on his table. Somewhere between the biscotti and the check, I complained that I needed a new bicycle since my beloved Schwinn, with its heart-shaped seat and handlebar bells, had been stolen that morning. I have no recollection of this conversation and was totally shocked when, a few days later, this complete stranger (your biological father, who, by the way, was only five feet seven inches tall, a good five inches shorter than your mother) showed up wheeling an old, rusty clunker of a bike, intended for me. I still didn't see it as a romantic gesture, just one of those "random acts of kindness" things you read about in magazines.

2. That I was Jewish. During this first encounter, your Biological Father (your B.F.) asked me if I was "Spanish or Jewish or what?" I can only assume it was because of

my dark eyes and hair. I picked Jewish, because I didn't speak any Spanish and because I was so used to lying about where I came from that the answers just sort of tumbled out of me. At the age of twenty-five, it wasn't as if I really had to worry that someone would report me to the Dutch authorities. By then we had been missing for fourteen years. Mom and I were old news. (Incidentally, on my side alone you are a quarter Italian, a quarter Irish, and half German.)

3. That my father died of _____ when I was _____ years old. Though this came up in a later conversation, it's hard to remember exactly what I told him. Usually, I said *lung cancer* and *nine,* although sometimes, just to mix it up, I said *cerebral aneurysm* and *fifteen,* because it thrilled me to think of knowing my father until I was in high school. In actuality, at the point that your B.F. and I knew each other, my father was very much alive, in Philadelphia, with his new wife and family. I called him, just once, from Eragny-Oise, France, the day we were leaving town. My father sounded relieved that we were alive and well and equally relieved to tell me that his new wife had had a baby. He seemed so complete that I never called again. And just so you know, he was a pediatrician, not an elementary-school music teacher— and my mother was not a homeroom teacher at the same school, so that wasn't how they met. Mom was an internationally ranked psychic. They met at a mutual friend's murder party, where everyone was supposed to bring a weapon. My father brought his pocketknife, which he always carried with him. My mother brought a guitar string, D for death. She didn't play the guitar.

4. That I grew up in Philadelphia, Pennsylvania. I picked Philadelphia because it's five hours away from my real hometown, and because it happened to be the place my

father settled after my parents divorced. Also, I knew the city landscape (tall buildings, a winding river, and a starless sky), since I'd been there once, briefly, when I was a little girl. In actuality, my formative years were spent in Pittsburgh, the same town that I am slated to be buried in, but you already know that if you are reading this. Incidentally, there's a space in the family plot for you, too. But you'll have many years before you have to worry about that.

5. That I wasn't smart. Granted, I never got a high school diploma or a college degree, but I was homeschooled from the age of eleven on, since your grandmother moved me around so frequently. I did attend a few English-speaking schools from time to time—like in England, of course, and in Ireland—but it's hard to make friends without a past. Most of what I know, I taught myself, which includes a little bit of Dutch, a little bit of German, psychology (Erik Erikson is my favorite), philosophy, aesthetics, sign language, massage, French and Italian cuisine, and everything about the Torah and Jewish customs. The latter backfired when it turned out your B.F.'s Father (your B.G.F.) was anti-Semitic and forbade his son to ever see me again. It was no use saying after the fact that I was Spanish.

6. That I drove him away by being so in love with him, when he was too young to really know what love meant. These are the words he used when we broke up after dating for three months. As is probably becoming clear to you now, most of what I told your B.F. were lies or, if I'm being kind to myself, truths spoken in code. We didn't know each other, or at least, he didn't really know me. I never mentioned what I dreamt about (seeing my father again), or what I cared about (having a family again), and we certainly said nothing about love.

7. That we were too young to have a baby. I was twenty-five, and he was twenty-three. "Old enough to use protection," as my mother muttered, when she heard the news of my pregnancy in the same breath as that of our breakup. Deep down, I think I just wanted you, and nothing else really mattered.

These are the truths that you should know if I'm not around to tell them myself. As you can see in my *Last Will and Testament*, I've decided to name my friend Holly as your new guardian. She loves you, and you love her, and so far, she hasn't been able to have children. But you should know your biological father is out there, probably still living in the Netherlands, if you ever want to find him. If you're wondering why I didn't leave you to my cousin Alecia, it's because Alecia happens to hate children—all children, not you in particular, so try not to take it personally. The important part to remember, even if things have been hard since we came back to the States, is that your life has not been short on love, kiddo.

Which brings me to why we came back. I might as well address it here, since I'm sure Alecia, in the midst of planning her wedding, may not have understood. It was not just because she asked me to be a bridesmaid, although I did want to be here for that, and it was not just because of a Barbie doll, though that was sort of a sign, as was my dream about Uncle Frank—or rather, Uncle Frank's toes. But the real sign came when my elementary school teacher found me—the one I'd had for sixth grade back in Pittsburgh. She said that she couldn't forget me, since I was kidnapped the year she was my teacher, and for sixteen years she'd been waiting for me to pop up on the Internet. To Miss Otlin (now Mrs. Hamm), Di Linzer had never become Old News. When I finally did emerge (on the "Our Staff" page of Wellington Spa in

London, England), she just "had to" e-mail me, to make sure I was okay. I replied a little more enthusiastically than I felt that day, as I'd just been fired (long story), but I promised that pictures of you, the one accomplishment I had to show for my years away, would be forthcoming. Almost immediately, she wrote again just to say that she wished she had kept my vocabulary word journal I'd turned in the year of my disappearance, but she'd handed it over to the police. "They were beautiful entries," she wrote, that showed me to be a "very sensitive young girl who was wise beyond her years." It all came back to me, then. Not just that there was a time in my life when I had two parents who seemed to be bursting with love, if not for each other, then certainly for me. But that there was a time in my life when I said too much, and all of it was the truth. That's how I knew it was time to go home.

CHAPTER I

The Beginning of the End of Me

I should probably back up and explain what made me compose the *Seven Misconceptions* in the first place, along with my *Last Will and Testament*. The short answer is easy enough: I wrote them down when I was afraid that my death was a heck of a lot closer than "someday," that the time frame which constituted The Rest of My Life was less an era and more an instant. I am still not sure if this conviction came from the physical symptoms occurring at the time, or the fresh realization that both of my parents were dead and, logically, I must be next. Every time I imagined leaving my son, Max, just two years old, I began committing all that I could remember to paper. And once I started, I realized that I also had to explain what was going on with my cousin, Alecia. Not just because, outside of my mother, she knew me best, but also because, when Max and I came from England to crash at her apartment for the two months before her wedding, everything changed for her as well. "The Beginning of the End—of Me!" she has since joked.

And so, if I am going to backtrack, I may as well start one humid day, early August, when Alecia and her fiancé, Ben, picked us up at the Pittsburgh airport. After ten hours of traveling, Max was in remarkably good spirits: high-fiving the flight attendants on the way out of the plane and, despite that he hadn't seen them in over a year, gleefully kicking his legs in his stroller at the sight of my cousin and her mate. When Max asked, "We in Pittsburgh?" Ben staggered backward a few steps, as if blown away that my son could actually speak.

In baggage claim, after my fourth suitcase had been retrieved, Ben joked, "Jesus, are you guys moving in?" and I glanced up from my carpetbag, elbow deep, just in time to catch Alecia's brown eyes flashing with panic that may have been mirroring my own. It seemed far too early to have to explain. Still rooting around in my oversized purse, I mumbled, "Housewarming gift's here somewhere" and wished I could dazzle them by producing a full-size floor lamp from the bag, à la Mary Poppins. Instead, my hands found the edge of a small box, which I offered with apology and high hopes.

"*A Ken doll?*" Alecia asked, after ripping off the paper rather unceremoniously.

"Outback Ken." I did my best to make my voice sound like Crocodile Dundee's: "He likes a bit of adventure, mate."

I'm still not sure why Alecia acted so utterly baffled when for years—actual adult years—of our lives we'd written letters as our Barbie doll alter egos.

"For Meg to marry," I said. "Remember?"

"If Meg isn't a doll, she's going to be a little disappointed in her mail-order groom." Ben laughed as he threw another suitcase onto our cart.

"Building a tower!" Max said and then clapped.

I explained to Ben how none of our Ken dolls were actually named Ken. They were Brian or Kevin or Lance or Derek. "And we could never find one good enough for Meg." Meg, of course, belonged to Alecia.

Ben nodded solemnly. "I'm pretty sure I saw all of them in the album."

"Oh, you kept it!" I turned to Alecia.

"Well, yeah, I kept it. But it's not like I've looked at it in years. I don't even know where my dolls went." Alecia glanced over her shoulder as if someone might recognize her.

"Am I remembering wrong? Meg is still single, right?" I asked.

"That's all about to change." Ben wrapped an arm around Alecia, who glared at him. But I laughed, even if I wasn't supposed to.

"Make tower higher?" Max asked, pointing at the suitcases.

"Oh, Boo. We're done. This is all we brought."

Ben glanced at Alecia, and then asked it again: "How long are you guys staying?"

"Indefinitely?" I asked and then watched as their smiles turned plastic, not unlike Outback Ken's eternal grin. "Just until I get on my feet," I added, never imagining just how long that would actually take.

HOLLY, BEN'S TWIN SISTER, happens to be a doctor and thus, often makes people rate their pain on a scale of one to ten. Even if you're just talking about a chore you have to get done or complaining of someone being a pain in the ass, she loves to quantify it in numbers.

So, I put Ben on the spot one day and made him rate the pain of Max and I moving in. It wasn't that I didn't care about Alecia's perception of things, but she had such an inflated sense of discomfort (the premarital counseling required by her church was often labeled a ten, the traffic on Route 28 a ten and a half) that I was certain we ranked well above natural childbirth. We'd been there for about a month, and yes, the timing of the question was a bit calculated, considering he'd just dipped a wooden spoon into my homemade Bolognese sauce for tasting. The way his eyes closed and his head swayed to the side could only be described as swooning. *Zero,* I thought. *Say zero.*

"Three," Ben finally said, opening his eyes. "At any given time. But it's tough because pain is a very fluid thing. Like, you being here right now? It's great."

Which meant that at other times, our presence must've reached at least a six, understandable, of course, in a cramped apartment such as this one, but a letdown all the same. Alecia would've pointed out that Max woke us up at seven o'clock on Saturday mornings, and how his Matchbox cars had tripped each one of us at least twice, and how he'd broken her favorite vase before it was even unwrapped. Still, it wouldn't have rocked me in quite the same way. After all, Alecia and I had the history of our entire childhood, not just sharing Barbie dolls, but everything else as well. As surrogate sisters, we were supposed to find each other's presence both completely exasperating and altogether comforting.

The disappointing part was that it was Ben calling us painful. Ben who loved my cooking, who'd called me brilliant, or at least, said that my collages were. (I'd overheard him defending me one night, when Alecia was complaining about my habit of cannibalizing magazines for the purpose of art. "Just for once, I want to pick up a *People* and be able to read it without half of the words and advertisements missing!" she'd snapped.) It was possible I'd developed a crush on my soon-to-be cousin—the innocent kind of crush.

That day in the kitchen, as Ben went on about how his

pain was really a mere aggravation, not specific to Max or me per se, but toward any guest who might compromise his ritual of walking around naked at night, I realized for certain that my crush on him was most certainly not of the romantic variety. I didn't want to imagine him naked. Still, it was a confusing sort of affection.

Before sauce dripped all over the floor, I reached for the wooden spoon in his hand. "We're going to move out soon. I promise."

"Don't move. I mean, go when you're ready. But don't worry about me. I love having Max here. It's great practice for us. And thanks to you, I've gained five pounds," Ben added, patting his new gut. "You didn't ask me the pain of living with Alecia, which is also a very fluid thing. And I'm marrying her."

I still didn't ask, even if his eyes were goading me to. It seemed more than disloyal: I was suddenly worried he might change his mind about her. And just to make sure he didn't change his mind about me, I kept cooking.

"OH, MY GOD, DI. This pork is *amazing,*" Ben said a few days later, early September, when we were sitting around the dining room table. "What did you *do* to it?"

"I brined it in salt water with twenty cloves of garlic." I laughed when he groaned.

"Baby, do you see this?" Ben turned to Alecia. "You can cut it with a butter knife. Who can cut pork with a butter knife?"

"Great. We get it. The meat is juicy. Ra-ra," Alecia said, spearing a carrot.

"Ra-ra!" Max cheered, waving his fork.

"So, Di, where'd you apply today?" Alecia asked.

The question always made me feel as if I was starring in

one of those reality shows where people were constantly fired or voted off. Next Alecia would ask me to pack my bags and leave the apartment immediately.

"The Dressbarn." I gave Max another bite of garlic pork. "But I think they want someone with retail experience."

Alecia curled her lip. I knew she wouldn't be happy, considering she'd begged me to apply at Banana Republic so I could get her a discount. "Is that why you're dressed for the farm?" she asked, with a nod toward my tank top and overalls.

"I wore a skirt and blouse for the interview, if that's what you mean." Lucky for me, peasant tops had come back into style, and an even flimsier version of my own could actually be found at some of Alecia's favorite stores. "And I don't think their dresses are actually manufactured in a barn."

"You're never going to get a job with your hair in braids." When I flipped my head around to show her it was just a single, she added, "One braid or two, it doesn't matter! And when you pull your hair back, you can see your bald spot!"

It was a disconcerting fact: I seemed to be losing my hair that summer and, as of a few weeks before, had even acquired a small bald patch. I'd been falsely assuming that no one else could see it.

"You should try Home Depot," Ben said. "Do you realize how many Olympians work there?" He had told me one night, when Alecia was working late, that he was considering a job change himself. That year, he was teaching ninth grade English at a Catholic high school. Alecia liked to say his consolation was that it was an all-girl school, but this was far from true. While he may have enjoyed the occasional pleated skirt/saddle shoe fantasy involving his fiancée (again, details I didn't want to know), when faced with actual ninth grade girls, who often approached his desk crying because they'd been graded too harshly, or crying because they'd been made to answer questions aloud on material they hadn't read, or crying for reasons that just weren't readily apparent to him, Ben said he would've happily traded those emotional girls for a roomful of dumb jocks throwing paper airplanes and making their armpits fart.

"You know what you should be? A nanny-finder," Alecia said. When I looked at her curiously, Alecia explained how wealthy families were so desperate that they often hired services to find them a nanny. "We're talking a thousand bucks in cash, just for the placement."

"One thousand dollars?" I repeated. Even Max must've known by the way I stopped trying to force-feed him peas that one thousand dollars would change everything.

"How do you know this?" Ben asked, laughing.

"Everyone at work is pregnant! Everyone's talking about child care." Alecia rolled her eyes. "Mazy Roberts was just asking me today if I know any nanny-finders."

"Hey, there she is!" I pointed at the TV set across the room, which was tuned to Alecia's station: a promo for the evening news team. First, there were images of the anchors Vanessa Phelps and Mazy Roberts giving cheesy smiles, and then it cut to a car going up in a ball of fire and a building collapsing, also engulfed in flames. *Because you want to know what happened today.*

"Something's missing," Ben said, rubbing his chin. "Maybe a picture of two nuclear warheads detonating?"

Alecia slapped his shoulder without taking her eyes off the screen. "Pretty soon, her job will be mine." She pointed to Vanessa Phelps. "She's already gained, like, twenty pounds and most of it has gone right to her ass."

I decided not to mention that it was the one part hidden by the news desk. The camera angles did a good job of concealing the anchorwoman's pregnant belly, too.

"She looks great to me," Ben said.

"So, what do you say, Di?" Alecia asked, as she grabbed the remote and shut off the TV. "A thousand bucks, and you won't even have to change one diaper."

I looked up from my plate, surprised. "I don't know any families. I don't know any nannies, either."

"With one phone call, I can hook you up with some desperate parents. And the rest is cake. You put an ad in the paper, and you've got a boatload of nannies to choose from."

I looked from my cousin, whose eyebrows made perfect arches, to Ben, who was nodding thoughtfully, as if it weren't a bad idea.

"Sure, it sounds great," I finally said, just to make them stop looking at me. "Sign me up."

CHAPTER 2

Near Blind

But I didn't really have serious intentions of becoming a nanny-finder, which was why, a day later, I ended up at Pottery Barn filling out a job application. (For whatever reason, the concept of mingling ceramics and a barn was more palatable to Alecia.) I'd just gotten to the part on the form that asked about retail experience, when the words suddenly wavered in front of me. I blinked, and the letters grew sharp again, except for everything to my left, which seemed to be missing.

"Is there something in my eye?" I asked, waving a hand out in front of me. "I can't see...."

"One moment, please," the clerk at the register said, before explaining to one of the customers that only the oven mitts with Christmas trees and gingerbread men on them were fifty percent off.

I opened and closed my left hand, which was beginning to feel numb. "I can't see anything out of my left eye."

"Did you lose a contact, hon?" an older woman asked from the checkout line.

"I don't wear contacts," I said, still looking down at my hand, which appeared to be moving normally, even if it felt dead. "Everything just went black in my left eye. And my hand feels funny."

Someone mentioned the word *stroke,* which seemed terribly wrong to me, considering I was only twenty-eight years old. I thought of Max, at his day care center probably stacking blocks or coloring, completely oblivious to the fact that his mother would die. Who was going to raise him? Would he remember me?

The sales clerk picked up a walkie-talkie. "Jill, we have a problem at the register. And we need a set of holiday oven mitts right away."

I felt myself being directed into a nearby cushioned deck chair positioned under a yellow beach umbrella. For whatever reason, people seemed to want to see me put my feet up. As I obediently reclined, someone handed me a rose-colored plastic champagne glass and insisted that I choke down water that tasted like the Allegheny River. Thankfully, the older woman had the sense to dig up an aspirin from the bottom of her leather purse, "just in case you're having a stroke."

The manager arrived, a stocky woman who reminded me of my sixth grade gym teacher. I'd once demonstrated to my only friend how all you needed to do was hyperventilate and, *voilà,* I was on the floor of the basketball court. Now, just like Miss Stevens did with her whistle, the manager swung her keys in circles and held up two fingers for me to identify.

"Two," I said.

"You're going to be just fine," she said confidently. *My right eye still works,* I wanted to protest, but the manager was already patting my leg and reassuring me that the paramedics would be there shortly.

"Oh no!" I said, lurching forward to jump off the chaise longue. "Really, that's not necessary." I could barely afford to send Max to day care. Paying for an ambulance was completely out of the question. As I bumped into a table set for a pool party, rose-colored plastic glasses clattered everywhere.

"Ma'am, please—they're already on their way!"

"You better stay and get checked out," the old lady added. "You could die!"

Bursting from the store, I managed to focus my one good eye in both directions. On the corner of Walnut Street, an ambulance turned, sirens blaring. *For me!* I realized with horror stepping off the curb. Startled by the horn of a Jaguar, I apologized with a wave of my dead hand and then broke into a sprint, running as if I really was the interloper that I'd been feeling like since returning to the States—the interloper I'd been feeling like for most of my life.

NOW WOULD PROBABLY BE a good time to elaborate on a few details that I left out of the *Seven Misconceptions,* details of my life just before Miss Otlin contacted me and I decided to fly back home, or at least, toward some vague conception of home. I had been renting the same flat on the north side of London that my mother, Roxanne, had died in, a once cozy apartment that had become too quiet, too dark, and musty since her ashes were scattered at sea, and Alecia and Ben, who'd come looking for me a few months earlier, had left to go back to the States. I had read somewhere that one shouldn't make any major changes for a year after the death of a loved one, so I waited out my sentence, plus a few months more, just hoping that inspiration would strike me.

Philadelphia came to mind, the city where my father's widow, Christine, and his daughter, Sophie—the half-sister I'd never met—were currently living. But it seemed too risky to count on them, when my mother had always told me that Christine was never anxious to be my stepmother in the first place. After my parents' divorce, my father had wanted me to live with him in Philly, but Christine wanted to send me to the Grier School, a boarding school in central Pennsylvania that she herself had attended. Dad won, and I was enrolled in Central Catholic instead, or at least, I would've been, if Mom hadn't kidnapped me first.

Briefly, I entertained the notion of moving to Miami, the place my former schoolteacher, Miss Otlin, now lived, but was dissuaded both by the heat and by the hurricanes. It was not enough of a clue that my only friends happened to reside in Pittsburgh. I am, of course, my mother's daughter, and thus, when figuring out where to go, I preferred to pay attention to more cosmic signs.

First, there was that prescient dream about my uncle Frank, Alecia's father, where I knew all of his thoughts intimately and, moreover, I knew he was dead because we both kept looking down at his toes, whose biggest nails had matching cracks right down the bluish center. (When I asked Alecia if she could verify the perplexing cracks in her very-much-alive father's toenails, she snapped that she found feet, all feet, even the ones with recent pedicures, completely revolting. *Discussion over.*) It was clear to me, though, that the Uncle Frank in the dream was disappointed, and not just because he had left so much unfinished business behind. His melancholy ran much deeper, and I knew, upon waking, that I had to warn him, but of what in particular I wasn't sure.

The second "sort of a sign" occurred when I was perusing the stock at Hamleys of London and found the Outback Ken. On a whim, I had wandered into the high-end toy store— past the stuffed animal sections, past the computer games department—and made a beeline for the Barbie dolls, the same way Alecia and I always did as children.

I had been thinking a lot about my cousin, and not the Alecia who was a news reporter and on the verge of getting married, but the Alecia who I had grown up with, the one who taught me all sorts of random things, like how to French kiss, and how to sneak out the bedroom window—along with information that, at five years her junior, I found much more pertinent to my life, such as the purpose of chewing gum when you don't even swallow it. ("Sometimes it just feels good to gnash your teeth.")

Browsing the doll section that day in Hamleys, I found a soft-bodied Bedtime Barbie (as if Barbie were meant to be a cuddle toy—*please!*). There was a Dutch Barbie, and English Barbie...and the nice-looking couple from the Outback. The Ken had blond hair, but Meg would get over it. So, I purchased the last missing doll in our cast of characters and wondered what it meant.

Two weeks later, I found out. After one of my massage clients brought a doctor's note certifying that his patient was suffering from cervical neck strain, most likely brought on by me and my ice-cold hands (truly absurd, when he came *in* with neck pain), I was let go without finishing the day. It was the same morning that Miss Otlin miraculously tracked me down—the Real Sign that things were about to change.

WITHIN TEN MINUTES, IT slowly came back, pins and needles of light in my left eye, so that at the beginning of Ellsworth Avenue, the parked cars looked as if they'd been painted on a canvas, but the farther down the block I ran, they appeared to take on their true shape in space. By the time I reached Holly's town house on Negley, my sight was restored, and when I reached out to press on the buzzer with my left hand, I felt the plastic beneath my fingertip. Still, my heart was slow to catch on. Even after I was sitting inside, telling her my story, my heart kept pace for a sprint.

Holly was my friend before I'd ever met her twin brother, Ben, and I owed our friendship to Alecia, who'd shown up on my mother's doorstep with Holly in tow. She'd been living abroad that year, practicing medicine and meeting her British husband, and happened to be the first person I'd ever met who, without actually being a relation, somehow compelled me to be honest. Holly was also notoriously calm in a crisis.

"Most likely it was an ocular migraine," she said when I finished speaking, and my shoulders instantly relaxed. "But you should go to the ER to be sure," she added. "They can't turn you away."

"But I feel fine now," I said, sitting on the bed, watching her pack. I'd been surprised to find her at home on a Friday afternoon, but it turned out she and her husband, Matthew, were leaving for London the next evening. *Matthew's mom fell again—Alecia's going to kill me,* Holly had explained all in one breath when she opened the door. There was something wrong about linking the two statements, but I knew what she meant. It wouldn't matter that Alecia's wedding was three weeks away; she would panic that Holly wouldn't make it back in time to be a bridesmaid.

"How could it have been a migraine if I never got a headache?" I asked, running my fingers over the books stacked on her night table. I loved that about Holly's place: every inch of the walls, every table, was covered in books. It was like visiting a library with comfortable furniture. Unlike Alecia and Ben, who preferred sofas with metal edges and silver feet, coffee tables that were glass, and lights with swiveling metal necks that reminded me of miniature robots.

"A small percentage of migraine sufferers never actually get the headache." Holly folded another sweater for the suitcase. "But they get all the symptoms of a TIA—a mini-stroke."

"How do we know I didn't just have a mini-stroke?"

"Well . . ." Holly hesitated. "We don't. That's why I think you should go to the ER." She picked up a toiletries bag and moved toward the master bathroom. I heard the swipe of the shower curtain, the rattle of bottles, and then she was back.

"Is there anything else it could've been?" I asked, moving toward the bookcase. One of the books caught my eye: *To the Lighthouse*. Ben had told me recently that Virginia Woolf's novel had inspired him to start a magazine—about faith. "One of the characters, Mr. Ramsey, talks about trying to get to the end of the alphabet of good thought," he said. "And I loved that. I decided I probably only live somewhere around the letter H, and that I'm probably stuck here because I just don't keep the faith—any faith. Although, if I did ever make it to Z, I'm sure I'd have to experience instantaneous death. Like what's-his-name in the Bible. Elijah. I bet he made it to Z."

I loved Ben's earnest idealism, loved that even his dreams sounded far-off and wistful; my goals were basic: get a job, get my own place—and if I were stuck at a letter it would probably be C for crisis.

Holly still hadn't spoken. "Maybe I have a brain tumor?" I suggested, turning away from the bookshelf.

"Sure. Or it could be MS. But I think it was an ocular migraine." Holly sounded almost annoyed, and I knew it was just because she didn't want anything to be wrong. "What about your family history?" she added.

I blinked. My life as part of a family seemed like very distant history, and I couldn't imagine how that might be important to me now. A childhood moment came to mind: a long car trip to the Jersey shore. After traveling for hours, my parents pulled over on the side of the highway to switch places in the car, so whichever one was driving could get a chance to sleep. From the brief moment that their doors slammed to the time that they climbed back in, I woke up, terrified that they were leaving me alone, in the dark, to fend for myself. Then both doors opened again, and Dad and Mom settled into the right places, along with my world.

"I mean, any family history of migraine?" Holly asked.

"My mother never got headaches...or random attacks of blindness." When she didn't answer right away, I asked, "So, what do I do now?"

"Start taking an aspirin every day. Promise me that if this happens again, you'll go to the ER. They have to take care of you, insurance or not."

"I promise." I glanced back at Holly. "So, could this have anything to do with why my hair keeps falling out?"

"That's just stress." Holly's voice was confident as she zipped her suitcase shut.

"Can one go completely bald from stress?" I asked.

Holly opened her mouth to speak and then hesitated.

"Because I'd rather just go gray," I added, and she laughed.

CHAPTER 3

The Fitting

I didn't tell Alecia what had happened, which was probably my first mistake. If I'd really thought about it, maybe she could've called Uncle Frank and borrowed some money on my behalf, maybe I could've gotten health insurance right away and taken care of whatever was on the verge of exploding inside me. Instead, after picking up Max from day care and heading back to the apartment, I roasted garlic for bruschetta, steamed the asparagus, and whipped up a honey soy glaze for two pounds of salmon. I've always been good with denial. After all, it's just another form of lying.

The next day, however, I had to face Walnut Street once again, when Max and I met Holly and Alecia at the wedding boutique just a few blocks down from Pottery Barn. Our bridesmaids' dresses were finally in, or—as Alecia wouldn't stop calling them—*the costumes*.

"What happened to wearing whatever you want?" Holly

asked grimly, after I zipped up the side of her red taffeta sheath.

"There are certain things my father likes to see at a wedding," Alecia replied. "Like a group of women all wearing the same dress." At the sight of Holly's scowl, Alecia added, "Deal with it!"

"Hold still, please," said the woman with pins coming out of her mouth, as I leaned over to hand Max his sippy cup. So far, we'd been reprimanded twice by the gray-haired spinster-seamstress, who told us not to touch anything—not the bodice, not the skirts, not the hems of our dresses—because of the oils on our hands. *"Oils?"* Alecia had repeated, insulted.

"I guess I never imagined you'd pick red." Holly sighed, touching her hair that was just an orangey shade of the same color.

I'd never imagined it, either, but the dress did make me feel glamorous. Earlier Alecia had said, "See how good you can look, Di, when your clothes actually fit you?"

"Well, I really wanted black, but Daddy wouldn't let me. Besides, it's *crimson*."

"How is Uncle Frank feeling these days?" I asked.

"Fine. Absolutely fine." Alecia's eyes darted around until they settled on her own frock, which was hanging in plastic on the outside of a fitting room. "He just had a stress test. His heart is perfect."

"Why did his doctor order a stress test?" Holly asked, her eyebrows furrowing. "Was he having chest pain?"

"Of course not! He feels great! Can everyone just stop obsessing about his toes for ten minutes? *Max!*" she yelped, when he accidentally knocked over a stack of shoeboxes in the corner. "Our shoes are in!" she suddenly trilled a moment later, holding up a pair of crimson pumps that reminded me of Dorothy's red heels in *The Wizard of Oz*.

"Shoes," I said, my voice flat. "Alecia, this is getting awfully expensive..."

She shook her head, still admiring the shoes. "Not to worry—I got you a gig!"

"A gig?" I repeated, smiling uncertainly. "What exactly will I be performing?"

She dropped the pumps carelessly back into a box and opened up her fingers in the air, like twin fireworks. *"Family First."*

I blinked. "I don't get it."

"I passed your name around at work, and Mazy Roberts wants to set up an interview. She is *desperate*"—Alecia clasped her hands together mock-dramatically—"for someone to find her a good nanny."

"Mazy Roberts?" Holly laughed with disbelief. "The anchorwoman?"

I stared at my cousin. "And you told her—"

"About Family First." She gave me a devilish grin. "Your company."

"You're crazy!"

"Ma'am, please! Hold still!" the seamstress barked.

"A thousand bucks, Di!" Alecia sang, as she reached for her dress. "You need a job. How hard could it be?"

"You'll need help with that!" the seamstress said, practically choking on her pins as Alecia hoisted her wedding dress over one arm and moved toward the fitting room.

"I can handle it," she snapped.

"I am done lying about who I am," I protested.

"No one said you had to lie. You just have to find her a nanny."

"Perhaps you'd like to wash your hands!" the seamstress called, still crouched at my hem.

"My hands are not oily, thank you very much. And *he's* the one who keeps touching your mirror," Alecia said, pointing at Max, who was now making his stuffed blue horse kiss his reflection.

"Come away from the mirror, Boo," I said. "Why don't you play with your Matchbox cars, instead?"

Holly turned and raised her brows at me. "So, Mazy Roberts wants you to find her a nanny," she said, marveling, as if we were talking about Gwyneth Paltrow.

It was a surprise to me, too: until that moment, I hadn't understood how badly Alecia must've wanted Max and me to move out.

Standing outside Alecia's stall, I could hear her grunting and swearing under her breath—it must've been harder than she imagined, climbing into a spaghetti strap, silk sheath by herself. Eventually Holly asked, "What do you want for your wedding?"

"Oh gosh, anything!" Alecia said, breathless, even though Ben and I watched her check the online registry nightly to see what had already been purchased. The apartment was becoming so crowded with presents sent in advance that they'd begun opening one each night. "People have sent the weirdest things—like one of my dad's friends sent us a slab of glass. Just a big slab. We have no idea what we're supposed to do with it."

"Maybe it's a window?" Holly suggested.

"I'm glad you didn't say some freak gave you an Outback Ken," I said.

"That was weird, too, Di. But the worst one came from my father's girlfriend, Becca. She sent me my mother's book of poems—first edition—and called it a gift!"

"Aunt Maddie wrote great poems," I said, in lieu of my usual line, which was "You should really invite your mother to the wedding."

Alecia snorted inside her dressing room stall. "And my dad really likes this Becca woman. They've been together three years. I think she might be the one—or at least, the third." More laughter, followed by the sudden, yet unmistakable, sound of ripping cloth.

The seamstress stiffened. "What was that?"

When she pulled back the fitting room curtain, Alecia's face looked sheepish. "Just my dress."

"Oh, my gosh, Alecia—you're beautiful!" I said.

"Alecia, you're the perfect bride." Holly moved to hug her.

"What's bride means?" Max asked, running toward us.

"It means Alecia gets to be a princess for a day," I said.

"Watch the tail!" Alecia bent down, swiping her arms, apparently trying to stop a stuffed-horse assault, and something ripped again.

"Stop moving! Keep your arms down at your sides!" the seamstress commanded. "I need to assess the damage."

Standing at attention, we stared at her in the mirror while the seamstress examined the back of the dress. Even Max was enthralled: He kept making his horse's tail wag over and over in her honor.

"Daddy's going to be blown away," Alecia said, absently touching her neck.

Holly and I locked eyes. Wasn't she going to mention Ben?

A middle-aged woman opened the door to the dressing area. "Oh, I'm sorry—I was looking for my daughter." She turned to leave, hesitated, and looked back. "You're not Alecia Axtel from Channel Four Action News, are you?"

"I am," Alecia said with a grin.

"Oh, my gosh—I have to find my daughter. We love *Taking Action for You!*"

They loved *Taking Action for You,* and Alecia loved being a celebrity. She didn't even do the *Taking Action* stints anymore but, of course, it didn't stop her from soaking up the attention. They'd given her job to Kate Frisbee when Alecia left for England for a year. Since her return, her boss, Art, had made her the six o'clock news reporter. These days Alecia got all the "Live" shots. And she often complained that Kate had made a mess of her new position. Now it wasn't about taking action; it was about informing the public that a particular pencil sharpener had been recalled for making pencils too sharp.

"You look so lovely!" the woman went on. "When's the wedding?"

"Three weeks," Alecia said, her cheeks glowing. "I would shake your hand, but I'm not allowed to lift my arms."

I lifted my own arms, just to try it out, and realized there was a price tag dangling from my side-zipper. I gasped.

"Oh, don't let me disturb you for another second! Enjoy this magical time!" the woman added in a singsong as she ducked out of the room.

Alecia immediately lost her smile. She turned and looked at me. My eyes were watering and I couldn't seem to stop swallowing.

"Di, are you all right?" Holly asked, and then said to Alecia: "She looks as if she just ingested pesticide."

"This dress is two hundred and fifty dollars," I said.

"That doesn't include alterations," the seamstress added.

"I told you—" Alecia started.

"No. You didn't." I shook my head. "I can't possibly be in your wedding."

Holly glanced at me and then back to Alecia. "Um, Alecia, Di might not be able to afford the dress, because she really has to save up for some health insurance."

"Health insurance? She can't be in my wedding because she's gotta buy *health insurance*?"

"What if she was in an emergency? She has Max to think about. He hasn't even been immunized—has he, Di?"

It was ironic, I know, that I hadn't immunized my son,

when my own father was a pediatrician who, after divorcing my free spirit mother, had gone on to marry a scientist who specialized in vaccine development. Or maybe it wasn't ironic at all. Maybe it was just rebellion. I glanced at Max, who was now crawling around under one of the dressing tables. "Well, it's just that I read something about vaccines giving you autism—"

"Therimasol has never been proven to cause autism. As for the MMR—"

"What the hell are we talking about here?" Alecia asked. "Vaccines? Autism? I'll pay for the dress, all right?"

"Are you sure?" I asked.

"Of course, I'm sure. I should've offered before." Half-smiling, she turned to Holly. "What about you? Should I pay for yours, too?"

"No, no. I got it. It's just…" Holly hesitated. "I found out last night that I have to go to England for a couple of weeks."

"England?"

"My mother-in-law fell and broke her wrist, and Matthew wants to help her move into an apartment. We're leaving tonight."

"You're *leaving*? Three weeks before our wedding? She's *always* falling! You don't even like her."

"I know, I know, and I would stay, but … Matthew needs me. And—I'm going to be ovulating next week. We kind of have to be together if we want anything to happen."

"That's your excuse? You're *ovulating*?"

"Please, stop thrashing!" the seamstress ordered.

"You can't wait until next month to get pregnant?" Alecia added.

"We've been trying for the last year! We're supposed to see the fertility specialist in November, and I keep hoping we'll be able to cancel the appointment. But, Alecia, I promise we'll make it back for your wedding. Okay?" Holly glanced at the seamstress before reaching out to touch Alecia. "Okay?" she added, giving her shoulder a squeeze.

Alecia looked at herself in the mirror. She must've decided that, even in Vera Wang, she looked unattractive when she grimaced, because she suddenly smiled. "Do me a favor— don't turn into one of those couples who start referring to each other as Mom and Dad even when the kids aren't around."

"I'd just be so happy if we were parents. Matthew could call me Mom for the rest of my life."

Alecia turned to me and rolled her eyes. Luckily, Holly didn't catch her in the mirror.

"CAN YOU BELIEVE HER?" Alecia said afterwards, as we pushed Max in his stroller toward the flower shop on South Aiken Avenue. Holly had left for the airport right after the fitting. "I mean, seriously. How thoughtless can you get?"

"She'll make it back."

"Well, she has to. Ben isn't going to want to get married without his twin by his side."

We were nearing an intersection when I halted. "Can we maybe not take Walnut? I kind of want to avoid running into anyone from Pottery Barn."

"I guess we can go up and over," Alecia decided, and we crossed the street.

"Ever think of going back to see your old house?" I asked. We were only a few blocks from the stone mansion that Alecia had grown up in, before Uncle Frank's business relocated them to New York. I'd loved sleepovers in my cousin's bedroom, with its twin French provincial beds, sprigs of Laura Ashley flowers on the wall, and matching pink carpet. But the rest of the house had a museum-esque chill. Alecia must've felt it, too, because she always preferred to stay at my parents': a crumbling Victorian ten minutes away in Highland Park that my father was perpetually restoring himself.

"I went." She shrugged. "It looks exactly the same."

Unlike my parents' house which was now, according to Alecia, a personal care home for the elderly. My mother, I knew, would've gotten a kick out of the current residents, old enough to be ghosts. Early on, she'd pronounced the place "deliciously haunted," an asset to her that equaled the wainscoting in the living room.

"Has Ben seen where you grew up?" I asked.

"Oh, God, no." Her answer shouldn't have surprised me: Alecia preferred not to dwell on the past for fear she might remember it.

"What does he say about inviting your mom to the wedding?" I asked.

"That it's my decision."

"My mom would've loved to watch you get married."

"Roxanne hated weddings."

"True," I admitted. *So many hopes just waiting to be dashed,* my mother used to say. "But yours would've been the exception."

Alecia laughed.

"There's hardly any of us left," I said, thinking of my parents, and Ben's mother, and our grandparents, all gone. "And Maddie's your *mother*."

Alecia groaned. "Stop reminding me, okay?"

We'd reached South Aiken Avenue, where a smattering of fallen leaves made little tornadoes in the wind. Max screamed with delight and shouted, "Mama, look!"

"I see, Boo! The leaves should be peaking just in time for your wedding," I added to Alecia, pushing his stroller up onto the sidewalk.

"Don't mention that to Ben," Alecia said. "He'll just get upset that we aren't having it outside."

When she'd suggested that they might get married at Hartwood Acres, a park with a mansion on the grounds to hold the reception, her father wouldn't hear of it. Uncle Frank wasn't going to drag all of his friends from New York to Pittsburgh for a "crappy wedding in a park," even if the tents alone would cost thousands. He claimed he wasn't against outdoor weddings, but he preferred vistas and great views, which should at least include cliffs with water crashing over them. If that weren't available, he'd settle for a church, but none of the newer ones. To my taste, Alecia had picked the perfect chapel: one with tall spires and Gothic buttresses—something right out of *The Sound of Music*. Alecia loved it, too, if it weren't for the premarital counseling they were required to attend. They'd been forced to become "members" just because they wanted to use the building. "As if it were a goddamn country club," she'd said.

"How's Pastor Nate doing?" I asked, half-joking, and Alecia let go of a sigh.

"The man sounds like he's got TB!" she sniped. "I'm serious—he's always hacking!" she added, when I shot her a look.

She rolled her eyes. "He wants us to take the Myers-Briggs personality *test*." She emphasized the word, as if it were yet another challenge to their compatibility.

She'd told me about their first painful visit with the minister, how she'd shown up fifteen minutes late, and he seemed to hold it against her; how he wouldn't stop coughing through the entire session—she was certain he was contagious even though he blamed it on his blood pressure pill—and how he'd asked questions about their shared past, their family histories, and their future plans—"prying," Alecia called it. She'd decided early on not to give in on anything, while Ben seemed compelled to fill up the silence with everything short of his birth. He told the pastor about his idea for the magazine, which would feature poems and essays from people of all faiths, about faith—and doubt. He talked about how his parents and sister were all doctors, but he preferred to weave his way through career paths that so far had included film school student, TV news editor, seminary student, writer, and now, high school English teacher. And Ben talked about how happy his sister, Holly, and her husband, Matthew, were and what a "solid" relationship his parents had until his mother's death.

Finally, Pastor Nate focused his gaze on Alecia, who tapped her feet and stammered that her parents were also happily married...up until her mother's nervous breakdown. "But my dad has been happily married since."

"Your dad has been happily married many times," Ben said.

"You know you're still allowed to get married, even if you didn't have the best role models," Pastor Nate told them. "And how do you both feel about getting married in a church? Is it just a place to have a wedding?"

They glanced at each other sheepishly.

"Lately, yes," Ben said.

"This is really an amazing...structure," Alecia said, looking up at the flaking paint of the ceiling as if it were an Italian fresco. "We just love the architecture."

"I think a wedding in a church is a good place to start the rest of our lives from," Ben said. "I've...kind of gotten away from it all. Organized religion. But I want to get back. I've probably been waiting to be Called back. And that hasn't happened yet."

"Ben, I think everyone would like to be personally invited

by God. But sometimes you have to just show up," Pastor Nate said wryly.

I had laughed. I, like Ben, tended to pursue God the way I pursued jobs—in fits and starts and without much success, which was probably why I ended up relying on my sixth sense to tell me what to do.

We were finally nearing the flower shop, when Alecia asked suspiciously, "What happened at Pottery Barn, anyway? When you went to apply?"

"Oh, there was just, this...little incident." I laughed. Alecia waited. "That involved me going blind."

"You went blind?"

"What's blinds means?" Max asked.

"In Pottery Barn. It was nothing." I waved my hand: *la-dee-da*. "I'm fine now. Blind is when you can't see, sweetie. That's right!" I added, when Max covered up his eyes with his hands. "Where's Max? Has anyone seen Max?"

"Does Holly know?" Alecia asked, and then her eyes widened. "That's why she wants you to get health insurance!"

"I'm *fine*. It wasn't a big deal. *There he is!*" I sang, and Max, no longer invisible, collapsed into giggles. "Hey, look!" I pointed behind him, to a doll in the window of a toy shop. The Ken had floppy brown hair and wore a bathing suit.

"Did Holly say you were fine?"

"*Yes.* Absolutely." I tapped on the window. "Look, his surfboard is included. Maybe Meg would like him."

Alecia stopped and stared, as if she might actually be considering it.

Here is what Alecia wouldn't admit about our Barbie dolls: that they were us, before we knew what we wanted to be. Meg was a reporter, and Jean was a mom, and they were best friends, even if Meg thought Jean was pathologically unambitious. "Should we buy him?" I asked, when we hadn't moved from our spot on the sidewalk.

Alecia blinked, as if coming to. "For who?"

"Meg! You didn't seem that excited about Outback Ken."

"Earth to Di: save your money for health insurance."

I shook my head as we started to walk again. "No one will ever be good enough for Meg, I suppose."

"That guy was too tan! Hasn't he heard of skin cancer? And what's with all that hair? It'll get wrapped around his surfboard."

"Meg was always such a snob."

BY THE TIME WE got to the flower shop, Max was asleep. As I struggled to get the stroller in through the front door, Alecia marched up to the counter and tapped the little bell over and over until someone appeared: a middle-aged woman who reeked of talcum powder.

"I understand there's a problem with the calla lilies?" Alecia demanded loudly. "Someone left a message on my machine."

"There's a shortage, I'm afraid, and I can't be certain they'll arrive before your wedding." The woman placed a flower catalog the size of a phone book on the counter between them. "Perhaps you'd like to select something else—something that's in season?" she suggested, opening the volume.

"I don't care what's 'in season'! I want what I paid for!"

I parked Max next to a potted plant and then rushed to join them. Thankfully, the store was otherwise empty.

"Apparently callas aren't in season." Alecia folded her arms across her chest.

"I heard." I pointed to one of the photos in the binder. "What about this 'mixed fall bouquet'? I like the berries."

"Very autumn, if we added some colorful leaves," the saleswoman added.

"Sure. Maybe we could add some sticks, too," Alecia said, her voice rising. "How about some squirrels to ride on my shoulder?"

The woman behind the counter just pursed her lips, adjusted her bifocals, and kept flipping the plastic pages in the book of flowers. "Perhaps a lovely cascade of white roses?"

Alecia leaned forward and raised an eyebrow. I knew that it wasn't the roses that had piqued her interest: it was the word *cascade*. Alecia was a sucker for marketing.

"Or what about hydrangeas?" I asked. "We could dye them red, to match the dresses."

"I have no idea what hydrangeas look like."

"Well, we have some pink ones right over there, if you'd like to check them out," the woman said, pointing to the front window.

"Yes, thank you, we will," I said, tugging on Alecia's arm and leading her away, as if to avoid a potential bar brawl. The front door to the store jangled, and another customer walked in: a gray-haired man in a pinstripe suit, a man just tall enough to catch my attention.

"These? You like these? They look like pink snowballs! Like . . . cotton candy! Di, think sophistication."

I watched as the customer strode across the room and then leaned against the counter. He seemed overly familiar with the saleslady. Either the man ordered flowers a lot, or he liked women, all women, even stout ones who wore glasses on chains around their necks and smelled like baby powder. When he turned around to point out something near us— probably not the hydrangeas, but possibly the lilies—I gasped and clutched Alecia's hand.

"Holy shit, I know him," I whispered.

She turned to look. "Mazy Roberts's husband?"

My eyebrows must've furrowed, because Alecia suddenly asked me if I was planning on having them waxed before the wedding. "Whose husband?" I asked.

"Mazy Roberts! That's her husband. Stop staring!" Alecia whispered.

We both turned around and looked at the bucket of flowers in the window.

"Does he know you?" I asked out of the corner of my mouth.

"We only met once at a company picnic. It was a while ago. He was really good at volleyball," she added, sounding perplexed, as if someone with gray hair shouldn't be good at anything but a wheelchair race.

"I think we met in a dream."

"Oh, no." Alecia groaned.

I knew that she didn't want to hear this, the same way she didn't want to hear about Uncle Frank's toes or that I saw our grandma Hazel's ghost standing in my bedroom when I was nine. And here's why: a part of her believed me.

"So, what's wrong with him?" she asked.

Channeling my mother, I squinted at him for a moment, trying to recall his dream-self, which was really more a montage— of blue sky, insanely green grass, a flutter of birds, and his face: eyes closed and looking peaceful. Finally I stood up straighter and took a guess. "It's his heart."

"Have you ever gotten a good premonition? Just once?" Alecia asked.

Apparently, Mr. Roberts liked his notes to arrive with his own handwriting. *Nice touch,* I thought, watching him compose the tiny card, seal the envelope, and slide it across the counter.

"We'll send them today," the saleswoman said with a sickly smile, and then he was walking toward us on his way to the exit.

"Ladies," he said with a nod and a smile, ambling around the stroller without even looking down. If the man had had a hat, he probably would've tipped it.

He must not have recognized Alecia as his wife's colleague. He was too sure of himself, too charismatic, not to mention hasty. When I glanced over at Alecia, she was staring at me.

"You're blushing," she said.

CHAPTER 4

Family First

A *thousand bucks, and you won't even have to change one diaper*, Alecia had promised me. It sounded too good to be true but, desperate to prove to Alecia that I was making every attempt to earn money and move out—and perhaps a tiny bit curious about Mazy Roberts's husband—I let myself be talked into it, which is how I ended up in the wealthy suburb of Fox Chapel on Wednesday afternoon, passing through the iron gates marked "Catalano." Luckily, the oak-tree-lined driveway was at least half a mile long, giving me time to rehearse my story.

I worked for Family First, a company which, according to Alecia, "understands the pressures on working parents to find an experienced nanny with good values." The slogan was Ben's idea, but he might've been joking: *Why waste time interviewing drug addicts, child molesters, and Internet predators when we can do that for you?* If I could pull it off, then maybe I could do other placements, and then maybe, once I could afford a website, I could do all the "intakes" over the Internet and wouldn't have to worry about day care for Max—wouldn't have to worry if I wanted to wear my hair in braids.

My thoughts skidded to a halt when a dog materialized and lunged for the front of Alecia's BMW. Startled, I swerved left into the grass and slammed on the brakes, stopping just short of a tree. Relaxing my grip on the steering wheel, I sat back in my seat with a nervous laugh, thinking of the last thing Alecia had said to me: *Don't get caught.* She hadn't meant caught in the sham of Family First. In a testament to how badly she wanted me out of her apartment, Alecia had loaned me her car, when I didn't even have a driver's license yet. And here I was, not even twenty minutes later, on the verge of animal manslaughter. Except that, out the window, the yellow Lab had never even left his side of the lawn. Instead, he panted and staggered in circles. I shook my head in commiseration. *Right there with you, buddy.*

It wasn't until I'd parked in front of the enormous white manor that I noticed the landscapers out front, digging a trench that led from the driveway up to the front door, where the sidewalk should've been. The way the two men held their shovels and stared into the mud, they appeared to be looking for gold.

In the rearview mirror, I applied a fresh coat of red lipstick, trying not to pay attention to the ridiculous red felt hat on my head. It was Alecia's idea—*Very House of Windsor,* she'd pronounced; I still wasn't sure where the hat had actually come from.

When I finished, the pair of landscapers on the front lawn were staring at me. The burly one leaned on a shovel and squinted, while the slender one held up a hand to shield the sun from his eyes. *It's now or never.* I opened the door to the BMW and, wobbling on borrowed heels, stepped into the Indian summer heat. I wished I hadn't worn panty hose,

Alecia's wool suit, or these torturous shoes. Navigating the chasm between the driveway and the front door was going to be a feat.

"What, you can't even apologize?" the redhead called out—the slight one, who, I noticed, also had bad acne.

"Excuse me?" I asked.

"Your car." He pointed. "Back there. You turfed up the lawn with your tires. Who do you think is gonna have to fix that?"

"It was either the lawn or the dog." Gingerly, I put a high heel onto the grass the way Jesus might have tested the water to see if it would hold him. The spike of my heel sunk into the soil, but I had no choice. The landscapers watched my unsteady progress across the lawn; their stares made me feel naked in this hip-hugging suit.

In preparation for her wedding, Alecia had exercised her way into a size 0, which to me was not really a size, except maybe in outerspace where one could be weightless. Insisting my clothes were "too gypsy-ish," she'd fished out one of her old size 4's and I'd stuffed myself into the skirt, holding it together with safety pins the way I had in the early months when I was pregnant with Max. The jacket seemed easy enough: I kept it open. But now I felt exposed: my blouse too thin, my bra too obvious.

"Hell-*o*," the heavyset guy said, after I wobbled past him.

"Next time, hit the dog," his buddy said.

These men were just a couple of jumpsuits shy of being convicts. I was glad I'd left holes in the lawn. Maybe they would get blamed.

I reached the front door and rang the doorbell before I could lose my nerve. In the pause that followed, I thought of Max, finger painting on the floor of the kitchen when I left, since the day care had closed due to a water leak. What if he wiped his hands on Alecia's flowered armchairs or touched one of the lamps? Alecia would kill him. Just the other night when Max shrieked and threw a piece of steak across the table, Alecia shook her head and said in a voice so full of disappointment, "You've changed, Max." How would Alecia handle one of his real tantrums? It was definitely a mistake to have left them alone together.

Before I could slip off the high heels and run, the door swung open. "Oh!" I said, startled. "I thought— I was looking for— Is this the Catalano-Roberts's residence?"

"Just Catalano, no hyphen. Come in. You must be Di," the blond woman said brusquely. I probably shouldn't have been surprised, considering Alecia had told me it was Mazy Roberts who needed the nanny, yet somehow I never expected this icon of Pittsburgh news to appear—without makeup and gray at her roots—quite so ordinary.

"I've heard such wonderful things about your service," Mazy said, her voice growing warmer as she led the way through a marble foyer with a crystal chandelier. I imagined parties in this room: ladies in swishy dresses, men in tuxedos, and ballroom dancing.

"Well, we do our best," I said.

Mazy cocked her head to the side. "I thought you'd be English. Alecia said you just moved here from England."

"Well, yes, my mother took me to live there when I was eleven." *Never use the word* kidnapped *in front of people looking for a nanny,* Alecia had instructed me. *And especially not with a smile. You always look like you're endorsing it.*

"Oh, how nice!" Mazy said.

We passed by one living room with an iron stove, dark wood, and lots of books, and kept walking into another living room, whose ceiling was two stories high and filled with light from each one of its thirty windows. Two flowered sofas took up most of the royal blue Persian rug, and at the far end of the room, the fireplace looked large enough to burn redwoods.

"Please have a seat. We'll wait here until Augustus is ready. Can I get you some tea?" Mazy asked.

I said yes to the tea, figuring that Mazy wasn't someone you said no to. I also knew that I better be sitting when she returned, but both sofas were covered in an avalanche of pillows that could easily suffocate a small child. I went to settle on the four-foot-long leather ottoman instead, but as soon as I bent at the waist, one of the pins holding my skirt together popped. As I was fumbling to get myself back together, I couldn't help overhearing two male voices conversing in the other room.

"I don't know what kind of business you're running here, Dave. When I hired you I thought this was a professional organization. I thought you had experience."

"We do—or I do…Sometimes it's hard when your crew—"

"Who hired the crew, Dave? Did I? Did I hire the crew? I don't think so. I think that was you, Dave."

Mopping my face on the sleeve of my jacket, I took a deep breath and exhaled. *I come highly recommended.*

"You came highly recommended, Dave."

"Look, this is something fixable. We can pack the walkway with extra crushed stone, and the water will fall away from the house."

"The stones are going to settle over time, Dave. Do I want a wet basement? Do I look like I want to put in a sump pump? I don't think so, Dave."

When Mazy reappeared carrying a tray with a pot of tea and chocolate digestive biscuits, I couldn't help feeling guilty for not being British. As she placed the tray on the ottoman, Mazy shot me a curious glance, and all at once I realized it was the wrong place to sit. After tossing aside a few pillows, Mazy sat down on one of the sofas, and I tried to gracefully get up and do the same, difficult in the skirt.

"So I gather most of your experience is abroad?" Mazy asked, once we were facing each other on opposite sofas.

"Yes, I . . . basically grew up there." I looked up to meet Mazy's brown eyes. Of course, she must've been waiting for something more, something about First Family (or was it Family First?) something about all the happy parents and nannies I had placed together like a dating service, but I couldn't think of anything to say. Thankfully, the swinging door to the right of the living room opened and two men walked in—one broad-shouldered and strikingly gray, in khaki shorts, sandals, and a white polo shirt; the other, tan and lanky and wearing dusty work boots. The three of us could've comprised The Tall Club.

Looking just a bit sheepish, the landscaper gave me a polite wave and clomped out the door. Meanwhile, the other man walked toward me with an outstretched hand. I stood up, startled to recognize him once again.

"Augustus Catalano," he introduced himself.

"Di Linzer. I guess we met."

"Have we?" he asked, raising an eyebrow.

"Not officially. I saw you in the flower shop last week." Even without the pinstripe suit, he had a handshake that could own the Western world. He let go of my hand, and I clenched it a few times, trying to get the blood to circulate again.

"Who were you buying flowers for?" Mazy asked from across the room.

Augustus kept his eyes on me. "What?"

"Who were you *buying flowers* for?"

"Harriet."

"I didn't realize Secretaries' Day was last week," she said.

He turned. "Sometimes it's just nice to say thank you."

So, he was a wife-cheater. *Lovely,* I thought.

"Now, Di, where did you come from?" Augustus asked, gazing at me again.

"Not England," Mazy said.

Apologetically, I explained, once again, that I'd only spent most of the last seventeen years there.

"From Pittsburgh originally?" Augustus asked.

"Yeah—I—grew up in Highland Park. And my father—he died here," I blurted. My cheeks suddenly felt warm: I'd meant to say that he lived here.

Augustus stopped in the middle of a nod. "Your father *died* here?"

"At the Exxon on the corner of Forbes and McKee in Oakland?" I said, trying desperately to modulate my tone into upbeat. It was always hard not to sound a little bit crazy when talking about my father's death. But I had thought about it a lot, about the pivotal choices we make in life, which are usually the very same ones that appear not to matter. Like where to buy gas, or a bottle of water, and at precisely what time. "He was a doctor, and he was supposed to give a talk at Pitt, and I guess he got thirsty on his way to the medical school, or maybe he was afraid his lips would get dry during the talk, but he stopped to buy a bottle of water, and apparently this suicidal guy went on a shooting rampage in the convenience store. My dad never made it out."

Of course, the more rapidly I spoke, the wider Augustus's blue eyes got. "I heard about that," he said. "That was recent, wasn't it?"

"Two years ago."

"Are you hearing this, Mazy?" Augustus asked.

But Mazy seemed distracted by something out the window, and I turned to see what she was staring at. In the yard, Dave appeared to be shoveling without an actual shovel and without actual dirt. Either he was miming to motivate his crew or simply making a teaching point.

"Didn't you do the story on that one, Mazy?" Augustus asked.

Mazy looked up. "On bottled water?"

"On the guy who went crazy at the gas station."

"Oh, yes." She appeared more interested in the show going on outside. But then a moment later she asked if I was related to Alecia, so she must've been listening after all.

"She's my cousin," I said.

"Well. That explains the hundred dollar application fee," Mazy muttered under her breath, finally turning away from the window.

"Why don't we come into the dining room? Okay, Mazy?" Augustus asked.

Apparently, the tea party was over. With Mazy in tow, I followed Augustus through the swinging door into the dining room, the same claustrophobic setting where Dave had been eviscerated minutes before. It was a dark room, with burgundy wainscoting and a long, dark cherry table flanked by built-in shelves full of decorative china on one side and yet another fireplace on the other. There was even a spotlight above a painting of a landscape.

Augustus gestured for me to take a seat at the head of the table, while he and Mazy pulled out chairs on the opposite sides. I felt like a boardroom executive, or a lawyer, until it occurred to me that I *forgot the clipboard*. My heart stalled and revved all at once, like a car engine riding the clutch. After patting my suit pockets, I looked frantically around my seat and under the table. I was Mary Poppins without the carpetbag, an ad executive without the slide show. *Get a grip,* I could hear Alecia saying in my head. *It's just a fucking clipboard.*

"Everything all right?" Augustus asked, bending down toward the floor, with one sandaled foot stretched toward me. "Lose a contact?"

"Oh!" I gasped, noticing his great toe, whose nail had a crack down the center like shattered glass. *Just like Uncle Frank's cadaver.* "Your . . ." I pointed lamely at his feet.

I heard Mazy's voice from somewhere above the table. "What's happening?"

"I know. Ugly as sin." Augustus sat back and lifted his leg, apparently showing me the uneven sole of his sandal. "Masai Barefoot Technology. Would you believe they cost me three hundred bucks? They're supposed to continuously exercise my quads." He laughed. "Don't worry. I don't wear them out in public."

I stared at his toes, which he was wiggling. Was it possible that the cadaver in my dream was actually Augustus Catalano, before we'd ever met? Why had I assumed the feet belonged to my uncle when I had no distinct memory of ever seeing him without his shoes on?

"What's *happening*?" Mazy asked again, her voice sharper.

"Mazy, relax."

Imagine someone normal and act like her! Alecia would say, snapping her fingers. "I'm so sorry." I straightened up again and shook my head. "Why don't we get started?"

I explained how the intake was essentially a four-page questionnaire designed to find them their ideal candidate. "But I left my clipboard in the car"—which could've been in the driveway or stolen for all I cared, because I sure as hell was not traipsing across the lawn again to find out—"so I'm just going to try to do this from memory." I paused, trying to come up with just one of the forty questions that Alecia and I had concocted this morning. "Okay, now, try to imagine your dream nanny. Who is she? We know she's out there, so don't hesitate to tell me all your goals and dreams."

Glancing at her husband, Mazy opened her mouth to speak.

"Hold that thought!" I said. "Could I just get something to write on? And maybe something to write with?"

It wasn't until Augustus returned with a yellow pad of Post-it notes and a pen that Mazy tried again. "Well…do you want to tell her or should I…?" she asked her husband.

Suddenly I felt like a small child, and these were my parents, who were about to tell me some very bad news. I should've known. Everything bad always happens at the dining room table. Like my parents telling me they were going to separate for a while, and possibly divorce. Like my father telling me that he was moving from Pittsburgh to Philadelphia to be closer to Christine, and that he was taking me with him. Like my mother telling me that she had cancer and was going to die. I was pretty sure that when Armageddon arrived it would somehow involve the dining room table.

"Mazy and I are getting a divorce," Augustus said.

"Oh, I'm sorry!" I said.

"Our son is having some problems with it."

"Adjustment disorder," Mazy said.

"We need someone who can handle him," Augustus said.

"Someone who can give him his medications."

I thought of having to give my mother the IV morphine at the end, to keep her calm when she couldn't breathe.

"My ideal nanny would be someone with a nursing background," Mazy said.

"Get real, Mazy. She's never going to find a nanny who is a nurse," Augustus said.

"She asked who my dream nanny would be!"

"What if they just have experience giving medications to loved ones?" I asked. Since Mazy was looking so blank, I added, "When my mom was dying, I gave her a lot of medications. And I'm not a nurse."

"How long was she sick?" Mazy asked.

"Gosh, not even a year," I said, picturing her jaundiced from liver cancer, lying in bed.

"Oh, that's still plenty of experience," Mazy said, sounding bright.

My eyebrows furrowed. "So your son is…" Flustered, I consulted my blank notepad. "Terminally ill?" I looked up again, just in time to see both parents' faces fall.

"Our son is diabetic," Augustus said, his voice stiff.

"Ah. Diabetes." I wrote that down. "So, I guess he's on insulin? Will he need someone to give it to him?"

"Well, he's been taught how to do it, but lately he's stopped giving it to himself. He's always in the ER—and twice the pediatric ICU," Augustus said.

"Seeking his father's attention," Mazy said.

"It's you he wants. He's a mama's boy."

"If he wanted my attention, why would he insist on staying with you?"

"Maybe he doesn't like what's-his-name," Augustus suggested and then added, "What is his name?"

I stared at the words *diabetes* and *give meds* on my notepad, remembering the times I had to hold Max down to get him to take his Amoxil when he had an ear infection. I couldn't even imagine having to hold him down every day to stick him with needles. My thoughts trailed off when one of the landscapers walked into the dining room wearing a green T-shirt and baggy shorts that made his legs look like sticks. *Kermit the Frog,* I thought.

"Who's this?" the kid asked, his blue eyes darting around the room.

"Where are your manners?" Mazy said, before turning to me. "This is our Gusty—Augustus the third." I should've known he wasn't one of the landscapers: his sandy blond hair was too clean, and he looked young, fourteen, if that. "Gusty, this is Diana."

"Diotima," I said.

"Diotima?" Augustus the senior said, looking at me with

intrigue now. "Not Plato's Diotima? The wise woman who taught Socrates what love means?"

I could feel my face heating up. No one ever knew the obscure reference. "That's the one." I smiled until I caught the look on Mazy's face: something more than anger. She was stricken. *Relax, lady. I'm going bald.*

To take the attention off myself, I consulted my Post-it notes again: *Insulin...Adjustment disorder...Doesn't like what's-his-name...* I looked up. "And how many children will be needing a nanny?"

"A nanny?" Gusty echoed.

"A caretaker, sweetheart. Did you take your medicine?" Mazy asked.

"You're a nanny?" Gusty asked.

"Oh, no no. I am just the person who finds the nanny," I said. "That's my business. I just find the nanny and get paid one time, in one lump sum, and that's that, and then you never see me again."

Gusty punched a fist at the wall, which made a bang out of proportion to any damage. The wallpaper was left intact. Still, he had enough power to make a picture fall with a loud clatter.

"Oh, my God!" Mazy said, jumping up from her chair. "Gusty, what's the matter with you?"

When Gusty didn't reply, Augustus just shook his head as his wife scrambled to collect the framed photograph off the floor. "I'm so sorry—he's not usually like this," Mazy said. "This is our other son, Jason," she added, holding up a black-and-white of a handsome young man. He looked very smart, unless that was just the thick-rimmed glasses. Despite Mazy's reverence, it seemed best not to ask if the other son was dead.

"So, I'm sorry, you were looking for part-time or full-time?"

"Full-time with sleepovers," both parents said in unison.

"I travel and his mother works very late. It's really what drove us apart," Augustus said.

"Sure, that's what drove us apart," Mazy said.

"And what's the pay? I mean, what should I tell the nanny?"

"Whatever it takes," Augustus said.

"Why are you doing this to me?" Gusty shouted before running out of the room.

After that, I capped my pen and collected my small pile of Post-its, telling Mazy and Augustus that I had all the information I needed, and that if I found any unanswered questions from the original intake form, I'd just call. "So who will be staying here?" I asked, and Mazy's pupils dilated in panic. "I mean, if I have questions, whom should I contact?" I quickly added. "And where?" Both parents replied by handing me business cards complete with cell, work, and fax numbers along with e-mail addresses.

After leading me back through the marble foyer, Mazy seemed to hesitate at the front door. "Alecia never mentioned that you were related, and no one from work even knows about Augustus and me...."

I felt sorry for this woman: for the dark circles under her eyes, for her failing marriage, and for the way she was pleading. I assured her that everything would be kept strictly confidential—it was Family First policy.

CHAPTER 5

The Telegram

"You might've warned me that I was supposed to be British," I said to Alecia later that night. Max was asleep and Ben was stuck at the high school for Back to School Night. (Miraculously, Alecia—and her furniture—had survived her first foray into babysitting.) We'd been watching *The Sound of Music,* pausing the movie just after the concert where the Von Trapp Family Singers never show up to take their bow. Alecia brought out two bowls of light ice cream and sat down beside me on the couch.

"I mentioned you were well traveled. I never said you had an *accent,*" Alecia replied. "If anything, Mazy's always struck me as a little xenophobic. So, give me *details,*" she added, as if we were in high school, talking about boys. It didn't occur to me until later that Alecia not only respected Mazy's influence at the station but looked up to her, as well.

"I forgot the clipboard." It seemed to sum everything up.

Alecia inhaled sharply. "Did they . . . ?"

"Suspect I was a fraud? Yes. Hire me? Yes. They were desperate."

She squealed and slapped me on the arm. "Why didn't you say so?"

"I don't know if I want the job." I took a mouthful of ice cream. "The son is a terror."

"You're not the nanny, remember?" Alecia said.

I thought of Mr. Catalano's toes again, and wondered what it had meant. Was I now obligated to warn him of something, and if so, of what exactly? Impending death and an eternity of melancholy over unresolved conflict? *Yeah, right.* "I'm not sure I would wish that family on any nanny," I said, picking up the remote to resume the movie.

"Oh, I hate the next part. Fast-forward?" she asked.

It was getting late, so I hit the button, and we watched as the characters silently flew through the climax: the nuns helping them escape from the Nazis, Liesl's ex-boyfriend Rolfe turning a gun on the captain. *Hello. Goodbye.* I wondered if it was true that the moment you died, everything you'd ever said and done would be presented to you in the fast-forward version of your life. But even that would take longer than a flash. Maybe it was more a sensory collage of voices, and colors, and everything you'd ever loved. "We're at the end," I realized. The von Trapps were hiking high in the Swiss Alps.

Alecia shrugged as the credits rolled. "It always disturbed me that they just left their beautiful house on the water and ran for the hills with the whole world after them."

"I loved that they were all together, though." *A mother and a father and their seven children.* It was a miracle, really, that one family unit could have survived intact. I looked at her. "Maybe you just hate it because Rolfe turned into such a weenie."

She sighed. "Yeah, maybe."

I knew she must've been thinking about Mom and me. She'd told me before that our disappearance classified as "the biggest fucking letdown of my life," though, from the way she told it, I was never really sure if it was because we were gone or because we'd ruined her birthday.

Here's how the story went: three weeks before Alecia's big day, her father sat down on her Laura Ashley bedspread and told her to imagine her dream party. Frank wanted her "sweet sixteen" to be special: if she wanted it to be on a yacht, they could use his yacht. If she wanted to rent the ballroom of his country club, he would throw her a dance, and if she wanted the Violent Femmes to play for her, he would try to arrange it. Alecia thought for a moment and then told him, whatever it was, she wanted to be surprised.

When Alecia got home from school that day, my father's car was in the driveway, which meant he and I were in on the festivities, but not my mother. My newly divorced parents had a custody battle in the works, ever since my father had decided he was moving across the state—and wanted to take me with him.

Even at the time, Alecia knew it was strange that her best friend was five years younger, but she always liked the way I looked up to her, even as I towered over her. Besides, I was mature for my age. Alecia assumed it was because of my height, or maybe it was because of my premonitions, and that I'd even seen a ghost once—just our grandma Hazel, "but a dead woman all the same." Or maybe it was because I knew how to keep secrets, which included everything from Alecia's lost virginity to her mother's suicide attempts.

On her sixteenth birthday, when she opened the front door to the house, the first thing Alecia became aware of was that it didn't smell like anything in particular—not garlic; not roast beef; not one of Veronique's chocolate cakes. There was a hint of Windex and Pledge in the air. From the kitchen, she could hear my father, her uncle Gabe, shouting about something.

"Don't tell me that you don't know where they are! She's your friend. She must've told you!"

"Lower your voice, Gabe. Okay?" Frank said. "Maddie, do you know where they went?" he added more gently.

Maddie folded her arms across the front of her pink bathrobe and stared at the floor, while Alecia stood on the threshold of the kitchen and waited to be noticed. After three years of high school, she didn't know why it still infuriated her, the way her mother always acted awake yet unconscious. She could sit for hours in the unfinished basement, watching the spiders climbing up the walls. "I told you, I have no idea where they went," Maddie finally said. "Did you try the mall?"

"They aren't at the mall!" Gabe said, his voice cracking with rage and panic. "Their clothes are gone! Di's stuffed animals and her dolls. The police found Roxanne's car at the airport. Now where the hell did they go?"

"What happened to Di?" Alecia asked, startling the men in the room. Her mother, as usual, looked blank.

Alecia flinched when my father came toward her in two strides. He was always such a mild-mannered man, with a quiet voice, and a big smile; Alecia had never seen him so furious. "Allie, where did Di say she was going? Did she tell you that her mother was planning on taking her away?"

"Like . . . on a vacation?"

"To anywhere! They disappeared! They're gone!" Gabe shouted. "The police think they probably left the country."

Alecia couldn't figure out why he would've notified the police, when I'd left with my own mother—couldn't figure out why everyone kept using the word *kidnapped*. Suddenly, she remembered that my mother had said she wanted to take

me on a trip to England that summer. In nearly the same moment, Maddie actually took her eyes off her bedroom slippers
and asked, "Where'd they go, Allie?" It seemed like the first
question her mother had directed toward her in months,
which was probably why Alecia answered.

"Spain. Di said they were going to take a vacation to
Spain." She hadn't planned on lying, but the act of defiance
immediately made her feel better. Alecia loved my mother
more than her own, she later said, and felt strangely aban-
doned when we left without her. The lie made her feel included, as if we'd planned it in advance.

"Spain?" Alecia's father repeated. "Who does she know in
Spain?"

"No one. She doesn't even speak Spanish!" my father
erupted.

"Alecia, are you telling the truth?" Frank asked. "This is
serious business. We're going to be notifying international
authorities."

"She said they were going to Spain!" Alecia insisted. "She
said it was a vacation! That's all I know!"

She must've been a convincing actress, because after that,
the police were called, the Spanish authorities were notified,
and, of course, Mom and I never turned up.

In the days to come, my father hired a private detective,
who eventually hunted down Clyde Johnson of London,
England. The actor admitted that my mother and I had lived
in his flat for several months, that he'd even helped Roxanne
get a visa, but we'd parted ways not long after, and he didn't
know where we went. Eventually, my father gave up. It
wasn't until seven years later, when Alecia was twenty-three
and living in Scranton, Pennsylvania, working as a weekend
anchor in a Podunk station, that she finally received a letter
from me, or rather, from Jean. *Hey, Meg! Long time no see!* At
the age of eighteen, I could've returned to the States without

anyone claiming me for custody, but I was too afraid—afraid that if I temporarily left my mother, she would lump me with the rest of the world, and disappear on me, too.

And, so, for the next seven years, we remained pen pals, or at least our Barbie dolls did, until Alecia decided to fly overseas and track me down after my father's death. She picked a good year to find me, because, at that point, my mother was dying of cancer and I actually needed her there. Alecia probably needed me, too, though she would never admit it.

Alecia licked her spoon and studied me, as if she'd read my thought. "How long had you guys been planning to leave?"

Startled, I stared at her. "It wasn't like I was Thelma and Mom was Louise. *We* weren't planning anything. One morning, I woke up for school and she said I wasn't going. That's how I found out."

"You never stopped and said, 'What about Dad?' "

"Of course, I did! But Mom said he wasn't ever going to let me see her again."

Alecia made a face. "You must've known that wasn't true."

"Dad was fighting for full custody! He and Christine wanted me in Philadelphia. And Mom was standing there, packed, with two airplane tickets. If I'd said no, she would've left without me." The truth was, Mom simply said, "Let's go, kiddo," and I went. It was the choice that rendered me incapable of making my own decisions ever since.

Alecia raised one of her perfect eyebrows. "Yet you had time to type up the telegram?"

"Telegram?"

"The one that arrived two days after you disappeared." I could feel my forehead crinkling in confusion, which made Alecia talk faster. "You typed it on your Strawberry

Shortcake stationery? From Jean to Meg? I never showed it to the police."

"Well, that's good." I scratched my head. My recollection may have been vague, but I was fairly certain that, considering I didn't know where we were going or how long we were staying, the telegram couldn't have conveyed any vital information. "Once the case was closed, did you ever tell my father, you know, that I wrote to you?"

Alecia put down her spoon and when she spoke, the words came out slowly. "I don't think the case was ever closed, Di. I never told anyone where you were. It was supposed to be a secret. I thought."

"Well, it was." My voice was glum. "It was." I reached for my ice cream, even though I wasn't hungry anymore.

"I mean, whenever you sent me another letter, it was always from a different return address," Alecia added. "And they were few and far between."

That was my trick: I would wait until we were on the verge of leaving for another town before I would write to Alecia. I always trusted that she wouldn't sic the authorities on us, yet I often daydreamed that my father might appear before we could move again.

Alecia put down her bowl. "You know what? I still have it. The telegram!"

I watched, shaking my head, as she walked over to the hall closet and then disappeared inside. I thought of Miss Otlin again, turning my vocabulary word journal over to the Pittsburgh police, which was funny to imagine, only because, as I recalled, the only secret the writing exercises gave away was the one of my parents' unraveling marriage, which wasn't much of a secret.

I thought of the three pictures I'd carried with me through fourteen different moves. The one of my parents on their wedding day: Roxanne in an empire waist dress, with a wreath of roses in her black hair, looking very Juliet to Gabe's Romeo in Birkenstocks, the same pair of sandals that he wore with everything from his hospital white coat to his blue suit. The photo of my father and me, standing proudly in front of the tall cabinet that we'd made together, after I'd read *The Chronicles of Narnia* and begged my parents for a wardrobe. We worked together in my father's wood shop in the garage, where he loved to spend hours on his weekends off, much to my mother's chagrin. He'd let me pick every detail, like the stain and the knobs, and where I wanted each shelf to go. I could still smell the cedar lining. The last picture was of Gabe alone: his hand, resting on his chin, and his blue eyes, lost in thoughts. *Of me.* Or, knowing my father, not of me. More likely, of *organic chemistry,* and *gene mutations,* and *immunizations,* and *pediatrics, woodworking,* and sometimes *cooking experiments,* which usually went wrong, and maybe even his *youth,* which meant growing up in Pittsburgh.

"He's buried here!" I suddenly remembered. "You have to take me to his grave!"

"It was actually a big ordeal to get him buried in the family plot—even though it was written in his will!" Alecia stuck her head out of the closet. "Christine and—" She caught herself and stopped. "They didn't want to drive five hours to visit him."

"It's okay to say 'Sophie,'" I said and watched as her eyes widened. "It's not like she's the other woman. She's my half-sister." Once Alecia disappeared into the closet again, I added, "What were they like together?"

"Gabe and Christine?"

I looked at my jagged nails. "Dad and Sophie."

There was a pause. Inside the closet, the boxes stopped shifting. "Oh, you know . . . normal. She wanted to be a doctor, just like him."

I shook my head. She'd taken my job: to be anything my

father said I could be. "I thought about going back some-time," I admitted. "Just to . . . see if they would welcome me. And Max." It wasn't until I said this aloud that I realized how badly this was everything that I wanted: a bit of normalcy for my son. A *family*.

"Go back?" Alecia stuck her head out of the closet. "To Philly?" When I nodded, her eyes opened larger. "I didn't know that you'd ever been."

"Just once. When Dad first introduced me to Christine." I had a single memory of spring in Rittenhouse Square: sitting on a bench in the shade next to my father, and watching tree branches waving in the breeze overhead—wondering if one snapped loose, was it really possible to kill me? (I'd recently read *The Secret Garden,* and the idea of Colin losing his mother to a gardening accident had made an impression on me.) "I want us to live here," Dad said, and I jerked my head upward, certain I had heard a branch crack.

Alecia was staring at me, perplexed, as if she couldn't imagine what I had in common with two virtual strangers. *Just my father.* "So, the funeral, it was held in Pittsburgh, then?" I asked. It worked: she headed back inside the closet again.

"And there was a separate memorial service later in Philadelphia, which I didn't attend because my mom was going to be there." Alecia's laugh sounded muffled, as if her head was inside a box.

"Why didn't anyone come and find me? I mean—before he died."

"I never knew you wanted to be found. Once you turned eighteen, you could've come back. You could've come back *anytime*."

"It wasn't that simple," I muttered. I was glad that Alecia, in the closet, couldn't see the shame on my face. "Is that what Dad thought? That I wanted to be missing?"

"Honestly, after you left, we all just . . . drifted apart. Your dad got remarried, my mom took off for Portland, and Dad and I moved to New York. I saw Uncle Gabe maybe once a year or so. And he didn't talk about you. It seemed to upset him too much. But we all knew that he missed you. Christine once said that right around your birthday, he would get in an awful funk, and no one could get near him."

The tragedy of our situation struck me all at once: the separation and the longing and the waste of it all. "Why did he give up?" I finally asked.

Alecia emerged from the closet carrying an egg crate filled with papers, and for a second, I thought she hadn't heard me. But she was biting her lip in hesitation. "It was years before you ever wrote to me. Christine decided it was time. She wanted him to fully focus on their new family for a change. At least, that's what my dad said." Alecia set the crate down on the coffee table.

It was time. His wife had ordered him to give up, and he had obeyed. But could I blame him? Hadn't I done the same thing to him? "So, Dad forgot me."

Alecia shook her head. "He let you go. He had to." She handed me a sheet of pink notepaper. "Here. See for yourself. It's what you sent me, the night you disappeared."

NIGHT TELEGRAM: TO MEG

ITS LATE STOP JEFF DECIDED STOP TOLD ME OVER
CANDLELIT DINNER STOP HE IS THE NEW SENIOR CO-
ORDINATOR OF OPERATIONS AND COMMUNICATIONS
EXCLAMATION STOP WE ARE BOTH VERY EXCITED YET
SAD TO LEAVE STOP ITS A SECRET STOP NO ONE EX-
CEPT FOR YOU CAN KNOW STOP LOVE JEAN

"So, who's Jeff?" she asked, hand on her hip.

I stared at the telegram and stared at her.

"One of Roxanne's lovers?" she asked, raising an eyebrow. As if my mother had taken more than … well, twelve in her lifetime, including my father. Plus one more, "The Mistake," as she always called it, which I'd always believed was a one-night stand that my father found out about, and which had caused him to promptly call for a divorce and rush off to Christine, whom he'd known forever. When I'd once asked my mother for more details about her mystery lover, she insisted, "It was a mistake, not an affair. We're talking about a kiss here." I'd looked at her doubtfully, and she added, "Well, French!" My mother made it clear that while she was not in love with The Mistake, my father had fallen in love with Christine.

"Malibu Ken? Remember him?" I said. "That was Jeff."

Alecia blinked. "But what's a—a senior coordinator of operations and communications?"

"Didn't Uncle Frank have that job title for a while?"

"He might have. But what did this mean?" She snatched the pink paper from my hand and shook it. "What did they all mean?"

Suddenly, I understood. She thought it was a code, thought that I'd kept her in the loop, except there was no loop, and there was no code: only me, being kidnapped and going along with it.

She unfolded another letter, this one dated nearly ten years later, so there must've been no particular order to the egg crate. " 'Dear Meg, Sorry to hear about how things ended with you and Ted Winslow. But Ben sounds great—a writer! Wow!' " She looked up when I laughed. "What?"

"Nothing, it's just—you must've written to Jean about a guy named Ben. Was that a coincidence?" I squinted, trying to read her face. "You weren't writing about real people, were you?"

"I was writing about me!" she snapped. "And everyone in my life. Who the hell were you writing about?"

I swallowed. "Malibu Ken and Hispanic Barbie."

"No, you weren't." She fumbled around in her egg crate, until she came up with a postcard. " 'Dear Meg, Today turned out to be a perfect Saturday once the rain was over. Jeff and I ran out to buy bushes to plant along our back fence. We also met our new neighbor and welcomed him with pumpkin bread....' " She looked up and tapped the letter as if it was an official court document. "Did you ever welcome a new neighbor with pumpkin bread?"

"We were always the new neighbors. And we were never welcome." I couldn't stand the pained expression on her face. "I was just...imagining things."

"So, these were all lies?"

"More or less."

She lifted the crate about an inch off the table and then dropped it, which made me jump. "Remind me to burn this crap," she muttered, before storming off to her bedroom and slamming the door.

I just stood there, staring at the box of lies, wondering why I hadn't even opened my mouth to apologize or defend myself. But what could I say? That it was a story, not a lie, and that all these tall tales kept me going for years. If I couldn't have a family, well, then, I'd make one up.

In the end, I decided the best defense was to pretend they'd never been written, and I picked up the egg crate and carried it to the closet. Except that a small book on the shelf caught my eye: *The Magic Lantern*. So, Alecia had been lying when she said she'd chucked her mother's book of poems. And lying, I saw when I opened the door to the hall closet, when she said she couldn't remember where her dolls were anymore. Her pink, plastic Barbie doll suitcase was sitting on the top shelf. It was all right here: everything she couldn't let go and couldn't bear to part with. So, I found a spot for my old lies, and left them there, too.

CHAPTER 6

The Oldest News in the Book

It was Saturday, one week later, and I still hadn't found Mazy Roberts a nanny, but she hadn't called, either—or, for that matter, mailed Alecia's "application fee"—to confirm that I had the job. Perhaps, I hoped, I'd only imagined her intent to employ me. In the meantime, I kept busy, dropping off more applications around Shadyside—at the bagel shop, and Feathers, the upscale bedding store—but it seemed no one was hiring, or at least, no one was hiring *me*.

When I got back to the apartment just before noon, Ben was typing on his laptop, Max was staring at Elmo on TV, while Alecia fretted about her upcoming baby shower that afternoon: apparently, she didn't know what it was that she'd purchased online for the mother-to-be. "I mean, what the hell is this?" she asked, lifting up her unwrapped gift, which resembled a quilted diaper bag on the bottom, with a shirt sewn on the top.

"Bunting," I said, slipping out of my jean jacket. "A traveling outfit."

"But it's just for emergencies, if he or she turns out to be a mermaid," Ben said, and I laughed, but Alecia only scowled, as she squinted at the tag on the side of the yellow bunting marked *Not suitable for sleeping*.

"What else does a baby do besides sleep?" she asked.

"Feeds. Burps. Cries," Ben said.

"So, she's supposed to put this kid in the outfit for the two minutes he's awake and then wrestle him out of it?"

I went to inspect the outfit myself. "Um, Alecia...?" I held up the label on the matching yellow hat that read, *Fire hazard*.

"Fantastic." Her laugh sounded jagged. "I picked a flammable jumper."

"Well, it's not like the baby will be smoking in his crib," Ben said with a snicker. He had a great snicker, with a lot of belly behind it, despite his thin frame.

"I don't know how many more of these showers I can take," Alecia muttered. "All these giddy women forced to watch some poor soul opening embarrassing gifts like a breast pump. And everyone has to talk about babies, even if you don't have one." She straightened up, struck by a thought. "I could bring Max! He fits with the theme."

"He's not a bundt cake," I said.

"You could come, too! You'd be my buffers! You know I hate showers!" she added, pleading.

"But you want a wedding shower, don't you?" Ben asked, and I might've kicked him, except that I was across the room, riffling through a stack of catalogs to butcher for my next collage. When Holly left the country one week ago, she and I had ended up canceling Alecia's surprise shower—which was a relief, because hardly anyone had agreed to come.

"Of course...not," Alecia said, and I exhaled. "Why do

we have to pretend that the biggest transitions in life are magical? The only people who get into baby showers are mothers. And women who plan to be mothers someday."

Ben looked up from his laptop and cocked his head to the side, as if trying to hear her correctly. "You . . . don't want to be a mother someday?" The smile was slow to leave his face.

At least the baby was out of the bag now, or however that expression went. I dropped the catalogs and went to get Max, whose show was ending. *This episode of Sesame Street was brought to you by the letter Z.*

"You knew that," Alecia said.

"No, I didn't know that." Ben shut his laptop. "Since when?"

She shrugged. "Since, like, my whole life."

Max started to howl as soon as I shut off the TV. "Come on, kiddo. Let's go for a walk. Go get your shoes."

"Tell him, Di," Alecia said, and her eyes pleaded with me to stay. She turned back to Ben, who'd just stood up off the sofa.

Max began begging for the remote, which he loved to pretend was a cell phone. I surrendered and then glanced back at my cousin, still waiting. "I knew, but . . ." *I'm not the one who matters.*

Alecia looked at Ben. "You never told me that you wanted to have children," she said.

"Sure I did."

"Nope."

"Well, I guess I just assumed . . ."

I grabbed a handful of Matchbox cars and stuffed them in the diaper bag. If I could just find Max's shoes, we'd be gone.

"When Pastor Nate asked us if we had the same ideas on family—" Ben started.

"It was none of his business!"

Ben ran his fingers through his hair then stopped and

pointed a finger at me. "What about at that photographer's studio? You were there, Di. Didn't Alecia say she wanted to have wedding pictures to show our children?"

I stopped in the middle of double-knotting Max's sneaker and glanced back at Alecia. "You did say that."

But I had known at the time that it was just a ploy to get Ben to agree to hire the photographer. Alecia asked what the point of the wedding was if they didn't take any pictures of it, which got him going about the importance of vows. That's when Alecia blurted out that she wanted pictures as a record for their children.

"I was referring to our figurative children."

"What does that mean?" Ben asked, pacing back and forth again. "What on earth is a figurative child?"

"It was just something to say." Alecia stared back at him and then erupted. "I just got a promotion! I've never been in such great shape in my life! A child would ruin everything. Look at Di."

I was in the middle of tugging on Max's arm, trying to get him to follow me out the door, but of course, he was resisting mightily. "Excuse me?" I asked.

"Ever since he came along, you don't have much of a life."

"He *is* my life," I said, accidentally letting go of Max, who immediately stumbled backward and knocked over one of the wrapped wedding gifts. Inside the box, the contents shattered, and then the apartment grew quiet. I quickly scooped up Max before he could start to cry.

"Great. That was probably one whole place setting," Alecia muttered.

"What do you say, Boo?" I asked, too annoyed to apologize for myself.

"Sorry," Max said, and buried his face in my shoulder.

Ben scowled at Alecia. "You don't even know what he broke."

"Whatever it was, it was valuable."

"You don't know what's valuable." Ben grabbed his keys off the table, headed for the front door to the apartment, and slammed it on his way out. Seconds later, everything went quiet again.

"On that happy note..." I muttered, picking up the stroller.

"You knew I didn't want to have children, right?" Alecia asked.

"Of course I knew." Then I took Max's hand and we left for the park. This time, he was smart enough not to protest.

Raining Babies

Unfortunately, we needed a car to actually get ourselves to the park—either that, or a bus schedule—so we took a walk through the streets of Shadyside instead. Deliberately avoiding the shopping area, I pointed Max's stroller toward Amberson Avenue, where sprawling, old houses perched on leafless green lawns. Any young mother unloading groceries from a Mercedes or heading out for a run was subject to my scrutiny. *What did she do to end up with all of this?* I kept wondering. And, *How does it feel?* Not unlike inhabiting Alecia's apartment for the last six weeks.

Watching Alecia with Ben, it was hard to imagine the two of them ever falling in love in the first place. Alecia had told me the story of how it happened five years ago, back at WZBE in New York City, where she was a reporter and sometimes Saturday morning anchorwoman, and Ben was editing newsreels.

"I need a beehive," Alecia said, rapping on the glass door to his office one day.

"A beehive?" Ben repeated, squinting at her. He kept his cubicle as dark as a cave. Later, he told her that he needed the dimness to watch the tapes the way radiologists sit in the dark to read films. But Alecia had taken one look at Ben's jeans and black T-shirt bearing the chronically depressed face of Morrissey and knew this was one gloomy guy. In her head, she called him The Guy Who Won't Smile.

"Yeah, a beehive—like now! Right away! Yesterday!" She snapped her fingers, trying to wake him up. "My anaphylaxis awareness piece is going on in fifty minutes. I need background footage of bees! Lots of them!"

Ben scratched his head and looked at the ceiling. "I might have one of a small boy getting consumed by an entire hive. He swells up and turns purple and just drops dead."

"Perfect!" Alecia said, her face lighting up.

"Oh, wait. I was kidding." Ben chuckled. "But I saw it once in a movie—*My Girl*. 1991. Macaulay Culkin, when he was, like, eight years old? Maybe you could—"

Alecia lost her smile. "I am going on the air in less than an hour, and you're talking to me about Macaulay Culkin? I'll be back!" she said, storming out.

"I'll be here!" Ben called after her.

Twenty minutes later, she found him monkeying with the final cuts of her beehive tape, and she leaned against his desk to wait. Suddenly, his hair didn't seem quite so red and his hunched shoulders became just the natural posture of a tall person stuck in a tight box.

As they started talking, Alecia found out that Ben was miserable because he had gone to NYU for film school and that the last thing he wanted to do was edit newsreels when he had visions of Sundance in his head. Besides that, he was lonely. He knew only a handful of people in the city. He showed her his Video Hits Visa card and called it "a metaphor for my existence."

Alecia confessed that she was only in New York City because her father had made some calls. "My career choice was actually his idea," she found herself saying. "I wanted to become an actress, but he picked journalism, saying I'd make a much better reporter." When she remembered that her doll Meg had been a reporter, it started to sound promising.

"You think he was right?" Ben asked.

Alecia shrugged. "Being in front of the camera is kind of like acting. I always have to look like I care about something."

Ben laughed, hard, as if she were kidding.

Little did he know, I thought now, ambling past another lovely stone mansion, whose empty front porch swing drifted upward, as the wind shifted. Max laughed and pointed, as if a ghost were kicking up its legs and gliding back and forth. That was the strange thing about this section of Shadyside: I never saw parents outside playing with their children, never saw anyone enjoying his porch swing on a fall afternoon. It had been the same way when Alecia was growing up. I often had the sense that the Axtels were a family who lived independently of their community and of one another—which may have explained the indifference she had to her own mother, and the separatist way she treated Ben now.

Maybe I was just jealous. Maybe I wanted love to float into my life like a buzzing bee. Though I had the distinct impression that sooner or later, no matter who you were and what you owned, you'd end up purple and misshapen and fighting for air.

WHILE MAX AND I were out walking, Alecia was getting ready for the baby shower. She'd just finished blow-drying her hair when the phone rang. It was her father, who'd gotten her message about the missing calla lilies and wanted to sue the shop. "They knew when you ordered the flowers that they weren't in season, am I right?"

She took a deep breath. "It's going to be fine, Daddy. I've switched it to a cascade of red roses. Call off the lawyers."

"As long as you're happy," Frank said, his voice suddenly down-to-business—she could imagine what might be coming next. "Listen, I never got those papers. When exactly did you send them?"

Alecia shifted from one foot to another. "I mailed them last week."

"Regular mail? Didn't I tell you to FedEx it?"

"I forgot." It was easier to blame the U.S. Postal Service than admit that, between the dress fittings and the premarital counseling, she hadn't actually gotten the papers sent off yet. Easier to blame the U.S. Postal Service than admit that Ben had refused to sign the prenuptial agreement that her father was insisting on. ("You're kidding, right?" Ben had said laughing with disbelief, when she'd presented him with the documents.) She had to agree with him: there was something disturbing about starting your marriage by assuming the worst.

"Well, it better get here soon," Frank said, irritated.

She hoped it would, too, before the postmaster got sued. Alecia had asked me recently if I thought that Uncle Frank really meant it when he told her that, without a signed prenup, he would write her out of his will. (She never liked to imagine Life Without Daddy, but the idea of five million dollars being wasted on homeless people and hurricane victims, instead of herself, was completely unbearable.) I told her I thought he had to be bluffing, but Alecia wasn't convinced. He'd used the same threat when she wanted to move to LA after sophomore year of college. Only this time, he'd said with a facetious laugh, "Not that your inheritance should matter, when you have a man like Ben to take care of you." How could he be so supportive and manipulative at the same time? she wondered. And what did he have against Ben? "It's because he's a teacher, right?" she'd said to her father, and he laughed.

"I'm just happy he's done with the whole seminary thing," Frank said. "You would've made a lousy minister's wife, kiddo."

She hadn't dared tell Frank about Ben's latest idea—a magazine, tentatively titled *The Burning Tree,* after the restaurant in Maine where they'd gotten engaged. Maybe Alecia would've been more enthusiastic if the magazine was about food rather than faith.

"Seriously," Frank was saying over the phone. "It's just a real hassle to split up your assets when things go sour. You remember Deserai, right? And Marcie? Learn from my mistakes, kiddo. I don't care about him—I care about *you*." He chuckled then, and his voice grew warmer. "It's been a long time coming, eh?"

"The . . . wedding?" Alecia said, confused, since her father was always asking her, *What's the rush?*

"Anchoring!" Frank said, so he must have listened to the last part of her voice mail message, when she said the position would soon be hers.

"Oh. Right."

"Don't 'oh, right' me, kiddo. If it weren't for me, you would've spent the last ten years living in your car, in downtown LA, collecting rejections right and left."

"We don't know that. I did a good job as Nellie, didn't I?" She meant in her high school musical, *South Pacific.*

Frank started to laugh. "Let's not argue about this, all right? I'm happy for you. You've worked hard, and you're well on your way to being the next Katie Couric."

She wanted to ask him if he'd heard from her mother anytime recently, or if he'd bothered to tell her about the wedding. But for some reason, she was afraid of what he might say. Besides, Max and I had just returned to the apartment, so she quickly said goodbye to her father, while I let go of Max, who rushed straight for his Matchbox cars.

"I'm sorry," she said, after hanging up the phone.

I folded my arms across my chest and waited.

"About that whole not-having-a-life thing—it seemed like you took it the wrong way."

"I took it the way you meant it."

She glanced away. "I've been trying to help you . . ."

"Get a job—not a life."

"It came out wrong. There's just . . . a lot of stress right now with the wedding, and the stupid papers—that was Daddy again, wondering where they were." She threw up a hand. "What would you do?"

I knew it was too easy for me to have an opinion, when I had no inheritance to speak of, when my own father had "let me go." But she'd asked. "I would say to hell with the money. Don't let him manipulate you like that."

"I just—I want—" Alecia stopped, shook her head, and glanced at her watch.

I leaned forward. "What is it that you want?"

But Alecia never answered me. Instead, the buzzer rang—*Saved by the bell,* I thought—and she rushed to push the button on the intercom. "Come on up!" she called.

Here is what she wouldn't confess to me at the time: that what she wanted most was to be taken care of—financially (which, at the time, meant Bank of Daddy); cosmetically (which meant Richard, her hair stylist who refused to let her try a new look: "If it ain't broke, don't fix it"); and sometimes, even gastronomically ("I like not having to think about dinner," she'd said once, watching me cook). This was hard for her to admit when she thought such basic longings were generally reserved for children or trophy wives rather than career-driven women. And besides, there was even another level of security that she had only vaguely begun to identify and often attributed to people who were "freakishly serene in the face of tragedy"—a peaceful state of mind which probably involved a lot of meditation and, at this point in her life, required too much effort.

THE LOBBY-CALLER TURNED out to be Fran Dubnicay, Action News medical reporter, who made it up to the apartment in a matter of moments. "Oh, hello!" she said, obviously surprised to find me on the other side of the open door.

Alecia often said that Fran took her job so seriously that she forgot she wasn't really a doctor, had no medical background whatsoever, and was completely and technically unqualified for the job. Unfortunately, she also lived three blocks away from my cousin and often wanted to carpool to work-related events.

"You're not still living here, are you?" Fran added, as I led the way into the living room.

"We are," I said, with forced cheerfulness. I wasn't sure which was worse: that Alecia must've been complaining about us to her colleagues, or that she had reinvented me as a British nanny-finder extraordinaire. "Alecia will be out in a second." At least, I hoped. She'd just disappeared into the bathroom with an entire duffel bag that turned out to be full of makeup. "Ready for the next baby shower?" I added, and Fran shrugged.

It had started the weekend before with Tonya, the Saturday morning news anchor, who was due in three weeks with either a Shontay or a Patrice—Alecia had grumbled that most of the scintillating conversation had revolved around which it might be. Tonya had told them she wanted to be surprised. "There are no good surprises in medicine," Fran said ominously, which made a gloom descend over the party until Alecia asked, "When did *you* graduate from medical school, Fran?"

"Who's this one for?" I asked.

"Kate Frisbee," Fran answered, which explained why Alecia had no interest in attending the shower: she still hadn't gotten over Kate's usurping the starring role on the *Taking Action for You* news segment. "I'm just hoping there will be men there," Fran admitted with a sheepish grin.

Poor Fran, Ben usually said, anytime he was subjected to her on-screen persona—which wasn't all that different from the real Fran: translucent skin, mousy brown hair, and a trench coat that managed to make her look a hundred pounds overweight, instead of the forty that she was.

"I didn't know men went to baby showers," I said.

"Well, sure—if they're invited! Vanessa's going to have men at her shower—at least, that's what I heard," Fran added quickly. Alecia would say that Fran heard a lot of things, and most of them were untrue. Fran hyped miracle drugs that made you quit smoking, lose wrinkles, and orgasm faster, and then—when new side effects were discovered—she lambasted doctors for recklessly prescribing them—even if they wouldn't be on the market for ten more years.

"Ready?" Alecia called, appearing from the hallway. Her red lipstick matched the flowers on her dress. "Are you coming, too?" she asked me, sounding so hopeful that I actually found myself smiling.

"Not a chance."

* * *

By Alecia's account I made the right decision: most of the ride out to the South Hills, Fran spent lamenting the lack of single men in Pittsburgh—and lamenting Tom-the-Cameraman's recent gastric-bypass surgery.

"I should've asked him out when he was fat," she said with a sigh. "I'm never going to meet anyone."

"You'll meet someone," Alecia said, hoping she sounded convincing. "Maybe you already know him. Ben and I were friends before anything happened."

"How long did it take for him to ask you out?"

"A while. I was actually dating someone else. But it wasn't serious or anything." Meaning that she and Ted Winslow, the other backup Saturday morning anchor, hadn't slept together yet. Her father liked him, or at least, liked what he saw of Ted on TV. Ted looked good above the waist. It wasn't unusual for her co-anchor to sit behind the news desk wearing a pinstripe suit on top, and ripped shorts and smelly sneakers on the bottom.

"So, how did you know Ben was The One?" Fran asked.

"Oh, it's a little hard to say," Alecia said, stalling. She turned on her headlights and pretended to concentrate on the road taking them through Fort Pitt Tunnel. "It was really more of an evolution than a moment."

She was lying, of course, but the truth was complicated. She couldn't really explain how three weeks after they became friends, Ben arrived to work giddy—so giddy that Alecia became annoyed, imagining he'd gotten a girlfriend or at least gotten laid over the weekend. When she ran into him in the station's lunchroom and asked, "What is with you?" Ben said he couldn't tell her—it was too weird. "Does it have to do with a certain woman?" Alecia asked and then felt embarrassed, because she thought Ben would think she meant herself. "Or maybe a certain man?" she added, just in case he was gay. "It has to do with my *life*," Ben said urgently, but when she pressed him for more details, he would only shake his head. For two weeks, he became The Guy Who Has a Secret, until finally, she cornered him again in the cafeteria.

"Everyone wants to know what your problem is," Alecia said, plunking down her tray of food during a break between the nine o'clock and noon broadcasts. "They sent me to find out."

"What my problem is?" Ben repeated.

"Mr. Happy-Happy-La-La-La," Alecia said, suddenly realizing how annoyed she'd been that he wasn't giddy over her.

"Who is this 'everyone'?" Ben asked. "Have we met?"

She leaned forward and said in a low voice, "I want to know what happened to you."

Ben leaned forward and said in an equally low voice, "I had a vision."

"A vision?" Alecia repeated, a little too loudly. They both looked around. No one was paying attention. Ted Winslow was studying the selections in the vending machine and hadn't even noticed them.

"My sister said it may have been a temporal lobe seizure," Ben said, absently tearing off a piece of his empty Styrofoam coffee cup and flicking it across the table.

"Did you...shake and foam at the mouth?"

"Nothing like that." Ben paused and swallowed. "It was just a moment in time. I was suddenly, fully aware that I was created for a purpose."

"But what exactly did you see?" Alecia prompted, unconsciously tilting her ear toward him.

Ben leaned forward again and whispered, "God."

Alecia sat back, horrified.

"The only trouble is, now I have to figure out what I'm going to do about it," Ben said, and by then his coffee cup was a pile of confetti.

"Have you seen a neurologist?" Alecia asked.

Later that morning, the floor director called in sick, and Alecia found herself under Ben's direction when she sat down to anchor. She wanted to say something, anything, to get his attention, which was bizarre because she already had his full attention, at least every time she was supposed to speak after a break, when he would point to the appropriate camera and say, "Alecia in ten seconds..."

During one of those commercial interludes, Ted Winslow said, "I think Ben found his new calling."

"Oh, Ben has a new calling all right. He had a vision," Alecia said.

"Always wanted to be the floor director, Ben?" Ted asked with a wink.

"It's why I went to NYU," Ben shot back and then looked at Alecia with those steady blue eyes until she felt guilty.

After the show, she stopped by his glass cubicle to apologize, but he was already gone. When he didn't show up for work the next day, she called up Human Resources and got his address, which was practically in another country: Brooklyn.

When Ben came to his apartment door and found Alecia, he didn't look happy or mad. In fact, she was pretty sure she'd just woken him up from a nap. His hair was sticking up in back and even his eyebrows had bed head. "I'm sorry I made fun of you," she blurted. *I took the subway for you,* she wanted to add. When Ben didn't move to let her in, she went on, "I was just trying to—oh, you know. It's like when you're on the playground and you throw rocks at the person you want to... look, can I just come in?"

"Little different," Ben said wryly, but he let her inside and took her coat and offered her a glass of cider. He sat down beside her on the sofa and watched her drink her cider. When she was done, she put the glass down on the coffee table.

"So," he said. "Everyone wants to know what the hell you're doing here?"

With a sudden surge of giddiness, Alecia started to laugh—the laugh that struck her unexpectedly, and always at the worst times, like at her uncle Gabe's funeral, when his second wife, Christine, started to sob loudly. That day in Ben's living room, Alecia laughed so hard that the words wouldn't come out, and she was waving her hands in circles trying to gesture something that made sense, until finally he took her hands, just so that she would stop moving them. "No, really, what are you doing here?" Ben asked.

"I want to hear more about your vision."

"No, you don't," he said. "You don't believe in visions."

She looked at their hands and then up at his face. "Convince me."

And so, they talked, for hours. Later, his twin sister, Holly, accused Alecia of being "turned off" by Ben's Calling. But his vision, or his moment of clarity, or whatever it was that led him to quit his job at the station, move to Shadyside, and enroll at the Pittsburgh Theological Seminary only attracted Alecia to Ben more. She'd always been surrounded by people who wanted something—her father wanted more houses, more cars, more wives, and, someday, for his only daughter to have the biggest damn wedding in the world. She'd never met someone who just believed in something.

But then Ben's mother died suddenly, in a car accident, and Alecia's uncle Gabe was randomly shot to death in a convenience store, and Ben's faith started to falter. It wasn't Alecia who discouraged Ben from the ministry; it was life.

I MIGHT AS WELL confess: despite Alecia's theory that all women with children love baby showers, I had never been to one. When I was pregnant with Max, the timing was not ideal. Even if we'd had friends to invite, Max was due just as my mother was—in her words—"coming down with a touch of cancer," turning yellower by the day, and thus, the last thing we were thinking about was a theme party. Watching Alecia attend Saturday after Saturday, I understood how strange her obligation must've felt. Not only did she and Fran have to stay up late as the messengers of death and tragedy on the news but in the morning, they had to float from haven to haven to celebrate the possibilities of birth. And they had to smile nonstop.

In the backyard of Kate Frisbee's sister's house, rag dolls and balloons were tied to vines of ivy in the trees. Blue hydrangeas sat on the table. And from the porch light, teddy bears dangled on the ends of satin ribbons. It took Alecia a second to realize everyone was congratulating her.

"Is she pregnant?" she heard Heidi ask. Heidi's greatest asset was her hair, which was long and honey blond. Unfortunately, it couldn't offset her worst asset, which was her pumpkin head.

"No, I am not pregnant," Alecia said. *You wish.* "I'm just taking over Vanessa's anchoring spot while she's gone."

"Is that official?" Heidi asked.

"It's official," Alecia said, although when Art had taken her into his office the week before he'd said, "Let's keep this on the down low until I make the announcement."

"But she's getting married in two weeks," Vanessa said. "I bet she'll be pregnant in no time. It's in the water."

"Ha! Don't count on it," Alecia said, looking around for the alcohol. She spotted a crystal bowl filled with pink liquid, but the punch, it turned out, was spiked only with Sprite. In the future, she'd have to remember to bring her own flask.

And so, the baby talk began. Not only was Vanessa pregnant, and Tonya, but Elaine, the meteorologist, and her husband, Keith, were "trying." Alecia couldn't be the only one who didn't want to imagine them trying, but for some reason Elaine felt compelled to tell everyone about their latest adventures in scheduled sex.

"Is it possible I was born without a single maternal instinct?" Alecia had wondered, watching me share my glass of cider with Max one morning. "Because nothing is entirely your own?" I'd asked, before taking another swallow from the glass. Alecia had made a face: "Because you're drinking *his* backwash." If marriage, to Alecia, meant risking your identity, then motherhood meant surrendering your dignity. I'd held up my glass—which did, in fact, contain visible bits of Max's mac-n-cheese—and said, "Trust me, there's more to it than this." But Alecia only looked as if she was about to be sick.

It was the same way at Kate's party: as the ladies swapped stories of procreation, queasiness hit her suddenly—but not unexpectedly, given the ten mini spinach quiches she'd just downed like a drunk surreptitiously doing shots. She quickly excused herself from the picnic table and rushed into the house before she could vomit.

In the bathroom, she gripped the edge of the sink and panted in front of the mirror. Her face was red and puffy; her hair so golden that, suddenly, she looked unfamiliar to herself.

"Ben says I've gone too blond," she'd confessed, twirling a lock of hair during one of our recent coffee outings. "He liked it better black."

"Ben's not into hair dye." I shrugged. "It looks great."

"Sometimes, I just want to be me again...." She'd sighed and then met my eyes. "But I can't make any radical changes before the wedding. Richard won't let me. And Art would have a *fit*." I must've looked skeptical that her boss would even care because she put down her coffee a moment later and erupted, "I just can't! There's too much at stake!"

"Well, it's your hair," I'd said, a line my mother had delivered after a head-shaving incident during my adolescent

Goth phase and henceforth applied to every aspect of my life she didn't approve of but probably wouldn't kill me. (E.g., "I'm pregnant." "Well, it's your hair.")

That day in the coffee shop, Alecia had grudgingly snickered, recognizing the Roxanne-ism. But in the bathroom at Kate Frisbee's baby shower, she panicked at the sight of her foreign blond self. "It's my hair; it's my hair; it's my hair," she whispered to herself, like a mantra, as she splashed cold water on her face, until the nausea finally passed. Then she reached to wipe her hands dry on a towel that she realized belatedly was covered in a large string of mucous. *Yet another reason not to have children,* she thought. *They blow snot into your hand towels and hang them back up.*

BACK AT THE PICNIC table, the topic had digressed from the best kind of breast pump to Mazy Roberts and her impending divorce.

"Her husband cheated on her with the family friend's daughter," Vanessa said.

Everyone groaned or sighed, except for Heidi, who giggled. "Am I the only one who thinks he looks like George Clooney?"

This was the first that Alecia had heard of the divorce, but she wasn't entirely surprised. "Where is Mazy?" she asked.

"She's not coming. She sent her regrets and a gift," Vanessa said, pointing to the table overflowing with presents, which apparently reminded Kate that she was ready to open them. They made their way back toward the table, where the lady of honor sat in a decorated chair, with a paper crown on her head of long curls. Someone asked what the baby would be named. "Andrew, but we're calling him Drew, not Andy—see?" Kate said, holding up a new blanket embroidered with the name Drew, as if it were proof.

The next gift, "Baby's First Computer!" was from Elaine, who cleared her throat for one of her high-pitched announcements. (The meteorologist stood all of about five feet tall and, according to Alecia, was constantly offended by people calling her "the weather girl.") "This little guy is going to be the smartest baby in the world, because his mommy and his daddy are so very bright," Elaine said to a collective murmur of agreement.

"Actually, in statistics the next generation regresses further to the mean of the population," Fran said.

"What does that mean?" Kate asked, smiling, a brownie hovering near her mouth.

"Every generation is dumber than the one before," Fran replied.

The conversation around the table stopped. Kate lost her smile.

For the first time all day, Alecia laughed.

CHAPTER 8

Acting Guardian

It was Saturday, one week later, when I woke up to the sound of dishes clanging in the kitchen. Sunlight streamed across the futon's yellow comforter, and the clock radio said eight-thirty A.M., which meant Max had let me oversleep for a change. I rolled onto my side and found him, red-cheeked and drooling, nuzzled up against me. His nose was running, and his forehead felt warm. When I tried to pick the goop from his eye, Max did a brief rendition of his tonsil-baring, shoulder-heaving cry before squirming away.

"Okay, okay. I'll stop. Be right back, Boo," I said, climbing out of bed.

In the living room, boxes of wrapped presents were strewn all over the floor. If only they'd get it over with and start opening the rest of the gifts. We still hadn't found out what was broken.

I stopped in the doorway of the kitchen. Alecia was at the sink, doing the dishes. "Oh, you don't want to do that," I blurted, when she opened the dishwasher, a knife in one hand. "You're supposed to rinse them by hand or it dulls the blades and causes them to rust." She looked at the knife in her grasp and then at me, as if considering whether to charge. Thankfully, she dropped it into the sink instead. "Is something wrong?" I asked. It had to be Ben. He'd been acting differently since their fight the weekend before—not watching her on the news every night, not making jokes at her expense. In fact, he'd been awfully subdued with me, too, I realized: on Tuesday, my roast duck had elicited a formal "Thank you for cooking," and nothing more.

"Yeah, Di, something's wrong. Something's very wrong." Alecia grabbed an envelope off the counter and thrust it at me. "I found this under the dining room table when I was cleaning up."

After slipping the card out, I looked at its cover, a picture of yellow baby booties over the Hallmark inscription: *Savor each magical moment.* "I don't get it."

"Here, let me help," Alecia said, snatching the card away. She opened it and read, " 'Dear Allie, Congratulations on your *happy news*! I was so surprised when I got Di's invitation to the *baby* shower!' " Alecia's enthusiasm was so exaggerated that it made me wince. " 'Sorry I won't be able to make it, but I'm still in *rehab*! Thanks for thinking of me, though. It's always nice to get mail. Love, *Mom*.' " Alecia set the letter down and glared at me.

"Aunt Maddie's in rehab?" I repeated. It was hard to imagine Aunt Maddie making a habit out of anything, considering all the years that she refused to take her medication on a regular basis. "I'm just not a pill taker," she'd told me once, when I was a child, as she pointed to the array on her bedside table.

"You invited her to a baby shower—for me?" Alecia added.

"I invited her to a wedding shower. I don't know where she got the idea—"

"How could you do that to me?" She shoved the dishwasher rack back inside and slammed the door shut.

"I forgot you hate showers. But we had to cancel it anyway, since Holly left—"

"How could you invite my mother to anything?"

"What's going on?" Ben asked, appearing from the living room. He was holding Max, who was either nuzzling his shoulder or just wiping his nose on it.

"She invited my mother to Pittsburgh!"

"But it says right here that she's not coming," I said, reaching for the envelope, as if presenting evidence to a judge.

"So, what's the matter?" he asked.

Alecia rolled her eyes before turning back to me. "Is there some reason you never put an ad in the paper to find Mazy's family a nanny?"

My eyelids sprang open. "They were a complete mess!"

"So, now you're judging them?"

"I'm not judging them—I just don't want to work for them!"

It was like the attack in Pottery Barn: maybe if I pretended that it never happened, that I'd never gone blind or never seen Augustus Catalano's cadaver toes, then I didn't have to act on it.

"Mama?" Max asked, worry in his voice. I never raised my voice in front of him.

"Why don't we go find some trucks to play with," Ben said.

"He needs some Tylenol first," I said.

"I did you a favor!" Alecia snapped. "I made *phone calls* to friends on your behalf, and what have you done besides *that*?" She pointed to my latest piece of collage art therapy, a montage of couples in love: brides and grooms, soldiers and girls-back-home, and even two toddlers kissing, all amidst a background of raining flowers, peonies and poppies and crocuses and lilacs. And at the center, an ever-so-tiny letter Z, inspired by Ben's latest quest. I wasn't sure if he'd noticed it yet.

"I have given you a place to live for over a month, and how do you repay me? You invite my crazy mother to a goddamn baby shower!"

"A baby shower?" Ben repeated, stooping down to hand the medicine cup to Max, who took it like a shot. He always loved the taste of medicine, the cherrier the better.

"First of all, it wasn't a baby shower," I said to Ben and then turned back to Alecia. "And second of all, she's not even coming."

"That's not the point!"

The phone rang, and all of us looked at the cordless receiver, which was empty.

"I'll find it," Ben said, wandering off with Max in tow.

"You shouldn't have invited her. It wasn't your place." Alecia waved her arm around in a circle and added, "This isn't your place. These aren't your knives!"

Somehow, I made my sagging mouth say, "Look, I'm sorry. Max and I will move out right after the wedding."

"In two weeks?"

"Well, after that, you'll be in Fiji for two weeks. That gives me a month. I'm sure, by then, I can get a job and an apartment...." I trailed off, because Alecia was shaking her head.

"We're rescheduling the honeymoon. Vanessa could give birth at any time, and I have to be available to anchor."

"What about all that money you spent on the trip?" I asked. "You can just postpone it like that?"

"I bought vacation insurance," Alecia said, so flippantly that suddenly I was infuriated.

Ben must have found the phone buried somewhere in the

sofa, because the ringing suddenly stopped. "Hello? ... Oh, certainly. It's for you, Di," he called. "Augustus Catalano?"

I stared at Alecia, whose face suddenly became smug, as if she'd personally arranged the call. When Ben returned to the kitchen and handed me the phone, I reached for it gingerly. "Mr. Catalano?"

"Please, call me Augustus," he said. "How's it going?"

"Oh ... pretty good. How're you?" It was only after I glanced up and caught Alecia's eye that I remembered that this wasn't a casual phone call.

"I'm fine. I'll be even better when you tell me you've found me a nanny."

I couldn't tell him that I hadn't even started looking. Not when his voice was so deep and perfect and just begging to be pleased. "Well ... I've gotten some leads, but as it turns out, none of them are really appropriate." I walked away from Ben and Alecia, who were both watching me now.

"Oh, come on. Try me."

"No, really. I can't see any of them ... fitting in well with your family."

"Di, at this point, I just need a warm body."

"With all due respect, if you had just wanted a warm body, you wouldn't be hiring me."

"Well, what are my options here? Tell me about the nannies you've interviewed. My standards are not all that high. You'd be surprised."

I walked into the bathroom and shut the door. "Um ... let me see ... Joyce has been a nanny for a family for the last five years but the youngest one is now in kindergarten and doesn't need her anymore. Her references all checked out— they loved her." I cleared my throat.

"Great. When can she start?"

"In twenty-one days when she gets out of rehab." On the end of the line, there was only silence, and I kept talking to fill it up. "Um…who else do I have…" I began to pace between the toilet and the sink. "There's Ginny, a sweet Southern belle whose specialty is diabetic cooking. But unfortunately she's just joined a convent, and the nuns won't let her out."

"The nuns won't let her out," Augustus repeated slowly. "Listen, we're kind of on a time crunch. I'm leaving for Boston today. I can't leave my son alone. He'll end up in the ER."

"What about his brother?"

"Who, Jason? He's an ER physician," Augustus said. "He's very busy. He doesn't have time to babysit."

"I see."

"Listen, Di, I would be willing to pay the finder's fee if you could just fill in until you find somebody else."

"Oh no. I have quite a few clients, and I can't be everyone's nanny until I find them the right nanny. I would have to be in a million places at once."

"Double the finder's fee. Consider it a retainer. You can eat whatever you like. Stay in the guest suite. Drive one of my cars. You just need to keep Gusty out of the ER."

"My two-year-old has a fever."

"I don't mind if you bring your son," Augustus said. "All you have to do is be here."

After hanging up the phone, I walked into the living room, where Alecia and Ben were facing each other in mirrored hands-on-the-hips stances. Their voices were low and urgent. "Well, what do you expect me to say?" Alecia asked.

"Just give me a chance—" Ben stopped, noticing me.

I scratched my head and glanced away. It occurred to me then that Augustus's invitation was an opportunity rather than a predicament—a chance to escape the apartment, at least for a little while. "Max and I need a ride to Fox Chapel," I said. "As soon as possible."

* * *

BEN TOOK US IN the Honda, which was a relief, since I was always afraid Max would throw up in Alecia's BMW. Sometimes I even felt underdressed for her car, like earlier, when Alecia saw my dressed-down outfit and said, "You're wearing that?" In Ben's Honda, I could wear my ripped jeans and slightly shrunken Superman T-shirt without feeling apologetic.

"So, why did you do it?" Ben asked, as he drove along the winding lanes of Fox Chapel, past the oak trees leading to the Presbyterian church, past the endless green of the golf course. "Why'd you invite her mother?"

"I was having a hard time coming up with a guest list for the shower. When I saw Aunt Maddie's address in Alecia's book, I just... really wanted to see her again. She *is* my father's little sister—'crazy' or not." I looked at him. "It was selfish, I know."

He shrugged.

"I have very few memories of my life in the States before my mother took me away. Of course, Aunt Maddie's not exactly the one to fill them in for me," I added with a laugh.

"What do you remember?" Ben asked.

"Oh, gosh. Nothing," I said automatically, and then, suddenly, a memory surfaced, as vivid as any movie. The setting: our kitchen; the menu: grilled cheeseburgers, so it must've been summer. It was the year before everything bad happened. Mom had been telling us about smile exercises: if we didn't feel like getting out of bed in the morning, we should stand before a mirror and smile ten times in a row. "What if I'm too tired to smile?" I asked. "Smile even if you don't mean it. You'll feel like doing anything," she replied. So, I tried it, right there, and even though I was only at about the fourth smile, I started laughing so hard that I was falling off my chair. My father kept eating his corn on the cob, methodically crunching down each row. My mother had recently banned all scientific journals and woodworking magazines from the dinner table, and he seemed to be taking it out on the corn. "Try it, Dad!" I said, head tilted back, laughs just burbling from my throat, and my mother gave him one of her glorious grins. "Go for it, Gabe."

"I'd rather not," my father said.

"That's precisely why you should be doing it!" my mother said.

"Do it, Dad!" I said, and possibly because I was the one begging, or because he wanted to prove my mother wrong, or because the faster he got it over with, the faster he could return to his rambling thoughts, my father put down his fork with an exasperated sigh and began to smile.

"Both sides of your mouth, Gabe."

"Show your teeth, Dad!" I said.

As my father's cheeks balled up and down, along with his rising and falling lips, we counted. For the first few, he might as well have been doing push-ups. But at number five, my father involuntarily chuckled. By nine, his shoulders were shaking and his stomach heaved, and the noises that came out of him were that of unmistakable hysteria. I leaned back in my seat, so thrilled that I let go of the table and toppled to the floor. My mother shrieked as they both stood up, and then, after seeing I was okay, they stumbled against each other, laughing even harder.

"You must miss them," Ben said, watching me wipe away a few tears, which, until that second, I'd thought were of the laughing variety.

"Well, yeah." My chuckles faded into silence. Missing didn't even come close. The worst part was that, if I'd only had the guts to leave my mother for just a little while, before she got sick, I could've seen my father again. "I never imagined that my dad would die before I could get back to the States," I said, my throat tight.

"And the way that he died," Ben added. "Who would've imagined that? Alecia doesn't talk about it much anymore, but she hasn't gotten over it, either. She still hates him."

"God?" I asked, twirling one of my braids.

"The kid," Ben said, instead of *the killer*.

I'd hated him, too, for a couple of weeks. Then it seemed futile, considering he was dead, too. "Why is she wasting her energy hating a dead guy?"

"Why does Alecia do anything she does?" His laugh didn't sound happy.

We came to a fork in the road. To the left, a stone fence along a shady lane, and to the right, more rolling green lawns that made me wish I played golf. I pointed to the left, and, as we passed a sign marked *Shady Side Academy,* I wondered if the brick building on the hilltop was actually Gusty's school. Soon, we were pulling up at the iron gates of the Catalano residence.

"Wow," Ben said, as we made our way toward the white manor. This time, the kamikaze dog was nowhere in sight.

"I know." Closing my eyes for just a second, I waved my hand out the window. The oak trees were making a shushing sound in the breeze.

When I opened my eyes again, Ben was parking just outside the four-car garage. I woke Max and lifted him out of his car seat, while Ben grabbed our bags and pillows out of the back.

"When are you coming back?" Ben asked, shutting the hatchback.

"I have no idea," I said, suddenly daunted.

We stood there staring at each other, as if we both knew that the next time we saw each other again, everything would be different. "Well . . . go get 'em, kid," Ben finally said, and I laughed as he hugged me, then got in the car and drove off.

USING THE HALF-ASSEMBLED new stone walkway, Max and I made our way to the front door. I carried two duffel bags and two pillows, and Max clutched his blanket and floppy blue horse.

"Big fan of Underoos?" someone called from a bed of mulch under the dining room window.

"Excuse me?" I asked, startled to find one of the landscapers smiling at me with a nod toward my Superman T-shirt. It was the boss, Dave, I remembered, the one who got interrogated in the dining room. He was crouched by a bush next to an overturned wheelbarrow of mulch. His employees were working, too, I realized, over in the rose garden not fifteen feet away.

"You know, Underoos. That . . . underwear . . . Made you feel like a superhero underneath your regular clothes. I was Batman." Dave stood up.

"I grew up in England. I never had Underoos." This was, of course, another lie. I got my first pair before we left Pittsburgh.

"You don't talk English," Dave said.

"What language do you think that I'm speaking?" I asked slowly, which made the other two landscapers whoop with laughter, and one of them holler, *Dickhead!*

"I mean . . . you know what I mean," Dave said, turning red, and suddenly I felt bad, but not bad enough to admit that mine were Wonder Woman.

"Thanks for not parking on the lawn this time!" one of the landscapers called out, the bitter one with bad acne who'd chewed me out the other week.

"You the new lady of the house?" the tubby guy shouted.

"I'm the nanny," I found myself shouting back. "I mean, I'm filling in for the nanny. Until I can find the nanny…" My voice trailed off. They all stared at me, including Dave. Including Max, for that matter. "Any of you know a nanny?" I added. They said no, and I nodded, resigned.

This time when I rang the bell, it was Augustus who answered the door. "Oh, Jesus, we have pillows," he said, rushing to grab one of my bags. He set it on the floor of the marble foyer. Shutting the door behind us, he added, "Well, that's a new look." All at once, I understood why my ratty outfit had horrified Alecia.

"Shouldn't you already be at the airport?" I asked.

"Rearranged my flight… hey, buddy!" Augustus shouted and waved at Max. Apparently Augustus was one of those men who shout at children, as if limited vocabulary was tantamount to deafness. "How old are you?"

"Max, tell him how old you are," I said, as he clung to my leg and buried his face against my jeans. "He's two," I finally said, when he wouldn't even humor me by holding up his fingers.

"You're so big!" Augustus shouted again, crouching down, which made Max's lips collapse into a frown.

"I…am…not big!" Max shouted back, before starting to howl.

"I'm sorry," I said, as Augustus, looking bewildered, stood up. If he was offended, he didn't say so and instead just told us to follow him into the master bedroom. Thankfully Max ended his outburst with a few pitiful whimpers and then took my hand.

The bedroom was more like a third living room that happened to have a king-size bed in it. There was a chaise longue and an easy chair next to yet another fireplace. The wallpaper matched the tasteful yellow-rose trellis on the bedspread. On the bed lay an open suitcase with dress shirts and ties piled next to it. For some reason, just seeing Augustus's open suitcase made my face heat up, as though I'd caught him in his boxers. I tried to concentrate on his instructions instead, when and where Gusty needed to be at school, what time he needed to be woken up, how he wasn't to be left alone for too long on his computer, and how he had to be reminded to check his blood sugar four times a day and take his insulin with every meal.

"When are you coming back?" I asked, crossing my arms over the giant S on my shirt, feeling like Augustus's daughter or lover; I wasn't sure which. If only we weren't having this conversation in the bedroom.

"Don't know. This trial could take a few days or a week." Augustus snapped his suitcase shut.

"You're a lawyer?"

"I'm an expert witness. I do consulting."

"You must always have to be in the right place at the right time," I joked.

A flicker of confusion seemed to cross Augustus's face, but all he said was "I really can't discuss it."

"Wouldn't Gusty rather be staying with his mother?" I asked.

Augustus's eyebrows shot up. I felt like I was Max shouting, *I am not big,* right in his face. "Gusty is not comfortable at his mother's place, for various reasons—no, no, no!" Augustus shouted at Max, who'd just picked up a china figurine off the marble coffee table in the sitting area.

Quickly moving to intercept my son, I asked, "Would Mazy want to sleep here? I mean, since you won't be here?"

Augustus waited to reply until I'd successfully distracted Max with Stanley, his stuffed horse, and pried the figurine from his hand. "Actually, we were doing that for the last six months," he said finally, watching me set the china piece on the mantel. "We wanted things to be the least disruptive for

Gusty. But that's not going to work long-term. We both want to move on."

Who gets custody of Gusty when you're gone? I thought. *The house?*

"You are his acting guardian, therefore..." Augustus handed me a cell phone and a notarized document stating that for the next three weeks, while under my care, I was allowed to get him medical treatment if need be. "Make sure to bring this to the hospital if he goes into hypoglycemic shock. And, of course, use the cell to give me a call."

I was too distracted by the dates on the letter to fret about his casual use of the word *shock*. "But this says through October ninth. I didn't agree to stay here for three weeks. My cousin is getting married on the first. I have to be in her wedding."

"I'll be back before then. I'm just not sure how long this case will take. Di, if there's one thing I like, it's to play it safe." He put a gentle hand on my shoulder. "Let me show you where you'll be."

THE GUEST SUITE WAS on the opposite side of the house, off the kitchen. Augustus left us alone for a few minutes so that we could unpack. Even Max seemed temporarily enthralled by the space. He let go of his horse and ran right up to the floor-to-ceiling mirror and tried to hug himself. I could've collapsed onto the fluffy white duvet covering the sleigh bed but opted to check out the bathroom instead, where white columns led the way to a round granite tub. There were even two toilets, which reminded me of the flat my mother and I had once shared in Paris, the spring that I turned sixteen, thanks to one of her friends. It was a blissful time, where we ate crusty bread and runny cheeses and drank red wine with dinner every night—actual vacationing, rather than hiding out.

After pressing my face into the soft towels and assessing the water pressure, I used the cell phone to quickly dial Alecia, who seemed less than pleased to hear my voice: "You're calling me already? It's been, what, fifteen minutes?"

"I thought you should have my new cell phone number—in case of an emergency. I'm in the bathroom," I added in a whisper. "The tub is *amazing*. I can't wait to use it."

"You're calling me from the john," Alecia said flatly.

"I'm not actually on the—"

"Goodbye, Di."

I snapped the phone shut and left the bathroom. Max was on the floor, cuddling his blue horse and staring glassy-eyed at the ceiling fan going round and round overhead.

"Oh, Boo, don't you want to nap on the bed?" I asked, stooping down to stroke his blond hair. I couldn't really blame him for wanting to crash right there. The sea foam carpet was so plush, it could've been a mattress. Max didn't answer, only blinked and made a sighing noise as he fixed his blue eyes on me. His watchfulness made me pause, made me remember him as a newborn, that first moment I held him. He was astonishingly awake and alert and curious, even in his first few minutes of life. Even now, when I looked in his eyes, I was often surprised to see tiny reflections of myself in there, as if I was everything to him. Until Max, I never knew what it meant to hold someone's gaze.

After covering him with his blanket and kissing both Max and Stanley the horse, I whispered that I'd be back in just a little while. In the kitchen, Augustus was giving Gusty instructions like a drill sergeant.

"I don't feel so hot," Gusty said, rubbing his forehead.

"You feel fine," Augustus said, an order. "Why don't you offer Di a drink?" he added, noticing me now. "You remember Di, don't you?"

"Hi, Gusty," I said.

"Would you like a drink?" Gusty asked, sounding vaguely robotic.

"Oh, no, no, no." I shouldn't have protested so emphatically. Suddenly, I was thirsty. "I mean, yes, but I can get it myself."

My answer was unacceptable to Augustus, who insisted on offering me cider, Pepsi or Coke, beer or wine, papaya juice, a bloody Mary. I said that a Coke would be fine, and, before I could stop him, Gusty poured my soda into a glass.

Once Augustus had pointed out the emergency money hidden in the back of the dish cabinet, he was gone with his matching luggage. Gusty peered outside and said gloomily, "My mom is not going to be happy."

Following his gaze out the window, I assumed he was talking about the overgrown rose trellis, or that the pool out back was covered with leaves, though why should his mother care if she didn't really run this house anymore? "She didn't want Dad to hire you," he added. "She wanted to use a more professional company."

"I can understand that."

"She said you didn't know what you were doing. She thought you were *strange*."

"Well, she could be right," I said cheerfully and then clapped my hands together. "How about a tour?"

So, he gave me a tour. I found out that the living room with all the books was actually called the library, and that the living room with the ottoman and the thirty windows was called the Great Room, but the kitchen was still just called the kitchen, even if it had tile on the walls and an eight-burner stove.

From the glass French doors overlooking the flagstone patio, we stared into the backyard. It was going to rain. Clouds were beginning to overtake the blue sky, the wind kicked up, and even more leaves were scattering into the oval pool.

"Do you spend much time in the pool?" I asked.

"Did my dad tell you to ask me that?" Gusty asked, instantly agitated. "God, that's all he ever says. 'Go swim, Gusty. Turn off the computer and swim.' " His hands balled into fists. " 'Who wanted the pool, Gusty? Did I want the pool? I don't think so. You wanted the pool, Gusty.' Who wants to go swimming alone?" Gusty shouted, startling me. "I wanted a dog. Not a fucking pool."

"But...you have a dog," I said, and this time it was Gusty's turn to stare at me. "The yellow Lab. I almost ran him over the first day I was here."

Gusty shook his head. "I'm not allowed to have a dog. Dad said if I can't keep myself out of the hospital, I can't possibly take care of an animal."

"Mama?" Max called, wandering into the kitchen in his overalls and bare feet.

"Who is this?" Gusty asked, his eyes widening in amazement, as if I'd presented him with the dog he'd always wanted.

"I'm hungry," Max said.

"Okay, Boo. But where are your socks? Go get your socks, and then I'll make something to eat."

"Is he staying here, too?" Gusty asked, as my son tramped back to the guest suite.

"As long as I'm here."

His hunched shoulders, the ones he'd been wearing as earmuffs, dropped a little.

We both turned back to the window. Leaves were blowing across the lawn. Autumn was coming, then winter, and soon, Max and I would have no place to go.

Gusty turned and met my eyes. "You want to know something that really scares me?" he asked, and I nodded slowly.

"When they took the cover off that pool at the beginning of the summer, that water was *black*. Then the pool people came and played with the chemicals until it was like, aqua-colored. But it's the same water!" He began to laugh, a squeaky guffaw. "They never switched it. Isn't that gross?"

Just hearing him chuckle for the first time was such a relief that I joined in, even if it wasn't that gross or that funny. I desperately wanted a reason to laugh. My mother, in less than five smiles, could transform an uncomfortable situation into something splendid and memorable. At this moment, I would've settled for quick and painless.

CHAPTER 9

Magical Time

What I didn't know when I called Alecia from the bathroom of the guest suite was that I'd interrupted her in the middle of a last-minute, frenetic effort to escape the apartment before Ben could return from dropping me off in Fox Chapel.

"We're gonna have to find a compromise," Ben had whispered the first night after the baby shower, as he spooned Alecia in bed. My cousin had simply shut her eyes and pretended to drift off, so that she wouldn't have to ask the next, obvious question, which was *How the hell are we gonna do that? Get a dog—or half a baby?* Perhaps a similar thought had occurred to him the next day, because she, too, had noticed he'd been acting funny ever since: staying late at school—supposedly to work on "the magazine"—avoiding her at home and on the news. He didn't even crack a smile that day when she quizzed him on which Winnie-the-Pooh character Fran most resembled. (Eeyore, of course, with occasional shades of Piglet, whenever new studies were released that suggested yet another drug might be *d-d-d-dangerous*.) "You said *I* was Eeyore," Ben had replied, sounding testy. "Just when we first met. You're much more Tiggerish now," Alecia said, a remark that made him scowl. She'd forgotten that Holly had once diagnosed Tigger with ADHD. "Who am I?" I had asked, to which Ben immediately answered, "Well, Kanga, of course." Alecia could tell by the way his forehead lines disappeared that Kanga was exactly what he wanted: Mother Earth, who not only loved children, but knew how to make succulent pork chops.

And then there was Max: was it her imagination, or had Ben been extra helpful with my son, as if to prove what a great father he'd be, if Alecia would just give in?

Somehow, they'd managed to put off The Talk for the last week. (Even their premarital counseling session had been miraculously canceled when Pastor Nate left a message that he was being treated for pneumonia. "I *told* you the man was dying," Alecia had said, sounding strangely triumphant.) She'd just gotten dressed in her favorite skinny jeans, silk T-shirt, and ballet flats, when her stomach started churning all over again, and her heart, rather than beating, began vibrating, instead. *Leave, now,* it occurred to her. She remembered the story she'd reported on of the bride who'd faked her own abduction to avoid walking down the aisle. At the time, Alecia had ridiculed the woman, but now, fleeing a situation seemed like a perfectly reasonable alternative to confrontation. She gathered twelve pairs of pants into her duffel bag and planned to disappear—not to Arizona, like the AWOL bride, but amongst the clothing racks at Banana Republic. The store was having a Donate Pants Campaign: for every old pair that Alecia donated, she would get 15 percent off a new pair. Maybe shopping would make the shaking in her fingers go away. And maybe it would help her let go of the thought that had been chasing her all week: *What if there isn't a compromise?*

Ben walked in the door, then, and she rushed toward him trying to speak, but her chest was heaving too fast to get the words out.

"What is it, baby?" Ben asked, taking her into his arms.

She buried her face into his shoulder. She loved his flannel shirt. Loved his shoulders. She'd been stupid to think of running away.

"Is this about your mother?" Ben asked, rubbing her back. "Because I really don't think that Di meant—"

"This is about us!" Alecia erupted. "You and me!"

"Baby, calm down." Ben stroked her shoulders. "It's going to be all right. Okay? It's going to be fine," he added in a whisper, kissing her neck.

And suddenly, she was kissing him back, and unbuckling his pants, and he was lifting her shirt over her head, and then they were stripping down, in the middle of the kitchen. Just before she could worry that he wanted to make love to her right there on the dirty floor, Ben scooped her up, carried her across the apartment, pushed her pile of makeup aside, and threw her down on the bed.

When it was over, they were sweaty and smiling. Finally, the quaking inside her had left.

"See, this is why—" Alecia started to say and then stopped. *This is why it's great not having children. We can have sex in the middle of the afternoon.*

"This is why, what?" Ben asked, smiling, as he pulled her off the bed and turned up the radio. Before she could even finish pulling on her bathrobe, he started spinning her around to the song that had just come on, "Dance Me to the End of Love."

"Who is this—Billie Holiday?" They hadn't danced in ages, or at least, not since they'd graduated from their *Intro to Ballroom* class over the summer.

"It's actually Madeleine Peyroux," Ben said, pulling her head to his cheek and swaying in time to the music like a military man in a 1940's dance hall.

She allowed him to spin her around until Madeleine sang, "Dance me to the children, who are asking to be born . . ." and she broke away, saying, "I have to get dressed."

"Alecia," Ben said, the weight of the world in his voice.

"What do you want for lunch?" Alecia asked, tightening the sash on her robe, but he'd grabbed her arm and wouldn't let go.

"Alecia," Ben said again, and she let him drag her back over to the edge of the bed. He looked so depressed all of a sudden that she wanted to comfort him.

"What is it, baby?" Alecia wrapped her arms around him and leaned her head on his shoulder.

"Don't you think we need to talk?"

"About what?"

"You know what."

Alecia rubbed Ben's back and neck, even his scalp, until he removed her hands from his head, pushed her backward onto the bed, and lay down on top of her. Alecia laughed until Ben stared her into silence with the same steady blue eyes that had first claimed her in the newsroom. He stroked her hair, and even her brows, what was left of them, since Richard had suggested she start waxing them into trim punctuation marks.

"Why do you want to marry me?" Ben asked.

"Because I love you!" She immediately regretted the snap in her voice.

Ben rolled off her and onto his back. "Remember that

time when we were first dating, when we walked on the beach at Coney Island and skipped stones? And the sun was so bright?"

"Yeah," Alecia said. *It's all in the wrist,* Ben had told her, as he got better and better at the flick and release. He threw his stones wildly, and they'd obey: skipping two then three then four times before disappearing underwater. Meanwhile, Alecia kept hurling her rocks with a definitive, single thunk, which made both of them laugh. "That was nice," she said.

"I miss that—that...uncertainty," Ben said. "Would you like me? Would you even love me? Would I get this rock to glide across the water's surface before it sank?"

Alecia sighed. "Ben, marriage is not going to be like that. I mean, not that it can't be exciting or unpredictable, but..." She shook her head.

"Can I tell you why I want to have children?" Ben asked, turning to look at her again. "They give you that uncertainty back. From the moment you meet your children, they're just entirely unpredictable. You have no idea who they'll become. It's just like at the beginning, when things were new with us, and we didn't know what we'd become...."

"So, you want to live vicariously through your children."

"No. No, you're missing the—it would be an adventure—for us, as a couple—to find out what happens next—"

"What if I couldn't have children? Would you hate me for it?"

"Of course not. But I'd want us to try."

"Look, maybe I told you *one time* that I wanted to have children, but I don't. You told me for an entire *year* that you planned on becoming a minister, and now you're not."

"What does that have to do with anything?" Ben asked.

"Things change," Alecia said with a shrug.

"Like you would've been a great minister's wife."

"Don't blame it on me! I am sick to death of everyone assuming that it was my fault that your vision went away, that it's my fault that you never follow through on anything—"

"How can you say that?"

"Every time I turn around, you pick something new. This week it's fatherhood and a magazine. Next week, it's golf."

The phone rang, and Alecia held his gaze for a second longer, before breaking away to read the caller ID on the cordless: her boss.

Art carried the title of general manager—or GM—at WTAE and was a man, Alecia had explained early on, who could be won over by food. (She'd asked me to make some "treats" that she might drop off at his office—garlic and goat cheese dip and those slices of French bread, for example— which was what he was sampling when he offered her the position of co-anchor.) Art also had a weakness for women with blond hair, which explained why the anchors at the station, Mazy and Vanessa, along with the field reporters, Alecia and Heidi, were all various shades of the same color.

"Oh, good. You're not busy," Art said, when she picked up the phone, making Alecia roll her eyes. "Listen, I've got big problems. Heidi is thinking about quitting."

"I'm sorry. What's the problem?"

"She's supposed to work tomorrow morning."

Alecia groaned. Now she understood: Art had holes in his schedule. "I just want to remind you that my wedding is in two weeks. What do you need?"

"Well, for starters, I need a reporter tomorrow. Are Sundays still a problem for you?"

Alecia had told her boss several times that her fiancé was no longer studying to be a minister, that in fact they rarely attended church, but she knew Art still held it against her. "Sundays never were a problem for me, Art."

"Good, good. The other thing is…" Art cleared his

throat—or, more precisely, coughed and sputtered for what seemed to be a full minute. "She's only leaving if I make you anchor," he finally managed to say. "It turns out that Heidi really wanted Vanessa's spot."

"Art, repeat after me: Ba-bye, Heidi." There was a pause. "She sucks as a reporter."

"She does, she does," Art said quickly. "But she has me convinced that it's because she's a much better anchor. And I watched her audition tapes from when she was back in Millersville. She was much more relaxed."

"So, she was relaxed! She was probably filming in someone's garage!" Alecia snapped. "Did you forget that I worked in Manhattan, Art? Pittsburgh is small potatoes for me! And you said yourself how impressed you've been with me."

"You're a fabulous reporter, Alecia, but the more I think of it, I don't know if I can afford to lose you in the field."

"No." Her voice turned so deep and menacing that Ben's eyebrows went up. He stood up to get dressed, grabbing his pants off the chair like a man reaching for armor. "If you give my spot to Heidi—"

"I think you're both forgetting that it's Vanessa's spot, and she won't be on maternity leave forever!" Art said. "Vanessa's coming back! I think you ladies are getting all worked up over—"

"If you give my spot to Heidi, I quit. And you'll have just as many holes in your schedule." Alecia hung up.

"Alecia." Ben stared at her. "Tell me you didn't just hang up on your boss."

"He's actually thinking about giving my job to Heidi!"

"He's going to make Heidi an anchor?" Ben's eyes grew even wider. "Wow. He really is an equal opportunity employer."

"What's her disability? Ugliness?" Alecia asked, jamming her feet into her slippers.

The phone rang. The caller ID said WTAE again. "You get it." Alecia tossed the cordless onto the edge of the bed. "Tell him I've gone to a dress-fitting."

"Alecia, I'm not going to..."

She walked out of the bedroom and slammed the door to the bathroom. Her heart was pounding, and nausea overwhelmed her. It had to be the pressure. The pressure was giving her an ulcer. Art promised she would be anchor. And she had told everyone.

Ben knocked on the bathroom door. "He said to tell you you're anchor, the second Vanessa goes into labor. But you have to work in the field tomorrow or you're fired."

Alecia opened the door, suddenly laughing so hysterically there were tears in her eyes. "Oh, thank God." She hugged Ben hard, but he still looked afraid of her. Or maybe he was just hurt. "Oh, sweetie. I'm sorry. I didn't mean anything I said."

"You meant every word of it," Ben said.

"I just didn't want to be blamed for your lack of conviction."

"Thanks," Ben said, throwing up his hands and backing away. "This is really helping."

"Oh, come on. You're the one who said I'd be a terrible minister's wife," Alecia called after him. Actually, her father had said that, too. It was possibly the first time he and Ben had agreed on anything.

When he didn't answer, she shut off the tap water and went to find him. He was fully dressed and sitting on the end of the bed, staring straight ahead. "Baby, you know I love you, right?" she asked from the doorway.

Watching him watch the window—*had he even heard her?*—Alecia was reminded of her own parents, who must've married with such high hopes—although it was hard to imagine—and of *my* parents who'd shocked everyone, or at least, shocked Alecia, when they announced their divorce. "Yours was the fun house," she'd often told me, "where we were all happy." She thought of my mother's anti-wedding sentiments, a fatalism that Alecia had never shared until that very moment when Ben finally sounded out her words like a man learning to read: "I know that you love me." She knew, then, that it wasn't going to be enough.

CHAPTER 10

First Night

I waited until I'd fed Max a peanut butter and jelly sandwich and he was happily coloring at the kitchen table with Gusty, then I went to investigate the pantry for dinner ingredients. I was in the mood for garlic, maybe in a Bolognese sauce over pasta with a side of garlic bread, but as soon as I discovered the cans of crushed tomatoes and boxes of linguine, I remembered Gusty's diabetes.

"Are you on a special diet?" I asked, coming out of the pantry, which was the size of the guest room Max and I had been sharing at Alecia's apartment.

"Not really." Gusty picked up a crayon.

"Shouldn't you be?"

"Look, I know how to handle my sugars. I've been dealing with this since I was two." Gusty didn't even look up. "Max, what color is my skin?"

Max stared at Gusty's pale arm and said, "Skin."

"Right. So why are you coloring everyone's face and arms blue?"

Max considered this for a moment before picking up another crayon and coloring someone's cheeks chartreuse.

"Okay, I just... might believe that you know what you're doing if you didn't end up in the hospital so much," I said in one breath. "Do you deliberately go into shock to get your parents' attention?"

"Yeah, I do it to get their attention," Gusty said. "That's all I want. *More* attention." I thought of the way his father harped on him to go swimming and realized this was a boy who might rather be left alone. "If everything doesn't go perfectly, my parents have no patience for it," Gusty added, reaching for another crayon. "They're the ones who have a problem with my diabetes, not me."

He must've been annoyed because now he, too, was coloring people green.

"Are you hungry for anything in particular?" I asked, giving up on the diet.

Gusty looked up at the ceiling. "I'd like a nice steak. Medium rare," he decided, rocking back in his chair until the front legs were off the ground.

"Okay, good. That helps." I searched the stainless steel fridge, only to find that it was surprisingly empty, save for fifteen different kinds of beverages, thirty condiments, eggs, and asparagus. Maybe I'd make hollandaise. Except there was no lemon juice, and no steak for that matter. "We might have to go to the grocery store. Your dad was saying that he'd leave us a car...?"

"We can take mine."

I stared at him. "Your... car? You're what, fourteen?"

"I'm thirteen," Gusty said. "I'll be fourteen in November, though." When I could only shake my head at him, he leaned forward, letting his chair legs hit the floor with a bang. "Well, what am I gonna say, no thanks? I don't want a Porsche, I'm too young, and I can't drive yet? Dad's the one who drives it all the time! He's put loads of miles on the car; it probably won't be worth anything by the time I get it."

"Oh, it'll be worth something," I said dryly.

"Great, now you hate me, too." Gusty slammed his hands down on the table, which made Max stop coloring and stare at him.

"No one hates you, Gusty," I said.

Max reached over to give him a gentle pat on the arm. "It's okay, Boo," he said. At least Gusty's shoulders relaxed, and one side of his mouth turned up in a reluctant half-smile.

"So, who wants to go to the grocery store?" I asked.

Gusty informed me that there was actually another pantry in the basement along with three freezers, which may or may not contain beef tenderloin, so Max and I followed him downstairs instead. I was relieved, as the thought of driving a thirteen-year-old's Porsche without a license had been unnerving.

The basement reminded me of movies I'd seen that had been set in New York lofts. There was a pool table, bar, and big-screen TV at the foot of the stairs. On one side of the endless room a mirrored gym looked equipped enough to handle the Steelers, while the uncarpeted section at the other end, with its multitude of freezers and shelves of canned goods, looked ready to satisfy a local homeless shelter or the Steelers after practice. *Maybe we could camp here,* I thought, rooting through frozen lamb chops and lobster in one of the chest freezers until I finally came upon a package of steaks.

"You could hide a dead body in here," I said, shutting the lid of the freezer.

Gusty's eyes darted around the room, as if he'd been waiting for me to stumble upon one. I looked around, too, at the leather sofa and the jukebox, until we both seemed to simultaneously notice Max waving at something or someone in the corner.

"Who is he waving to?" Gusty asked nervously, pointing at Max, who was now walking back toward the sofa.

"I don't know," I said thoughtfully. "Max, who're you waving to?"

"That man," Max said, laughing as he passed the pool table and kept going toward the bar.

"What man?" Gusty asked. "Does he see someone?"

I hoped the invisible person was my father, who, so far, had yet to appear to me and say goodbye. (Not entirely surprising, since Dad was never quite convinced of the existence of spirits, despite that my mother saw them all the time.) But perhaps Max would get luckier than me. After all, children are supposed to be more clairvoyant than adults.

Max finally stopped underneath a photo hanging on the wall. It was of an elderly man with a gray mustache, blue eyes, and a friendly smile—Gusty's face on an old man, I realized. "Hello!" Max said, still laughing as if they were sharing a joke.

"That's my grandfather. How does he know my grandfather?" Gusty looked as if he was about to cry.

"Oh, he doesn't know him," I said. "Max, come back here. You're scaring Gusty."

"I'm not scared. I just thought..." Gusty trailed off, watching Max, who was still pointing at the picture. "Sometimes I hear noises down here. Or, like, a light will be left on and no one's been in the basement. My dad says that our house can't be haunted, because it's brand-new."

"Oh, it can be haunted," I said, which made Gusty's eyes widen. "But I've never met an unfriendly ghost."

Gusty gulped. "You've met...*ghosts*?"

"Only relatives. And not lately." I moved across the room

to get Max. "My mother, on the other hand, could see spirits who weren't in the family. But they were always polite, she said."

"Polite," Gusty repeated, eyes still wide.

"Well, if you had something to say from the afterlife, wouldn't you be?" I asked, scooping up Max, so that he could get a better look at the picture. "This is Gusty's grandfather. Hi, Gusty's grandfather!" I said, waving. "Your dad's dad?" I asked, tossing the question behind me.

"Augustus the first," Gusty said as he went to get the frozen steaks off the top of the freezer. "He used to watch me when my parents were out. But he died last June."

"Unexpectedly?" I asked and then hated myself for asking such a stupid question. "I mean, was he sick for a long time?"

"He was totally fine! I mean, he never even needed a caddy when he played golf. Then one day he just fell down," Gusty said. "In the middle of a sentence."

"Who was he talking to?"

"Me."

When I turned and looked at him, this skinny-legged misfit who seemed so miserable, it took my entire willpower not to reach over and hug him. But I knew it would be inappropriate; we'd just met, after all, and besides, he would probably take it as a sign of pity. Max was wriggling in my arms, demanding my attention again.

"So, who's been staying with you since your grandfather died?" I asked as we made our way up from the basement, following Max, who'd rushed for the stairs as soon as I let him go.

"Once they had my mom's mom come and stay, but she was too drunk to notice me, and I ended up in the ER."

When we made it back into the well-lit foyer, I felt more at ease, leaving our conversation behind, along with the chilly basement. Except that the front hall marble, squeaking under my sneakers, wasn't much cozier. It wasn't a warm house, that was for sure.

Hours later, after nightfall had enveloped the many windows of the mansion, and Max and his blue horse were set up to sleep on the floor of the guest room like he wanted, I made a late dinner: steak, pan-seared then roasted in the oven, mushroom risotto, asparagus with hollandaise sauce (since I'd discovered some lemon juice at the back of the fridge), and chocolate chip cookies from scratch.

"Are you a chef or something?" Gusty asked, watching me give the risotto a final stir.

"I just like to cook." I checked the mixer to see how the cookie dough was coming together. "I'm actually a masseuse."

"What does that mean? People pay you to, like, touch them?"

"They used to." After seeing the look on his face, I chose not to tell him that I also handled all the bikini waxes at the London spa.

"There's raw egg in that!" Gusty shouted, just as I lifted a spoonful of the dough to my mouth. He reminded me of Augustus, when Max grabbed the china figurine.

"So?" I asked, hesitating for just a moment.

"So, you could get sick from it! My mom always says that."

"You've never tasted raw cookie dough before?" I couldn't get Gusty a dog or even a life, but I could definitely offer him this one small pleasure. "Oh, it's so good. Taste it."

"No way," Gusty said, so emphatic that I finally shrugged and put the spoon into my own mouth. "And just so you know, cookies aren't good for my diabetes."

I stopped chewing.

"Just kidding. I mean, I'm not, but I'll have one when it's

cooked," Gusty said. He waited until I'd reached for a second bite to add, "Geez, you're like my grandma offering me my first beer."

"Cookies and beer are not the same thing," I said with a full mouth.

Gusty laughed, until I handed him a set of silverware, then he shut right up. In fact, he looked so confused that I realized he didn't know what to do with the forks and knives. "It's for the table. Dinner's ready."

"Oh, okay, sure. We just . . . don't do that anymore."

"Eat with utensils?"

"No, eat sitting down. We mostly eat standing up. And never together, unless Dad has a friend over, and then we eat in the dining room. I hate the dining room."

"So, what are your dad's friends like?" I asked, using pot holders to carry the risotto to the kitchen table.

Gusty opened a drawer and came up with cloth napkins. "Dr. Berger plays pool with my dad, and sometimes they let me play, too. And Dr. Locklear used to be my shrink, when I was little."

"When you were little?" I repeated. "What are you now?"

"Like, in elementary school. My parents thought I needed to talk to someone about having diabetes." Gusty rolled his eyes as he set the forks onto the table. "I think *they* needed to talk to someone about having a kid with diabetes."

"Do you have any friends your own age?"

He shook his head and pulled out a chair. "Every once in a while, Pastor Krasinowski comes over with his family. But his kids are kind of weird."

I thought about Augustus Catalano's toes again. In light of his imminent death, inviting a pastor over for dinner had to be a good thing. "Is your father a religious man?"

"He gives a lot of money to the church. But my mom says he's just trying to buy his way into heaven. She says he always throws his money down instead of his heart. This is really good, by the way," he added, finally taking a bite of the meat.

It was good. I was pleased with how creamy the risotto turned out. And I couldn't help admiring the colors of the food on the plate. The bright green asparagus, the yellow sauce, the slightly red center to the meat. If only I'd remembered carrots in the risotto for just a touch of orange. All that was missing was Ben's dramatic reaction.

"My dad likes to sponsor people, and it used to drive Mom crazy. She said all she would have to do is flip through his checkbook to see who he was hanging around with."

"Sponsor people?" I asked, taking a sip of water. On second thought, maybe all that was missing was someone to turn it into red wine.

"Say you had a really good idea, and he liked it? He'd give you money to make it happen. My mom calls him a dream parasite. She says he invests in other people's dreams because he has none of his own."

I thought of Ben's magazine, how he'd told me that the start-up costs were several thousand dollars.

"That's how Mom found out that something was going on with Stacey Locklear."

"Who is Stacey Locklear?"

"Dr. Locklear's daughter! My mom checked the book, and he'd donated all this money to Stacey's law school. I guess they were boyfriend and girlfriend, or something."

Which pretty much answered my next question: *Would Ben have to sleep with Augustus Catalano to get sponsored?* "Her last name is Locklear—as in Heather?" When Gusty only stared at me blankly, I added, "The actress."

"I don't think they're related." Gusty picked up an asparagus spear. "My dad says that he and Mom were planning on getting a divorce even before he and Stacey started going out. But Jason's pissed."

"Jason," I echoed.

"My brother," Gusty said. And then, matter-of-factly: "He hates me."

"Why would you say that?"

"Because it's the truth. He says I'm spoiled. But it's not my fault that my parents made all their money later. Besides, they only give me whatever I want to bribe me. I'm not stupid."

"I'm sure your parents don't want to bribe you," I said.

"Sure, they do. Mom says Jason's just depressed because he's in residency. And before that, she said he was depressed because he was working so hard at Johns Hopkins medical school. Before that, she said he was depressed because he was trying to get into medical school. He's actually a little better now that he's met Valerie. She's a neurologist. They fell in love when they found out they both hate exactly the same things. Like snorkeling and country music and stupid people."

"That's . . . so romantic," I said, jumping up, remembering the cookies.

Gusty was quiet for a moment, watching as I quickly pulled the cookie sheet out of the oven. They were still gooey. *Perfect,* I thought.

"I like eating in the kitchen," Gusty said. "I don't know why Dad likes the dining room so much. Dad keeps talking about getting a chef."

"How often does your dad go away?" I asked, returning to the table.

"All the time for work. Plus, he's up in Boston twice a month at least. That's where Stacey lives."

"Has he ever thought of moving up there?"

"He can't leave the state if he wants joint custody."

"What about your mom?"

"She can't leave, either. Not because of me. The news.

God, this was so good," Gusty added with a groan, taking his last bite of risotto. "Hey, you should be our chef!"

I can't imagine what my face must've done, because he looked so apologetic a moment later. "I mean...I didn't mean it like that."

"Like what? I took it as a compliment, Gusty," I said, which was both the truth and a lie. I took it as an answer—or at least, a temporary one.

"Okay, I just...didn't mean...as long as you're not offended," Gusty said.

"I won't be offended, if you help me clean up," I said with a smile.

"What about the cookies?"

"First we do the dishes, then cookies." Watching Gusty happily jump up to load the dishwasher, possibly for the first time in his life, it occurred to me that maybe a few chores wouldn't kill him.

LATER ON, WHEN I went to peek on Max, sleeping on the floor of the guest suite, there was an unfamiliar beeping noise coming from the bathroom. I followed the sound all the way over to the ledge of the sink, where my forgotten cell phone was now signaling my very first text message: "Found out what was broken." I dialed my cousin, who sounded surprised to hear from me, if not dazed.

"So, what's the damage?" I asked. We were already accumulating quite a tab, since Max had accidentally destroyed her Waterford crystal vase a couple of weeks ago.

"Oh...pretty significant, I'd say."

She told me about The Talk, and the makeup sex, and Art's phone call, and how, when it was all over, she made the mistake of asking Ben if he was planning on picking up his tux.

"Look, Alecia . . ." He'd hesitated. "Maybe we need to just take this a little slower."

She'd blinked. "Take what a little slower?"

"Maybe we need to postpone the wedding."

"No!" I said, the same thing Alecia cried out as she backed away from him.

"I don't know if I can go through with it," Ben said.

"Okay. Okay. Okay." Alecia had stopped backing up. "No tux. Your suit is fine."

"I don't know if I can go through with it," he said again.

"I asked him if this had something to do with you," Alecia confessed presently, and I nearly dropped the phone.

"Me?" My voice echoed off the tiled walls and floors, and in the bedroom, Max groaned in his sleep.

"Well, he practically orgasms whenever you make dinner."

The cell phone felt hot, making my shaky palm moist. "What did he *say?*"

"That he wants to have children, and I don't. That it's kind of a deal breaker."

I winced.

"I told him how my mom never wanted to have children—and look what happened to her after I came along. *Crazy.*"

"You didn't cause Aunt Maddie's mental illness," I said.

"Well, she sure as hell wasn't crazy when Daddy married her! And I'm not going to have a kid and risk passing along any of my wacko genes. Ben said, in that case, we could consider adoption—as if that's a compromise. A child is a child!" She let go of a breath of air. "You should've seen the way he looked at me before he left: like I was a complete stranger."

"Oh, Alecia," I started.

"I opened all the gifts. I thought it would make me feel better!" she added when I gasped: there were over a hundred of them left to unwrap.

"What was that massive box by the window?" I couldn't help asking.

"A Weber grill." Her voice was flat. "The thing is, it was everything I'd registered for and nothing that I wanted."

There was a knock on the door to the guest suite: I'd forgotten Gusty had wanted to watch a movie.

"You kept a list of what everyone gave you, right?" I quickly asked. "For the thank-you notes?"

There was a pause, and when she spoke again, it was as if the weight of the situation had finally landed on her. "Oh. *Fuck*."

THREE HOURS LATER, AFTER we'd watched a movie and Gusty had gone upstairs to sleep, I soaked in the tub reading Augustus's *Architectural Digest*. Afterwards, I slipped between the lace-trimmed sheets of the sleigh bed and finally fell asleep, too, until I woke up abruptly from a dream about a peach orchard. I'd been wandering around through row after row of trees, trying to find the one without any fruit—the magical one, all twisting trunk, slender branches, and a perfect crown of blue-green leaves. Just as I came upon a clearing, a young man appeared and told me to follow him back to a table that was set for a picnic entirely of peaches. He was tall and slim, with dark brown hair and deep-set eyes, and it wasn't until he'd fed me five bushels of the fruit, so juicy it dripped down my face, that I looked up and realized he was the one who'd killed my father.

Startled awake, I threw back the duvet cover and ran. For a second, in the bright light of the bathroom, I was confused. I hadn't thrown up in years, and there were *two* toilets to choose from. But my stomach urged me into a decision, and I lifted the lid just in time.

"Mama?" Max whispered through the door, once I'd

progressed from vomiting, to dry heaves and diarrhea, to just diarrhea. I was sweating and dizzy, but at least the retching had stopped. It seemed like I'd been trapped in this bathroom for hours.

"Mama's sick, Boo. Are you okay?"

"I'm scared," he said with a whimper.

"Well, cuddle Stanley," I said. "And bring Mama her toothbrush."

Back in bed, I was too worn out to do more than rub Max's back when he curled up next to me. *Thank God, Gusty didn't eat the raw cookie dough,* I thought, pressing a cool rag to my head. My bowels were making rumbling sounds but the worst of it was over. With a sigh, I let myself relax. After all, I'd wake up if the diarrhea hit again, and if I got the chance to sleep this off, all the better. Gusty would understand if I didn't cook him breakfast. *Thank God, he didn't eat—*

I sat up in bed. "Oh, my God."

Max didn't even stir when I jumped out of bed, grabbed my bathrobe, and ran out. *I forgot about the hollandaise. There were raw eggs in the hollandaise.* Who knew if Gusty had collapsed in the opposite wing of the house as a result of my deadly gourmet cooking?

I sprinted through the kitchen and Great Room, into the marble foyer, and then took the stairs to the second floor two at a time. At the top, there were so many doors to choose from, I spun in a circle, before calling out, "Gusty?"

"In here" came a slightly muffled voice at the far end of the hall.

I should've followed the smell, it occurred to me outside his bathroom door. I hesitated, then asked if he was decent. Then I pushed open the door—trying not to inhale—and found him lying on the floor by the toilet.

"Can you take me to the hospital?" he asked in a feeble voice. "My sugar is over five hundred."

CHAPTER 11

Collage Art Therapy

t wasn't until nine A.M. on Sunday that a frizzy-haired nurse finally appeared outside the ICU to solemnly report that I would now be allowed to enter. She reminded me of the Beefeaters outside the Tower of London, those guards who kept track of Her Majesty's prisoners and the Crown Jewels. Only this guard's nametag said "Bernice," her scrub top was covered in purple bears, and she seemed distinctly perturbed that I was holding the hand of a two-year-old. "What's this?" she asked, noticing Max on the threshold of the unit. An odd question from someone employed at the Children's Hospital, I thought. We'd just spent the last several hours trying to nap on the vinyl waiting room sofas, and it wouldn't be long before Max started showing signs of sleep deprivation. Once the whining, the shrieking, and the kicking began, we would all suffer. I informed Bernice that I was Gusty's acting guardian and Max's mother, and I really couldn't possibly abandon either one of them. Miraculously, the ICU doors swung open at that moment and there stood another nurse, whose face broke into a smile so wide that her eyes nearly disappeared. "Look at those apple cheeks!" she said, before rescuing Max from the other nurse's angry glare. In fact, an hour later I realized that I hadn't seen my son since Nurse Polly had started parading him around the dismal unit trying to make people smile.

"Is this going to get you fired?" I turned from watching Polly and Max to Gusty, who was lying in bed, hooked up to IV fluids and an insulin drip.

"I can't get fired." I folded my arms across my chest. "I'm not your nanny."

"That's right. I forgot. What did you call yourself downstairs?"

"A temporary caretaker." This was how I'd described myself to Dr. Kimble, the ER attending, in the middle of the night.

"You said something about owning your own company."

"Well, I do," I said, only, after last night, I couldn't for the life of me remember what it was called. *Family Match?*

"Is it an LLC?" Gusty asked.

I blinked.

"Are you incorporated?" Gusty asked.

"I'll let you know."

The cell phone in my pocket rang, ending the interrogation. Except that my stomach dropped when I saw the name on the caller ID screen. Of course, it was Augustus Catalano. He'd given me a cell expressly for this purpose. "Hi, Mr. Catalano," I said, picking up.

"Please, Di. I won't be fifty until next month. You make me feel so old. Call me Augustus."

"Right, well, Augustus, I better be quick." I turned away from Bernice, who had entered the room and was gesticulating wildly to the sign that said cell phones weren't allowed on the unit. "We're here in the ICU—"

"Oh, God," Augustus said.

"But everyone's okay. We're all okay. Gusty just has a mild case of . . ." I hesitated, trying to remember the initials everyone kept using.

"DKA," Gusty called. "Tell him why," he added, and I waved at him to keep quiet.

"Dr. Kimble thinks he may be in for just twenty-four to thirty-six hours," I went on. "We'll probably be home before you're even back from Boston."

"Tell him not to come back," Gusty piped up.

"Gusty says he's feeling better already and not to come back," I said.

"I wasn't planning on it," Augustus said.

"Ma'am, you're going to have to hang up," Bernice ordered.

Where's Polly when you need her? I looked out of the doorway and answered my own question. The friendly nurse was sneaking Max a packet of graham crackers and a juice box from the small refrigerator.

"I better get off the phone—they're not letting me use it. Do you want the number, so you can call the nurses' station?" I asked.

"I already have it. Trust me, this isn't the first time."

"Your dad is sorry to hear you're sick," I said, after hanging up.

"I'll bet," Gusty said with a snort. "When were you going to tell about the car?" he added. "Getting it towed."

During the flurry of arterial blood gases and lab work, stat drips and differential diagnoses that included "food poisoning—possible salmonella," I'd apparently missed all the pages warning the owner of the Porsche to promptly remove the car from the emergency vehicle lane.

"I'll get around to it. Should I call your mother, do you think?" I asked, slumping into the recliner next to him.

"I already did. She's not coming." Gusty reached over to turn on the TV, the morning news broadcast. We both stared at the screen, stared at Alecia, despite the fact that it was Sunday, and Alecia never worked on Sundays. She was on the street talking into a microphone about a house fire in Cranberry Township that started from a deep fat fryer left unattended. "The question remains, in this day and age, with obesity rates rising and Pittsburgh now ranked one of the fattest cities in our nation, should we even be allowed to own and operate deep fat fryers? It's a question Nancy Fielding will be asking herself for a long time to come. Back to you, Mazy and Vanessa."

You should've bitten into a French fry, and maybe stepped over some steaming rubble, Ben would probably joke later.

The image cut back to the station, though, where the pair of blond anchors, one natural, one obviously dyed, sat smiling behind the news desk, as if Alecia had just been talking about the Oscar Mayer Wienermobile coming to town instead of the conflagration of Nancy Fielding's home. But I was thinking of my cousin. Alecia had looked so pale, faintly green. Was she ill? A startling rush of certainty came over me—the same feeling I'd had at the sight of Augustus Catalano's telltale toes—except that, in this case, the premonition thrilled me: Alecia was *pregnant*.

"My mom said she can't come when the news is over because she's gotta go to a barbecue. That lady there is having a baby." Gusty pointed at Vanessa Phelps, on the screen. "It's her party."

How many times in the last few weeks had Alecia complained of feeling nauseous? How many times had she said, "It's just the pressure getting to me"? *Ben is going to be so happy!* I blinked. "Did you say your mom isn't coming to see you in the ICU because she's going to a *barbecue*?"

Gusty shrugged. Bernice was back. We watched as she

pricked his finger and announced that he was down to two hundred twelve. "Now we're getting somewhere. Better add the dextrose back to my drip. And tell Dr. Kimble I want out of here by tomorrow morning," he added, making her roll her eyes. "How did I get assigned to you, Bernice? What happened to Polly?"

"She's preoccupied with your little friend," Bernice said, jutting her head in the direction of Max, who was in the middle of high-fiving a hulking security guard.

"Tell Polly to come back and take care of me," Gusty said.

"You're behaving like a Raja." I'd learned the word from reading *The Secret Garden* at least twenty times as a child. The crippled boy Colin was always ordering people around.

"Bernice knows I'm kidding. Right, Bernice?" Gusty asked.

Bernice shook her head and said only, "Gusty's our frequent flier."

Suddenly, it occurred to me just how sad this was, that Gusty considered these people his friends, that he seemed more comfortable in an ICU than at his own house.

GUSTY'S LUNCH TRAY WAS just arriving when Nurse Polly finally returned with Max, so I took him on a field trip to the hospital cafeteria. Afterwards, we stopped in at the gift shop to buy Gusty some magazines. As soon as Max saw the *Get Well* balloons, he wouldn't stop whining until I bought him a silver one bearing the face of Cookie Monster. Still hoping to get through the day without a Max Meltdown, I knew better than to say no.

Back in the ICU, as soon as I saw Gusty's face, I regretted not buying one for him, too.

"Hey, a balloon!" he exclaimed. "No one's ever brought me a balloon before. Not since I was like two."

"My balloon," Max said, tugging on its yellow string. "Mine."

"Yes, Boo, it's yours, but you might have to share it with Gusty." I stooped down just as Max's face collapsed and, from nowhere, the tears began.

"I ... don't ... wanna share!"

"Oh, geez, I'm not gonna take your balloon. I don't even like Cookie Monster," Gusty said.

"My balloon!" Max repeated, delirious with fatigue. When I took him in my arms, he buried his head in my shoulder, his wails pathetic and faltering: *"Ma-ha-hiiii-nnnnn ..."*

Of course, Max's meltdown occurred just as another doctor arrived in the doorway. He wore the usual garb: white coat, blue scrubs, and a stethoscope slung around the neck, and his face seemed molded into a smile that bordered on a grimace, possibly on account of the screaming child. "I'm sorry, I was looking for—oh, Gusty!"

"What are you doing here?" Gusty asked. "Did Bernice tell you I'm here? Because that's a HIPAA violation. I could sue."

"Mom told me, asshole," the doctor said, nostrils flaring, smile-grimace gone.

Jason, I realized, kissing the tears still stuck to Max's cheeks. His body heaved with the aftershocks of a good sob, but at least the sight of a visitor had made him curious enough to stop crying.

"What'd you do this time—conveniently forget to take your insulin again?" Jason asked.

"It wasn't my fault! Ask her," Gusty said, pointing to me. When Jason's eyebrows furrowed, Gusty added with a flourish, "My nanny."

"Hi, I'm Di." I waved my free hand. "I may have accidentally poisoned him last night."

Jason looked at me and then back to Gusty. "You have a nanny? Christ, you're fourteen."

"Not until November, actually," Gusty said. "And could you please not swear in front of them?"

"We'll wait outside," I said.

"You can't leave!" Gusty said. "I want you to stay!"

I hesitated and turned back.

"I should never have let her talk me into coming over here." Jason took off his glasses to wipe them on his shirt. "She wanted me to talk some sense into you."

"Who, Mom? Try telling *her* not to divorce *Dad*."

"You don't get it. Dad's an asshole."

"You're just mad because Stacey Locklear's not *your* girl-friend."

Jason's eyes dilated and his mouth hung open for just a second. "I don't—she's half his—I've got Val," he stammered. "And stop blaming Mom. You've been doing this long before she left Dad. One of these times, you'll end up dead."

"Shouldn't you be getting back to your *own* ER?" Gusty asked him.

"Actually, my shift is over, so I'm on my way home."

"Well, thanks for stopping by," Gusty said, flopping backward in bed. "Tell Mom I took everything you said to heart, and I'll never let it happen again."

"You're such a little prick—sorry," Jason said, barely glancing in my direction.

"Nice meeting you!" I called, as he walked out the door.

I didn't know what to say after that, so I busied myself with getting Max settled down on the recliner for a nap. Once he was asleep, it seemed best to focus on something other than Jason's visit, so I told Gusty about Collage Art Therapy, how he should look for quotes in the magazines that best charac-terized how he was feeling or who he was as a person, and, once I could get him some poster board, he could glue it on in an artistic way.

Gusty looked at the stack of magazines on his tray and then looked back at me. "I don't think the words that I would spell out should really be made into a poster," he said.

"Why not? If you're angry, be angry."

He narrowed his eyes at me. "Are you a shrink?"

"No, but I want to be one when I grow up." It was true. There were so many things I still wanted to be. "What about you? What do you want to be when you grow up?"

"You heard Jason. I'm not going to live long enough to be anything," Gusty said.

"Dr. Kimble said last night that you'd be going home tomorrow."

Gusty shrugged. "Whoop dee do."

"Would you rather stay here?"

"It's better than school. Better than getting shoved into lockers or getting tripped at an assembly. At least here, everyone's nice to me."

"Gusty, these people are here to take care of you."

"I know that. It's not like I want to be here. I just said it was better than school. Better than home, too."

"Well, where would you really like to be?"

When Gusty leaned back in his bed and held his arms behind his neck, I realized that he hadn't answered because he was about to cry. "I don't want to be anywhere," he said.

"Do you want to die?"

Gusty shrugged. "It would be easier. Not having to deal anymore."

I stared at him, thinking about the kid again, the one who'd killed my father. The newspapers had said he was depressed. "Do you feel like hurting anyone other than yourself?"

Gusty sat up. "God, no—what do you think?"

I shrugged.

"No way! I only"—he looked away—"hate me." Glancing back, Gusty must've seen the concern on my face, because he hastily added, "But it's not like I'd kill myself."

"You will live," I said. His eyebrows went up. "I mean, I see you into adulthood."

"You see me," Gusty said. "Like, in the future?" His laugh sounded nervous. "What are you, a witch, or something?"

"Not a witch, just . . . I get visions sometimes—just a quick image of the future. It runs in my family." I thought of my mother, how she would press her lips together and stare off, narrowing her eyes at something behind you, until finally she'd stand up straighter and sigh, which meant you were finally going to get an answer about the future. Even if my father didn't believe in ghosts, he knew when to listen to my mother's hunches. Sometimes, he even dared to call them "predictions."

"I saw you at the Indy 500 changing tires on a racecar. You were wearing a jumpsuit."

"Me?" Gusty said, obviously intrigued. "That's pretty weird."

"Well, I've been wrong before. Maybe it just means . . . you're supposed to be on a team," I said, realizing it as I said it. "Does your school have any you could try out for?"

"Yeah, right. I'd make a great football player," Gusty said, showing me a scrawny bicep.

"You could run cross-country."

"Tryouts were in August. Besides, I hate running. I always get this bad taste in my mouth." Gusty held out his arm so Bernice, who had just returned, could inspect his IV site. "I tried out for baseball one year. But my sugar went low at the tryouts, and they called an ambulance because I passed out. It was so embarrassing."

"So eat a granola bar before you exercise, and lower your

insulin dose," Bernice said, pressing buttons on the IV pump to make it stop beeping. "Come on, Gusty. You think there are no diabetic athletes?"

"I am aware that there are diabetic athletes, Bernice, but they probably *like* sports."

After she left, Gusty said, "It might be neat to be a land-scaper, though."

"You mean like the guys at the house?" I thought of Dave appearing from behind a mulch mound to ask if I was a fan of Underoos.

Gusty shrugged. "They all have stupid nicknames and stuff. Like, even the dog."

"What dog?" So, I hadn't imagined one after all.

"Dave's dog—the yellow Lab. Her name is Taco, because one time they went to Taco Bell, and she ate Hobbes's taco."

"Hobbes?"

"The short guy with red hair. His real name is Calvin but they call him Hobbes because they all have to have stupid nicknames. That's a rule. Like the big, huge guy, they call him TJ Hooker, because he likes hookers. The dog's real name isn't even Taco. It's Lacey. But she had to have a stupid nickname, too."

"How do you know all this?"

"They've been there all summer. They had to redo that sidewalk five times."

"Maybe you could get a job with them."

Gusty shook his head. "My dad would never let me. He thinks they're idiots." He sighed. "Dad won't let me do any-thing. Like, I wanted to leave Shady Side Academy to join cyber-school—"

"Cyber-school?" I repeated. "Where is that held? Outer space?"

"Close. On the Internet," Gusty said. "I could get my GED that way, which would be cool because I love hanging out on the computer, but Dad said no. He said I won't get into prep school with a degree from cyber-school."

"I don't understand. Aren't you *in* prep school?"

"He wants me to go away to another prep school after this one, a boarding school, for an extra year of high school, so that I'll be extra prepared for college. If I go to Choate, I'll be assured of getting into the Ivy League."

"Oh, my God. *More* high school?" It seemed like the last thing that would do any good for a kid who preferred the intensive care unit to gym class. "Let me talk to your dad. When he gets back from his trip, okay? I'll say something."

"Really?" Gusty said, his face breaking into the first real smile since he'd seen Max yesterday. "I'll say something, too. I'll tell him he should hire you to be our chef. I won't even mention the whole food-poisoning thing."

"Deal," I said, holding out my hand.

It didn't occur to me until after we shook on it that I probably shouldn't be making deals with a thirteen-year-old boy.

CHAPTER 12

Two Bars

Later, after Max had woken up from his nap, and Gusty was eating his dinner, I left them watching *SpongeBob SquarePants* and went for a walk. It wouldn't be long before visiting hours were over but, suddenly, I needed to take a quick breath of air that belonged to the sky, rather than the ICU, needed a moment of silence from the cacophony of beeps generated by nearly every piece of surrounding equipment.

Pulling out my cell phone, I dialed Alecia."Hey! How're you feeling?" I asked automatically. It was the same thing everyone wanted to know when I was pregnant with Max.

"How am I feeling?" she repeated. "Why would you ask me that? You never ask me how I'm feeling."

"I saw you on the news this morning," I said. "You looked sort of sick."

"Thanks!" Alecia snapped. "Is that why you called? To tell me I looked like shit on TV?"

"No, I just . . . actually I was wondering—"

"Ben never came home last night," she blurted, before I could ask. "I just got in from work a few minutes ago, and the apartment looks . . . ransacked."

"Ransacked?" I repeated. "In what way?"

"It's just . . . random stuff. Some of my shoes were out of their boxes. And my makeup is on the bedroom floor. And Ben's old stereo speakers are out of the closet. And my egg crate—the one with your letters—isn't where I left it. Someone dumped the box upside down on the dining room table."

"Have you called the police?"

"Well, the wedding gifts are still here. Nothing's *missing*."

"Except for Ben."

"Ben must've done this, obviously. But what was he looking for? Oh, God, I'm getting another call—*Fran*," Alecia added with a groan. "She's going to want to carpool to Vanessa's party. Christ. I have to get rid of her."

"Ah. Right. I heard about the big *barbecue*," I said, hoping she'd ask me how we were doing.

"Don't be fooled. The beer and men are only decoys. It's just another goddamn baby shower. I gotta go."

"Tell Mazy that Gusty says hello!" I called, but there was only a dial tone in reply.

HERE'S WHAT I DIDN'T know at the time: that Alecia had just returned home from the drugstore, having completed a mission for "prescription strength antacid stomach relief," and a pregnancy test, even though she knew she couldn't possibly be pregnant. She'd missed her period but it was pharmacologically induced: Holly had told her to start the next pill pack early, so she wouldn't have to have her period on her wedding day.

Alecia hung up with me too late to catch Fran's call and only bothered to listen to the first half of her message—long enough to hear the salient point, however, which was that Vanessa's baby shower had been canceled just an hour before kickoff. Good thing, too, because she had more important things to do, like pee on a stick.

The pregnancy test directions said it would take two minutes for a result. Before she could even look at her watch, Alecia accidentally fumbled the urine-soaked dipstick onto the floor. Scrambling around under the sink, she finally retrieved the stick, just as the apartment phone began to ring. Retreating to the dining room, she reached for the receiver she'd left on the table moments ago: *Art WTAE. Jesus Christ.* Her boss could wait.

"Two minutes!" Alecia said aloud. "I just need two fucking minutes!" She set the cordless down, walked into the kitchen, and rummaged through the refrigerator, until she came up with an unopened bottle of San Pellegrino. Ben was always making fun of her disdain for tap water, but she loved the decadence of bubbles.

"You may have heard that Vanessa's barbecue was canceled," Art's voice was rambling on the answering machine.

"Thank God for that!" Alecia shouted, rooting through a drawer for a bottle top opener.

"Her water broke. She's in labor—on her way to the hospital right now. I'm going to need you to anchor the news tomorrow."

Alecia paused, suddenly grasping the green bottle as if it were a buoy. She'd been waiting for this opportunity for weeks—years, really—so why did she have the sensation that she'd just been tossed off a boat into freezing-cold waters? *Long time coming, eh?* She could hear her father's voice in her mind. *I am so proud of you, kiddo.*

"Heidi has already left me about six messages—she's

ready to fill in for Vanessa, if you're not. So, call me back tonight and let me know. Doesn't matter what time."

Alecia shook her head, coming to. "I'm ready!" she called, running to grab the phone, still gripping the bottle by the neck.

But when she stepped back into the dining room, she saw it: Frank's prenuptial agreement out of its envelope, lying on the table, and open to the back page where she'd forged Ben's signature. *Oh, fuck. Oh, God. Oh, no.* Spots came into her vision, as bubbles of panic popped in her brain. Her legs felt weak, but somehow she made herself set the bottle down and stagger back to the bathroom to find the pregnancy test, whose two little windows were decorated with matching symmetrical bars. For half a second, she couldn't remember what that might mean. *Two bars . . . two bars . . .* Alecia checked the instructions and promptly vomited.

CHAPTER 13

The Show
Must Go On

After taking a taxi back to Fox Chapel Sunday night, Max and I had spent the better part of Monday in the Catalano kitchen, waiting for Gusty to get home from the hospital. We read books, ate pancakes, drew pictures, and raced Matchbox cars—and would've considered taking a dip in the pool, if it weren't for the landscaper-convicts working out back. Meanwhile, Gusty killed time in the ICU, waiting for his mother to bring him back to Augustus's house—Gusty's idea, in lieu of a taxi. "She's just gotta get here before three o'clock. After that, they charge my insurance another day," he said.

"It depresses me that you know that," I said.

Meanwhile, Alecia was in the dressing room at WTAE, basically a women's bathroom with extra mirrors.

Stupid, stupid test, she thought. Why did they even allow such things the market? It was like having a home cancer detection kit.

She checked her watch: an hour and a half until showtime.

She would have to scan her scripts, check for any typos, write up any additional stories, track the opening, and make herself look presentable, the most challenging of tasks. *This can't be happening,* she thought, but her face seemed to say otherwise. It was washed out and greenish; her eyes ringed by dark circles (*reverse eye shadow!*) and new crow's-feet that had magically appeared. *Thank God for Estée Lauder.*

Alecia had told me once that each year she wrote off two hundred dollars on her income taxes for makeup, which led me to ask if it was the most important part of her job. The foundation, tanning lotion, eyebrow pencil, blush, lipstick, and gloss just helped put her in the right spirit of things, she'd explained, like an actor who only felt like a priest if he practiced his lines wearing a collar. Besides, she had very sensitive skin, she'd said. She needed to buy the expensive brands or her face would break out.

But when Alecia opened her duffel bag full of cosmetics, she gasped when she saw that it contained nothing but pants, twelve fucking pairs of pants. An image popped into her head: her makeup, piled like a mountain, on the floor by her bed. She now remembered dumping out the duffel herself to make room for the pants. The bag seemed to tilt and sway as she rifled though it, searching for even a measly tube of Mac lipstick. She ran into one of the toilet stalls and vomited, which at least helped make the spinning go away. *What if I puke on television?* It suddenly occurred to her, as her heart clanged in her chest. *At least it isn't sweeps month.*

Coming out of the stall, Alecia staggered back over to the counter in front of the mirrors, slumped into her chair, and gathered all the pants into a pile. They made for a nice pillow.

The dressing room door opened and Alecia heard a clack of high heels followed by Mazy's voice, "Well, well. If it isn't the nanny-finder's *cousin.*"

"Wha . . . ?" She tried to pick her head up. "Oh." Catching

a glimpse of herself in the mirror, Alecia quickly wiped the splash of vomit off her bottom lip. "Thank you for hiring her."

"*I* didn't." Mazy's voice was surprisingly venomous. "My husband hired her against my wishes. And my *son*—whom she's supposed to be taking care of—ended up in the ICU last night."

Alecia blinked. "Oh, my God."

"She's lucky he's all right. What're those—pants?" Mazy added, standing next to her, rattling her hair spray before sending up a cloud of aerosol that made Alecia cough.

Somehow she found enough oxygen to explain the Banana Republic Donate Pants Campaign. "Next time, I think I might just stick to Goodwill." Things went to Goodwill in garbage bags, not her flowered duffel made expressly for five hundred dollars' worth of makeup. She glanced over at Mazy, who didn't appear to be listening. "I'm really sorry about your son," Alecia started, wondering how to segue from the ICU into eyeliner. Was it completely inappropriate to ask if she could share?

"Thank you. He'll be all right. This isn't the first time it's happened," Mazy muttered, brushing off one of her eyebrows with a manicured finger. "Art wants us out at the desk in five, so that we can track the voice-over," she said, practically running over Elaine, the meteorologist, as she left the dressing room. *Too late*.

Elaine dumped a bag on the counter before heading into the bathroom herself. "Did you hear? Vanessa had a little girl," she called in her shrill, squeaky voice. "Seven pounds, eight ounces."

"Oh!" Alecia singsonged, as she reached for her cell phone to speed-dial Ben. "That's gr-eat!"

Of course, he still wasn't back at the apartment, and no one answered at Holly's house, either. Alecia stared at her phone. There was only one cell bar, but there was no time to stand outside the building, trying to get a better signal. Before the phone could die on her, she dialed Holly, first at her home, then at her office.

"She's with a patient," the nurse said.

"This is an emergency. I'm family."

Even if they weren't going to be related, after all, it worked. Within a few seconds, Holly picked up. "Alecia? Are you okay?"

God, it was the question of the day. "No, actually."

"I'm so sorry. I just—don't know what to say."

"Sorry about what?" Alecia asked.

"Oh…" Holly hesitated. "We got home from England, and Ben was here…"

"He told you that he doesn't want to marry me?" Alecia asked.

A toilet flushed. *Fuck.* She'd forgotten about Elaine.

"He didn't say for sure," Holly stammered.

Alecia waved and smiled at Elaine, who'd just exited her stall and was now plugging in her curling iron. "Listen, I can't really talk right now. I just need a favor. I'm about to go on the air, and I forgot my makeup."

There was a pause. "Um, Alecia, I'm seeing patients right now."

"Well, if you could get here by five-thirty—I'm going on the air at six. You might want to leave now, though. Traffic is horrendous."

"I can't bring you your makeup bag. I have evening hours."

"Is this about Ben?"

"This has nothing to do with Ben! I've been out of the country, and I have a waiting room full of patients who are sick."

"So, tell them it's an emergency!"

"I don't think bringing someone lipstick and blush across town constitutes an emergency."

So that was what Holly thought of Alecia and her career: lipstick and blush.

Alecia took a deep breath and tried to smile. Elaine was curling her bangs and holding out a melted tube of CoverGirl in a shade that would look terrific on Alecia if she wanted to look like she'd been eating dog doo. If anyone needed a stylist more than Alecia, it was Elaine. "Okay, well, then—"

"Alecia," Holly said, gentler now. "Can't you borrow some makeup from someone? Or find a nearby convenience store?"

"No, no, no. Listen, forget it. Thanks anyway. Take care of all those coughs and colds."

Alecia's cell phone battery died after that, just as Rich Davis, the sports reporter, hollered through the dressing room door that everyone was waiting for her to record the voice-over. Alecia blotted her face on a pair of pants and headed out to the news desk. This ritual of pre-taping the opening lines, when the rest of the newscast was live, was to avoid any opening bloopers—and besides, they could get the newsreels perfectly in sync with their voices, something which didn't always happen during the show.

Behind the desk, Mazy was waiting for her. Rich started singing, "Here she comes, Miss America," as Alecia walked toward the blue screen.

"Fuck off, Rich," she said, putting her earpiece in her ear and clipping the microphone to her shirt before taking a seat beside Mazy.

"Where's your script?" Mazy asked, raising an eyebrow. Her makeup and hair were perfect, but she was still scary as hell.

"Oh…" Alecia looked around, as if one might be tucked

under the desk. "In New York, someone always handed us our scripts."

"Well, in Pittsburgh, you print them out for yourself," Mazy said.

"Can't you ladies share?" came the sound guy's voice in Alecia's earpiece.

Mazy let out a huff as she moved her paper over two whole millimeters, so that Alecia had to crane her neck to see it. When her elbow accidentally brushed Mazy's sleeve, she turned and glared at Alecia, as if she was trying to cheat on a test. "I hope someone told you that we don't have stylists in Pittsburgh, either," Mazy added, looking Alecia up and down, just as the opening music started in their earpieces.

"And go," the sound guy said.

"The Steelers do it again!" Mazy said, her face lit up with her voice, even though the cameras weren't rolling. "Big Ben goes long to beat the Ravens!"

"Teens find out that diet pills are no joke when a local cheerleader drops dead!" Alecia tried to mimic Mazy's enthusiasm. "And a local politician blows out his knee—"

"My line," Mazy interrupted. "Start over."

The music stopped. In her earpiece, Alecia could hear the sound of rewinding.

"Mazy, would it be possible to borrow any of your makeup?" Alecia whispered, even though the sound guy could hear everything through her microphone. "I seem to have forgotten mine."

Mazy's eyebrows flew up, although her forehead never wrinkled. "You've got some nerve."

Alecia smiled as she sheepishly admitted, "I know."

"Sending us your *cousin,* who—by the way—was positively *thrilled* by the attention Auggie gave her at the interview."

Alecia stared at her. "I can't imagine that..." She trailed off, thinking of the flower shop and my blush-at-first-sight.

The music started. "And go," said the faceless voice in her ear.

"The Steelers do it again!" Mazy said with such gusto that Alecia couldn't help but be impressed. "Big Ben goes long to beat the Ravens!"

"Teens find out that diet pills are no joke when a local cheerleader drops dead!" Alecia chimed in.

"And a local politician blows out his knee while doing high kicks in his office. Details coming up at six!" Mazy finished.

In Alecia's right ear, she heard the sound guy say, "Perfect. Thanks, ladies."

She looked over at Mazy to make one more plea, but Mazy had already removed her microphone and was stalking off toward the newsroom without even a glance in Alecia's direction.

GUSTY FINALLY RETURNED AROUND four-thirty (after Mazy sent a town car, rather than herself), and I was rooting through the refrigerator, wondering what to make for dinner that wouldn't kill him, when my cell phone rang.

"Hello?"

There was a pause, and when Alecia finally spoke, I wasn't sure whether she was crying or being strangled. "Di, please...I need...your..."

Help. She needed help. "Are you okay?"

"No! I need my..." She gasped. "Makeup."

I tilted my head to the side, straining to hear something more. "You want to make up? With Ben?"

"My cosmetics!" she hissed. "I left them at the apartment. Can you bring them to me?"

I scratched my head, baffled.

"You'll need to find a suitcase," she added, when I still hadn't spoken.

"Suitcase for what—your *makeup*? Oh, geez." I looked at my watch and then looked out the window. Directly outside, a dump truck was parked on the lawn. "We'll make it," I said.

WHAT HAPPENED AFTER WE hung up seemed like a miracle to Alecia. One moment, she was fielding phone calls from the distraught parent of a teen who'd been on the squad with the dead cheerleader and wanted to give a sound bite for the newscast. ("I'm so sorry for your loss," Alecia said. "You do understand that we're taping this call?") The next moment Bob from security was paging her to say that she had a guest in the front lobby.

"Already?" she said, jumping up from her desk. "Be right down!"

She pressed the button for the elevator, and when that didn't arrive in three seconds, she took the stairs as fast as her high heels would allow. She burst into the front lobby, startling Bob, who gasped when the stairwell door opened with a bang.

"Where is she?" Alecia asked, panting, and Bob pointed across the room . . . but it wasn't at me. A woman in a blue cotton capedress was looking at a framed picture of the space shuttle, and even from behind, the slouch of her shoulders was startlingly familiar.

"M-Maddie?" Alecia called.

When the woman turned, Alecia was horrified. Her mother looked terrible: bloodshot eyes, gray hair, and wrinkles. Lots of them. More than Alecia's father had. More than her *grandfather* had.

"Hey, Allie," Maddie said with a watery smile. She hugged the shoulders of her pilgrim dress as if she'd just noticed the air-conditioning. "What's up?"

"What are you—what's going—where's Di? Are you *Amish* now?" she blurted, before Maddie could answer.

Her mother's eyebrows rose along with her apple cheeks. "You think I took a horse all the way from Oregon?" she said with a chuckle. She glanced down at the gathered skirts of her dress and then up again. "I just like the look. Did you get the card that I sent?"

"Yes, it came. Thank you. Listen, now really isn't the time..."

But Maddie wasn't paying attention. She was peering around the lobby at the TV paraphernalia, all the framed images of various important events in history. Alecia looked, too, for the first time. "Boy, I can't believe it," Maddie said, impressed. "You actually work here. It's really wild for me, you know?"

"Yes, it's wild. Very wild. How did you—find me?"

Maddie's eyes lit up. "Google!"

Google. Of course. She would have to remember to tell Art to take her off the WTAE website in the future. It wasn't as if she ever got fan mail—just the occasional letter from a bitter viewer, who wrote to tell her to gain weight. "What are you doing here?"

"Well, I just got in to town. And I went to your apartment, and no one was there. So, I figured I'd come see you here!"

"This is my daughter," Maddie said to Bob. "I haven't seen her in fourteen years."

"You know what? I kinda see the resemblance between you two," Bob said, pointing back and forth.

Alecia glared at him.

"Oh, no. She's so much prettier," Maddie said. "Look at you, Allie! You turned out great!"

"Chip off the old block," Bob said.

"So, when are you due?"

Alecia felt her throat close off. "I'm *not* pregnant."

"I'm sorry. I thought Di invited me to a baby shower." Maddie slapped her head. "You know, it was funny, I was telling my therapist that I had no idea what you were up to these days, but I assumed you must be married with children, by now. I told her how you just turned thirty-five—"

"Thirty-*three*."

"—And right after our conversation, I got Di's invitation out of the blue. I just put two and two together—"

"You didn't put anything together, Mother. It was a wedding shower. And you missed it."

"You're getting married! That's great! Or . . . did I miss that, too?"

"Mother!" Alecia clenched her fists. "You missed my entire life! You can't just show up now and expect a *tour*!"

"I was in La La Land for most of her childhood," Maddie said to Bob, as if La La Land were a sabbatical in France. "Her father and my brother were always locking me up in the loony bin. I'm better now, though," she added, blowing her bangs off her forehead.

"Well, that's great!" Bob said cheerfully.

"You were just in rehab!" Alecia snapped.

"It was a small relapse." Then, to Bob: "When I get depressed, I drink."

Over Maddie's head, the wall clock said five-thirty, and Alecia inhaled and clamped a hand over her mouth. "She's about to go on the air," Bob said to Maddie.

"Could we at least meet for a cup of coffee later?" Maddie suggested. "After your show?"

"Yes, Mother, yes," Alecia hastily agreed—anything to make her mother go.

"Here—let me give you the number at my hotel," Maddie

said, laying a card on Bob's security counter, as if she were inviting him over for a tryst rather than Alecia for coffee. "I'm really looking forward to hanging out," she added.

"Me, too," Alecia said, nodding eagerly so that Maddie would keep walking away.

"Amish," Alecia heard her say to herself with a disbelieving chuckle as she finally ambled out the lobby doors.

CHAPTER 14

Pro Lawn Service

After I explained Alecia's situation to Gusty, the three of us marched outside with a tray of iced tea. With his chain saw, Dave was tending to a fallen tree at the edge of the property, but his minions were spreading mulch right near the rose garden.

"Hel-*lo,*" the big guy—TJ Who Likes Hookers—said, looking me up and down after I'd whistled from the front doorstep and held up a glass.

"Where were you this summer when it was ninety degrees?" said the skinny guy—his nickname was Hobbes, I recalled—as they approached the house in sweaty T-shirts and shorts.

I set the tray on the front stoop. I was hoping to get Dave's attention, but he was engrossed in his tree. In the distance, I could hear him whooping for joy as a branch fell.

"I think we've seen you before, right?" TJ nodded to Gusty.

"That's because I live here. Hey, what happened to our bushes?" Gusty asked, pointing to the front of the house.

"The Big Man wanted them gone. He wants to replace them with something smaller," TJ said. "He forgot those suckers have *roots*."

Hobbes explained that the only way to remove the yew bushes was to chain them to the back of the dump truck, step on the gas, and wait for the ground to let go of them. "There was a specific reason we waited until the Sunday he was out of town."

No wonder the lawn was all turfed up. I pointed to the side of the truck, which said *Pro Lawn Service*. "And you guys are supposed to be the pros?"

"It just means we're for lawn care, not against it," Hobbes said.

We all looked over at Dave, whose noises were becoming even more enthusiastic as wood sprayed out from under the blade of his chain saw. I couldn't help staring for a second. It was like watching joy that I couldn't quite comprehend.

"Big truck," Max said, pointing. At least he seemed to remember the task at hand.

"That's right, buddy," TJ said, reaching over to pinch his cheek and leaving a fingerprint of dirt in the process.

"Do you need a special license to drive that thing?" I don't know why I asked, when I didn't even have one, special or otherwise.

"The truck? Nah. It's not *that* big," TJ said.

"Would it be possible to speak to whoever's in charge?" I asked.

"He's getting off on his chain saw over there," Hobbes said.

"Hey, dickhead!" TJ shouted, but Dave kept sawing and *wooo-hooo*-ing as his bare arms and chest shook with the vibrations from the saw.

"So, when's quittin' time?" I asked the landscapers.

"Whenever we finish the mulch," Hobbes said, sounding thoughtful even as he was spitting tobacco.

"What about the walkway?" Gusty asked. "Are you ever going to finish that?"

"If it's not done by the time the Big Man gets back from his trip, we're screwed. Or at least, Dave is," Hobbes said.

Finally, the engine on the chain saw stopped. Dave looked around until he finally spotted his workers lounging on the front step. "Hey, assholes! Pick up a rake!" he shouted. "Shovel something!"

"The nanny wants to speak to whoever's in charge!" TJ shouted back. "I told her that was you, jackass!"

After setting down the chain saw, Dave walked toward us, wiping his face on the shirt that was in his hand. I tried not to stare at his chest, which was quite muscular given how slender he was. He took off his baseball cap, revealing matted-down hat-hair. "Sorry about these idiots. We're obviously still ironing out some issues of boss/employee respect." He held out a hand for me to shake. "What's up?"

"I'm Di, and this is Max, and this is Gusty, and we were wondering if it would be possible to borrow the dump truck for an hour or two?"

Dave laughed. I didn't.

"You're kidding, right?" he asked.

"I wish I was." I explained how we'd been left with the Porsche, which had been towed outside the emergency room when Gusty was rushed to the hospital the night before, how my cousin was going to be making her debut on Channel Four as an anchorwoman, how she'd forgotten her makeup, and how we had to get it to her in the next seventy minutes.

"No," Dave said, losing his smile. "No, no, no."

"I could have it back by six-thirty."

"We're using the truck. That's why it's *here*."

"But we dumped all the mulch out," TJ said.

"Let me remind you that after you finish spreading the mulch, which should take about forty minutes, tops, then you're going to fill up the back of the dump truck with brush. Remember?"

TJ rolled his eyes and then looked at me. "Which one is your cousin?"

"Alecia Axtel. You probably wouldn't know—"

"Oh, I know her. I know all the hot ones." And then, to Dave: "Come on, man. You have to let her take it."

"What if I got it right back?" I asked Dave.

"That dump truck is a *death trap*," he said, so emphatically that it made Max reach for my hand. "There aren't any seat belts. You couldn't strap him to anything." He pointed to Max.

"Why are we allowed to drive—"

"Because you're expendable." Dave didn't let Hobbes finish.

Looking at Dave's suddenly stern face, I was beginning to regret asking. It was as if I'd just ruined his orgasm.

"Okay, I'm sorry. You're right. I'll call my cousin back and tell her—"

"I'll take you myself," Dave said.

I stopped in the middle of collecting the empty glasses of tea off the stoop and looked up. "But . . . in what?"

"My pickup." It must've been parked on the far side of the garage, out of view of where he was pointing. "It's got a small backseat for these two." Dave jerked his head toward Gusty and Max.

"Can you take us to pick up the Porsche afterwards?" Gusty asked, hands on his hips.

"Don't push it, kid."

*　*　*

"WHAT WAS WRONG WITH that oak tree?" I asked Dave, once Max was secured in his car seat, and we were finally winding our way down Fox Chapel Road. "The one you were cutting up?"

"Back there? That was a sycamore. Got struck by lightning."

"A sycamore?" I repeated, surprised. That meant they were all sycamores, every single one of those stately trees shading the driveway. It occurred to me that for most of my life I'd been calling every non–pine tree an oak. "And what will you do with the wood?"

"Catalano will burn it in one of his eight fireplaces," Dave said, sipping a mug of something black—coffee, I supposed.

"We actually only have four fireplaces," Gusty said from the backseat.

"Oh, really? Just four?" Dave said, with a little smile as he raised the mug to his lips again.

It wasn't until Gusty leaned forward and asked, his voice full of awe, "Is that chewing tobacco?" that I realized Dave's mug apparently wasn't filled with coffee, but instead a revolting concoction of phlegm and tobacco. *Ick.* "Can I try some?" Gusty added.

"No way," Dave said. "It's bad for you."

"Dave here is not going to die with his own teeth or neck or voice box," I added.

"Thanks," he said grimly, easing the car around a bend in the road. "So, where am I taking you again? WTAE?"

"Right." I held up the directions. "But first we have to stop at my cousin's apartment in Shadyside."

"Great," Dave said, stepping on the gas pedal. At least he wasn't turning around. "He payin' you well, or what?"

"Who, Gusty's dad?" I asked, rolling up my window since, in the back, Max was squinting from the wind in his eyes. "I'm sure he will. He . . . said he would."

Dave chuckled. "But you haven't gotten a dime yet, am I right? He'll give you half of what he promises, so ask for double and you'll get close to what you're owed."

"It's called bargaining. Everybody does that," Gusty said, but Dave only shook his head in reply.

"So, how do you like being a nanny?" he asked, moments later, once we were inching along the Highland Park Bridge in rush-hour traffic.

"My only charge was to keep Gusty out of the hospital," I said.

"Well done," Dave said, chuckling. He could make fun of me all day long, just as long as he kept driving.

"Gusty's been watching you guys all summer," I added. "In fact, just yesterday, when he was in the intensive care unit, near death, he told me that the one thing that would make him really happy would be a chance to work with you."

Dave turned and stared at me the way people in movies did who were only pretending to drive their cars. "With who?" he asked.

"With you! With Pro Lawn Service! Watch the road!"

Dave laughed. "Wait a sec—you're serious? Oh, man. You all need help."

"I really do want to be a landscaper," Gusty said, pressing himself up between the seats. "Why is that funny?"

"You've been hanging out with her too long." Dave jerked his head in my direction and then glanced in the rearview mirror again. "What do you say, kid? Is your mom a nut?"

"A nut!" Max said like a cheer. Then he laughed the way he always did when everyone else was laughing, and he didn't know why.

*   *   *

AFTER RETRIEVING MY PASSPORT and stuffing Alecia's makeup into the first duffel I could find—pink leather and large enough to fit a thirty-two-inch TV set—I jumped back into the car and told Dave to floor it. Between the traffic and construction leading into the city, we were suddenly down to twenty-five minutes.

"No pressure, but if we don't make it to the station in time, my cousin will never forgive me."

"We better not get killed then. Or she'll be really mad," Dave said.

I looked at him and laughed. He had no idea how true that was.

"You know, I've never seen my mom at work," Gusty said. "I've seen her on TV, but it's not like she's ever taken me around the station or anything. She took me to the company picnic once, and everyone said I looked too young to be a doctor. I was *twelve* at the time. Green!"

"So, you look wise for your years," I said, as Dave stepped on the gas after the light turned.

"No. It's because she only talks about Jason. They'd never heard of me."

"Sure they had. You're the sick one," I said.

Gusty sat forward and stared at me. "I'm the *sick* one?"

I nodded. "Jason's the doctor, and Gusty is the diabetic. They couldn't very well say, 'Hey, aren't you the kid who she's always rushing off to see in the ICU?' That's why they pretended to confuse you with your older brother."

"But . . . I don't want to be 'the sick one.' "

"So, don't be." I shrugged.

"Don't be sick? Don't have diabetes?"

"No, I mean—you've got diabetes. Just . . . get a life."

"*Get a life?* I'm thirteen and I'm not allowed to do anything! He won't even let me be a landscaper."

"Don't bring me into this," Dave said.

"Never mind. I'm the one who needs a life. Right, Max?"

"Backhoe!" Max called from his car seat. We were passing a construction site.

"That's right, Boo." Ben had taught him the difference between backhoes, front loaders, and bulldozers. Max preferred backhoes to any other piece of equipment.

"Smart kid," Dave said, impressed.

"Get a life. I can't believe you just said that," Gusty said.

"It was just projection. Do you know what projection is?"

"Come on. I was in therapy for five years."

WHEN WE PEELED INTO the WTAE parking lot at ten to six, Gusty yelled, "Watch out for the Quaker lady!" and Dave quickly jerked the steering wheel to the left, toward a row of white vans instead. Once he'd thrown the truck in park, I unbuckled my seat belt, opened the back door, and pulled Max out of his car seat. When I turned around, Gusty was already standing on the sidewalk holding the pink duffel. I was impressed. At least he didn't have masculinity issues.

"So, you'll wait for us, then?" I asked Dave.

He shrugged. "I'll be here. Or if I'm not, I went to get something to eat."

I remembered the emergency money in my pocket. "Can I buy you dinner?"

He cocked his head to the side and the corners of his mouth turned up. "Okay. Sure."

I pulled out the wad of cash and fished out a twenty. "Will this cover it, you think?" It wasn't until I held it out to him—and caught his crestfallen expression—that I realized my gaffe.

Dave looked at my hand and then to me. "Forget it. I got money."

Then we ran. Across the parking lot, up the stairs, and into the lobby, until we came across a security guard, who sputtered as he set down his glass of water. "Whoa, whoa, whoa! You can't go up there!" The neck of the guard's shirt was so tight that his jowls sagged over it. He looked ready to have a heart attack at any moment.

"We're here for Alecia Axtel," I said.

"Well, you can forget it. She's about to go on the air."

"But she's expecting us, Bob," I said, reading the name on his badge. "So why don't you give her a call and tell her we're down here?"

"That's what the last lady said, too. And Ms. Axtel wasn't expecting her, either."

"Do you know who my mother is?" Gusty asked.

"Who's your mother, kid?"

"Mazy Roberts."

"No, kiddin'." Bob gave him an exaggerated once-over. "You look a little young to be a doctor."

"I'm the sick one," Gusty said, shooting a sideways glance at me.

"Oh—the—oh . . . heck, go on up," Bob said, mopping his brow.

As we got off on the third floor, a petite woman with brown lips, big hair, and giant heels gasped from down the hallway. *"You made it!"* she squealed. I looked behind me even though no one else had been on the elevator with us. Apparently the woman was confusing me for someone else, though she did look awfully familiar. Had she grown up on my street in Highland Park?

"Oh, wait, you're the weather girl," I realized.

"I'm a meteorologist," the weather girl said, brusque despite the soprano voice. "Alecia's in there." She pointed to a door marked *Dressing Room*.

"If it's okay, I'm going to go find my mom," Gusty said.

"Who's your mom?" the weather girl asked, and once Gusty replied, she told him to follow her.

The first thing I heard when I opened the dressing room door was the sound of retching, which reminded me of when my mother was sick. Vomiting had always seemed like the worst sort of torture, especially if you happened to be dying on top of it all.

"Alecia?" I called.

"Di? You made it?" Her voice was infused with relief. I couldn't help feeling relieved myself.

"We made it." I placed the contents of Alecia's makeup bag on the counter, catching a glimpse of myself in the mirror. The fluorescent lights made me look as if I hadn't slept in a year.

When the bathroom door opened and Alecia staggered toward me, I tried not to stare. Her cheeks looked pale, and there was some vomit in her hair. Slumping into a seat, she said absently, "Oh, hey, Max."

I glanced over to see him pulling a curling iron down off the counter. "Max, leave that alone."

"Oh, it's not plugged in."

"Are you okay?" I asked.

Alecia shook her head and started to weep.

"Hey," I said, looking around for a box of tissues but found only a roll of toilet paper on the counter. It was hard to believe this was a TV station in a metropolitan city, maybe not a major one, but a city all the same. Alecia had probably seen better-equipped dressing rooms at Uncle Frank's country club. "Hey, come on. It's all right."

"Nothing is all right, Di. My mother showed up. The wedding is off. Ben and I are breaking up—oh yeah, and I'm pregnant," Alecia added, with a jagged laugh.

I slapped my thigh. "I knew you were pregnant!"

"Which is ironic because he's dumping me because I won't get pregnant," she finished.

"Ben doesn't know about the baby? Don't you think he should?" I added, when Alecia kept shaking her head.

"It's not a baby yet!" she snapped.

"Stop." I blotted the tears streaming down Alecia's face. "Your eyes are getting puffier."

Gently, I began to cover Alecia's face with foundation, a nice light bronze. She shut her eyes again and her shoulders sagged. In the meantime, Max entertained himself by jumping on a pile of pants like they were leaves.

"Can you believe my mother actually showed up here?" Alecia asked, under closed lids. "She was dressed in one of those capedresses, like Amish people wear. She's not even Mennonite—she likes the look!"

"Aunt Maddie?" I stopped sponging her face for just a second. *Watch out for the Quaker!* Gusty had yelled.

"She had the nerve to ask me when the baby was due! In front of *Bob*!"

I uncapped the eyeliner. "What would make her think—"

"She got mixed up! She told her therapist that I must be married with children by now—she thought I was thirty-*five*!"

I pursed my lips and kept painting, even though the eyeliner was starting to smear from Alecia's tears. "It could've been worse," I said finally. "Imagine if she'd come dressed as the Pope, or an undersea diver, or a French maid . . ."

"Or my mother," Alecia said, with a hiccup.

"Exactly. She could've worn her pink bathrobe," I said. "This is progress."

"What the hell am I gonna do?" Alecia asked with a sniff.

"Right now? You're going to sit here, and you're going to stop crying so I can finish your makeup. And then you're going to go give the news."

"Di…" Alecia reached out and took my hand. "I can't thank you—"

"Thank me later," I said. "I'm trying to make you look good."

WHEN IT WAS ALL said and done, Alecia seemed impressed. A good thing, too, because a second later a male voice called through the dressing room door, "Axtel, get your ass out to the desk. You're on in ten minutes!"

Alecia sighed. "It's showtime," she muttered under her breath as she stood up.

"Showtime!" Max echoed, waving his beloved miniature backhoe.

Then we left the dressing room and ran down the hall to the newsroom. I didn't know why we were running after Alecia, except that I felt as if I had to see her get as far as her seat, and then the whole ordeal would be out of my hands. As soon as we got into the room, which was dark except for the well-lit desks in front of a blue screen, I picked up Max and told him that we could only whisper from now on.

"Where's my backhoe?" Max asked in his best inside voice, which was still quite loud.

Unfortunately, we'd left it in the dressing room. "We'll have to get it later, Boo."

The door opened behind us, and I overheard Mazy saying to Gusty, "And this is where we film."

"Awesome! Can I stay and watch?"

"Well…" Mazy hesitated. Her eyes narrowed when she saw me, though maybe she was just adjusting her eyes to the light.

"If you want, you can even sit next to your mom at the desk while she's giving the news," said a bald man wearing a headset and mouthpiece.

"No! Really?" Gusty sounded happy. "Would the home viewers be able to see me?"

"We won't point the camera at you. 'Course, when it's time for Rich to do sports, you'll have to get up."

"Can I, Mom?"

"It might be distracting to me to have him at the desk, Jeff," Mazy said.

"*Nothing* distracts you, Mazy. You're too good," Jeff replied.

I grinned at him. *Good man.*

MAX AND I WERE ushered to another room filled with desks and phones and TV monitors so we could watch Alecia's debut. Jeff had said we could stay, but he was obviously childless if he thought a two-year-old boy could restrain himself from yelling, "Backhoe!" in the middle of a live broadcast.

"They let me sit behind the desk!" Gusty said, once he'd found us afterwards. "I watched all their lines on the monitors! And, like, all the commercials in between!"

Amazingly, Mazy actually had a Mona-Lisa hint of a smile playing at her lips and her eyes almost looked...pleased. Alecia smiled at me, her face washed in relief, and I gave her two thumbs up.

I watched now as the guy everyone was calling Art, who'd just come out from one of the glass booths, shook her hand and congratulated her. *The boss,* I remembered.

"I love how you guys are just, like, putting on a show." Gusty swung his arms with glee. "You have the coolest job, Mom!"

It's been a long time since this woman was admired by her son, I thought, watching Mazy's cheeks turn red.

"Maybe you'll go into broadcast journalism yourself, kid," Art suggested.

"I don't think so. I want to drive a truck, so I can travel all over the country."

"Gusty, please." Mazy's laugh sounded embarrassed. "We aren't sending you to Shady Side Academy so you can become a truck driver."

"Just for a few years, Mom." Gusty looked around at his audience. "I can't rent a car until I turn twenty-five, but I can drive an oil tanker when I'm eighteen, isn't that funny?"

I didn't know why he would need to cruise around in an oil tanker when he already had a car. But it seemed best not to bring up the Porsche right now, considering it was in an impound lot.

"Aren't you going to introduce me to the rest of your family?" Art asked Mazy. "Is this cute little fella your grandson?" He pointed at Max.

"My *grandson*?"

"Sorry, Mazy—you're not old enough to be a grandmother yet, are you?" Art slapped his leg and laughed loudly, until Mazy managed to muster up a ghoulish smile. I shushed Max, who was grinning and clapping.

"This is my cousin and her son," Alecia said.

"Well, that's great!" Art smiled and looked at the small crowd of them. "We always welcome families here. Right, Mazy?"

"Right, Art."

After we'd mumbled our thank-yous and looked at our feet for long enough, Art finally walked back into his glass cubicle.

"Can I push buttons?" Max pointed across the room at the "control center," which wasn't much of a control center at all, just a giant, flat image on the wall of complicated-appearing silver equipment with plenty of gadgets and knobs.

"There're no buttons to push, Max. It's just a picture," Alecia said.

"Hold on, it's *fake*?" Gusty said with disbelief. "*That's* the famous control center? What's the point?"

"If it looks as though we're reporting from a spaceship, then we *must* have an eye on everything," Alecia said with a laugh. "Come on, I'll show you."

Once they walked off to go investigate, Mazy turned and glared at me. "How's the nanny search coming, Di?"

"Great." When I nodded, the bones in my neck cracked.

"Enjoying the house?"

I hesitated, wondering what the right answer was. *Not at all?* "It's a lovely house."

"Did Augustus tell you who found it?"

I hesitated. "Um . . . you?"

"I got it for less than the asking price. Auggie never even liked it! He said we didn't have enough children to fill up all the rooms. I said, fine, we'll have another kid. Who do you think put Auggie through business school? Me. That is *my* house."

"It's a lovely house," I said again. There was something about the woman's rage that reminded me of Alecia. A feeling welled up, too desperate to be called hope. *Please, please, please don't let Alecia turn out like this bitter woman.*

"So, tell me, Di. What are you, really?" She folded her arms across her chest. "Not exactly a nanny-finder, I presume?"

I couldn't think of what the truth really was anymore. If I wasn't a nanny-finder, what was I? A masseuse, a bikini waxer, a chef? A witch, as Gusty had accused me of? For a moment, it actually sounded promising, the mingling of career and religion. "I'm a mom," I finally said, the only honest answer I could come up with.

Mazy didn't have a reply to that. We were both watching Gusty across the room, where, in the control center, he spoke animatedly into a ballpoint pen. Meanwhile, Alecia was holding Max up, so that he could lunge at the buttons that weren't really buttons. Perplexed and pleased, I cocked my head to the side: my cousin had never willingly touched my son before. What did it mean for her future? And what did it mean for mine? I stared at them, suddenly disconcerted by how much fun Max was having without me. Was Mazy having the same self-centered thought as we stood side by side, watching our boys?

"It was really nice of you to let him sit at the news desk," I said. "Gusty's thrilled to see what you do." When I was met with silence, I turned and realized Mazy had walked back into her glass office and shut the door. "I'll tell him you said goodbye," I said, under my breath.

"HOW'D YOU EVEN GET here?" Alecia asked, as she walked Max and me out to the parking lot between broadcasts. The horizon was tinged with streaks of pink, and a flock of birds rippled across the sky. Rush hour was over, the mild breeze felt soft and peaceful and vaguely familiar.

"Dave the landscaper gave us a ride." I shielded my eyes from the setting sun with the back of my hand. "He might be out having dinner right now, but he said he'd come back for us."

"Dave the landscaper?"

"He even promised to take us to the tow lot to pick up the Porsche afterwards."

"Dave the landscaper?"

"Right." Why did she keep repeating his name and title like that?

"Di, are you crazy? What do you think Mr. Catalano is going to say when Gusty tells him you hitched a ride to the TV station with his groundskeeper?"

"He's not really the groundskeeper," I said flatly, although, technically, I suppose he was. Still, it made him sound so hired-helpless. "And he's the one who got us to your apartment so I could get the makeup. He's the one who nearly wrecked his truck trying to get us here on time. So, when he drives up, be more than civil. Try to gush a little bit."

"I'm sorry I ... put you in a bad position." Alecia sighed and ran her fingers through her hair. "Thank you for coming. Thank you for not ... holding it against me."

"Holding what against you?"

"Everything." She looked up from her feet. "You don't have to move out, if you don't want. I mean, stay as long as you need to."

Max tugged on her arm and told her his favorite nonsense joke that he'd made up himself: "Rutabaga stuffed with dirty socks." He giggled.

"Rutabaga stuffed with ... eyeballs," Alecia replied, and he laughed harder.

"Thanks for the offer," I said. "But let's just see how it goes." Dave was pulling up. I glanced over my shoulder, looking for Gusty, who'd promised to meet us outside.

"So, you must be the famous anchorwoman," Dave said, climbing out of the pickup.

"You must be the famous Dave," Alecia said, beaming at him. "How can I thank you?"

He shrugged. "Don't have to. Your cousin is going to take me out to dinner." Dave smiled, his bottom teeth steeped in tar.

"Oh, that's wonderful!" Alecia turned and grinned at me like a Cheshire cat. *You told me to gush,* her eyes were saying.

"Where's the kid?" he asked.

"He went back to say goodbye to his mom. Come on, Max!" I added, as he ran around in circles, still giggling.

"I'll send him out. Di, call me later." Alecia was still smiling. "Dave, it was a pleasure."

He waved. We both watched her go. "She is something," Dave said.

"Yes," I agreed, wondering how the hell I was going to get out of dinner with him.

"So, I'll make you a deal," he said, as if reading my mind. "I take you all the way out past the airport to get the Porsche. You let me drive it home."

I laughed. "Yeah, right." After watching him saw through that tree today, I could only imagine what he'd do to a gas pedal in a car that did zero to sixty in less than five seconds. He'd managed to hit ninety in the pickup between two traffic lights.

"Think about it. If you total his Porsche, your life is over. You could never pay it back," Dave said. "You and Max and the kid can drive home in the pickup, and I'll just meet you all back at the house."

I hesitated. What if he got in a fender bender or, worse, stole it? "What if I wrecked your truck? How would that be any better?"

"Simple," Dave said, putting a hand on my shoulder. "I won't press charges."

I looked at his hand and wondered, for the briefest of seconds, how his love of chain saws and fast cars would translate in bed. But then, it was hard to envision him driving the Porsche without simultaneously imagining his mug of brown sludge tipping out of the cup holder onto one of Augustus's seats. "I'm afraid I just couldn't risk it—the upholstery, you understand."

He took his hand back. "What the hell do you think I'm gonna do to the upholstery?"

I pointed to the container of Copenhagen in the top pocket of his T-shirt. "I would be afraid you might . . . spill your spit cup." My face was heating up again.

"Oh, Christ." He pulled out the round container and tossed it into a nearby trash can. "There. Done. His upholstery is safe. Now, can I take the Porsche?"

"Are you going to let Gusty work with you?"

"Catalano is a prick," Dave said, shaking his head. "I'm not babysitting his kid."

"It wouldn't be babysitting—"

"I'm not doing that man any favors. He doesn't even know the names of his own trees," Dave muttered, and I could hear the disdain in his voice. Or maybe it was a jab at me for not knowing the difference between a sycamore and an oak.

"Okay. You can take the Porsche," I said finally. "As long as Gusty promises not to say a word."

LATER ON THAT NIGHT, as Gusty, Max, and I were waiting in Fox Chapel for Dave to reappear with the car, Alecia unlocked the door to her apartment in Shadyside and found Ben sitting on the sofa and watching TV. She was struck by a combination of relief and dread that was similar, I imagined, to finally getting a diagnosis. They couldn't really be breaking up if he was here, she thought. Unless he was here so they could really break up.

"I'm so glad you're back," she said, injecting hope into her voice, even as she saw the luggage—his luggage—blocking the entryway. After scooting his bag out of the way with her foot, she made her way to the sofa and plopped next to him. Ben's shoulders remained hunched, as if the Pottery Barn pillows were swallowing him, and he didn't take his eyes off the TV. "I had an idea—it just hit me on the way home from work—did you see me tonight?" she added brightly.

When Ben finally turned, he looked startled to see her. Though maybe it was just her makeup. He'd always said he never got used to her coming home from work looking like she'd been street-walking. "Sorry, no, I was...watching something else."

Alecia's eyes focused in front of them where some unfortunate soul was getting tackled on the TV. *When did he start to like football?* she wondered but didn't want to ask for fear Ben's reply would be an accusation of all the things they didn't know about each other. "Well, you missed my debut as an anchor in Pittsburgh. Vanessa went into labor—not on the air, thank God—and Maddie showed up in the lobby of WTAE five minutes before I was supposed to go on. And Art *wondered* why I seemed a bit frazzled."

"Your...*Maddie*?" Ben sat up. "Is she . . . ?"

"Still crazy? Yeah." She leaned over to touch his shoulder and then rubbed the soft flannel shirt on his arm. "Look, sweetie, here's my idea: we elope. To Fiji."

Ben reached for the remote and shut off the TV.

"Just you and me on the beach in our bare feet," Alecia added. "No witnesses. No tux. No dancing. No father-in-law. Well? Isn't that what you wanted?" She let her hand slide off of him as he stood up and began to pace.

"When were you going to tell me you'd forged my signature on the prenuptial agreement?" he asked. "The night before the wedding? Or at our divorce hearing?"

"Well, I didn't know what to do. Every time Daddy would call, he'd ask if it was signed. It wasn't anything personal—"

"Of course it was personal! Your father hates me!"

"That's not true. Daddy just wants us to be prepared for the worst."

"You forged my name." He laughed in disbelief. "How can I trust you?"

"It was a mistake. I'm sorry. Okay? I never sent it back to him."

Ben ran his hands through his hair again, and his eyes

hesitated before meeting hers. "I meant what I said the other day. I can't go through with it."

"Sweetie, come on. I just got carried away with all the plans..."

"You've been carried away with your career, too, ever since we got back from England. Your life is a battle, Alecia."

"I've had to fight hard to get where I want to be." She folded her arms across her chest. "It's what you do when you have a dream. You work for it."

"I'm not against work." When she made a face, he added, "Do I think work *equals* life? No." Ben straightened. "I can't give you what you want."

She looked up at him, confused. "Why? What do I want?"

"Someone successful. Or, at the very least, ambitious."

If anything, she thought grimly, he had *too much* ambition: every other year he dreamed up something new. And besides, she was having trouble defining success these days: Was it just a list of accomplishments with all the items—including happiness—neatly ticked off? Lately Alecia was beginning to wonder if she even wanted to be successful anymore—or, for that matter, if she was capable of being truly happy. ("I'm missing something vital," she told me later. "Yeah," I said. "Your mother." But no, it was different—some basic inspiration, like Ben had had, when they first became friends. She thought of Pastor Nate asking them if a church was just a place to have a wedding. *What about the world?* she imagined him saying. *Is it just a place to have a life?*)

"I just wish you'd pick one thing and stick to it for a while," she said to Ben. "You follow your every whim."

"And you hide behind your career. You couldn't even take a honeymoon."

"It was just an issue of timing."

"Life is an issue of timing!" Ben exhaled and sat on the

coffee table, facing her. "If you stripped away your life on TV, who would you be? And what would you really want?"

She leaned forward and caressed his cheek. "I would really want you."

Ben closed his eyes as her hand stroked his face. "It shouldn't be this hard," he finally said. His eyes opened, and he stared at her for a moment. "In the beginning . . . I was just so sure about you and me. Now, I just . . . can't remember what the signs were anymore."

Shaking his head wearily, Ben stood up off the table and then hesitated in the front hall for just a second before reaching for his suitcase. "Look, I'll get the rest of my things later, okay? I'm going to stay at Holly's for a little while."

Alecia rose from the sofa and followed him. Her legs felt strangely unsteady, while her heart banged in her chest. "You can't go now!" she blurted, thinking of her pregnancy, just as his hand touched the doorknob. "I need—more time—to figure things out . . ."

"To figure *what* out?" Ben asked, turning around to face her again.

She swallowed, searching for her answer. She couldn't tell him and let him make the decision for her. But how could she not? Ben set down his suitcase and waited.

"If you could just . . . give me a week," she said.

"How will things look any different in a week? How will you be any different?"

She hesitated. It would be too easy to let him decide, to have him stay. They couldn't get married just because she was pregnant; the idea was repugnant to her.

"Don't you see?" Ben said, unbolting the lock. "We're out of time."

"Baby, wait," Alecia said, pressing herself against the door before he could open it. "Let's figure this out." She slid her arms around his waist. "Please."

For a moment, Ben didn't move. She kissed him under the chin, wishing she'd thought to do this back on the couch. Ben swallowed and still didn't move. *Stay,* she insisted telepathically.

Outside the living room windows, a siren wailed, a car stereo thrummed, and a drunk laughed hysterically. Finally, Ben tilted his head down and met her lips with his own. It wasn't quite a chaste kiss, and it wasn't quite distant; it was a tender goodbye. "I have figured this out," he said softly, untangling himself from her embrace before stooping down to pick up his suitcase again. The siren grew closer, the bass louder—unless that was the blood pushing through Alecia's brain—and the drunk girl's laugh was transformed into the cackle of three hundred guests, called off in the final moments. "If you want help getting these gifts back—"

"I don't care about the gifts!" she said. "I care about you!"

"I'm sorry."

She watched him reach for the handle, watched as he didn't even look at her one last time before leaving her with the biggest mess of her life to clean up.

Gone, she thought, hugging herself in the doorway. *Just like everybody else.*

CHAPTER 15

New Deal

It was Wednesday afternoon, two days later, and the house was quiet. Max was napping, and Gusty had assured me that he would be using the computer in his room for schoolwork until lunch was ready. I stood at the kitchen counter, chopping up hearts of palm for a salad, when the screen door suddenly rattled open.

"Anybody home?" Augustus called, coming inside from the deck. He wore khaki pants and a white golf shirt that made his skin look tan. His face relaxed into a smile when he noticed me standing there, one hand over my heart. "Hi, Di. Did I scare you?"

"Just surprised me." I wasn't nervous because he'd struck me as handsome, but rather because the Master of the House was home, and I was waiting for him to discover piece by piece everything that had gone wrong. "When did you get back?" I added. There had been an unexplained pile of mail on the kitchen counter that morning, but I'd incorrectly assumed Gusty was responsible.

"Early—before you all were up. Played a round of golf and took Gusty's Porsche out for a spin. Listen, thanks for getting it washed. It looks great."

"Oh, sure." Apparently I hadn't ruined the transmission after all. And I would have to thank Dave for cleaning the car. I'd been especially hard on him when he showed up with the Porsche after ten o'clock on Monday night.

"Where'd you take it, anyway?"

"The car? Oh...that place..." I snapped my finger and pointed vaguely beyond his shoulder.

"Down the road? The one on the left?" Augustus reached for a handful of mail.

I nodded slowly, just in case he had something against the place on the left. "And where do you play golf?" It's something I've learned from my life on the run: a good way to distract someone from a lie is to ask him a question about himself.

"Oakmont Country Club. A buddy of mine—Gusty's old shrink, Craig Locklear—is a member."

"Oh, Stacey's dad."

Augustus stopped sorting through the pile and stared at me. "Do you *know* the Locklear family?"

"I don't. Gusty and Jason were both saying something about you and Stacey."

"When did you and Jason meet?"

"He came to visit Gusty at the hospital."

"Must've been quite a visit if he was talking about Stacey and me."

"It was short, actually."

He didn't ask me to elaborate. Instead, he cocked his head to the side and looked at something behind me. When he spoke again, his voice sounded perplexed. "My grill . . . seems to be smoking."

"Oh, that's—Gusty's veggie burger!" I put down my knife, grabbed a plate and spatula, and pushed past him. Outside, gray plumes of smoke billowed out of the grill and stung my eyes as I lifted the lid to search for a charred ball of protein matter.

"I thought it was broken," Augustus said, just behind me.

"You needed a new propane tank."

"And I had one?"

"In the basement." I turned around and saw his befuddled expression. "You've got everything down there."

He looked down at the black burger in the center of the plate. "So, I understand you're a great cook."

We both laughed.

Back inside, Gusty wandered into the kitchen, just as I was scraping his plate into the trash. "How about I throw some tuna and olives in your salad, instead?" I asked. "It'll be a salad niçoise."

"That's okay. I'm not that hungry." He yawned and stretched. "Kind of filled up on chips, anyway."

"Chips?" I looked to Augustus for a reaction, but he didn't even glance up from his phone bill. *Mental note: Remove chips from house.*

"Get any homework done, pal?" Augustus finally asked, tossing aside another envelope.

"It's done," Gusty said, even though I knew he hadn't picked up a schoolbook since I'd been here, and I suspected he'd really just been playing video games.

"Well, good, because I got us tickets to watch the Penguins tomorrow night."

"Hockey?" Gusty sounded doubtful.

"Yeah, hockey. And quality time with your dad. Buck up." Augustus laughed.

Gusty picked up the tickets and made a face while he examined them. "Who were you originally supposed to go with?"

"You. Only you. Were the tickets free? Yes. But I never made plans with anyone else." He glanced at me. "Can you believe this kid?"

I looked at Gusty and raised my eyebrows: *Thank him, you ungrateful Raja.*

"Thanks, Dad. I've always wanted to go to a hockey game." His voice sounded robotic again, but at least the smile looked real. "I'll leave you two alone now. You probably have *lots* of things to talk about." Gusty saluted me before moving off toward the Great Room, which meant this was probably my cue to convince his father to let him do landscaping. Gusty didn't seem to care that Dave wasn't interested in hiring him. *He likes you. If you ask him again, I bet he'll agree,* he'd told me.

"Actually, can I talk to you for a moment, Di?" Augustus asked, gesturing toward the kitchen table. At least I wasn't going to be forced to take a stand in the court of the dining room. I took the seat across from him and folded my hands on the granite tabletop, steeling myself for the worst.

"Well, I'll cut to the chase," Augustus said. "Gusty loves you."

I felt my face heat up, both pleased and worried by the compliment. Love was obviously a sign of Gusty's desperation; it meant that he was depending on me to fix everything. I hoped I wouldn't let him down.

"The last time he raved about anyone, it was his grandfather. They were each other's best babysitter."

"Yeah, I'm . . . sorry about your father."

"Thank you," Augustus said. He leaned forward and added urgently: "Gusty doesn't want any other nanny."

"The thing is, I'm not really a nanny."

"He said that, apparently notwithstanding veggie burgers, you're an unbelievable cook."

"I am, yes." *Notwithstanding salmonella, too.*

"Well, what would it take to make you mine?"

I blinked in near disbelief. After six weeks of searching, here it was: an actual, legitimate job offer involving something that I was good at. *My first miracle.* "Will there be health benefits?"

"Benefits?" Augustus sounded surprised. "This is all under the table, Di. I'm talking about cash."

I thought of my conversation with Dave, how he'd said that Catalano would try to get away with paying me half of whatever I asked for. "What exactly is the offer?"

"Name your price."

Holly had said an MRI of my brain would cost around thirty-five hundred dollars, so I asked for that per month. "But I need the first month up front. And I still keep the finder's fee. You promised to double it."

"I see," Augustus said, rubbing his chin. "You realize that's . . . forty thousand a year? Much more than the going rate of a full-time live-in nanny. Gusty is only here half of the time, which is about how often I'll need you to cook. Most cooks, by the way, don't move in with their two-year-olds."

I looked down at my folded hands and thought of Dave again. Was it too early to back down?

"Listen, if you take the job, you'll still have plenty of time off for your personal life. Are you married?" I shook my head. "Great." Augustus smiled. "I mean, in the sense that you'll be fully able to attend to us when we need you. And, of course, if you aren't willing to be our nanny, you'll still have to find us one, which could take you a while. Gusty has to approve of her, you understand."

So, it was a trap. "How much are you willing to pay me?"

"Two thousand a month."

I thought of Dave again. *Ask for double and then everybody wins.* "Three thousand, if I'm the interim nanny. Two thousand once I'm just the cook."

"Deal."

"What about when Gusty's not here—do you want me to make meals for you?"

He hesitated for a moment. "What I'd really like is for you to teach me. No, really," he said, after I accidentally chuckled. "I can't make a thing. I have all this food . . ."

"And all this kitchen . . ." I added.

"And I only eat cold cereal."

"Or takeout!" Gusty called out from the Great Room. I'd forgotten about him. He'd probably been eavesdropping on our whole conversation waiting for me to put in the Pro Lawn Service plug.

"Or takeout," Augustus agreed. "Thanks, pal!"

"Well, I'd be happy to teach you."

"Terrific." He pushed back his chair, preparing to stand up. "Then I guess we have a—"

"There's just one more thing," I blurted.

"Shoot."

"Gusty was really hoping to be able to work landscaping with Pro Lawn Service."

Augustus settled back into his seat and stared at me.

"You know, mowing lawns, pulling up weeds, planting things. I thought it could be good for him to get outside—"

"No. Absolutely not. If he needs to get outside, he can swim in the pool."

"For another couple of weeks until it's covered!" Gusty shouted from behind one of the flowered sofas.

"If you want to get outside, you can take a walk in the woods," Augustus shouted back.

"I hate you! I hate you and I hate Mom and I hate hockey!"

We both listened to the stomp of Gusty's feet across the wood floor and up the stairs, followed by the slam of his door.

"Ah, the joys of parenthood. You'll love it when Max tells you he hates you for the first time." I was probably supposed to laugh but couldn't. "Which reminds me…" His brows furrowed. "Do you know where this came from?" He placed a container of Copenhagen on the table between us. "I found it in the Porsche."

Too stunned to answer, I simply shook my head.

"You weren't buying Gusty chewing tobacco, were you?"

"No, of course not. Maybe…one of the car wash guys left it behind?"

"They got in my Porsche?" Augustus's eyebrows shot up.

"To vacuum. Someone got in to vacuum…I think."

Augustus narrowed his eyes at me for just a second before his face relaxed again. "Good. We have a deal. My new cook." His handshake was gentler than when we first met, but it still felt like he meant it. "What's for dinner tonight?"

I hesitated. "I've really just been taking it meal by meal. Finding things that won't drive up Gusty's blood sugar. Is there something you'd like?"

"More salmon, my doctor tells me. My good cholesterol is too low. Is that…a problem?" he asked, since I was scratching my head, wondering how the hell I was going to get to the grocery store. It was too late to admit after all this that I didn't even have a driver's license.

"It's just…driving the Porsche makes me nervous. And I'd have to get to the store."

"I'll take you, then."

"When Max wakes up from his nap?" I asked.

Augustus's smile turned into a wince. "Why don't you just give me a list, and I'll make a run. We'll make tonight my first lesson."

CHAPTER 16

Cooking Lessons

Augustus showed up for his first lesson as if we were about to go hiking: the same white polo shirt, shorts, and funky sandals from our first meeting. Cadaverous toenails aside, I liked the idea that he was a sandal kind of guy. It made him seem more like an "Auggie"—and was vaguely reminiscent of my father, who'd lived and died in his Birkenstocks.

"I have to say, I was relieved when I saw your shopping list," he said, placing a Whole Foods bag on the counter. "I panicked for about a minute thinking I'd just hired a cook who'd want me to buy bean sprouts, and wheat germ, and tofu..."

"I don't happen to like tofu," I said. "Neither does Max."

"Thank God for that."

"Rutabaga stuffed with tofu sneezes," Max said at the kitchen table, where he was coloring with his no-mess magic markers. I pretended to retch, which made Max laugh hysterically and Auggie look at me curiously.

"I never even asked if you eat meat."

"I do eat meat. And, more importantly, I cook meat." I smiled when Auggie exhaled noisily. "But I don't wear fur."

He snapped his fingers. "Darn. Remind me to return that coat...."

I laughed and told him that he could relax; I'd abided by his two requirements, namely that the food should be both "stupidly easy" to prepare and fast, something that he could whip up in under a half hour.

"But something that'll still impress the ladies," he added now.

"By ladies, you mean Stacey," I translated.

"Unfortunately, not Stacey. She's found herself a new young lawyer." He sighed. "You'd think when a guy buys you a building, it would mean something, but apparently she wanted a ring, not a couple of classrooms."

"You bought her a building?"

"Well, it was really just a hallway. I made her acceptance to law school contingent on that. Luckily, it's my alma mater. If they want to name a north wing after me, I suppose it's all right."

" 'If I had a million dollars, I'd buy your love,' " I sang, as I unpacked the grocery bags, placing the main ingredients on the counter: basil, garlic, parmesan, roasted pine nuts, and oil.

Auggie raised an eyebrow. "Barenaked Ladies fan, eh? See, I would've pegged you differently." He rubbed his chin, studying me. "I would've thought... The Dead? Joni Mitchell? No?"

"What gave you that impression? The braid?" I asked, laughing.

"The braid. The blue fish tattoo," he said, nodding at my left shoulder.

I adjusted the spaghetti strap on my tank top, so it wasn't sliding down my arm.

"What's dead means?" Max asked, from the table.

"It means…" I hesitated. Just the other day, he'd asked Ben the opposite question: *What's life means?* Ben had said that he would let him know when he figured it out. "It's a band, sweetie. A group of people who sing and play instruments."

"So, I should probably pay attention," Auggie said. "What are we making here?"

"Pesto. If you're a purist you mince the basil by hand. If you want stupidly easy, throw it all into your food processor." He watched as I loaded up the Cuisinart. "So, let me get this straight: without you, this woman wouldn't have even gotten into law school?"

He shrugged. "She made it as far as the wait list."

"Was she appropriately horrified by your grand gesture?" I pushed the button: a quick on, quick off.

"I much prefer to be anonymous with my random acts of kindness." Auggie shook his head and leaned on the counter. "It used to drive Mazy out of her mind."

"Buying buildings for hot women? I can't imagine why." I headed back toward the stove.

"It wasn't always about a girl. She got mad when I didn't go to church, but I tithed. Because I didn't serve soup in a homeless shelter with her, but I donated the money to give a couple of folks their first home. Mazy said I did it all for the tax write-off."

"Why did you do it?" I asked, rummaging in the cabinet for an appropriate pasta pot.

"For the tax write-off. Plus, I figured it had to count for something, karma-wise."

"Gusty said you like to sponsor people," I said, thinking of Ben and his magazine again. I handed him a pot.

"Yet another thing that drove my ex crazy. What am I doing with this?"

"It's for the pasta. You can boil water, can't you?" He laughed and nodded. I opened the last grocery bag to retrieve the salmon and explained how we'd cook it: fill up a pan with cold salt water, lay the fish in it, and turn up the heat. "As soon as the water boils, we'll shut off the heat and let the salmon sit in the water for ten minutes. Then we'll make our sauce."

Augustus squinted one eye at me. "Sauce sounds hard."

"It's just dill, lemon juice, and sour cream. Couldn't be easier," I said. "Oh—go easy over there. If you overprocess the basil, it'll lose all its taste. Just do gentle pulses."

"Gentle pulses." He grinned. "Got it."

"So, how often do you invest in other people's dreams?" I asked, moving back to check on the pasta. "Because I have this friend who wants to start a magazine."

He winced. "Magazines are tough. They're kind of like restaurants. More than ninety percent fail in the first year. Should we taste it?" He lifted the wooden spoon, took a bite, and then offered it to me.

"Too dry. And not enough garlic." I reached for the garlic press while handing him the oil.

"My thoughts exactly. Tell me when to stop," he added, pouring. "So, who is this friend with a dream?"

"My cousin's ex-fiancé."

"Ex-fiancé," he mused. "Is he a loser, or what?"

"No, he's awesome—or I wouldn't have mentioned it. The magazine is about faith. Stop!"

He put down the oil. "So, if he's your cousin's ex, are you going to go for it?"

I blinked. "Go for what?"

"Him. The guy. He sounds available now. Am I right?" He nudged me.

My face and neck were growing warm. "I don't love him like that."

Auggie's eyebrows went up. "So, you admit you have a thing for this guy?"

"You're an instigator," I said, pulsing the pesto myself this time. "It's platonic. My cousin's pregnant with his baby."

"Nah. It's not platonic. Not if you're pitching a magazine about faith." Augustus sampled another bite of the pesto. I knew we must've been getting somewhere this time, because he shut his eyes, as if to fully appreciate the taste, he had to block out the four other senses. I watched his face, as if waiting for him to wake up. "Bring him out to the house. I'd like to meet him." He opened his eyes, which were shockingly blue. "Find out what your type is."

CHAPTER 17

Hitching a Ride

It was Thursday night, my first evening off. Max and I had only been gone for six days, and yet it already felt like a year. So much had happened, and so much hadn't happened—specifically, the symptoms from Pottery Barn, which thankfully hadn't repeated themselves in over three weeks. Still, I hadn't forgotten, at least not at night, when I'd go to shut my eyes and the panic would invade my chest. My most important prayers rang through my mind to the tune of that Smiths song, "Please Please Please." *Please please please don't let me be separated from Max,* I'd say over and over. In the days of my parents' divorce, the song was: *Please please please, let him come back,* before it was, *Please please please, let us come back,* and then, when my mother got sick, it became, *Please please please let her live,* which, of course, didn't happen, either. At this rate, I could sing the line, "Lord knows it would be the first time," without exaggerating. Unless God counted that moment I found Maddie facedown next to the toilet and thought, *Please please please, don't let her be dead,* and it turned out she wasn't. If each of us only got one prayer to come true, Alecia would've declared that I'd wasted it. Ben would've told me that prayers were not the same as wishes. Sometimes, though, when you weren't sure if anyone was listening, it was hard to tell the difference.

I knew Holly would listen, though, so I called and made two doctors' appointments—one for myself and one for Max. She'd been after me long enough to get my son immunized. And for some reason, I had decided that I could stop worrying about myself if she would simply lay hands on me and pronounce me "fine," if not "healed."

Once Augustus and Gusty had left for the hockey game, Max and I went out to the driveway, where Hobbes and TJ were loading up the back of a big pickup truck. Dave leaned against the cab as he surveyed a clipboard.

"Didn't we have a deal?" I asked.

Dave straightened and took the pencil from his mouth. "Say what?"

I opened my palm to show him the container of Copenhagen. "You left this in the Porsche, and Aug—Mr. Catalano found it. Didn't you promise me that you wouldn't chew tobacco in his car?"

"I promised you that I wouldn't ruin his seats. I don't remember promising not to dip." Dave tucked the pencil behind his ear and then hoisted a mammoth Gatorade jug into the back of the truck. "Sorry, though. It must've slipped out of my back pocket."

"Your jeans were tight," I said. "Nothing was getting out of that back pocket without some help."

Dave turned, looking startled, while TJ burst out laughing.

"I mean . . ." My face was heating up.

"There are no accidents," Hobbes added.

"Hey, assholes, try getting back to work."

"It's time to go," TJ said, tapping his wrist where a watch might have been.

"Well, then, get in the truck," Dave said. He scowled when Hobbes held out his hands for the keys. "I'm the boss. I drive." Dave turned back to me. "I thought the deal was that you were going to take me out to dinner."

"We—I—yes," I stammered. "Soon."

"So, did he fire you?" TJ asked.

"I'm going to be his personal cook."

"His personal cook." Dave shook his head. "Fantastic." He turned to Hobbes and TJ. "Somebody get in the back."

"Excuse me," I said, before Dave could shut his truck door, "but would Max and I fit?"

He shifted around, his green eyes wide. "You need a car of your own, lady." At least he didn't say I needed help this time.

"Max and I have doctors' appointments in Aspinwall at five-thirty. It's right down the road. You wouldn't have to wait or anything. We have a ride home." After the office visit, Holly was having us over for dinner.

"Hey, loser, you live in Aspinwall, remember?" TJ said to Dave.

"It's the least you could do for trying to screw up her future," Hobbes added.

"Fine. But that means both of you are in the flatbed. Max gets the backseat." He jerked his head toward me. "She's shotgun."

"I can ride in the flatbed," I offered.

"No way," Dave muttered. "You're somebody's mother."

IT TOOK US A while to get on the road because Dave had to install Max's car seat, and Hobbes and TJ had started a round of rock, paper, scissors for no particular reason that I could see, except to avoid the inevitable. I felt kind of bad making them lie down in compost, but I wasn't about to volunteer twice, considering that, in preparation for my doctor's appointment, I'd already showered and was even wearing a denim skirt with my white peasant blouse. Finally, we were all aboard and Dave peeled out.

"Keep your heads down!" he called out the back hatch. "I don't need another citation."

As the truck sped along, whipping around the turns of the road, I pressed my face to the window and looked at the endless sky, breaking through the trees.

"What are those gigantic trees?" I pointed at the ones I always called "really big pines."

"Norway spruces."

"Did you hear that, Max? Those trees are called Norway spruces," I called behind me.

"Broccoli!" Max loved to classify all trees as broccoli and all broccoli as trees.

"I think you'd find that a Norway spruce would be pretty tough to eat, kiddo," Dave said, reaching for his spit cup. Even if he was gross and had possibly tried to sabotage my career, at least he was nice to my son.

"Do you have children?" I asked, which made him laugh.

"God, I hope not." He glanced at me.

"How'd you figure out the car seat so quickly?"

"Nieces and nephews. Whole bunch of them. The oldest is, like, thirteen."

Gusty's age, I thought. "Gusty's age." I waited a beat to let it sink in. "Would you ever reconsider hiring him as an employee? It wouldn't be babysitting."

"I don't care what it would be. I got enough liability with these two." Dave jerked his head toward the back where TJ and Hobbes were throwing grass in the air.

"You're right," I said with a sigh. "His dad won't let him do it, anyway."

"What do you mean? I thought this was Catalano's idea."

"It was Gusty's. And I promised I'd talk to his father, who said no; and I've talked to you, who said no—twice now; so I'll tell him to come up with something else. He's got that pool in the back. Maybe I could get him really excited about doing laps."

"Laps." Dave took the next bend in the road so hard that my knee brushed up against his muddy shorts. I tried to scoot away but couldn't. "Why is it up to you to get him excited about doing anything?"

"Well, it's not. I just want to help...." I shuddered as he picked up the mug and spit into it. "Don't you like to taste your food?" I blurted.

"I can taste."

"Remind me never to cook for you."

"I didn't ask you to cook for me, lady. Keep cookin' for Catalano."

I tossed my braid behind my back again and stared out the window.

"So, why do you care so much about the kid—Gusty?"

I shrugged. "He's got diabetes. He's had some trouble regulating his sugar. I thought he might just like to get outside and..." Maybe I'd read *The Secret Garden* too many times as a child.

We pulled up at the stoplight on Freeport Road when Dave turned and looked at me. "Tell Gusty we start at seven A.M."

"Really?" I could've hugged him, but cheered instead. "Hooray!"

From the backseat, Max clapped the way he did whenever anyone said "Hooray!"

"Tell him he's going to get a Stupid Nickname," Dave added.

CHAPTER 18

Doctor's Appointment

From the moment the woman in the pink pants and teddy bear shirt put the blood pressure cuff around my arm and pumped it up, I knew I shouldn't have brushed off the blindness. I could feel it in the pumping—in my face, in my chest, all over my body. The tighter it got, the more certain I was that whatever happened three weeks ago was not a fluke. It was a warning. When the moment ended with a hiss, it surprised me. "One twenty over eighty," the girl said and then marked it in the chart. I remembered from when my mother was sick that one twenty over eighty meant everything was okay, at least for now.

There was a Max-size skeleton set up on the floor, and Max curiously approached it and stuck his fingers in the sockets where some poor child's eyes used to be. Unless it was only plastic, I realized belatedly. God, it was horrible to be here. The waiting room alone had been an ordeal: the questions on the forms, the empty blanks where Max's immunization record should've been, the multiple requests for insurance cards that we didn't have. Never did I feel as much of an outsider as when the receptionist behind the desk at the doctor's office stamped my chart *SELF PAY*.

I took a deep breath and tried not to listen to the somewhat muffled conversation Holly was having in the room next door. "So, what's the word, Doc?" The voice probably belonged to the man who'd been sitting next to me in the waiting room, the one who was so thin he looked cold. In the pause that followed, I imagined Holly taking a deep breath. Then her own voice quieted into the low but steady notes of Bad News Breaking.

I looked at Max, who was comparing his hands to the skeleton's and grinning. I looked down at my own hands. Was my left index finger tingling or was I just imagining it?

"Lung cancer?" the man next door repeated.

I fidgeted and ran my fingers through my hair, and five strands came out on my fingers. *Oh, God*. Why had I come? Things were getting better—I was getting better. Max and I had been invited to live in a lovely home, and I was going to be making more money than I'd ever had in my entire life. Most of all, I was getting a family back, even if it didn't happen to be my own. What the hell was I doing here except trolling for bad news?

"...not hopeless," I heard Holly say through the wall. And, "...not easy."

"Ain't it the truth. Don't get old, Doc."

"Well, if I don't get old, then I'm dead, Harry."

"Just make sure you go quickly in the end," he said.

Yes, that was a great idea. *Go quickly*. I jumped off the examining table and grabbed Max's arm.

"Bones!" he screamed, letting his legs go limp so that he slumped to the floor.

"The skeleton stays here," I said. "We're going."

"My skel-e-ton!" Max wailed. "Mine!"

"Hush, Boo. Hush! Be quiet. Max, *please*—"

The door opened. "Who's afraid of a little old skeleton?" Holly asked, with a big grin on her face as she stooped to the floor. Somehow, I found my own smile and felt my shoulders relax. Even Max, still on his belly on the floor, stopped kicking and beamed, tantrum instantly forgotten.

"Come here, little man!" Holly said, and he scrambled up off the floor and ran to her with open arms. "You are so big!" She scooped him up and rocked him back and forth.

"How was England?" I asked, smiling, as I watched them.

"Not quite a vacation," she said, turning to me with a grin. "And how's the mama? Any more headaches?"

"I never got a headache, remember? I just went blind and numb."

"Oh, right." I wished Holly didn't look so immediately worried. She lowered Max to the floor and opened my blank chart before gesturing at me to get back on the examining table. I moved slowly, as if approaching a gangplank.

"But good news!" I said, while Holly skimmed my intake form. "I should be able to afford my MRI. I got a job while you were gone! I'm sort of a nanny, but just temporarily. My real job is 'personal chef.' "

"Whose personal chef?" Holly looked up with wide eyes, as if waiting for me to say, *Sting's!*

"Augustus Catalano—Mazy Roberts's ex. He wants me to live at his house and cook for him. And his son," I said. Holly put a finger to her lips, and I was quiet while she listened to my neck with a stethoscope.

"And his son," Holly belatedly echoed with a laugh as she lowered the stethoscope. "What's the father like? Follow my finger with your eyes."

"Tall. Taller than me."

"So, you can wear heels! Push me away."

"Right." I pushed against her, palm to palm.

"Hold on," she said, slowly lowering her hand. "You're in love with your employer?"

"No."

"You noticed his height." She pointed at me. "You have deduced that, if you kissed him, you wouldn't have to crouch down to do so."

I laughed, wishing my cheeks weren't giving me away. So, it was true: I happened to be intrigued. But what was the harm? The same formula had worked for Maria and Captain von Trapp. *Maria was a freaking nun, not a single mother,* Alecia would say.

"It's just…a nice working environment. No benefits, though," I added, watching my legs kick, one then the other, as Holly tapped my knees with her reflex hammer. There was a new smudge of dirt on my thigh from when I'd brushed up against Dave in the pickup truck. I thought his legs were tan; apparently, they were just grimy.

"Try to stare at that picture so I can get a good look at your retina."

It was hard to stare at anything when Holly was shining a bright light in my eyes, but somehow I managed.

"Looks good," she said finally, stepping away, and then all I could see were white spots in my vision. After that, the neurological exam got funny. Holly made me walk on my tiptoes, and then walk as if I were taking a sobriety test, heel to toe, and then I had to touch my nose and then touch Holly's finger, and then touch my nose. Max giggled as I flipped my hands back and forth, quickly.

"What exactly are you checking for?"

"Disdiadokinesis. Cerebellar function. Yours appears to be intact."

"So, that's good then. And I'm okay?"

"I think," Holly said, instead of yes. She scratched her

head. "I'm still standing by my theory that it was just an atypical migraine without the headache. Nevertheless—"

"So, I can stop taking the aspirin and forget the MRI?"

"*Nevertheless,* I think we should still make sure you don't have MS or ..."

"A brain tumor."

Holly allowed it with a half nod. "Or any ischemic changes in your brain." *Whatever that meant.* "Listen, Di ..." she hesitated. "I'll pay for it."

I waved the idea away. "Please. I can get the money."

"Alecia's father?" she suggested.

"Uncle Frank?" I said, surprised. "I haven't talked to him in ages."

"Has Alecia, since ...?" Holly winced.

"Somehow I doubt it."

"I ran into her in the lobby of my other office on Tuesday. She seemed skittish," Holly said, sounding perplexed. "She said she had an appointment with the gynecologist upstairs. I told her about how I'm supposed to see the fertility specialist next week, and she looked . . . so strange. Like I'd just told her the saddest news."

"She probably felt bad."

"For *me*?"

"No, for her—for the situation! There you are—wanting a baby—and there she is ..." Holly stared at me, just as I felt my own eyes widening. "Not that I'm saying she's—"

"Pregnant," Holly blurted, pointing her pen at me. "Of course!"

"She might not be ..." I bit my lip. "... anymore."

"She never went upstairs to the appointment! We talked for a few minutes, and then she practically fled the building." Holly tucked her pen behind her ear. "It all makes sense, now ..."

"You can't tell Ben," I grabbed her arm. "Please."

"He's my brother!"

"Doctor-patient confidentiality!"

"She's not my patient!"

"But I am *afflicted* with this big mouth!" I cupped my chin. "It's a terrible condition. If you told anyone anything I said—it might be fatal."

Holly shook her head and sighed. "He's my brother."

"I will *make her* tell him. I promise."

Holly nodded, finally, and uncrossed her arms. Glancing down, she seemed to notice my chart once again. "So, what are we going to do about your MRI?"

"I've got a paying job now," I reminded her. "And I get the feeling they're both going to want me around for a while."

She nodded, considering this. "Just be careful, okay?"

"Be careful of what?" I asked, knowing we weren't talking about my health anymore.

"I'm sorry. You don't need my advice."

"Medical advice, yes," I said, and Holly laughed.

"Oh, no, Max, you don't want to touch that!" I blurted before he could stick his whole hand in the biohazardous waste container. "I was thinking of giving him his shots today, but now I don't think I'm ready," I added in one breath, as Holly steered him back toward the skeleton.

"You want my medical advice? You should immunize Max. He's going to survive the shot." She patted my arm. "And so will you, Mama."

CHAPTER 19

The Pitch

The next morning, after Gusty left for school, I tried calling Alecia, but the outgoing message on her voice mail said that she would be out of town until Sunday. Holly had never actually promised to keep Alecia's secret, and I wanted to catch my cousin before Ben caught her first. A few hours later, once Max was down for his afternoon nap, I tried her cell phone and this time was rewarded with her voice.

"Where *are* you?" I blurted in a hushed whisper, calling from the cavernous bathroom again. Auggie was working from home that day, and I didn't want to be caught chatting in the kitchen.

"Pittsburgh Airport. Sitting on the tarmac." There was a yawn in her voice.

"But it's Friday—what about work?"

Alecia groaned and explained: Mazy wanted to give another reporter a shot at anchoring the next few nights—"to check the chemistry," as Art had delicately put it. And then, in a whisper, he'd added, "She's going through a rough time, with the divorce and all."

"As if she's the only person at WTAE going through a freaking rough time! Just a second—they want to make sure I know how to work the emergency exit—yes, yes, I got it—we throw the door *out*," she said to someone. "When do we land in Philadelphia?"

"*Philadelphia?*" I sat up straighter, thinking of my father's widow, Christine, and my half-sister, or, as I usually thought of her, My Replacement.

"Hang on, 13F doesn't feel capable of performing the exit-row duties," Alecia said grimly. "The door is not *that* heavy."

"I can't believe you're going to Philadelphia without me," I said, thinking of the trip I would have to take one day soon, if only to sit down with Christine and listen to her memories of my father. And more: I wanted to know why he gave up on me, but I was too afraid of the answer. What if Alecia had been trying to make me feel better—what if it really hadn't been Christine's idea to end the search?

"It's just a layover," Alecia said. "I'm on my way to see Daddy. I figured I better tell him in person."

"You're telling *him* before Ben?"

"About the wedding!"

"What about the baby?"

"He'll never need to know about that." Her voice turned sharper: "You haven't said anything to Ben, have you?"

"No—I—no…" I trailed off, wondering how to tell her that at this very moment Ben was on his way to Auggie's house to pitch his magazine. The night before, at Holly's house, when I announced that Auggie was interested in becoming an investor, Ben just stared blankly and said, "Why?" I said that I didn't know, but that he might want to come up with a couple of good reasons before two o'clock. I knew Alecia wouldn't approve—that she would somehow see my arranging the meeting as a sign of betrayal—yet keeping it from her made me uneasy. In my mind, I formed my own pitch: *Good news about the magazine!*

"Because if Ben found out from someone other than me—"

"So you *are* going to tell him, right?"

In the pause that followed I could hear a car engine in the driveway, and Auggie's shoes moving across the kitchen floor. "They want me to hang up," Alecia muttered. "We're not even taxiing yet!"

"Enjoy the extra legroom," I said. "And good luck with that thousand-pound door." She laughed, and we hung up, just as the doorbell rang.

I'D ENVISIONED THAT THE meeting would be relaxed—heavy on the magazine concept and light on the business end. But as soon as Augustus emerged from his office, looking uncharacteristically formal in his gray slacks and white oxford, I realized that I'd miscalculated. It was a good thing Ben was wearing a suit.

"Augustus, this is my friend Ben," I said, leading the way through the marble foyer.

"Hello, hello!" Augustus grinned and pumped his hand. "Di told me that you have an idea that might be of some interest to me."

"I think you'll be very interested," Ben replied, reminding me of a stage actor playing Confident Man. He glanced at me and winked.

"Excellent. Why don't we . . ." Augustus pointed the opposite direction.

"Oh, not the dining room table!" I blurted. They both

stopped to look at me. "It's just … such a nice day. We could sit out back … ?"

Augustus made a face, so apparently the deck was out.

"There's even better light in the Great Room, then." It hadn't occurred to me until right at that moment, with both men staring at me like I'd lost my mind, that maybe I wasn't actually invited to this meeting.

"Why do we need light? We're not looking at artwork, Di."

"She has this thing about Armageddon and the dining room table," Ben said, throwing a weary hand up in the air.

"She does, does she?" At least Augustus was smiling now. "This, I would like to hear sometime." He motioned for an about-face: "The Great Room it is."

"Does anyone want anything to drink?" I asked, as they settled onto opposing couches, the same way Mazy and I had done just a few weeks prior.

"I'll have a beer. Ben?"

He hesitated. "Sure. Beer's fine."

I excused myself to the kitchen and opened the fridge to grab two Coronas, my ears straining to hear every word from the adjacent room.

"So, let me have it," Auggie said.

"*The Burning Tree:* a new magazine about the risk of faith"—Ben paused to inhale—"and its twin sister, doubt." He exhaled. "Unless you're an automaton or easily brainwashed, you can't have one without, at some point, the other. C. S. Lewis talks about how easily faith in God falls apart when stuff goes wrong. And then you're left wondering if 'the things I am believing are only a dream, or … I only dream that I believe them.'"

A loud sigh erupted from the baby monitor—Max sleep noises—and I quickly turned the volume down, so nothing would interfere with my eavesdropping. In the Great Room,

Ben cleared his throat. "Anyway, I got this idea that we could all come together, people of all religious backgrounds, to create a dialogue or just…an inspiration…or, the truth. Monthly. In a glossy and readable format. We'll include some art. No ads."

"No *ads*?" Auggie repeated. "Ben, Ben, Ben. For a print magazine, you're looking at half a million—maybe two hundred fifty thousand if you're lucky—in start-up costs just to get ten thousand subscribers. You're going to have to convince people to buy your magazine. And you're going to need advertisers to support the printing costs. This isn't the time to be too good for them. Where's your business plan?"

It occurred to me now that I'd overheard Auggie using the same condescending tone the day we officially met: *Do I want a wet basement, Dave? I don't think so.*

"If you keep going past the third page, it's attached…." Ben said. They were both quiet. I sliced a lime and squeezed a wedge into the top of each beer bottle. "As you can see, a lot of people are eager to contribute—"

"Money?" Auggie sounded incredulous.

"No, stories. Essays. Writing samples."

More silence. I went to the pantry to grab some chips.

"I don't think you've got any idea what you're getting into here, Ben. It's not possible to have an ad-free magazine."

I poured the chips in a bowl, grabbed the beer, and hurried back. *Screw the salsa, Ben needs me.*

"Think of *The Sun* magazine," Ben said. "They don't advertise."

"So, how is *The Burning Tree* not *The Sun* magazine? How is it unique, yet how is it the same? And…" Auggie glanced at the cover again and made a face. "Why is it called *The Burning Tree*?"

"Because burning bushes have never really spoken to me."

Auggie thought for a moment and then laughed. "Me neither." He glanced at me, standing next to the piano. "Di, come join us."

I hesitated, unsure which sofa to choose, but Auggie was patting the seat next to him, as if I was on his team. I handed Ben his beer, and he downed half before I even sat down. His face looked even more rumpled than it had ten minutes ago.

Auggie, though, seemed to relax now that I was back. He leaned into the pillows, crossed his foot over his knee, and even stretched an arm behind me, around the back of the sofa. "Seriously, who's your audience?" He sounded downright cheerful now. "Who do you think really wants to read this?"

"There're a lot of people, like me, who are . . . in between faiths, who aren't getting what they need from their places of worship. But they want a community." Ben stared at Auggie, who'd made a noise: something between a groan and a sigh. "Haven't you ever felt let down by your religion?" he added.

"Honestly? I'm not sure I think about it enough to be let down by it. And even if I felt like this"—Auggie shook the papers in his hand—"I don't know that I'd go looking for answers in a magazine."

Ben finished his beer in two swallows and then sat back into the mound of pillows. "Well, where would you go, then?"

"I don't know. If I cared enough . . . and I happened to have been raised Christian . . . maybe I'd join a Bible study. If I was Muslim, maybe I'd join—"

"But what if you don't believe that there is only one way to look at things? What if your idea of the truth is an integration of all faiths—or something in between?"

Auggie chuckled. "You're assuming that the truth can be found in religion. Maybe that's your problem."

"Take the Israelites in Egypt," Ben said, tearing off the Corona label. "There is absolutely no archaeological evidence that they were actually there. There's evidence of a flood. Evidence of a lot of other shit in the Bible, right? But no one can find any evidence that it was the Israelites who were enslaved in Egypt. What does that mean?"

"It means faith isn't something that you can prove," I said.

"But why couldn't the Bible just be a story, designed to send us a message about God? Does it matter if it's not the actual truth if it stands for the truth?"

"So...I'm trying to understand this, Ben." Auggie sounded confused but, thankfully, no longer irritated. "What the hell is this about, exactly?"

"Being part of a community, even when you're confused. Even when you still want to believe. Even when you *do* believe."

I thought of how badly and for how long I'd wanted a family, a real one, with two parents and, if not siblings, then cats and dogs and an extended family that didn't amount to an uncle who didn't seem to know I existed, and an aunt who'd rather be dead. Ben and I were essentially looking for the same thing, only I wanted a family and he wanted a whole neighborhood.

"If you ask me, you're thinking too much," Auggie said, reaching for a chip. "Take me, for instance. I'm as happy as I can possibly be. Do you think I'm sitting here worrying about whether the Israelites were actually in Egypt?"

Was he really happy, I wondered, given the state of his marriage and his relationship with his sons? At this moment, with his arm draped around the back of my sofa cushion, apparently the answer was yes. Ben, on the other hand, looked flattened: his suit—and his face—were creased in all the wrong places.

"Ever thought of just pursuing a career, Ben? Making a success of yourself? Maybe you'd sleep better at night."

Ben shrugged. "Ever thought of pursuing a higher power?"

I turned to Auggie. "Ben used to be in a seminary. He had a vision."

His eyebrows went up again. "Of God?"

Ben shook his head. "I saw myself. A better me. Whole." He slumped back on the couch with a noisy exhale. "God was kind of there, too. It was a fleeting moment."

"Funny, isn't it? Enlightenment is kind of like falling in love." Auggie sounded thoughtful. "The moment fades away, and you can barely remember how it happened, and yet you're expected to live your whole life in a new way. Without straying from some vague memory of . . . what, exactly?"

I scratched my head, perplexed. How was it possible that I'd reached the age of twenty-eight and hadn't experienced even a transient version of enlightenment with a man? I supposed I was lucky enough to have fallen completely head over heels for Max.

"So, what are you most afraid of here, Ben? The afterlife?" Auggie pointed his bottle at him. "Or just getting married?"

Ben looked at me, startled. I reached for a chip and shrugged. *Go ahead. Answer the question.*

"I want to get married," he said finally. "I just want it to be to the right person."

"And what's wrong with the woman—Alecia, right?— who you were supposed to marry? I mean, hell, if she's Di's sister—"

"Cousin," I said.

"Di's cousin, she's gotta be great." I smiled at Auggie.

"It's kind of complicated. She's just . . . really difficult."

"Ben, she's a woman, right?"

He sighed. "She signed this prenuptial agreement—"

"So, she's smart. Half of all marriages end in divorce."

"She didn't even want the damn thing. Her father insisted."

"So, she honors her parents."

Ben looked up from his empty beer bottle. "At the risk of losing me?"

"Be honest." Auggie cocked his head to the side. "Are you attracted to someone else?"

"I'm attracted to the idea of someone else, someone who's not so driven by her career. Someone who'd be a good mom."

Auggie looked at me and smiled. "Like Di here."

My face flushed, and I shook my head. *You instigator.*

Ben's ears were turning equally pink. "Yeah. Kind of like Di." He glanced at me and then quickly looked away. Auggie took a peek in my direction and winked, making me turn redder. It wasn't just that he was embarrassing Ben—or rather, both of us—it was the giddy sensation that Auggie might have been...*flirting with me?* Was that possible? Or was I merely confusing earnest approval with sexual tension?

"So, you're not attracted to Alecia anymore," Auggie went on.

"No, I'm very attracted to her." Ben ran his hand through his red hair. "That's part of the problem."

"I don't follow."

"C. S. Lewis once wrote something about the danger of following an impulse at all costs and calling it the right thing. I think that's what I've been doing."

"Following your instincts?" Auggie asked with a laugh. "And that's *bad*?"

"She doesn't want to have kids." Ben held out his right hand. "I want to have kids." He turned over his left.

"I thought she was already pregnant."

Ben dropped his arms. *"What?"*

Auggie frowned at me. "Didn't you say . . . ?"

"No. I didn't say that. No." I stared at Auggie until his eyebrows unknit.

"I'm wrong, then." He suddenly smiled and leaned into me. "Sorry about that."

"No problem." I looked at Ben, who'd grown even paler.

"Di, is she . . . ?"

"I have no idea," I said, which was almost the truth.

Ben waited. I folded my arms across my chest and stared back, until he finally shook his head. "Listen, thanks for the beer, and for the advice, but I gotta go."

"Well, wait a second. You're not just leaving after all this." Auggie stood up. "Let me go get my checkbook." When Ben's jaw sagged open in surprise, Auggie glanced at me and grinned. "A friend of Di's is a friend of mine."

I WALKED BEN OUT to the driveway, hands in my pockets. "Sorry Max wasn't awake. He would've liked seeing you."

Ben didn't even pretend to be listening. He just walked with giant strides across the trench where the walkway should've been, while I trailed behind, glancing around for the landscapers, who were probably still around back, cutting brush. At the Honda, he whirled around. "I'm going to ask you this one more time. Is Alecia pregnant?"

"I promise you that I—I really don't know."

"*Was* she pregnant, then?"

I looked at my feet for a long time. It was like that moment in the house, when I was forced to choose my sofa. Finally, I looked up. "No, she wasn't. I really don't know why Auggie said that."

"Right. Well. Thank you." Ben yanked on his door handle.

"Aren't you even going to look? The check!" I added, when his expression turned confused.

"I did. It was ten thousand."

"Dollars?"

"No, liras."

"Ben, that's . . . that's amazing!"

"I can't cash it." He reached in the front pocket of his suit jacket and took out the check.

"No—wait!" I said, before Ben could tear it in half.

"You don't get it. He's using me to try to buy you."

I thought of Stacey Locklear and the law school hallway. "I don't think so."

"There's no other plausible explanation for him to give me a dime after a conversation like that."

"I really think he liked you!"

"No, I really think he likes *you*." At least I'd kept him from ripping up the check. I watched as Ben replaced it in his pocket, got in the Honda, and slammed the door. He rolled down the window before backing out. "Don't fall for him, okay?"

"Why not?"

Ben's ears were turning colors again, as if I'd been trying to get him to admit that he was jealous. "If it were Holly out here instead of you, I'd tell her the same thing."

If it were Holly out here instead of me, she'd probably listen, I thought.

CHAPTER 20

Personal Cook

Later that night, after Max had already eaten his macaroni and cheese in the kitchen, Gusty went and called Augustus to the dining room for dinner. "Jesus, Di, we're just a family of two here," he said. The table looked set for a Thanksgiving feast: glazed carrots, wilted spinach, creamy garlic mashed potatoes, and the pork loin.

"I got carried away," I said sheepishly.

He glanced at me, looked away, and then back, his right eyebrow arching up. "No braids today?"

I touched my hair. "Oh! I was...feeling more bun-ish." I'd just discovered that with a side part and twist of hair at my neck, my bald spot was perfectly concealed.

"Bun-ish?" Auggie smiled. "And dress-ish, too?"

"Right." He meant my black jersey wrap dress, which I'd put on for no particular reason except that I desperately needed to do laundry. It was an outfit that even Alecia approved of, though she would've hated my accompanying flip-flops and, for that matter, the dangly earrings of tiny lapis stones, which I'd strung myself.

"You're not gonna like this, Dad, you're gonna love it!" Gusty cut into his pork ferociously. He hadn't even tried it yet, but I could've hugged him for the declaration.

The doorbell rang, and Auggie looked up from the plate he was loading. "Who could that be?"

"Eat up. I got it."

I passed through the kitchen, where Max was shooting his Matchbox cars across the floor, through the Great Room, and into the marble foyer. Through the window of the front door, I could see Mazy's face, distorted by the panes of glass. I hesitated and glanced toward the dining room before unlatching the dead bolt.

"Hi, Mazy," I said, after opening the door.

"Well. Look who it is." Mazy narrowed her eyes. "Find a nanny yet?"

"Not yet."

"Just making yourself at home?"

"I'm actually the cook—Gusty's personal cook."

"You're Auggie's personal fuck, you mean!"

"Mama?" Max called from across the foyer. I turned to see him standing there in his little overalls, holding out his hands as if the marble were water, and he couldn't possibly swim to me.

"Mazy!" Auggie said cheerfully, appearing from the dining room with Gusty behind. "What are you doing here?"

"What the hell is *she* doing here?" Mazy jutted her thumb in my direction.

"Frankly, that's none of your business."

"Anything that has to do with my son is my business!"

"Mama!" Max wailed, and I ran to pick him up.

Mazy turned to Gusty. "Get your things. We're going."

"But we just started dinner."

"Get your things, *we're going*!" Mazy shouted again, making Max flinch in my arms. "It's my weekend! It's my week! Did you forget?" Her eyes darted around. "Did everybody forget?"

As if avoiding gunfire, I pushed Max's head against my shoulder and ducked out of the foyer.

"Mazy, just calm down." I heard Auggie's soothing voice. "We forgot. I've been out of town—"

"You're always out of town. Gusty, go get your things!"

"But . . . I don't want to leave." His voice cracked. "I want to stay here with Dad."

"I don't care what you want!"

As I washed Max up in the enormous guest room tub, I found myself fighting back tears. There was something about the scene I'd just witnessed that felt very familiar, a memory of myself as a child being tugged back and forth. I'd always tried to forget the way my parents had argued. They'd been a mismatched couple on the surface but so belovedly quirky that they complemented each other perfectly. But now I thought of the battles that escalated when my father declared his love for Christine and moved to Philadelphia. How they screamed and slung their insults at every interaction, without even worrying about whether I was in the room. How it was almost a relief when my mother said we were going away, so that I wouldn't have to hear them fighting over me anymore. No wonder Gusty preferred the ICU.

Max stopped splashing and looked at me. "Mama, sad?"

"No, baby." When he still didn't smile, I admitted, "Well, Mama's a little sad, Boo. But Mama's happy about *you*." I caressed his cheek and then tickled him under the chin until he giggled again.

It wasn't just Gusty getting me down. I wished I could save Max, too, from life.

"THERE YOU ARE," AUGGIE said later, from the kitchen table, where he sat reading the *New York Times*. His glasses made him look older.

"How's Gusty?" I asked, sliding my hands toward my pockets before remembering the dress didn't have any.

"Gusty is gone." Auggie removed his glasses and we both stared at each other without smiling. "I'm sorry you were here to see it."

"I'm sorry Gusty was here to see it." I went for my pockets again and felt my hands skim down my hips. "How was dinner? I mean, after they left?"

Finally, he smiled and pushed the paper aside. "I was waiting for you. I can't eat all that by myself."

"Oh!" I glanced back at the guest suite where Max was sleeping.

"Can you handle the dining room? Or will that be the end of the world as we know it?"

I laughed as Auggie got up from the kitchen table and rummaged around in the cabinets. "I can handle it."

"You like Merlot?"

"Sure," I said, even though Merlot gave me a headache the next day. Half-dazed, I wandered into the dining room and took the seat where Gusty had been. No wonder he hated it. The table was huge. It looked as if we were expecting the board, all twenty members, to arrive for a meeting.

Auggie came through the swinging door with a single place setting and an uncorked bottle of wine. "Here we go," he said, pouring me a glass.

If only I weren't sitting in Gusty's seat. He'd been snatched from his barely touched dinner. I should've at least packed him some sugar-free lemon pudding to go. "It's just so dark in here," I said, helping myself to cold carrots.

"You're right. We need candles. Hold on—let me microwave that!" he added, when I picked up my fork.

I am eating dinner alone with Augustus Catalano by candlelight, it occurred to me moments later, when he'd returned from the kitchen, our plates steaming. After all the time I'd spent thinking about Auggie in the last week, I should've had clammy palms and a thrill in my chest. But how could he act so cheerful after what happened? He reminded me of Max, quickly reassured and then happy to splash in his tub, oblivious to the drama that he'd just been rescued from. Except that Max was two, not forty-nine.

"Everything okay, Di?" Auggie asked when I still hadn't taken a bite.

"I just feel sad about what happened tonight."

"I know. Me, too." He reached for his glass of wine. "Are you divorced?" I shook my head. "Well, avoid it, if you can. It's not for the faint of heart."

"I know. My parents were divorced. It got pretty ugly." I picked up a knife to cut my meat. "Do you...have any regrets?" I asked carefully, thinking of his infidelity.

"Sure. I regret marrying Mazy." He sighed. "Until Gusty goes to college, she'll never stop torturing me. I'm like a POW. I've been released, and I'd like to forget the war happened, but I'm still walking around with this goddamn limp."

"I think Gusty's the POW in this situation," I said, reaching for my glass of wine.

Auggie tilted his head and put his finger in the air. *Your point.*

I took a few swallows and put down my glass. "I was

actually wondering if you had any regrets about cheating on your wife?"

"Mazy and I were pretty much finished even before Stacey and I got going. And now that's history." He paused, took another swig of wine. "Along with my relationship with Jason. Who knew he'd been in love with her forever? Never did a thing about it. Hell, he's marrying someone else." Augustus chuckled. "You know what we need? A life makeover. One of those TV shows to come in and fix everything."

"With your sons?" I asked.

Auggie smiled as he swirled his wine in its glass. "I guess if I listen to you, all it should take for Gusty is to pull up a couple of weeds."

"It couldn't hurt." I poked a fork into my meat. "Are you morally opposed to him pulling up weeds?" I asked, between bites. "Do you not want him to work for anything? Or are you just worried about his diabetes?"

"I just want to see that kid go to college and not move back in."

I reached for a cold popover.

"Let me heat that up. Come on, hand it over," Auggie added when I hesitated. He took the plate from me again and disappeared, leaving me wondering why he was waiting on me like this, why it felt like a date. I looked down at the V-neckline of my wrap dress. *See what happens when you don't dress like Punky Brewster?* Alecia would say.

Auggie returned, bearing one popover. "His mother wouldn't like it. She'd be very upset if he were riding around with those clowns."

I thought about how even Dave had called his dump truck a death trap. "What if he never had to go anywhere? What if he was allowed to work right here, on this property only?

Gusty might really take to gardening. Maybe next summer, you wouldn't even have to *hire* Pro Lawn Service."

Slowly, a smile spread across Auggie's face. "Ever consider law school, Di? You argue a great case."

"No, not law." I sat back and fanned my chest, suddenly feeling flushed and restless. There was something about challenging Auggie that made me want to shove all the platters of food to the side of the boardroom table and climb into his lap.

"Ever think about doing something other than this? I mean, other than being a nanny-finder…or whatever it is you normally do," he added.

"Well, sure. I wanted to be a clinical psychologist. Or a champion ice-skater—" I stopped when Auggie laughed out loud. "I'm *serious*. I wanted to be a lot of things. But then I got pregnant with Max, and that pretty much changed everything."

He squinted, as if trying to see me clearly. "And how does Ben fit into the picture?"

I shrugged. "He's just a good guy who appreciates me."

"Ah. So, that's your type." He leaned across the table and stared at me. "Can I interest you in a glass of port?"

"I'd love it," I said with a smile, even though port gave me headaches, too. What did it matter, now, after all that Merlot? I reached over to collect the dishes.

"Leave it," he said.

I SAT ON THE sofa in the Great Room and watched him build me a fire as Miles Davis played on the sound system all over the house. A giddy feeling returned in full force: the racing heart, the jelly legs, the ache in my pelvis.

"How did you get so tall, Di?" Auggie asked, as he finally sank onto the cushion next to me.

"Mendelian genetics, I guess," I said, which made him

laugh again. We were touching thigh to thigh, or rather, skirt to pant leg. Leaning back against the mound of pillows, Auggie proposed a toast, even though I was already in the middle of a sip.

"To my personal fuck," he said.

I coughed and felt the port go up my nose.

"Are you okay?" When I couldn't answer, he rescued my glass and gave me a wallop on the back that made me cough harder. "Nod if you're okay or hold up your arms or—"

"I'm . . . okay," I finally managed.

"I'm really thrilled—you're a great cook," he tried again, so I must've heard him wrong the first time. "And Gusty's thrilled, too. Here's to . . . a great start."

"A great start," I agreed, clinking my glass to his.

"Careful now. Remember to swallow."

Easier said than done, since I was laughing. Somehow I got it down without another choking spell. "The port is so sweet," I said. "I didn't think you'd be into sweet."

"What'd you think I'd be into?"

"I don't know. Scotch on the rocks. A dry martini."

"Shaken, not stirred?"

"Exactly," I said, cracking up with laughter again. My head felt light.

He stared at me for a second before taking the port from my hand and placing both of our glasses on the ottoman. Then he pulled me toward him, one hand encircling my neck, the other sliding around the small of my back. For one terrified second, I felt as if I was being seized. "Is this okay?" he asked, lips against mine.

"Um . . ." I said, as he began to rub my neck, in the most expert of massages, and to kiss me. *Oh, to be touched!* How long had it been? Not pressed against, not nuzzled or caressed in nearly three years? Tingles shot through my spine as he ran his fingers up and down my neck. *I'm drunk,* I thought, but his hands were like small ovens, warming me all over, and if I made him stop, I'd be cold again.

"Stop," I whispered, without pulling away.

"You feel great," he said softly. He gently pushed me backward, his hand traveling up my skirt as he moved on top of me. An avalanche of pillows fell on my face, and I tossed them to the floor, one after the other.

"No, really, stop," I said, paying attention to myself this time. "I'm not here for this."

When he sat up, his face was surprised. "Well, I wasn't looking for this either, but—"

"I really need this job. I can't mess it up."

"You haven't messed anything up." The way he looked at me, with such kindness, made me hesitate for just a second. Then I glanced down and saw that my wrap dress was noticeably unwrapped below the waist.

"I'm sorry, I—didn't mean to kiss you," I said, yanking it closed. "I'm supposed to be warning you," I added, standing and stumbling around the ottoman.

"Warning me?" Auggie repeated, leaning back and putting his arm up on the pillows, where I should've been sitting.

I turned back too quickly and was forced to wait for the room to stop bobbing. "You're going to die very soon. I had a premonition about your toes."

"My toes?" He laughed. "Christ, how much did you drink? Sit, before you fall," he insisted, jumping up to guide me back down to the sofa. This time, our thighs weren't touching.

"It was before we ever met," I said, my head in my hands. "I had a dream that you were already dead. And you were really depressed because . . . well, probably because of your relationships with your sons. And possibly Mazy, too. You need to fix things with them. Otherwise . . ."

"Otherwise, what? They'll hate me more?" He rubbed my back, the way you might do for someone who happened to be heaving into a toilet. "Listen, Di, I'm sorry I've given you so much to drink. I'm sorry about . . . whatever just happened. Can we move past this?"

I opened my eyes and turned to look at him. "Do you believe me?"

"Do you know something that I don't know?" He smiled as he tucked some of my hair behind my ear. "Mazy's not planning on having me offed, is she?"

I shook my head. "But you have to . . . fix things. While you still have time."

He played with the same strands of my hair and kept staring at me as if he didn't know what to think.

"Mama?"

I straightened and saw Max standing in the kitchen in his blanket sleeper, holding Stanley the horse. "What's the matter, Boo?"

"I'm scared." Max whimpered. "Mama, come?"

"I'll be right there. You go back and lie down." I stood up and readjusted my skirt again.

Max didn't move. "Now?"

"Max, I'll be right there!" I ran my fingers through my hair as he started to cry. "I'm sorry, I have to—"

"Of course, go!" Auggie waved me away.

When I looked back from the kitchen, he was still sitting in the same position on the sofa staring into space.

CHAPTER 21

Frank's Cottage

Hours before Auggie and I were tangled up on the Great Room sofa, Alecia's connecting flight landed in Bangor, Maine. She waited until after she'd picked up the rental car and was headed along Route 1 toward Mount Desert Island to call for directions to one of her father's vacation homes—the autumn one, she thought of it, because it was the only time of the year that she found him there. It had been so many years since her last visit that she couldn't even picture the five-bedroom house overlooking the Sommes Sound that Frank liked to refer to as "the cottage."

At the end of a cobblestone driveway, away from the hope of any cell phone reception, Alecia found the house—from the front, a deceptively small bungalow, while from the back, its foundation sprang up from a cliff, and three stories of windows looked over the sea. Even if she had recalled these details of the outside, nothing appeared the same on the inside.

"You gutted it!" Alecia exclaimed, as soon as she saw the shiny, blond floors, the skylights and vaulted ceilings, and the sliding glass doors all along the back, where walls used to be.

"Half-a-million-dollar project," her father said, as he toweled off his nearly bald head. He must've just climbed out of the hot tub. "Everything is brand-new except for the stairs. They're a hundred years old—it seemed wrong to take them out."

"Wow!" she said, peering around the downstairs, which was easier to look at than her father's rapidly deteriorating body. Hadn't she just seen him last summer? Where did all of his hair go? And since when did he have a paunch? ("It occurred to me that maybe you were right," she told me later. "Maybe he is going to die.")

"Did you bring any sneakers with you?" her father asked, with a nod at her feet. She shifted back and forth in her suede ballet flats. "Thought we might go for a hike later. The views here are amazing."

"A hike?" Alecia repeated, her face screwed up in confusion. If they wanted a view, why wouldn't they just look out the window?

"It's like a walk," Frank said, pulling on a robe. "But when you're in the woods, in Maine, it's called hiking. Becca might've left a pair of boots behind. Did I tell you we broke up?"

Alecia blinked. "No."

"We broke up." He shrugged and then added, "Yours is the first door to the left at the top of the stairs. Need help with your bag?"

"No, no, no. I got it." She reached for her suitcase. If this had been a weekend trip with Ben, he would've made her compress everything into a backpack, but her father liked to see her in makeup, all five hundred dollars' worth.

People must've had much smaller feet one hundred years ago, she decided, balancing her way up one narrow and precariously tall step at a time. *Either that, or the house was previously owned by a family of fawns.*

As soon as she saw the buttery walls of her room, with its big, brass bed and breathtaking view of the waves that glittered across Sommes Sound, she fell in love with the place, crappy old stairs and all. After hoisting her suitcase onto the luggage rack and putting the contents away in the dresser drawers—a habit of hers that used to drive Ben crazy—she finally sat on the silk duvet cover and sighed. The sigh felt surprisingly good. Tentatively, she leaned back against the pillows. She hadn't felt such relief in days—*no, weeks*. Down the hall, she could hear the shower running in her father's bathroom, which meant there was plenty of time not to move or think.

Alecia looked up and stared out the window where a sailboat was drifting across the sound. The wind was starting to blow and, down on the dock, a gust of orange and yellow leaves were spilling out to sea. She thought of Ben quoting Ecclesiastes: "Better to have a hand full of quiet instead of two fists toiling and striving after wind." She thought of the newscast, of Mazy Roberts and her list of concerns. She thought of Art asking if she was okay. *What have I been doing? Toiling after wind?*

COMING BACK DOWNSTAIRS, SHE noticed her father was now dressed in khaki pants, a corduroy shirt, and notably unscuffed leather boots, while in the corner, an umbrella stand was filled with various sizes of gnarled yet glossy wooden walking sticks. She wondered if hiking was Becca's influence, the way sailing had been Monica's and sky-diving Deserai's. "So, what happened with Becca?" Alecia asked.

"We're through." Frank shrugged as he uncapped a bottle

of whiskey and poured himself a glass. Alecia was relieved. Whiskey and walking couldn't go together—unless that was where the sticks came in, to keep them upright.

"Since when?" she asked, folding her arms across her chest.

"Two nights ago."

"But I just talked to her two nights ago—she called to ask me when the rehearsal dinner was."

"It must've been after you talked. We broke up as I was on my way to the airport."

"Not by text message?"

"No, no, no. We talked." He took a sip, then admitted, "On the phone. But we talked."

"But what happened?" Alecia didn't know why she was shocked. After Frank's third divorce—the "final payout," he called it—he'd decided it was best not to merge assets anymore. Instead, he kept a serious girlfriend on retainer for years at a time. Becca had been around longer than the others.

He shrugged again, then said—in a way that reminded me of Auggie when Alecia told me the story later, "She wanted me to meet her parents. I don't meet parents. Then she wanted to know where things were headed if I wouldn't meet her parents. I told her I don't get married anymore. So, she ended it. Why do you look so surprised?"

"I'm not, I just . . . thought you really liked her."

"Well, I did, but . . ." He put his hands up as if to say *You win some; you lose some.* "What can I get you to drink, honey? San Pellegrino? White wine? I have a Chardonnay you'll love. Guy I know shipped it to me from Napa."

"Water's fine. *Not* sparkling." Frank's eyebrows dropped, and he squinted at her, probably the same expression she'd worn when he first mentioned hiking. "Well . . . maybe one glass of wine." She watched her father's face immediately brighten when she changed her mind. Alecia followed him into the kitchen. "I met someone for you on the plane. Seriously, Daddy, I got her number and everything. Her name's Alma." Alma had worn the same Ann Taylor periwinkle twinset that Alecia herself actually owned—the sweater set that always made Ben look at her twice and say, *You should wear that color more often.* And, as Alecia vomited into her airsickness bag during takeoff, Alma had patted her back and made sure she got some water. If there had been any fairness in life, she would've been Alecia's real mother. "She's really pretty," Alecia went on. "Smart. A new grandmother—"

"A grandmother? Uh uh. I don't date women my age. You know that."

"Isn't there something pathological about that? About us?" she added as an afterthought.

"You're not pathological, honey. You're getting married." She watched as he poured her wine and then set out a platter of food—Brie and crackers, shrimp and cocktail sauce, olives and pistachios.

"What if I'm having second thoughts?" she asked, reaching for a piece of cheese.

"About what—marriage? Forget them. You're gonna look beautiful. I can't wait to see you all dressed up. Cheers!" he said, and they clinked glasses. Before she could even take a sip, he said, "Oh, and you won't believe it. I was able to book Lana Jackson for part of the reception—the singer? Sounds just like Etta James." He popped an olive into his mouth.

"Ben won't sign the prenuptial agreement," she blurted.

"Tell him it's not negotiable. *I'll* tell him." Her father put down his glass of whiskey. "Hold on—you said it was signed."

Alecia shook her head and frowned.

"What's the matter, baby?" he asked, his voice both gentle

and cautious. Despite the half-smile on his face, he looked as if he knew something bad had happened.

"I don't know if I can go through with it. I don't know if I can marry him." She was parroting Ben's words. She looked up from swirling her glass of wine. "Maybe I wasn't meant to marry anyone. I mean, you don't marry anyone anymore. Maybe I shouldn't, either."

"Sweetie, you're going to be a beautiful bride. And even I got married a few times myself, right?"

"I don't want to end up like you and Mom."

"That's easy. Neither you nor Ben are nuts. You've got that going for you."

She followed him out of the kitchen and into the living room, where he set the platter of food on the coffee table and adjusted the lights. Outside, the water was white-capped, and the leaves burned against the sky. Maybe he was right. Maybe they should take a walk. She couldn't remember the last time she'd done anything so pointless.

"I never understood how you and Mom fell in love," she said, once her father had turned on the gas stove and sank into the leather recliner across from her.

"It was easy to fall in love in college. You met someone in a class and—bang."

"Bang," Alecia repeated. Was he talking about sex now? Because when she thought of the word *bang* and her mother, she could only imagine Maddie with a gun to her head. "You never suspected, you know . . ." Alecia waved a finger around her ear. *Loco?*

"Not at all. I mean, sure, her poems were a little dark. And she had issues with her mother. But who doesn't have issues with their mother? Besides, she was stunning, back then."

"Stunning," Alecia muttered, shaking her head. "You should see her now."

Frank's eyebrows rose. "You've seen your mother lately?"

"She showed up at the TV station out of the blue. Said she'd just gotten out of rehab. She looked...wrinkly."

"Well, a liter of vodka a day will do that to a person over time."

"Did *everyone* know Mom was an alcoholic?"

Frank shrugged. "If everyone means your uncle Gabe, your aunt Roxanne, and me, then yes."

"But I thought...she was just crazy."

"Not just." He shook his head and smiled. "I guess it was when you were in elementary school that my liquor cabinet started to disappear. I was pretty sure it wasn't Veronique, since she wasn't the one who had to be woken up for dinner every night." He shook his head as he looked out the window. "And, yet, she still wanted more children."

"Who, Mom?" Alecia craned her neck forward. "But I always thought that she wished she'd never had any."

"Oh, no. I was the roadblock there. But your mother broke me."

"*She* broke *you?*" Alecia repeated, scratching her head. It was the antithesis of how she'd always imagined things: Maddie didn't want her; therefore, Maddie ignored her. Frank, on the other hand, adored her...unless Alecia was mistaken about that, too.

"Later on, she was determined not to make you an only child, but she'd had her first...*episode* by then—you were about four at the time—and I said absolutely no more kids," Frank went on. "It was bad enough having to take care of her. After that, she started drinking. It kept her from being too manic, she said. And, of course, she never took her medication."

"She took *plenty* of medication after Roxanne and Di left," Alecia said, remembering the finale of her Sweet Sixteen/"Biggest Letdown of My Life" story: ten days after my mother and I disappeared, Maddie had her stomach pumped and spent the night on a ventilator.

"Well, yeah, the alcohol couldn't really fix the depression. Hence, the attempts."

The attempts. Alecia and I had both hated that euphemism growing up. We both had a shared memory of Veronique, the housekeeper, sitting us down in her pink bedroom after school one day. *She has made another attempt.* The way the grown-ups talked—or didn't talk—about it, Maddie could have been attempting to climb Mount Everest or could have been attempting to break out of jail.

"The only time she took her medication correctly was when we hospitalized her," he said. "And she'd be functional...for a while. But she couldn't write poems on the meds, so she'd stop taking them. Then, the drinking just kind of took over."

"I'm so confused. You never wanted children and Mom did?"

"Honey." Frank reached over the table to grab her hand. "You know you're the best thing that ever happened to me, right?"

It was silly, she knew, to doubt the depth of his love, when she was the one person he showed any constant affection for. Nevertheless, Alecia couldn't answer for fear of crying. How had Maddie gone from wanting her to total disinterest? How had her aunt Roxanne been more of a mother than her own? Her father stared at her as she gulped and wiped her eye. "How's Ben?" he finally asked.

"Um, he's, um...stressed out about the wedding. You know. A lot of people coming into town. Most of whom he doesn't know. And frankly, neither do I."

"I wanted to give you an engagement party in New York to introduce you both to everyone. As I recall, Ben said no, because he wanted to 'keep it simple.' Let me guess—now he's regretting it."

"No…not regretting it…just regretting me….I think the wedding is off." Alecia covered her face with her hands before he could see that she was crying.

"Are you fucking kidding me? That bastard." He slammed a fist against his leg.

"Well, he's…confused," she said, reaching for a tissue in the box on the end table.

"What the hell is he confused about?"

"I don't want to have children, and he does." She blew her nose noisily.

"How many does he want?"

"I don't know—four or five," Alecia said.

She was startled when her father started to laugh. "Doesn't he know that you're the fresh face of Channel Four Action News? Oh, honey," Frank said, walking around the coffee table to give her a hug. She'd buried her face against his shoulder when she heard him say, "Just give him one."

Alecia pulled away. "I can't do that."

"One," Dad said, holding up a single finger. "That's all."

"One *human being*. One of *me*!"

"Alecia, think about what you're saying."

"Think about what *you're* saying! You just finished telling me you never wanted children!"

"But I wanted to marry your mother, so I did what it took. Do you or don't you want to marry Ben?" It was as if she were sixteen again, before the *South Pacific* tryouts. *Do you or do you not want to play Nellie?* "Well?" he added, when she kept staring at the landscape behind his shoulder. A flock of geese was moving across the sky in a haphazard "W" as if they just couldn't get their act together.

"I want Ben," she said slowly.

"I didn't ask if you *want* him. Hell, I'd want Becca…and Monica and Deserai all at the same time. I asked if you want to *marry* him."

Alecia blinked. "I don't want to lose him."

Her father leaned forward and said in a quiet voice, "But you will."

Finally, she turned and met Frank's brown-eyed gaze. "You've lost everyone you've ever loved!" she snapped. "You can't give me advice!"

"Oh, no?" Frank sat back, annoyed. "I've shelled out a hundred grand on this wedding. As far as I'm concerned, I have *paid* for my right to give you advice."

Alecia folded her arms across her chest, hung her head, and waited.

"Now." Frank reached for his glass of whiskey again. "Where do you see yourself in five years?"

She glanced up from her jiggling foot. So, it was a job interview. She could handle a job interview: her father would be easier to win over than Art. "Lead anchor, I suppose . . . if Mazy retires . . ."

"Don't tell me what you think I want to hear. When you imagine yourself in five years, ten years, what are you doing? And who is by your side?" He took another sip and added cheerfully, "Me, I'd be right here on the edge of this cliff, by myself."

She looked up, startled by his declaration. "Are you sorry I'm here, then?"

Frank's eyebrows furrowed for just a second, and then he smiled. "From the moment you were born, I have never once been sorry you're here."

Alecia bit her fingernail, too afraid to smile back. Was it as easy as that, then? You turn into a parent as soon as you're facing your own child? But what would she have to give up?

"You can still have everything you've ever wanted," Frank said, as if reading her mind. "Just not at the same time. You will never meet anyone who 'has it all' who isn't compromising on something."

Alecia stared out the window again, trying to picture the future. *Everything she'd ever wanted.* Right now, she simply wanted the rushing inside her to stop. It seemed as if Ben had done enough dreaming for both of them, and she'd blamed him for it, blamed him for not taking care of her.

She met her father's eyes again. "What about *my* dreams?"

"There are plenty of anchorwomen with children."

"I mean acting."

"It's a little late for that, kiddo," Frank said, with a dismissive laugh. He glanced at his watch. "It's a little late, period. You want to put on some sneakers, before it gets dark?"

"Why didn't you let me go to LA?" Alecia blurted.

"That was a long time ago. You were a lot younger. Hell, I was a lot younger."

"You didn't think I would make it as an actress."

"No, I didn't." Her father looked at her steadily. "But you're good at the news!" he added, when she stood up off the sofa. "Just wait until you have a daughter someday—you won't let her move to LA when she's eighteen, either."

"I was twenty! And I am *not* having a daughter someday!" she retorted, stomping toward the stairs in her socked feet. But even as she said the words, she knew it was no longer the truth: something had let go inside of her. Her father had no regrets about having her. Maybe if she had this baby, the same would be true. At the very least, Ben would come back, and everything would be okay again. The funny thing about toiling after wind was how much effort it took, and how easily she could be distracted from what mattered most.

"I found a pair of Becca's boots in the hall closet," her father called from the living room, just as she reached the top of those hundred-year-old steps.

"I am *not* borrowing her boots!" Alecia whirled around, sending her foot sliding right off of the first narrow step.

Panicked, she lurched for the banister and missed. When her legs gave way, a knee—the right one—smacked the third step, and then she was falling, headfirst, down the stairs. The effects of momentum and gravity seemed to happen in slow motion.

Her father came running from the kitchen. "Allie? Are you okay?" she heard him shout. "My God! Allie?"

When she tried to use her arm to sit up, pain seared through her wrist. "My arm—I think I broke my—" Her voice choked on a sob. Everything hurt. Her ribs, her arms, her knee . . . And, *Oh, God, what about the baby?*

"Help me up—*ow!*" she screamed, when he reached for her. *"Not that hand!"*

As tears burned her eyes and dripped down her cheeks, Frank finally stopped shouting and stooped beside her. His voice grew softer, along with the tentative hand on her back. "What did you do?"

"I fell."

Her father blinked, apparently baffled into silence. It occurred to Alecia that he'd never seen her cry like this before, and she couldn't seem to stop. Since her hands hurt too much to hide behind, she brought her knees up to her chest and buried her face in her lap. Finally, he reached out and put a gentle hand on her back, the one part of her that didn't ache yet. "You really didn't want to go hiking, did you?" he asked.

CHAPTER 22

Aunt Maddie

It was so hard to sleep that night. All that wine and port should've knocked me out, but instead I tossed and turned, thinking of how I'd kissed the man of the house before I'd abruptly rejected him, before I'd told him that he was on the verge of death. *You're toast,* Alecia would say. At least once I was officially fired, I could return to her apartment, after all. Maybe it was a good thing: my cousin probably needed me more than Gusty did.

Ignoring the sounds of footsteps and the clatter of breakfast dishes in the sink Saturday morning, I hunkered down in the guest suite with Max, reading *The Adventures of Curious George* and waiting for the moment when Auggie would rap on the door and ask to have a word with me. But the moment never came. At last, the back door slammed, the house grew quiet, and, holding Max's hand, I emerged. Surprisingly, the dining room table had been cleared, the dishwasher was running, and the place was spotless. Stuck to the kitchen counter was a Post-it: *Di, Out of town until Tuesday night. Gusty is at his mother's until the end of the week. Saw the emergency money was <u>gone</u>, so here's another $200 should another <u>emergency</u> arise. A.*

So, apparently I still had a job, at least until Tuesday night.

"Backhoe!" Max yelled, peering out the glass of the French doors.

"You think we'll see a backhoe today?" I asked, putting the money back in its envelope.

"Right there! Look, Mama! Backhoe!" he insisted, jumping up and down, until finally, I went to look for myself. "See the backhoe? See?"

I could see. There was Hobbes in the driver's seat, using the long arm to move dirt in the backyard. "First breakfast. Then we'll go outside."

FALL HAD FINALLY ARRIVED, and it felt a heck of a lot like winter. I threw on a wool sweater and jeans and bundled Max in his fleece-lined jean jacket before we made our way across the leaf-strewn lawn toward the backhoe.

"What's going on here?" I shouted to TJ, who was possibly overseeing something, but from what I could tell, wasn't doing more than just standing there with his hands in the pockets of his jeans.

"Big man decided he wanted to terrace the backyard. Decides this just as the ground gets cold, but he wants it done now."

"What about the walkway?" I shivered in the wind.

"He wanted that done yesterday. Yo, boss!" TJ shouted. Then he whistled, jerking his head toward me. Dave, as usual, was consulting his clipboard over by the dump truck. His baseball cap was missing, and his sandy hair was tousled from the wind.

"Hey, good news!" I said, as he ambled toward me. "I convinced Aug—Mr. Catalano—to let Gusty work with you."

"Oh, yeah?" For some reason, Dave didn't look happy. "And how'd you do that?"

I thought of last night's mistaken kiss and looked away. "I just...lobbied for Gusty. But he's not allowed to work anywhere but on his own property. And nothing unsafe—I wouldn't have him operating a backhoe or anything." I was joking but Dave didn't smile.

"So, essentially you fought for his right to rake his own leaves?"

I blinked. He made it sound so stupid. *"And I won,"* I said.

"Backhoe!" Max yelled.

"Check it out—he's actually jumping for joy." TJ laughed and pointed at Max.

Dave signaled to Hobbes to cut the engine. "Let's give the little guy a shot," he shouted before turning to me. "Don't worry. Just pretend. I'm not going to let him operate it, either. What do you say, Max? You want to get in the backhoe?"

Max, who hadn't yet mastered the art of the nod, shook his head and smiled, which always meant yes.

"So, where is Gusty?" Dave asked, once they'd hoisted my son up into the operator's compartment with Hobbes. "I could use him today."

"He's at his mother's. But he'll be back later in the week. Can I still tell him it's okay?"

Dave didn't look at me, just kept watching Max from underneath his hair that flapped in the wind. "We're not going to be here much longer. Soon as the grading is done and that walkway is finished."

"But as long as you're here—you'll make him one of the team, right?"

Finally, he turned to me and smiled. "We know how to play nice."

As if in confirmation, Max laughed and squealed with glee as Hobbes let him crank one of the levers. Thankfully, nothing moved.

"Maybe we should hire him." TJ laughed.

"I'm sorry for holding you up. Max, we better get going!" I called. "Don't you want to go shopping?" Max shook his head—sans smile—while Dave looked at me and waved his hand in a circle, as if expecting more elaboration. "We're going back to Shadyside. We have the next couple of days off."

"And . . . ?" he prompted, as if he knew I'd left off the rest of it: that I was planning on using Alecia's computer to search for bus tickets to Philadelphia, using her phone to schedule my MRI, and using my windfall to buy myself some new underwear. I stared at him, confused. "You need a ride, right?" Dave added.

"Oh, no. Thank you. We're taking a cab. I got my paycheck. Okay, Max! Say goodbye to the backhoe! And say thank you to everyone."

"He's blowing me kisses now?" Dave asked.

"That's sign language for thank you. You don't touch your lips, you touch your chin," I added, when he started mimicking Max.

"Ah." Dave smiled and touched his chin with his hand, then made an arc toward me.

"You got it." My face suddenly felt warm, as if he were signing something intimate. His curls were blowing in the breeze again, and I had the strange urge to tell him that women would kill to have hair like his, especially those of us with bald spots. But before I could embarrass us both, I grabbed Max's hand and quickly retreated.

* * *

ON OUR WAY TO Shadyside, I stared at the window of the cab, thinking of Augustus. What was going to happen when he got back on Tuesday night? My chest kept fluttering with anxiety or anticipation, I wasn't sure which.

The cell phone in my coat pocket rang, and I checked the caller ID: Gusty.

"Hey! I'm glad you called. Listen, I worked it out with your dad. You're allowed to work with Pro Lawn Service—"

"I *am*?" His voice was shocked.

"But just on your own property."

There was a lag of silence. "Okay," he said. It was the same voice he'd used for the hockey tickets.

"Well, it's a start, right?"

"I guess." He paused, then said anxiously, "Di, you didn't—you're not . . . ?"

"What, Gusty?" I waited, thinking of Mazy. *You're not my dad's personal fuck?* "Say it," I ordered.

"My mom thinks you and my dad are . . . going out. But that's not true, right?"

"Right, Gusty." Thankfully, Max was too busy looking out the window to dispute me. The cabdriver had begun to swear as all of the traffic on Negley Run was merged into a single lane.

"I knew you wouldn't do that to me," Gusty said.

I scratched my head, imagining the von Trapp children shunning Maria instead of the Baroness. "What's that supposed to mean?"

"It's just . . . you're supposed to be there for me. Not for him."

Ah. The Raja strikes back. "I'm supposed to be there for your family, Gusty. And I am. Okay?"

I hung up after we said goodbye and stared out the window, where a line of excavators, dump trucks, and backhoes worked with near elegance to dismantle the earth. Funny how, before Max, I'd never noticed a single piece of construction equipment and now they were turning up everywhere.

ALECIA'S APARTMENT WAS DARK; the living room still cluttered with gifts and the hallway strewn with varying sizes of suitcases, as if, in the midst of running away, she hadn't been able to decide for how long. Seven messages waited on the machine: two cheerful ones from Maddie—*I'm leaving Tuesday. Still hoping to meet for coffee!*—one from the wedding boutique stating that the dresses were ready for pickup, and four from Ben—each one louder and more emphatic than the one before, until the final dejected recording: *I know about the baby. Please call me.*

I stared at the phone, wondering whom to call first: Ben or Alecia. In the end, I dialed Aunt Maddie at the hotel and made plans to meet for lunch.

WE GOT TO THAI Place just after noon. Max held my hand as I stood on the threshold of the dining room, scouring the patrons for someone who looked vaguely like Aunt Maddie. In my memory, she was slim with auburn hair and hazel eyes that were just a few shades grayer than my father's. Alecia had said that she didn't look like herself anymore, but I didn't quite believe it. Aunt Maddie had been beautiful, a skinnier version of Joan Crawford, and though she rarely smiled, when she did, it was striking.

"Are you Di?" said a voice behind me.

I turned to see a gray-haired woman in a gray cloak and, underneath, a flowered cotton capedress. *An elderly pilgrim,* I thought. It took me a moment to place her. *"Aunt Maddie?"* My father would've been sixty this year, which meant that Maddie was only turning fifty-six. She looked seventy.

"It *is* you!" Maddie hugged me. "I saw you walking in and could've sworn it was Roxanne." When she turned to Max, he beamed. "And who is this handsome little guy?"

"This is my son, Max."

"The spitting image of Gabe."

"Really?" I said doubtfully. Luckily, the hostess arrived.

"So, how does it feel to be back in the States?" Maddie asked, once we were settled into our booths. "Am I remembering wrong? Didn't you live in Europe for a while? Or did you come back to go to college here or something?"

"No, I never went to college—here or anywhere. Careful, Max!" I said, mopping up his wonton soup. "I came back from England after Mom died—"

"Roxanne?" Maddie looked up from her bowl.

"Don't you...remember? I sent you that letter? You wrote me back...?" *And why on earth did you write my mother—to reminisce?* Alecia would say later.

Maddie put down her spoon and shook her head, her eyes shining with tears. "You know what, I guess you must've told me, but I just...my memory is not what it used to be. I think ...I must've stored that away somewhere, not wanting to touch it." I winced when she blew her nose right into her cloth napkin. "That makes me very, very sad."

"I'm sorry, Aunt Maddie." I turned to Max, who had lowered his stuffed horse's nose into his soup and was making slurping noises. "Don't let Stanley taste the soup, Boo. Just pretend."

"First Gabe, now Roxanne." Maddie clenched her fist. "It just *sickens* me."

So, apparently she'd left that particular memory in an accessible place. I was relieved. "How'd you find out about my dad?"

"Frank called me. It was the first time we'd spoken in years. He wanted to let me know, in case I wanted to go to the memorial service. You would've thought she'd have let me in on the funeral arrangements, my own sister-in-law, but no. Not a goddamn *peep!*" Maddie's voice sharpened on the word.

"Who, Christine?"

"You know why, don't you?" When I shook my head, Maddie leaned forward and hissed, "Why Christine didn't call to tell me that my *own brother was murdered*?"

I glanced around at all the nearby diners, enjoying their spring rolls and Thai iced teas. I heard a smattering of words and laughter, *It goes on sale next week,* and, *They're growing up fast,* and, *You've gotta see it!* Whatever people were talking about, it wasn't murder. "She didn't want to ... upset you?" I suggested.

"She didn't want me to know what happened to the money."

"What money?"

"Gabe's money." Maddie sat back in her booth. "Gabe had a lot of money."

I thought of our Victorian in Highland Park, which was sprawling, to be sure, but, even at the time, was as decrepit as the current personal care boarders. "We never had money growing up. I mean, we had enough—"

"Your father was a doctor, sweetie. He had money; he just didn't spend it."

"Well, maybe he left it all to Christine."

"He didn't!" When Maddie slammed a fist on the table, the silverware jumped. "I know for a fact he didn't leave it all to her."

"Mama?" Max asked, his voice a question. *Is everything okay?*

Still looking at my aunt, I reached over to rub his back. "And you think ... Christine had you cut out of the will?"

"Not me! *You! It* was your money!"

"I think you're mistaken," I said quietly. The waitress appeared in order to pick up our soup bowls and replace them with our meals: red curry chicken for Maddie, eggplant basil for me. Max could eat off my plate.

"You were his little girl!" Maddie erupted, even though the waitress hadn't finished unloading her tray. "He knew you were going to come home someday."

"No, actually, he didn't," I insisted, picking up my fork. "He never came after me, and he never took me home, and he certainly didn't recognize me in his will."

"Because Christine took it all for that daughter of theirs— Little Miss Tongue Ring."

"Sophie?" My sinking heart grabbed hold of my throat for dear life and suddenly, it was hard to swallow.

Maddie didn't seem to even notice her meal. "I went up to Christine at the service. I said, 'Look, I don't expect anything.' Gabe and I hadn't really been on good terms for years, not since... well, not since you and your mom left, and he thought I had something to do with it. And certainly not since I moved away from Frank and Allie. But I said to Christine, 'Find her. Get a bounty hunter if you have to. She's out there, and she deserves her share.' But she didn't listen, did she? And you got *nothing*. Ask Alecia—she's got a copy of the will."

I put down my fork. "What are you saying? I was actually in my father's will?" Something surged in my chest. "You saw my name?"

Maddie nodded. "Slated to get a quarter of his estate, baby doll."

The fist on my throat opened up as my heart clanged to life. "Oh, my God." I inhaled. The cell phone in my coat pocket vibrated against my belly, and I fished it out of my pocket and saw the name *Catalano* on the caller ID screen.

"Di, are you okay?" Auggie asked when I answered.

"Fine, fine." It was hard to breathe normally. My name had been there. He hadn't forgotten me.

"Are we okay? You and I?" Auggie asked.

"Um, yeah, definitely, yes." The restaurant was growing noisier, and I held a hand over my free ear and turned from Maddie's gaze.

"I know I overstepped my bounds and I apologize." He paused, waiting for me to respond. "I wasn't sure if I was going to find a letter of resignation on the counter in the morning."

"No, no," I said, and the waitress, her pitcher poised, hesitated over our water glasses. "Yes, yes—go ahead, pour." I flapped my hand toward my glass. And to Auggie: "Everything's fine. Really."

"Where *are* you?"

"Out to lunch with my aunt."

"Enjoying the emergency money, are we?" he asked, and I laughed. "Well, I'm here in Minneapolis. Just got to the hotel. I'll be here till tomorrow night. Just wanted to make sure you were all right."

"I'm fine. Thank you. Have a good trip."

"So, who overstepped his bounds last night?" Maddie asked, once I'd snapped my cell phone shut. *Were we just on speakerphone?* The way Maddie smiled at me reminded me of a little devil—of Alecia, actually.

"Oh, no one."

"I guess I don't know—or maybe you told me—are you married?"

I shook my head.

"Is your phone friend married?" She pointed to my cell on the table, which Max was lunging for.

"Divorced." I slipped it back in my pocket.

"Good girl." Maddie nodded. "Your mother had a thing for a married man once," she said, which didn't surprise me. My mother had a thing for a lot of men.

"An organic chemistry professor," she added. "It didn't end well."

I cut up more eggplant for Max and asked, "What was my mother like when you met?"

"Oh, gosh. A free spirit, as always." Maddie sighed, thinking. "It was right after I'd graduated from college, and just before Frank and I were married. Gabe brought her to lunch at this outdoor café in Boston—they'd met at a friend of a friend's murder party, or something. There I was in this preppy outfit Frank's mother had given me—yellow argyle, if you can believe it—and your mother was wearing a bandanna, and those bangles, and flowy skirts. And she was beautiful, of course. So beautiful. I felt like . . . such a fraud. To be sitting there on Frank's arm, looking like his mother . . ." She trailed off, shaking her head. Suddenly, Maddie reached over, picked up Max's horse, and put it on her head, which made Max giggle in his booster seat.

"This is Stanley!" He pointed and waved.

"Hiya, Stanley," Maddie said, removing the horse and making it walk back toward Max. She looked over at me. "Your mother made me feel so normal, when no one else could. I loved that about her."

"Me, too," I said.

When Maddie spoke again, her voice trembled with emotion. "After she and Gabe were divorced, and she ran away with you, it was, by far, one of the greatest losses in my life—*paramount*." Maddie swallowed and looked at me. "But it probably saved me. Before then, it had never occurred to me that I could just . . . disappear. Without killing myself."

I nodded, thinking of how hard my father had worked to

rescue his little sister, and of how my mother had, inadvertently, managed to do so. "For what it's worth," I said, "I'm glad you decided to reappear."

Maddie's eyes were wet, even though she was smiling. "It's worth a lot."

CHAPTER 23

Bad Back

Max and I spent Saturday night at the apartment in Shadyside, which was disconcertingly quiet without Alecia and Ben. After lunch with Aunt Maddie, I'd tried calling my cousin several times but kept getting her voice mail instead. Uncle Frank had houses in New York, Maine, Tahoe, and Italy. Was she in another time zone—was I calling in the middle of the night? I wanted to talk to Ben, too, but Holly had told me he'd taken off for the weekend—home to Maryland, to see his father. Everyone was going home, it seemed, maybe even me: On Sunday morning, while Max watched cartoons, I searched online bus schedules—from Pittsburgh to Philadelphia. When Alecia returned, I would convince her to come with me. After all, she'd known my father's widow better than I, and the idea of showing up alone was too daunting. My cell phone rang, and I reached for it—hoping for my cousin but hearing Gusty's voice instead.

"I'm at work!" He sounded triumphant. "I'm riding around in the flatbed of a pickup truck."

"Gusty! Wha—no! I told you—who let you—is Dave there? Put Dave on the phone! Tell him to pull over."

"Dave's not here. He got hurt. We were working at Dad's house when he left to go to the emergency room. TJ said it was time to go to the next property."

"Is TJ aware that you weren't allowed to leave your father's lawn—does *Mazy* know where you are?"

"Mom's at a baby shower. She wanted me to come, too, but I told her I wasn't feeling well, so she let me stay home. That's when I left."

"Gusty, if your mother gets back, and you're not there—"

"I thought you'd be happy for me."

"I'm not *happy,* Gusty, because your parents are going to *freak out!*" I paced back and forth, my voice echoing off the wood floors. "It's not safe to be riding around in the back of a pickup—"

"Take it easy. He's slowing down…he's turning in the driveway. We're at the job now."

I exhaled. "Promise me you'll ride *inside* the pickup on the way home. Promise me you'll buckle your seat belt."

"Okay, I promise. Geez!" he said. "The only reason I called was because TJ told me to. He thought you'd want to know about Dave's back."

"Dave's back?"

"He thought you'd want to know that Dave threw his back out, and that he can't move."

I stopped pacing and stood up straighter. "Why would I want to know that?"

Gusty sounded sheepish. "I kind of told them how you were a professional massager and stuff."

"A masseuse."

"Yeah. That's what I mean. Listen, I gotta go. They're hooking me up to a leaf blower."

It probably wasn't the proper phraseology, but it sounded much more promising than hooking him up to an IV, and I found myself smiling.

LATER THAT AFTERNOON, MAX and I got off the bus in Aspinwall and walked the few blocks to Emerson Avenue. We stopped in front of a small Cape Cod with a maple tree out front, and I lifted Max up so he could ring the buzzer. A fat lady in a purple flowered housecoat answered the door.

How odd. I could've sworn this was the house Dave dropped TJ and Hobbes off at the day he took us to see Holly. The siding was the same—wooden shingle—and the end of the driveway was decorated with the same crooked red mailbox . . . but no, I was apparently mistaken. I must've been off by a house. "I'm so sorry . . ." Just then, from behind the big lady's legs, a yellow Lab—the same yellow Lab I'd nearly run over that day at the Catalanos—poked out its nose and began to sniff my feet. "We're here to see Dave?"

"He lives in the upstairs apartment." The woman eyed me suspiciously. "You'll have to go around the side. You'll see the other set of stairs. Lacey, stay!" she snapped at the dog. "He hurt his back, you know!" she called after us.

"That's exactly why we're here," I returned over my shoulder, as I took the iron-rung steps with Max on one hip and my bag of massage oils banging against the other.

At the top of the steps, there was no doorbell, so I knocked lightly. When footsteps failed to arrive within a minute, I checked the door handle and pushed. "Hello? Anybody home?" I imagined Dave stuck in bed, unable to move, like a spinal cord injury victim. "Don't get up!" I added. After setting Max on the yellow linoleum of the kitchen floor, I bent down to drop my bag. Glancing down the hall, I was startled to see Dave—surprisingly upright—standing there and staring at me.

"Oh!" I hadn't expected to find him without a shirt on, hadn't expected to find him looking so young and healthy and not at all like the invalid I'd come to save.

"Di," he said, still blinking at me without moving. It occurred to me then that I'd never heard him call me by my name before. I was "lady" or "she" or "somebody's mother" but not Di. Now, just realizing that he did know my name, after all, made me blush. Or maybe I was turning red because of the way he kept staring at me, like I'd just walked right into his dream.

"I didn't expect you to be standing. We heard about your back, didn't we, Max?" I asked, finally breaking his gaze to look at my son, who'd found a gold mine of remotes on the coffee table.

"You have a bad back," Max said.

"That's right, kiddo." He nodded, then looked at me. "I just took some more Percocet and a muscle relaxant, so I probably won't be able to stand for long. Did you . . . need a ride somewhere?"

"No, I'm—we're here because of your back." All at once it dawned on me just how odd it was that I'd come rushing over here like a paramedic. "I'm a masseuse. I brought my . . . equipment." My face was heating up even more. "Except that I don't own a table." *So we'll have to do this on a bed.* What the hell was I thinking? Who had talked me into this but a thirteen-year-old boy?

The corners of Dave's mouth were starting to turn up. "What about Max? Is he going to massage me, too?"

"Oh, no. It's Max's naptime. Right, Max?" I looked around. Max was making himself at home in the place. He'd already moved on from the six remotes to a poker set that he'd found on the floor. Now the chips were scattered all over the rug. "Oh, no, Max!"

"It's cool. I don't really play anymore. My nephew lost half the chips anyway. If he's really going to nap, there's another bedroom over here."

ONCE DAVE HAD STAGGERED off to his room, it took a while to actually get Max to settle down and sleep, with all the exploring he had to do. There was the plaid sofa with its multiple afghans, which Max tested for bounceability; the thick, yellow carpet, covered in dog hair, which he rolled around on as if he were Lacey herself; the posters on the walls—one of Jerome Bettis, one of a half-naked man emerging from a pond surrounded by lily pads and five naked female nymphs; and even a diploma from Penn State University. With its piles of clothes and trail of leaves scattered across the carpet, the place was dirty but homey.

Finally, I took Max into the second bedroom, which was set up as an office, and together we read *The Adventures of Dick and Jane*. As my mouth moved with the words, it occurred to me, *I am reading my son a book in a stranger's house*. Why had I let Gusty talk me into this? It couldn't have been because, for just a moment on the lawn yesterday, when Dave had been nice to my son, I'd found him marginally attractive?

Once Max was asleep on the daybed, I knocked on the door to Dave's room. He was lying faceup, staring at the ceiling.

"So, is this typical for you?" he asked, as I made my way toward his bed. "You just . . . show up unannounced, and tell someone you're going to massage them?"

"No, I just . . . heard about your back. And besides, I still had to thank you. For giving me a ride."

"Rides."

"I had to thank you for the rides, plural, then." I looked

around for a spot to put my portable CD player and lotions. The dresser was piled high with clothes, as was the floor. "Besides, I like to give massages. You should roll over, by the way."

"That could take a while." He groaned, shifting positions, and his eyes followed mine to the stack of filthy cups littering the night table. "I want you to know, I haven't dipped in two days."

"Yeah, then what are these?" I pushed them aside to set down my radio. The CD was from Scotland, *Skye Music,* and I waited for the first soulful notes of the bagpipes to begin.

"Cups from two days ago. Didn't know I'd be getting company."

"What made you quit?" I hesitated when I came to the candles in my bag. *No. No candles. Too romantic.*

"I don't know if I've quit. Just thought I'd see what it's like without it. Thought maybe I'd ask you to cook something for me. See if it's any good."

"Oh, it's good." I paused once again at the edge of the bed. He was lying on his stomach now, back exposed, cut off sweatpants covering most of his ass.

"Climb aboard, pretty lady."

"I'm not *mounting you.*" I laughed and selected a bottle of lotion from my bag. "Haven't you ever had a professional massage before?"

"Not in my bedroom."

I ignored that. "I guess I should ask you now—do you have any allergies to skin products?" He shook his head. "And any health problems I should be aware of?"

"Yeah, I threw my back out. I think we established that's why you're—yow! Your hands are cold!" He jumped when I touched him.

They'd said that in England, too, before they fired me. It didn't matter if I rubbed my hands together or ran them under hot water first; they stayed like ice. My nicest clients called me "Warm Heart."

"Your rhomboids are really tight." I pushed on the muscles just next to his shoulder blades, which made him jump and yelp again. My clients had always liked to hear me name the muscles as I rubbed them out. I'd never officially gone to a massage school, of course, but I'd checked out several books from the library on the subject and even taught myself all the muscles of the back and neck.

"Ow, ow, ow." Dave flinched as I moved up to his shoulders and started kneading.

"Your trapezius muscles are a mess."

"My lower back is the prob—lem—" He grunted when I pushed on a trigger point. "Damn, lady!"

"Go to your happy place," I ordered, pushing on the knot in his back until it popped, and his left arm flopped forward. "There we go. You're loosening up." His back was starting to sweat.

"Is my arm still attached?"

I laughed. "You're fine. You just need to relax. Listen to the music." The soothing sound of the bagpipes was starting to swell, but Dave was probably grunting too loud to hear it. "Come on, *re-lax,*" I insisted, pushing harder on his rhomboid, until he made another noise that sounded as if he'd been punched in the gut. "So, how'd you pick this house? Your landlady seems like a bit of a busybody."

"No kidding. One of the many reasons why I'm"—he grunted again—"moving. Jesus!"

"So, where are you moving to?" I reached over to squirt more lotion in my hand, being careful to keep one palm flat on his back, so as not to break contact with the patient. All the books recommended that.

"*Ohhh* yeah. *Ohhh* yeah. Now this feels great."

"I'm not doing anything."

"I know." He finally exhaled, noisily. "I don't know how to break it to you, but you're seriously hurting me, lady."

"You forgot to breathe. You're just not relaxed enough."

"Sweetheart, I'm drugged up. I couldn't be more relaxed." Dave rolled over with a groan, and I stood up straighter, instinctively grabbing my own back, which was starting to ache from bending over him. This time, he was the one who laughed. "Oh, Jesus, don't look like that."

"Like what?" I took a step away and he caught my hand.

"Like I just hurt your feelings or something." He tugged on my arm and then pulled me down to sit next to him.

"You realize you could kill a man with these hands?" Dave asked, examining them. "Crush him to bits." When he ran his thumb in a circle across my palm, I felt a tense spot release inside me: it could've been my back, could've been inside my rib cage.

I blinked, remembering it was my turn to speak. "You need to really just . . . feel the music."

"I should probably tell you now that the only thing in the world that makes me cry is the sound of a bagpipe."

"Seriously?"

"No." Dave laughed. "But my niece did that to me once. Took her on a two-hour drive to see the Highland Games, where, like, everyone's in Scottish garb and all you can hear throughout the whole forest is the sound of bagpipes. We pay for our tickets and get inside the park, and she turns and says this to me—that the bagpipes are the saddest sound in the world—before bursting into tears."

As he talked, I was surprised to see the two figures of myself in his eyes, the same way I usually saw myself in Max's gaze. I blinked again and realized that Dave was staring at me. "What?"

"Nothing." He reached up, as if to run his fingers through my hair.

"Oh no, you don't want to do that! I'm losing it!" I flipped my hair around to show him my bald spot.

Dave looked puzzled. "Well, I was going to say that you are a beautiful sight. But now that I know about the bald spot, I take it back."

I reached for the nearest pillow and clobbered him. Then I burst out laughing.

"My God, she laughs!"

I lowered the pillow, surprised. "I'm actually a really happy person. Or at least I used to be."

Dave looked amused. "What are you now?"

"Exhausted," I realized. It seemed to hit me all at once.

"So, take a rest." He patted the bed next to him. I hesitated and then shook my head. I couldn't nap next to Dave, no matter how nice he was. Not with Max a room away. It was only the night before that he'd wandered in on Auggie and me.

"Why didn't you ever get a stupid nickname?" I suddenly wondered, thinking of Auggie calling the landscapers "those clowns," when Dave was so far from it.

"You hear what they call me."

Dickhead. Loser. "Well, yeah, but . . . why don't you have a sillier nickname?"

Dave looked sheepish and told me that ever since I'd come along, they'd been calling him "Under-who?"

When did I come along? I wondered. "When did I come along?"

"You know, that day I asked if you were a fan of Underoos, and you were like, 'I'm sorry, asshole, but I grew up in England.' "

"I never called you an asshole!"

"Actually, I saw you before that, when you were inside the house. Your suit was just falling apart in the back, and your hair was coming out of your bun, and you had that funny hat on . . ." He smiled sheepishly.

So, Dave had been watching me all that time, when I hadn't even been paying attention. The way he was closing his eyes and wincing, as if pained to have admitted so much, made me feel guilty and sorry and flattered all at once. And when I leaned over and kissed him, I couldn't say whether I was doing it to make him feel better or me. As soon as Dave kissed me back, though—long and slow, with his hands on my face and in my hair, as if it were his job to keep every strand of it from tumbling across my face—I wanted him. He smelled like aftershave, even though he hadn't shaved, and he tasted like peppermint gum. How was it possible that his touch felt so chaste and so hot and so sweet all at once? It was as if all of my hair grew back in that kiss, and it might have gone on for longer if a yell from the other room hadn't startled us both.

"David?"

"Oh, shit," Dave said, sitting up. He winced and flopped back again.

"Is that your landlady?" I whispered.

"David?"

"Ma, I'm busy," Dave called.

"Mama?" Max, in the next room, sounded pitiful.

I hopped up from the bed and ran from the room to find the lady in the purple flowered muumuu standing in the hallway, and Max fearfully regarding her from the threshold of the office.

"I'm Nancy, David's mother." She smiled. "Would the little boy like to come downstairs for cookies? They're fresh baked."

"He's not—allowed to have cookies before dinner," I stammered.

Nancy looked at her watch. "It's only two-thirty in the afternoon."

"Ma, she said he's not allowed," Dave said, wandering out of his bedroom, still holding on to his back.

"Could you kindly introduce me to your friends, David?"

"This is Di, and this is Max."

Nancy didn't seem to process the introduction, because she asked a moment later, "Where's the little boy's father?"

"Ma!"

"He doesn't have one." I scooped Max up off the floor.

Nancy looked intrigued. "Artificial insemination?"

"*Not* artificial." I quickly turned my head to Max. "Should we find Stanley? Where'd you leave him?" Max pointed to the daybed, and I put him down so he could run and get his horse.

"Ma, I think it's time for you to leave."

"What about macaroni and cheese? Does he like macaroni and cheese?"

"No," I said, at the exact moment that Max appeared again at my feet.

"Macaroni?" he asked hopefully, as if I'd never fed him lunch.

"Max, I don't think so. You already ate."

"Macaroni and cheese? Now? Please? I'm hungry."

"It sounds like the little boy would like macaroni and cheese," Nancy translated triumphantly.

It was reassuring to discover that Max could be lured into a stranger's car with the promise of noodles smothered in Velveeta. I watched as Nancy took his hand. "We'll just be downstairs. You two have a nice time."

When the door closed after them, it occurred to me that Max hadn't even looked back to see if I was coming. It was just like at day care. How could he be comfortable with so many people who weren't me? Of course, it was probably better this way. If anything happened, Max would adapt. But why didn't that make me feel any better?

"Sorry about that," Dave said, returning from his bedroom. He pulled a T-shirt over his head.

"So, you live with your mother!" I said cheerfully.

"I live upstairs. I pay rent. She's just having trouble with boundaries and limits—especially now that I'm leaving."

"Where exactly are you going?"

"Ten minutes away. Ten freaking minutes. You'd think it was the end of the universe." He pulled on my elbow to get me to move toward the window. "See that house? Little Colonial four doors down? That's my sister's. She's lived there since she got married, fifteen years ago. None of us can seem to get away from Emerson Avenue. If my mom had her way, I'd stay here forever, or buy the place for sale next door, but I need land to put all my toys on."

"Toys," I repeated before my eyes widened. "That was your backhoe? Those are your trucks? How can you afford all that?"

"I'm thirty-two years old. Been living above my mom since I graduated college." He leaned against the windowsill, glanced at his feet. "At least the rent is stable." He looked up again. "Must seem kind of weird, huh?"

"No, not really. I lived with my mom until I was twenty-six."

"What finally got you out of the house?"

"She died."

His eyebrows shot up.

"No, no, really, it's fine," I said, trying to save him from coming up with the right thing to say. "I mean, it's not fine, it's just..." I backed away and stood in the middle of the living room. "I thought I was going to be okay with it. I had six months to prepare completely. And then, as soon as she died, I just...couldn't believe how lost I was without her." It was as if I'd suddenly become a single mom when it happened, because before that, I was just a girl, living with her mom and her baby.

"Thought you'd get all your grieving done in advance?"

"Maybe, I don't know." I hugged my shoulders. "I guess I thought I'd see her again. You know, in my dreams, or something. But she hasn't visited. And then my dad . . ."

"Where's your dad?" Dave asked kindly, and then suddenly, embarrassingly, I started to cry. I thought of Maddie saying that Little Miss Tongue Ring got my inheritance. But worse, she got my father.

"He died, too. Before I ever got to see him again. I'm so sorry." I wiped my face as Dave crossed the room toward me.

"No, this is cool. I love it when girls drop by to give me massages, and I make them cry. Maybe I'll call my niece up, and we can play the bagpipes again. It'll be a party."

I laughed into my hands as he hugged me.

"You okay, now?" he finally asked, once my shoulders stopped shaking.

"Yeah. I'm okay."

"You want to go find Max?" he asked. I nodded.

CHAPTER 24

A Revelation

While Max and I were finding our way back from Aspinwall later that afternoon, Alecia was traveling across town—from the Pittsburgh airport to the church where she and Ben were supposed to be married in just six days. With her right arm in a cast and her left wrist in a splint, maneuvering the steering wheel was more of a challenge than Alecia had anticipated. But it was the knee, packed into the most unbecoming of leg braces—extending from the bottom of her thigh to the top of her calf and involving three wide strips of Velcro—that bothered her most of all. Every time she pushed on the gas pedal, she winced and thought of Dr. Patel, the jerk in the Mount Desert Island ER who'd scoffed and said, "Just soft tissue injury," as if the purple swelling where her kneecap used to be was just a hangnail. The very same jerk who'd asked, right in front of her father, *Any way you could be pregnant?*

In East Liberty, she parked in a handicap spot then ·

grabbed her crutches out of the backseat, and limped her way toward the church office. Pastor Nate had canceled the last counseling session, and somebody needed to let him know that his services wouldn't be required next weekend.

When the cell phone rang in her pocket, she let it go again. So far, Ben had left a total of six messages on her voice mail. She had a feeling he knew, had a feeling her father may have been to blame. As soon as Patel had appeared with his sickening little smile—*You are indeed pregnant! Is good news or bad? You decide!*—Frank had threatened to call Ben right then: "The wedding is *on*." But Alecia had insisted that if her father got involved, she'd never speak to him again. *Leave all your money to the Sierra Club, I don't care,* she'd said, and for the first time, she realized that was true. The money had ruined everything. She had ruined everything.

"Didn't anyone call you from the prayer chain?" the secretary asked in a hushed voice, once Alecia had crutched her way into the church office and asked for Pastor Nate. "He's just been diagnosed with lung cancer—stage four," she added in a whisper, hazel eyes immediately filling with tears. "They thought it was pneumonia when they took him to the hospital."

"Lung cancer?" Alecia repeated, baffled.

"He never smoked a day in his life. It's just devastating," the secretary said, shaking her head.

Alecia thought of the tickle in his throat. "Where is he now?" she asked.

At Shadyside Hospital, nobody stopped her for an autograph. Nobody stopped her, period. Inside room 353, she found him lying in bed and coughing.

"Hey, Pastor Nate. It's Alecia Axtel. You were supposed to marry Ben and me this weekend?" she added, when he looked confused.

"That's right. Of course. Please, come in . . ." He watched as she lurched toward a seat by the bed.

"Nice flowers." She pointed to the arrangements that adorned every surface from the windowsill to the night table—there was even a potted plant on the floor.

"The congregation got carried away. Unfortunately, they tell me all the flowers are going to have to go. If everything goes according to plan, the chemo should destroy my immune system in the next day or two." He started coughing again.

Alecia pushed herself up from the plastic lounge chair and limped over to the corkboard where someone had tacked up family photos. It was easier to study the snapshots than study him. "Adorable kids," she said and meant it for a change. Finally, the hacking spell came to an end. Pastor Nate wiped his tearing eyes and lay back, appearing exhausted.

"So, um…how're you?" she asked, suddenly self-conscious for barging into his hospital room.

"I couldn't be better." Even if his eyes were tired, at least his smile seemed real. "How's Ben?"

"Ben's, you know—Ben's…" She forgot that she didn't have to pretend with Pastor Nate. "Ben called off the wedding." She watched as his eyes opened a little wider. "Yeah. So, don't worry about coming on Saturday. You're off the hook! I mean, you were already off the hook…" Pastor Nate chuckled. "He's probably right that it shouldn't be this hard," Alecia added.

His eyebrows furrowed. "That…what shouldn't be this hard?"

"Love, I guess."

"Love shouldn't. But life is hard. And marriage is hard. And if you're going to get married, you've got to hang your hat on more than just love." Alecia must've looked perplexed this time, because he added, "There's honesty, loyalty, integrity, your faith."

Alecia sat back down again and rubbed her splinted hand

over her hair. "Is it possible that I was born without any of that? That I'm... missing some key ingredient?"

"Basic spirituality?" Pastor Nate suggested.

Alecia slapped her good knee. "Basic spirituality! Yes! That's it. I mean, isn't it? Don't I need that?"

"Well, Alecia, I think everyone needs spirituality."

She nodded slowly, taking it all in: the cold tile floors, the adjustable bed, the pastor's thin, white legs barely covered by a thin, white blanket. One bony foot was even sticking out from underneath the flimsy covers, revealing a misshapen big toe. She cocked her head to the side and stared at the collection of purple blood underneath the cracked nail thinking—absurdly: *Di's dream*. "What happened there?"

For just a second, Pastor Nate looked bewildered, as if he were examining someone else's toe. "Cup fell on my foot." Alecia's eyebrows went up, and he laughed. "Not the blood of Christ. Just orange juice."

"Does it hurt?"

He shrugged. "Yeah, actually. But no one seems to think it's particularly important right now. Go figure."

It seemed hard to believe the man could actually be that sick when, save the pajamas and the nasal cannula of oxygen, he looked the way he always had: same well-groomed beard, same easy smile, same noisy cough. "Are you... mad at God?" she asked.

His expression grew thoughtful. "No, Alecia. I'm not mad at God," he finally said. "Are you?"

"I'm not even sure I believe in God," she said slowly, thinking of her father and Ben during their first inauspicious meeting five years before. ("Did Alecia tell you we're Nothing?" Frank had asked. He said it as if Nothing were a religion, like that time he said his favorite Jolly Rancher flavor was "Regular." The red-colored one, he'd meant.) But Ben had convinced Alecia, and she still believed—reluctantly—in both God and Ben. Even though life seemed so much easier back when she was Nothing.

She stood up again to test her weight on the braced leg. It seemed to hold. "How did Ben and I compare to other couples?"

"In what way?"

"I mean, when you met us, were you like, 'Whoa, this couple is doomed'?"

"Not at all."

"My father hated Ben from the start. He thought we were terrible together. I thought it was just because Ben doesn't care about money . . . but it was more than that." Alecia made her way to the window where, on the street below, she could see people rushing every which way—to catch a bus, to put money in the meter, maybe even to buy a wig or save a life. "Daddy doesn't like what he's not in control of, and he couldn't control Ben. Actually, Ben can't deal with it, either—not being in control," she realized. "He thought he had this big faith, and then it turned out he had hardly any convictions, that he's just waiting for proof. Proof that we're right together. He wants it to be so easy."

"How do you feel about not being in control?" Pastor Nate asked.

"I hate it!" Alecia whirled around. She'd learned early on that it didn't matter how perfectly she performed—memorizing her lines, getting the lead in *South Pacific,* passing her driver's test on the first go-round, achieving all As, remembering to use condoms. It didn't matter because at any moment, Alecia could come home from school and find her mother unconscious on the bathroom floor. She shook her head, remembering.

"What is it?" Pastor Nate asked.

"My mother was always trying to commit suicide. Like, at least once a year, she gave it another try. The first note I ever found was written in a pink Crayola marker—*my* pink Crayola marker, which she left right near it, drying out."

"And you thought your mother's depression was your fault?"

"Why would it have been my fault?"

"I don't know. You tell me." Pastor Nate started coughing again, but this spell was brief. "Why would it have been your fault, Alecia?"

"I don't know. I just . . . don't know what I did . . . to make her that way."

Pastor Nate shrugged again. "Probably nothing."

Alecia shook her head. She wanted there to be a reason. She realized she was in the same boat as Ben, struggling so hard to find answers from God. Why did he have to dissect his religion to the point that it became meaningless? Why couldn't he be satisfied just to cast a vote without worrying about which way it would all go in the end? She limped back to the plastic armchair and lowered herself into it. "What if I live an unhappy life because of my lack of spirituality?"

"Interesting." Pastor Nate sounded thoughtful. "Essentially you're equating no God with no happiness. That *is* basic spirituality."

Alecia blinked. "You really believe that?"

"This? No." He pointed to the IV pole and the drab room and the plastic furniture. "God? Yes. And so do you. It's pretty obvious."

"What about Ben and me? Is that obvious, too?"

Pastor Nate shook his head. "But you could pray about it. There's a little chapel on the first floor of the hospital. Stop in."

"What if I go in and feel nothing?"

"What if you go in and feel something?"

Alecia sighed. "No offense, but I think having faith is just too easy, if you know what I mean."

Pastor Nate looked at her so gravely that, for the first time, she recognized how sick he really was. "There is nothing easy about faith."

ALECIA NEVER MADE IT to the little chapel. Instead, she stopped to use the ladies' room right across the hall. Ever since she'd fallen down the steps, she couldn't pee without checking the toilet for blood, and every time she didn't see any, Alecia was surprised and confused by her own relief. *The kid is holding on.* Was she actually rooting for its survival— the thing that would steal her figure and, worse, her life?

After washing her hands at the sink, Alecia stared at herself in the mirror. She touched her yellow-blond hair, ran her splinted fingers through a clump of split ends. *Change. Change. Change,* something whispered inside her. She leaned forward to inspect her dark roots and then stepped back again to study the length: just below her shoulders. She'd been growing it out for the wedding, and Richard, her stylist, had assured her they could pull off a French twist with extensions if need be. But now she thought of Ben, how he'd always loved her hair short and black. In her mind, she heard my mother's wry voice: *It's your hair.*

Alecia grabbed her crutches and moved toward the door. Change was coming.

CHAPTER 25

New Look

When Max and I got back to Shadyside, I was surprised to find Alecia's apartment door unlocked and a single crutch on the floor of the front hall. "Hello?" I called, taking Max's hand.

"In here!" came a shout from the bathroom, followed by: *"Help!"*

At first sight, my cousin appeared to have been brutally attacked by Edward Scissorhands. There was the leg brace, of course, and the cast on her arm, but it was the sight of her neck that startled me most: no longer shrouded in blond hair, it looked vulnerable, as if at risk of suddenly snapping in two.

"Alecia! What happened to you?"

"I know! It's awful!" she said, near tears, holding up a pair of shears in a splinted hand. She had new bangs that were wickedly uneven and new, zigzagged layers, too—mostly black with jagged blond tips.

Max peered around my legs and clapped when he saw Alecia. "Funny hair!"

"What happened to . . . the rest of you!" I waved my hand toward her leg.

"I fell down the steps in Daddy's house—but I'm going to tell Art that it was a car wreck and that the paramedics had to cut my hair to see where to put in the stitches."

"You're going to tell your boss that the paramedics did this to you?" I said, cocking my head to the side so that her hair didn't seem quite so uneven. I searched my brain for the name of her stylist. "Was Richard sick today?"

"I don't have the energy for Richard," Alecia said with a groan, limping past me on her way to her bedroom. "The small talk, the painting, the foiling, the baking under a dryer—*more* small talk—before he even reaches for a pair of scissors. I was desperate to make a change!"

"Your desperation . . . shows," I said, glancing behind me for Max, who'd found the other crutch and was now pretending it was a horse.

Leaning against the door frame of her bedroom, I watched as Alecia stopped short at the sight of her wedding dress, which was hanging up over the mirror. Finally, she hobbled over and touched it through the plastic, as if she couldn't imagine where it had come from, couldn't imagine that it had actually been made for her. "Aunt Maddie and I picked it up," I said quietly. "She's leaving town tomorrow. She really wants to see you."

Alecia snorted. "They must've been some pretty expensive nonrefundable tickets for her to stick around."

"She said—" I stopped.

"That she's sorry for ruining my childhood?" Alecia suggested. "That she's sorry for leaving?"

I cleared my throat. "She said she saw my father's will. She said I was supposed to inherit some money."

"She's mistaken. Di, this is my mother we're talking about."

"Mistaken," I repeated.

"I never saw your name in his will. Everything went to Christine and Sophie." Alecia turned away from me again, just as her cell phone rang from somewhere in the other room. "It's probably Ben again—leave it!" she added, when I moved to answer it for her. "You didn't tell him, did you?" Her voice was suddenly sharp.

I halted and then slowly looked back. "I didn't tell him."

"Because I can't have him—I could miscarry tomorrow— I *should've* miscarried—and if that were the reason . . ." She trailed off, shaking her head. "I want him to come back for *me*."

I nodded, crossing the rug again to where Alecia was still standing and looking at herself in the mirror. Now that her hair was darker, we looked surprisingly similar—like family.

"What exactly were you envisioning here?" I asked, smoothing down one side of her hair.

"The way Ben always liked it, short and kind of framing my face. He used to call it 'an optical illusion of length' because he could still tuck it behind my ears." She met my eyes in the mirror. "We could dye the blond parts back to my natural color."

"Are you sure you don't want to call Richard?"

"I can't walk into his salon looking like this! You have to do it, Di."

Since I couldn't fix anything else—not Ben, or the baby, or the wedding, or her job—I agreed to save her hair.

CHAPTER 26

Give Them
What They Want

On Monday afternoon, as Max and I were running errands around Shadyside, Alecia was crutching her way into the lobby of WTAE preparing for her inaugural newscast as a brunette.

Behind the security desk, Bob jumped to his feet. "Jesus, Alecia! What the hell happened to you?"

"I was in a car wreck over the weekend." Alecia used her crutch to push the "up" button on the elevator.

"Oh, my God!" Bob moaned as if it had happened to him. "Whose fault?"

She stared at him, momentarily shocked. "Mine." The elevator doors closed.

The reaction in the newsroom wasn't much better: Elaine, the weather girl, gasped and hung up the phone in what appeared to be mid-conversation. Heidi glanced over and then stared, mouth sagging with surprise. The sound guy didn't seem to recognize her, just gave her a look: *Are you lost?*

Whistling loudly, Rich, the sports guy, bopped around the corner from the editing booths. Thankfully, the mere sight of her extinguished that intractable tune—*Pittsburgh's Go-in' to the Su-per Bowl.* "What the hell happened to you?"

"I was in a car accident over the weekend," Alecia announced. "In Maine."

"And they turned you into a pixie?" Heidi asked.

"No, she looks like that chick who stole all that shit—"

"Winona Ryder," the sound guy said. He turned to Alecia and asked, "What were you doing in Maine?"

"My father was ill, and I had to visit him." Alecia added in a louder voice, "He's so sick that Ben and I have decided to postpone the wedding. The doctors said that if he tried to walk me down the aisle, he'd have another heart attack."

"Did he have to have bypass surgery, or did they put in stents?" Fran asked.

Goddamn medical reporter. "Bypass," Alecia decided.

"Did they have to airlift him someplace?" Fran asked.

It was a good question. Surely they couldn't have done cardiothoracic surgery at the tiny Mount Desert Island Hospital, but where might they have flown him to? Thankfully, Art's office door opened with a bang, and she didn't have to answer. "*Alecia? Is that you?*"

"Yes, it's me. Hi!" She waved her crutch.

Art didn't smile in return. "Get in here."

Every eye seemed fixed on her movements as she lurched and swung her way across the newsroom toward his office. When her bad leg accidentally bumped the back of Heidi's chair, eliciting yet another titter of laughter from the bitch, she thought of Dr. Patel again. *Soft tissue injuries are sometimes worse than the breaks,* he'd said when fitting her for the hideous brace.

Inside Art's office, she watched as he slammed his door shut, pulled out a chair and—before Alecia could fall into it herself—sat down. Then, hands on both knees, he slowly leaned forward, eyebrows raised, and whispered, *"What happened to your hair?"*

"I was in a car wreck this weekend. They had to cut my hair to see where to put in the stitches. I would love a seat, thank you," she added, slumping into the other chair. Turning to rest her crutches against the window that faced the newsroom, she saw that everyone was still watching. "Could we maybe shut the shades?"

But Art was too agitated to listen. "Did you *tell them* you're on TV every night?" She hadn't, actually, but it had been the first thing Frank thought of when he found out she was getting a cast. *She's an anchorwoman in Pittsburgh—she can't wear a cast!*

"I told them, Art, but I don't think they cared."

He squinted as if the color hurt. "But why is it black?"

"Because it is. It's my hair."

"Oh, Jesus. Fuck." Art ran a hand over the top of his splotchy bald head. "I can't believe this."

"I'm just happy to be alive."

"But what about your hair?"

"I happen to like it."

The door opened, and Alecia's crutches clattered to the floor. "Oh, my God. They weren't kidding," Mazy said, her eyes blazing with . . . something Alecia couldn't identify. *Mirth? Horror?* The Botox made it so hard to tell.

"We're gonna have to get her a wig before six o' clock," Art said to Mazy. He snapped his fingers. "Tom's wife— doesn't she work for that beauty shop that does all the wigs for the Hillman Cancer Center? Maybe we could have him get one for her. As long as it's blond, no one will know the difference."

"But her hands are in casts!" Mazy said.

Alecia was beginning to feel like the mannequin in the

room. "I'm sure that won't be a big deal. They always did a great job of hiding Vanessa's pregnant belly."

Art wasn't paying attention. He'd already reached for the phone to call Tom out in the field. "Alecia was in a car wreck. They did something awful to her hair." He paused. "Yeah, *seriously*! We need a wig. Can Carol hook us up, or what?" Another pause and then Art hung up. "He's going to see what he can do."

Mazy folded her arms across her chest. "The cut isn't bad, but the *color* is awfully severe—"

"Black is actually my natural—" Alecia said.

"She looks like my tax guy!" Art erupted.

"A little makeup might help," Mazy said, sounding uncharacteristically wry.

"A lot of makeup—and a wig," Art insisted.

"Don't mind me," Alecia said with a little wave. "Pretend I'm not even here."

Art ran his hand over his head again, glanced anxiously at Mazy and then back to Alecia. "Listen, maybe you should take the night off. Get some rest. We'll let Heidi go on tonight, and tomorrow, if you're feeling better, give me a call. Let's get you a wheelchair," Art decided, opening the office door.

"I wasn't aware that being blond was part of my contract," Alecia said.

"It's not! It's not!— It's just . . . look at you!" Art swirled his hand in the general direction of her arms and legs before calling out the office door, "Jeff! Find Alecia a wheelchair!"

It was like being on the *Gong Show*. One moment, center stage, the next, ushered out of the building in a wheelchair by the sound guy.

"So, what really happened?" he asked, once they were alone in the elevator.

"I tripped and fell down some stairs."

"Drunk?"

"I wish." She sighed. "I was just wearing socks on slippery steps and . . . down I went."

"And your hair?"

Alecia shrugged. "I was ready for a change."

The door opened. "You look good. Very Audrey Hepburn in *Sabrina*." The sound guy gave her wheelchair a push into the lobby.

"You don't have to say that. But thanks . . . Jeff."

"You know my name!"

"Of course I know your name."

CHAPTER 27

It was six o'clock on Monday evening, and for some reason Alecia wasn't on TV. I watched, puzzled, as Mazy Roberts bantered with the sports guy, Rich, about the Steelers. Beside her, Heidi looked on with a smile plastered across her bowling ball face. I flipped to channel eleven and eight—even CNN. There was plenty of depressing stuff—a car bomb, a kidnapping, an entire family found dead in the wilderness—but nothing about Alecia.

I imagined her explanation later: *I never went to work, silly. I went shopping. You must've been mistaken.* The word reminded me of my lunch with Aunt Maddie and my father's estate: *Mistaken,* Alecia had said. *And the paramedics attacked you with scissors,* I thought now.

"Mama?" Max asked from the dining room table, where he was eating macaroni and cheese for the second time in less than forty-eight hours.

"Just a sec, Boo," I called, opening the door to the front

hall closet. There was less junk in it now that the luggage had been removed along with some of Ben's boxes. It didn't take me long to find Alecia's egg crate of files, with my old telegram lying on top, shoved behind a retired set of speakers. I carried the box back to the table and riffled through its contents, separating seven years of airmail envelopes from the more official-looking documents: one high school diploma, a contract for a wedding jazz band, Alecia's birth certificate, a prenuptial agreement, and finally, in a manila folder labeled "Death," my father's *Last Will and Testament*.

"What's that, Mama?" Max asked, when I unfolded the papers with shaking fingers.

"Opa's will, baby."

"Opa will what?"

I flipped through the pages of legalese, just hunting for my name. "A will is what Opa would've intended . . ." I trailed off, staring at the pages of bequests. There it was in boldface type. Just above Sophie Linzer and just below Christine. *Diotima Linzer,* one quarter of his estate. In the event that Christine was already dead, Sophie and I would split everything. And in the highly unlikely circumstance that Christine, Sophie, and I all happened to simultaneously expire (*Nuclear war?*), Alecia would inherit. "Oh, my God," I breathed.

"Opa will what?" Max asked again.

Staring at my name, I struggled to catch my breath, struggled not to let the tears into my voice. "This says what Opa would've wanted. He didn't forget about us, after all."

On the kitchen counter, my cell phone rang, and I rushed for it, imagining what I would say to Alecia. *How could you have kept this from me?*

"How are you?" *Auggie.*

"Furious." It wasn't just my hands: I was trembling on the inside.

"With me?"

"With my cousin. With . . . the world. Not with you." I exhaled, trying to recompose myself. "It's a long story."

"Try me."

The sound of such kindness made me frown, and I raised a hand to my temple, willing the tears not to come. When my voice came out it was a whisper. "Really. I can't."

There was a pause just long enough to make me think we'd lost the call. When he spoke up again, Auggie was back to business. "Well, I'm just leaving the Pittsburgh airport. The trial only lasted a day, so I'm back early. Did you eat yet?"

I hesitated, imagining constructing a last-minute meal from one of the freezers in the basement. "No, but . . . Max and I won't have a ride out there tonight."

"Ah, that's right. I forgot about Max," he said, instead of *I forgot you don't have a car*. "I'll pick you guys up. Say, eight o' clock?"

"That's his bedtime."

"Perfect."

It was far from perfect. Not only would dinner be frozen, but Max would be out of sorts if I kept him up late. But I couldn't worry about it then. The apartment door had just opened and Alecia was lurching toward me on crutches. I quickly hung up the phone with Auggie.

"I have to talk to you!" I blurted.

"Not now!" She moved toward the bathroom with surprising swiftness.

"All done, Mama!" Max called from his booster seat.

I hadn't even finished wiping off his face when I heard Alecia retching into the toilet. After lifting him out of his chair, I went to stand outside the bathroom door, wondering how I could possibly confront her. "I read somewhere that you can control nausea by pressing on your wrists," I called through the crack. "It's an acupuncture technique."

Alecia opened the door all the way and held up her arms: one wrist hidden in a cast, the other in a splint. "Thanks for the tip." She kicked the door shut.

Apparently a bath for Max was not going to happen right then, so I set him up with a video about Old MacDonald's farm and—trying to regain the momentum of my anger— paced around until Alecia finally emerged.

"Talk to Ben lately?" she asked, over her shoulder, as she crutched toward her bedroom. "Because his last voice mail message asked if I was still pregnant!"

"I swear to you, I never told him," I said, following behind.

She whirled around. "Well, guess what, Di, I didn't, either! And I called my father—neither did he! So, why don't you tell me the truth?"

"Why don't you tell me the truth about Dad's will?" I blurted. Alecia stared at me. "I found it in your closet. My name was there."

Alecia's shoulders sagged as she sighed. "That will was out-of-date, Di."

"So, there was another one?"

She didn't answer right away, just lowered herself into the suede recliner and started adjusting the Velcro straps on her knee brace. "Christine made him change it about ten years ago, so if he died, everything would go to her and vice versa—at least, that's what my dad said."

I folded my arms across my chest, trying to steel myself against the disappointment: Once again, this woman had insisted that my father forget me—and she won.

"But there's more . . ." Alecia took a deep breath. "He had a bunch of policies—life insurance, IRAs, you name it, he had it." Finally, she looked at me. "And you weren't named as a beneficiary to any of his assets."

I swallowed and glanced down at my feet. "Why didn't you say so before?"

"Because I was."

I craned my neck forward and stared at Alecia for a moment, until the truth finally caught up to my brain—or at least, my lungs. I stopped in the middle of a breath, whirled around, and left the room.

"Di!"

"Look, Mama, a combine harvester!" Max beamed.

I couldn't look, couldn't smile, couldn't do anything but try not to start screaming. My eyes darted around, searching for something to break. For just a second, I considered the china creamer, shaped like a cow, but it happened to be sitting on the lowest bookshelf, which meant Alecia didn't even care about it. I reached for the remote instead. "Bath time," I ordered, aiming as if it were a gun and the TV were Alecia's head.

My son's face immediately crumpled. "Old MacDonald's farm!" he wailed.

"Bath time!" I said louder, scooping him off the sofa as he kicked. When we turned around, Alecia was standing in the hallway, leaning on a crutch.

"You know I had nothing to do with it, right?" Alecia asked. "I was just as surprised as you are—"

"Why didn't you tell my father where I was?" I asked.

Her eyes grew larger, and her mouth fell open. "You were eighteen years old when you found me again—you could've called him yourself!"

And that was the real truth: It was my own fault that he'd let me go. I had been old enough to make a decision, my first one that wasn't my mother's—and I'd failed him. *Failed us.*

Max squirmed and howled in my arms the way I felt like doing.

"I'm sorry, Di, but I figured you had a reason—you wrote to me in *code*."

I shook my head, unable to think of a time when I'd done anything for reasons that were my own, but it must've been so.

"Down!" Max screamed, and when I finally let go, he ran for the living room.

"I'm sorry," she said again.

"Me, too," I admitted, finally meeting her eyes. "It's my fault Ben found out." I sighed. "He was over at the Catalanos' to pitch the magazine—"

Her dark eyes narrowed, and her brows made a perfect, scary V. "He came to the house?"

"Auggie—he likes to sponsor people," I stammered. "And I'd mentioned to him that you were pregnant, and he let it slip while Ben was over . . ."

"He, who?" Her eyes widened. "Your *boss* told Ben?" I nodded, slowly, and Alecia screeched, "Oh, my *God*! Why were you even—why the hell was Ben—*you love him*!" she erupted, slamming her crutch into the floor like the butt of a rifle.

"He's attractive, but . . . I'm working there. I doubt his divorce is even final—"

"Not your boss—Ben!" She waggled a finger at me. "That's why you were cooking every night."

"I was cooking for both of you—so you'd let me stay!"

"You laugh at all of his jokes. . . ."

"He's funny!" I said, smiling with disbelief.

"You set up meetings for his magazine! Christ!" She hobbled away from me.

"I was just trying to help," I called after her.

"It was none of your business!"

Just as she slammed the door to her bedroom, a cow mooed from the opposite direction. I turned and found Max standing by the TV and holding the remote. "Hey," I said, still shaking.

"Old MacDonald's farm," he replied, without a question in his voice.

LATER ON, ONCE MAX had finished his video and was tucked in on the futon, I showered, dressed, and then knocked on the door to Alecia's room. "I have to go in to work tonight," I said, leaning against the frame. "Max is asleep. Okay?"

There was a pause, then, "Open the door!"

I turned the handle and pushed. Alecia was sitting up in bed, on top of the covers, her knee elevated on a pillow. "You're going to work? Now?"

I folded my arms across my chest. "You'll be here, right?"

She nodded, slowly. "Are those my jeans?"

"No, they're mine. I bought them yesterday."

She squinted at me. "And that shirt…" It was sun-sleeved and V-necked, with a Japanese silkscreen of a tree across the front. "It's sexy." An accusation, not a compliment.

"It's just a T-shirt," I said, shrugging.

"What the hell is going on with you and Mazy's husband?"

"Nothing's going on…" I looked at my jagged nails, remembering that Alecia had wanted me to have them manicured before the wedding. "It's just dinner."

"Is the kid even going to be there?" I shook my head. "And now 'Auggie's' asking you to come in at eight o'clock at night and do what, exactly?"

"Teach him to cook."

Alecia shook her head and exhaled so gustily that her bangs fluttered. "Jesus, Di, how stupid are you?"

The buzzer rang in the front hall. "Thanks for your vote of confidence," I muttered and then shut her door with a bang.

"WHERE'S THE LITTLE GUY?" Auggie asked when I got in the car. It was pouring rain and at the last second, I'd grabbed one of Alecia's wool pashminas to drape over my shoulders. It was a lovely shade of rose but not much protection against the elements. *I'm not worried about the elements!* Alecia would say. I shook my head, trying to push her voice out of my mind.

"He's asleep. My cousin got home, after all. But I'll need you to drop me off later."

"No problem." When he put the car in drive and stepped on the gas, I took a deep breath and held it for an entire block of Centre Avenue.

"So, you sounded pretty upset on the phone earlier. Feeling any better?" he asked, flicking his windshield wipers to a higher speed.

"Not really." I stared at the wipers, beating to and fro, feeling as frenetic on the inside.

"You want to talk about it?"

"Not really." I glanced at him. "Sorry."

He shrugged. "Don't be."

"We should probably hit the grocery store . . ." I trailed off, as we passed it.

"Don't worry, I've got it covered."

He waited until we'd reached the Highland Park Bridge to ask me how Ben was.

"He's . . . a little overwhelmed." I looked at Auggie's profile. "Your conversation was the dose of reality that he really didn't want to hear."

"Good. Somebody needed to do it."

"Why did you give him the money?" I asked, when he was done merging onto Route 28.

He smiled. "Why not?"

"But you didn't like the concept."

"I liked his passion." There was silence inside the car.

"He thought you were trying to buy me," I admitted. More silence. "Were you trying to buy me?" I asked.

"If I were trying to buy you, I wouldn't have stopped at ten thousand."

It was a sweet compliment. I found myself smiling in the dark.

As we turned at the Catalano gates and made our way up the driveway, lined by sycamores, I saw the branches tossing in the wind and rain and imagined it was the same storm that whisked Dorothy to Oz.

We walked to the front door, under the motion-sensor lights, which illuminated a flagstone walkway. "They finished!" I said.

"What?" Auggie glanced at the flat stones in the ground. "Oh, yeah. *Finally.*"

I wondered if Dave's back was feeling better. Wondered what he thought of me, now that I'd barged in and kissed him and cried.

Auggie put the key in the lock, turned, and pushed the door open. "Mademoiselle," he said, reaching for my hand.

The house was dark inside, and I kept holding his hand as he flipped on a trail of lights from the marble foyer to the kitchen, where the table was already set for two.

"Figured you'd want to avoid the dining room." Auggie smiled and pulled out a chair. "Sit down. Put your feet up. I'll have dinner ready in a second."

"I thought—I was supposed to cook for you." Slowly I

sank in my seat and watched as he collected our empty plates to load with food at the kitchen island.

"Weren't you coming from the airport? How did you have time to do all this?" I asked, as he pulled a platter out of the refrigerator.

"Between you and me, the menu was 'stupidly easy.' It took me half an hour to pull this off."

I laughed when he finally brought my plate back: cold poached salmon topped with dill sauce, steamed asparagus, and the pasta—not leftovers, but the one meal I'd taught him how to cook. "Watch out for the pesto—it's got some kick this time," he said, lighting a candle in the center of the table.

"You can never use too much garlic," I said, smiling.

"My kind of woman." Auggie uncapped a bottle of white wine. The label said *Conundrum,* which seemed like a sign— of what, I didn't yet know.

"Oh!" I said, just as he was about to pour. "I, um . . . I'd rather not."

He laughed and filled up his own glass instead. "After last time, I don't blame you."

We clinked glasses before we ate—my water glass to his wine. "To . . . better days?" Auggie suggested, and I smiled.

"So, Ben was onto me," Auggie said, setting down his wine.

I lost my smile, stopped chewing.

"Not that I wanted to buy you. But I did want to buy something." He picked up a limp asparagus spear with his fingers and waved it around thoughtfully. "Something I can't really explain. Something a little less tangible than *stuff*."

"Your soul," I said.

He blinked. "You really think I'm gonna die, don't you?"

"Well, we're all going to die."

Auggie nodded slowly, as his eyes drifted away from my own. "I think that...I have been unusually lucky. Sometimes I just want to say, 'Thanks.' To whoever. Or whatever." He looked at me again. "Maybe I didn't want to buy my soul. Maybe it was just a...donation."

"*Korban Todah,*" I said, recalling something I'd learned when I'd been pretending to be Jewish. "An offering of thanksgiving. In the Torah, most sacrifices are to make up for something you've done wrong. But *Korban Todah* is just to say thank you to God for all the joy and abundance."

"Well, I don't know about joy...but certainly abundance." Auggie laughed. He dropped the asparagus and reached for the wine again. "I guess if I'm dying, I better enjoy myself now, huh?"

"Can I have some of that?" I asked.

THE FOOD WAS AWFUL: the salmon tasted like the ocean floor, the asparagus was mushy, and the pesto was so kicky that my nostrils burned. Still, the dinner was perfect: flickering candlelight and Auggie's blue eyes and the knowledge that it all had been prepared just for me.

"So, why do you need money so badly?" he asked, after I'd told him the story of finding out that my inheritance was not actually mine.

"Things have just been...tight." It wasn't the time to review my lack of education, my single motherhood, or my driving need for health insurance.

He leaned on his elbow, with his chin resting in his hand. "What's this woman got against you?"

"Who, Christine?" I took another sip of wine and set down the glass. "She probably just wanted to make sure her family was taken care of. Or maybe she saw me as my

mother's daughter—the enemy." I shrugged and then confessed, "People say I look just like my mother."

His chin didn't move from his hand as he smiled. In fact,
Auggie studied me for so long that I had to look away. "Did
her cheeks turn as pink as yours do?" he asked.

DESSERT TURNED OUT TO be even easier than dinner: a small
dish arranged with Pim's dark chocolate cookies. "I love
these things," Auggie said, popping one in his mouth. He
grabbed the remainder of the Conundrum and led the way
into the wood-paneled library. "Figured you might want to
avoid the Great Room," he said with a laugh, as he sat down
on the burgundy sofa and patted the seat next to him. I hesitated, setting the plate of cookies on the coffee table before finally sitting down.

"I think I scared you the other night," Auggie said.

"No, you didn't."

He leaned toward me with a raised eyebrow. "Then why
are you still wearing that blanket?"

I laughed and let the pashmina slip off one of my shoulders.

"So, Di . . ." He grabbed a cookie and slumped back on the
sofa next to me. "I like you."

"I think I like you, too," I said slowly.

"But you're worried about your job. Would it be enough
to know that I'll take great care of you?" When I didn't answer right away, he turned toward me. "You're worried
about something else." A statement.

"I, um, might have this brain tumor thing."

He laughed. "Did you have a dream about that, too?"

I shook my head.

"Come on. Seriously?"

"Yeah, seriously." I drained the rest of my wineglass.

Pursing his lips, Auggie stared straight ahead for a moment. "So, aside from the fact that I'm your boss, and aside from the fact that you may or may not have a brain tumor, and aside from the fact that you're not attracted to me—"

"That's not true," I said.

"And that I'm ancient—"

"You're really not."

"And that you have a boyfriend—"

"I don't."

He smiled. "Well, then it seems to me, if we're both dying, then I can think of one thing that we should be doing right now."

My face and neck were growing warm. I let the pashmina fall onto the sofa cushion behind us. "What's that?"

He stood up. "Dancing!"

THE SOUND SYSTEM, IT turned out, had a pantry entirely to itself. I waited for Auggie to return but ten minutes later, when he hadn't come back, I went looking for him and found him in the closet, swearing under his breath and holding two remotes.

"Wow. What a collection," I said, admiring the walls of CDs, which were actually alphabetized, from Alanis Morissette to Depeche Mode to Led Zeppelin to Sting.

"Too...many...buttons..."

I stood on my tiptoes, reached over his shoulder, and pressed one of them. The black box came to life, green digital letters appearing on the front. He looked at me from the corner of his eye. "First my grill and now my sound system?"

"I can wait out there." I jerked my head behind me.

He swatted my butt on the way out the door.

*   *   *

WHEN THE MUSIC FINALLY began, I was standing in the middle of the marble floor, under the chandelier, thinking of Maria's first dance with Captain von Trapp on the patio, when she blushes for the first time. Except that Auggie hadn't picked a waltz or the paso doble or even a ballroom number. Instead it was the Barenaked Ladies, singing, "If I Had a Million Dollars."

I tilted my head back and laughed as he took my arm, sliding a hand around my waist. "You're funny," I said.

As he spun me around, we sang to each other in alternating choruses:

"I'd build a tree fort in a yard!"

"You could help, it wouldn't be that hard!"

We twirled, we dipped, we shimmied and grooved, laughing and stumbling. And when the song was over, we kept on going to the rest of the album: the silly songs, the fast ones, and the ones that called for unabashedly loud singing. I hadn't felt so carefree since . . . the moment I'd kissed Dave.

Auggie pulled me closer and belted out the words to "What a Good Boy" so unself-consciously that I knew he, too, must've woken up feeling scared and strange and wondering when things were ever going to change. He ran his fingers through my hair, singing of penance and temptation. When the song was over, Auggie put a hand up to my cheek and caressed it.

"I really want to kiss you again," he said, and then did, tenderly. His shoulders were not Dave's shoulders, and his arms were not Dave's arms, but he knew how to kiss. And when he scooped me up to carry me to his bedroom, I didn't do anything but marvel that he was capable of doing so.

"Not—over the—threshold," I said, moments later, when

he banged my legs into the wall, not once, but three times. Auggie tried again, this time smacking my head against the doorway.

"Jesus!" he said, laughing and staggering ahead, until he finally hoisted me onto the bed.

"You sure know how to make a girl feel like a railroad tie," I said.

"A beautiful railroad tie." Auggie kissed my lips and neck and then, before I knew it, pulled my shirt over my head. I got started on the buttons of his shirt, working as if they were a very complicated puzzle. *A conundrum.* Auggie yanked his shirt off before leaning me backward on the bed. I was surprised by the weight of his hips on top of me.

His hands felt good—he was a better masseuse than I was—and I closed my eyes and sighed. Maybe it was too late to say no. He'd picked me up, after all, made me dinner, danced with me, and given me the best night I could remember in a long time. Then I thought of the walkway outside, of the two figures of myself in Dave's eyes, and of him telling me that I could kill a man with my hands, such a strange and lovely compliment.

I opened my eyes. "I don't think we should sleep together."

"Relax," Auggie whispered.

I'd told Dave the same thing—to relax—when I'd almost ripped off his arm during the massage. "I like someone else," I blurted. I wasn't sure how I felt about Dave, but I knew I wanted to find out, knew that it wouldn't be an option if I slept with Auggie that night, and knew that such an awkward moment called for declarations.

Auggie tilted his head back and looked at me. "Di, sweetie, he's very protective of you. And he's even attracted to you. But he's never going to want you."

Ben. I thought of Alecia again. Was it better or worse to let Auggie believe it?

"It would be the perfect ending to the perfect night," he added, nuzzling me.

I hesitated another moment, wondering if I should go ahead just to please him, as a thank-you for pleasing me. Not for the dinner or the wine or even the attention. Just those moments of joy, when we were dancing and nothing else mattered. I reached up to stroke his hair when my hand went numb.

"Uh oh." I blinked one eye closed and then the other, realizing everything to the left of me had turned into darkness. "It's happening again."

"What's happening again?"

"My eye. I can't see out of my left eye. And my hand is numb." My heart suddenly thumped faster than my breath could keep up with. I scooted out from underneath him, climbed off the bed, and felt around the floor with my feet. My shirt had to be around here somewhere—and, for that matter, my bra. "I need to go to the nearest ER," I said, zipping up my jeans.

"Hold on, hold on." Auggie struggled to sit up. His hair was sticking straight up. "You're completely serious here? Because I was thinking...that you weren't."

EVEN BEFORE MY VISION came back—in the car, fifteen minutes later—I knew it was a migraine, the kind Holly had told me about, the kind without the headache. After all, she'd put me through the neurological tests; she'd looked at the back of my eye and said everything seemed okay. My father had once told me: "In the good old days, we didn't have all these tests. We just had the physical exam"—and I had passed. But at the moment, it seemed best not to downplay my symptoms, when Auggie was relying on them to restore his own ego: maybe I hadn't just changed my mind in the middle of things; maybe I'd been suffering from a legitimate health crisis. Most of the ride was spent in silence, other than Auggie's few, cheerful attempts at diagnosis.

"You're too young for mini-strokes. I bet it's MS."

We merged onto Route 28.

"Should I have given you an aspirin back there?"

"I already took one."

More silence. We turned onto Washington Boulevard.

"Is it okay that I'm not taking you to the *nearest* ER?" He exhaled noisily. "Because Jason works there, and I can't...I just can't..."

"It's okay. I'm not blind anymore."

"No? Well, good! *Phew!*" He glanced my way, must've caught me glaring. "Not good?"

"Are you ever going to talk to Jason?" I asked, folding my arms across my chest.

"About what?"

"Anything! He's your son. You don't even have the balls to walk into his ER—"

"After midnight with another young girl on my arm? No way. It'll just be more ammunition." He was probably right. I watched as he turned into the emergency vehicle lane outside of Shadyside Hospital.

"You should still call him."

"And you should go in there." He pointed to the ER. "I'll find a space and meet you inside."

"You know what? I'm okay now. And I live right there." I pointed to the awning across the street, Alecia's building. The rain had even stopped. "I left my insurance card in my cousin's apartment. She'll come back with me."

Auggie looked relieved. "Promise?"

I nodded, reached over, and gave his arm a squeeze before

I climbed out. He rolled down the window and called after me, "I didn't hear you promise!"

"I promise," I said, which wasn't quite a lie, but of course, it wasn't quite the truth, either. All I knew was that I felt fine right now—even good—and migraines, as Holly had told me, notoriously got better after lying in a dark room. *Sleep now,* I told myself. *Tomorrow, you'll know what to do.*

CHAPTER 28

Philadelphia

The first conscious thoughts that struck me the next morning were not of Auggie or even of Dave. Instead, it was Alecia's voice, replaying in my mind, over and over: *How stupid are you?*

Holly, no doubt, would agree. I'd actually called her the night before, despite that it was midnight, despite that I had an inkling of what she might say. What I wanted to hear was something reassuring—some tune about ocular migraines being scary but benign, in lieu of Auggie's song: "Hey, Hey, You're Dying." Instead, she yelled at me for not going to the ER and yelled at me for being in bed with Augustus in the first place. "What kind of a man says that he can't take you to the nearest ER because someone might recognize him?" Twelve hours later, it was an easy question to answer. From now on, the only guy I needed to think about was Max, who happened to be asleep on the futon next to me. I rubbed a crusty eye and blinked at my son: blond hair, long lashes, cherub cheeks. He was utter perfection—my one, lovely accomplishment. I couldn't help but say a little prayer: *Help me protect him. From life.*

I could hear Alecia in the kitchen, her spoon clinking against the bottom of her cereal bowl. For a brief second, I considered getting up to join her for breakfast—maybe even telling her about last night—but then I thought of our argument and shut my eyes again. The gloom felt so heavy, unless it was just the aftereffects of the Conundrum.

The next time I squinted awake, Alecia was standing over me. I'd been dreaming of Philadelphia—and my father.

"Di! *Hello?*" Alecia called, practically shaking me with her voice.

I raised my eyebrows, wishing they had pulleys to tug my eyes open.

"Holly called. She wanted to know if you were alive. I told her you were, but then I thought I should check to be sure." She sounded begrudging, as if she'd hoped for otherwise.

"I'm fine," I croaked, surprised by the sunlight in the room. It was dark in the dream, wintertime, and my father wore wool socks with his Birkenstocks, despite the falling snow. We crossed each other on a city sidewalk, and he didn't recognize me, even after I said hello.

"What happened last night?" Alecia asked, hands on her hips.

Rolling away from her, I realized my bed was empty. "Where's Max?"

"Watching TV."

Before I could ask if she meant *Sesame Street* or one of her favorites—*E: True Hollywood Story*—she folded her arms across her chest and demanded, "So, what's up with Dave the landscaper?"

"D-Dave the landscaper?" I stuttered, sitting up on my elbow. My head felt swirly.

"Take him to dinner yet?"

"Not . . . yet," I said, rubbing my temple, trying to come to.

"Well, maybe you should. Unless, of course, you only like pursuing other people's husbands—and fiancés," she added.

My chin jerked up. Her eyes were as narrow as knife blades; mine felt wider than saucers, possibly even wider than side salad plates. "I didn't—I'm not after—why the hell are we even talking about 'Dave the landscaper'?"

"He called."

I stared at her. "What did he want?"

"He was downstairs and wanted to come up." She shrugged. "I let him up."

That meant that in a matter of seconds, he would be seeing me in my tank top and underpants. I moved my feet to the floor and waited for the wave of nausea to roll off me. "In the future, you might try asking me if I'm accepting visitors," I muttered, steadying myself on the bed.

"In the future, you won't be living in my apartment," Alecia said, moving back toward the door.

I waved my finger in the air, opened my mouth to say something, and accidentally burped instead. It was not the comeback I'd been searching for, but it did manage to make Alecia whirl back around.

"Look, I'm sorry that Ben found out—but frankly, you should've told him yourself," I said, stumbling across the room. "He would've wanted a baby, with or without you." There was a rap on the front door to the apartment. Alecia glanced behind her and then back to me. "And just so you know, the idea of Ben in any romantic way kind of turns my stomach," I added, riffling through my suitcase of dirty clothes for a pair of pants.

"Then why didn't you want us to end up together?" Her voice was quiet.

It took me a moment to answer, only because it was the

truth, as much as I hated myself for it. "I want you both to be happy," I finally said, meeting her eyes.

"Whatever that means," she muttered.

"You know what it means, and you both deserve it."

"But not each other," Alecia said.

I looked back down at the ball of clothes in my hand.

"I thought so," she said.

I LET HER ANSWER the door. For one thing, I needed another second to get dressed and run a comb through my hair. For another, I really didn't want to see him. When I'd said what I'd said to Auggie, Dave was a concept, a *maybe someday,* an excuse. Besides, I was embarrassed. Facing him—after not sleeping with Auggie because of him—was like bumping into a co-worker at the water cooler after you've engaged in accidental dream sex. I didn't even know Dave, couldn't recall quite what he looked like, and couldn't remember anything about him except for the way his lips felt against mine.

"Dave the landscaper!" I heard Alecia announce, when she opened the door.

"Alecia the—hey!—*whoa!*—new hair! It looks great!"

Alecia crutched backward to let him in. "Tell that to my boss. He says I have to get a wig before he'll let me back on the news."

"Isn't that considered *hair*-assment? Sorry, bad joke," Dave added, even though Alecia was laughing as I walked into the living room. At the sight of him in his jeans and gray T-shirt, something sprung up inside me. *So, that's what you look like.* Dave noticed me in the same instant.

"Hey." He swallowed.

My wave was so uncoordinated that I reminded myself of a scarecrow. "Hey."

"You have a backhoe?" Max asked, jumping off the sofa.

"Not with me, buddy."

"You have a bad back?"

"My back feels great now, thanks to your mom."

"You mean in spite of…" I glanced at Alecia. "I gave him the worst back massage of his life."

Her eyebrows scrunched in confusion. "Who?"

Before I could explain, the phone started ringing. As Alecia left in search of the cordless, I felt strangely unprotected. "So, um, how'd you find me?"

"How do you think?" He chuckled. "Felt a little funny about having a thirteen-year-old kid do my legwork, but I guess Gusty's the reason you came over in the first place, right?"

"Right." My cheeks felt warm. Dave was still looking at me, but I was looking at Max.

"I need your hat," Max said, standing on his tiptoes.

Dave took off his baseball cap and put it on my son, who giggled. "By the way, your phone's right there." He pointed to the faux-distressed bookcases, whose artfully gouged wood by Pottery Barn craftsmen always struck me as absurd, when Alecia hated actual antiques.

Just as I swiped the cordless off the top shelf and saw the caller ID—"Omni William Penn"—Alecia called from the kitchen, "Don't pick up!"

"It's Aunt Maddie," I said, as my aunt's voice filled up the apartment. "Hello? Hello? Oh…maybe I missed it…I was waiting for the beep. Well, listen, Allie. Today's the day. Flying back to Portland. I am still hoping to see you. If you get this message before, say, lunchtime, why don't you head on over to the hotel?"

"Did you hear that?" I asked, after a full minute of silence. Aunt Maddie had hung up, and Alecia still hadn't appeared in the living room. "She still wants to see you."

"Stay out of it, Di," Alecia said, finally coming around the corner. Her eyes darted around until they landed on the coffee table, where her zebra-print purse lay. After fitting its strap over her shoulder, she replaced her crutches back under her arms and hobbled toward us. "Dave, lovely to see you."

"You're *going*?"

It must've been the panic in my voice that made Alecia smile—the first real one I'd seen since last night or, for that matter, since I'd left the apartment nearly two weeks before. "I have to find a wig," she said.

"But what about—Philadelphia?" I blurted. The idea seemed to form inside my mouth, just as I was uttering the words.

She shook her head blankly. "Philadelphia?"

"You were supposed to take Max and me to the bus station. Remember?" I was pleading with my eyes.

Her smile turned into a smirk. "Well, maybe Dave can take you."

"Sure." Dave shrugged. "I'm off today."

"Perfect!" Alecia decided. "Isn't that perfect, Di?"

As she moved toward the door, I considered sneaking my foot in front of one of her crutches. But Dave was still watching me, so I smiled back, instead. "It's perfect."

And just like that, it was decided: Max and I were leaving for Philadelphia. It was time to find out what really happened after I left without saying goodbye.

CHAPTER 29

Basic Dread

Later, Alecia told me that it must have been the wig that made her change her mind: She couldn't get past the idea that doing the news in disguise somehow seemed cowardly. Or it may have been Art's warning, as he'd made it implicitly clear that the only way he'd agree to her return was if she looked exactly the same as she always had—thin, blond, unbroken. Or maybe it was the nearly whimsical idea of losing her career altogether. "Facing basic dread makes you fearless," Ben had once said, a quote from *The Careerfree Life,* which she knew wasn't true. "Try waking your mother up for dinner and not knowing if she'll be dead or alive, that's basic dread," she told me. "It didn't make me fearless, it made me *mad*." And now Maddie had shown up and wanted... what, exactly? Forgiveness? A relationship? Alecia wasn't about to let her off so easy. She looked at her watch: two hours until her mother would be going back to Portland. *Two hours to give her a piece of my mind.*

Except that, by the time she'd driven downtown, attempted to parallel park six times before resorting to a garage, and crutched her way into the lobby of the Omni William Penn hotel, Alecia wasn't even mad any longer. Instead, there was something else turning over inside her, panic, alternating with hope. Hope that her car wouldn't be towed from the "compact only" lane, hope that Maddie hadn't already left for the airport, and panic that her mother might actually be there.

"Madeleine Linzer," the concierge repeated, after Alecia asked him to dial her room. "I'm afraid she's just checked out."

"Oh." The engine inside her stopped. So, that was it. Maddie was gone. At least Alecia would be able to say that she'd tried.

"But we've got her suitcase behind the desk, so she can't be far," he added, glancing up from his computer screen. "I think I saw her going toward the dining room. Just over there."

She thanked him and started crutching again, past the couches and grand piano, past a cluster of bellhops, and into the main restaurant, an ornate room with high ceilings, chandeliers, and white tablecloths. It was just after two o'clock, which was probably why there wasn't a hostess or a waiter to be found, and why nearly every table was empty, except for one.

"Mom!" Alecia called with a wave of her splinted wrist. At least her injuries were mostly hidden beneath a bulky sweater, the widest khaki pants that she owned, and a coat.

If Maddie was surprised to see that she was on crutches, or even hurt by the things Alecia had said in the lobby of WTAE, her face didn't show it. Instead, the smile wrinkles were back. Maddie didn't jump up from her seat, but she did put down her pencil and wave her over. "Oh, Allie!" she exclaimed, as Alecia neared the table. "New hairdo! I love it!"

"Thanks." Alecia touched her hair, which once again surprised her when it stopped at the nape of her neck.

"You've got a wonderfully shaped skull." Maddie cocked her head to the side, studying her, as she struggled to sit down without tripping over the crutches. "I'm wondering who you got that from."

"Dad," Alecia said, just to make her stop staring.

"I don't know. Your grandma Hazel had a pretty great head. That's one of the few things that I remember. She really didn't need hair. What's with the crutches?"

"I fell."

"Ah—a klutz, huh? You definitely got that from my side." Maddie nodded as if to herself and then swiveled around in her seat. "Let me find Jimmy. He's my new buddy, since I've been hanging out in this dining room all week. Pretty swanky, huh? Unfortunately they only serve Starbucks, but, hey, what're you gonna do?"

Alecia glanced around and lowered her voice. "Isn't the restaurant closed?"

"Nah. It's a hotel. They'll serve you whenever. Hey! Jimmy!" Maddie suddenly bellowed, as a man appeared over by the empty buffet table, fifty feet away. "This is the girl I was telling you about," she added, as he neared them, holding a pitcher of water.

"Your mother is very proud of you," he said, turning over a water glass to fill it. He wore a tuxedo, and his black hair was slicked back from his forehead. He looked like he belonged in a black-and-white movie.

"Thank you," she replied, her hand flying up to touch her hair again.

"Should I bring you a menu?" Jimmy asked.

"Oh, no. Just a cup of coffee. Or no—tea. Earl Grey tea,"

she decided. She unzipped her jacket and shrugged her shoulders out of it.

"I watched you on the news every night last week," Maddie said, once Jimmy was gone. "You were incredible. Then what happened? They brought in this automaton who smiled when she was talking about a father who died trying to rescue his drowning daughter."

"It was my hair. They're not sure they want me back." Even as Alecia said it, she realized that wasn't true. She wasn't sure she wanted herself back. And maybe that included her job.

"Oh, come on. You look great!" Maddie leaned forward. "Is that Mazy woman as much of a bitch as she looks like on screen?"

"She can be." Alecia hesitated. "But I think she...has her reasons."

"She has her reasons?" Maddie sat back in her seat again and shook her head. "Boy, you're nice. How'd you turn out nice?"

Alecia blinked. "*Nice* is generally not a word associated with me, Mother," she finally said.

Maddie tilted her head back and laughed loudly. "Oh, Allie, forget about what everyone thinks."

"That's what I've been trying to do," she said, surprised by the tears that suddenly pricked her eyes.

"You, unfortunately, were blessed with your father's stubbornness and my...irritability. I felt sad sometimes, looking at you. It was like looking at me."

"Great." Alecia fumbled around inside her purse trying to find her sunglasses. "I made you sad." Jimmy was coming back. She'd only ordered tea, but for some reason he was carrying a whole tray—the pot, the cup, the creamer, the sugar, five sliced lemons, and a box containing a selection of twenty teas.

Maddie, of course, talked as though he wasn't even there.

"Oh, stop. You're taking it the wrong way. I just thought you might struggle more. But I hoped you wouldn't."

"Earl Grey," Alecia said loudly, hoping to signal a silence.

"You remind me of me with my own mother," Maddie went on, as Jimmy prepared her teapot with the right bag. "Everything your uncle Gabe did made him more perfect. Everything I did was wrong. She called me Mad Dog. He was the Good Eater."

"Mother, will you please stop talking?" Alecia whispered, once Jimmy had finally left them alone to steep.

Maddie looked confused. "O...*kay*."

"You don't talk when the waiter is around! Everyone knows that!"

Her eyes darted back and forth. "But...he's gone now."

"Yes, now he's gone. Before he wasn't. *Jimmy* doesn't need to know about the details of your dysfunctional upbringing. Or mine, for that matter!"

"Allie, I'm leaving for the airport in..." Maddie checked her watch. "Twenty minutes. I have a lot to say. Besides, Jimmy's my bud. I've spent a week in this dining room waiting for you."

"You didn't have to," Alecia mumbled, pouring her tea. It wasn't ready yet. The water was clear. Maybe she would eat one of the lemons, instead, something that used to make Ben shudder. "You could've left, you know."

Maddie reached for a lemon. Alecia blinked, watching her mother peel and eat it, like it was an orange.

"It was good to be back. I did a little exploring. Got out to the cemetery to see where Grandma and Grandpa were buried. Then I went to our old house in Point Breeze. Very depressing. But my therapist said it would be a good idea."

"Why was Grandma such 'an awful mother'?" Alecia

asked, transferring the tea bag from the pot to her own cup of hot water.

Maddie's eyes grew larger. "When did I say that?"

"You wrote it. In your journal."

"Well, it wasn't easy, living with Mother. She was very dramatic, always screaming and yelling and throwing things. Histrionic, Gabe called her, once he got a degree. She used to drive people away by just insisting they were out to do her in. I was one of those people." Maddie held up a finger. "And in the case of him and me, she really did love Gabe more. She told me so."

"But Dad always said how proud your mother was of you for publishing that book of poetry when you were, like, ten."

"I was sixteen. And Mother edited most of them. They weren't very good. She always wanted everything in iambic pentameter. I hated iambic pentameter."

"I forgot she taught English," Alecia said thoughtfully, reaching for a packet of sugar. "But you wanted to make amends with her, right? And you couldn't."

Maddie stared at her. "I really kept a journal? It's so strange all the years the alcohol just took off me. Sometimes I forget where I am."

"It had about two entries in it. About how much you loathed my father, and how much you loved him."

Maddie laughed. "That pretty much sums us up, doesn't it?"

"Dad cheated on you. Or at least, you said so in one of your entries."

"Well, shit, do you blame him?" Maddie reached for another lemon. "It's been suggested to me that I may have driven your father to philandering when I first assaulted your babysitter."

Alecia coughed on a mouthful of tea. "Who, Veronique?"

"Before that one. The German, Hilda. In retrospect, your father wouldn't have gone near her with a ten-foot pole. Too big-boned."

"God, Mom." So, this must've been what her father was talking about when he mentioned Maddie's "first episode." How strange to imagine they'd stayed together after that. She thought of bringing Ben home for the first time, when her father begged her not to marry him, or at least, never to purchase real estate as a couple. "Did Dad's parents ever say that you weren't right for each other? That you'd make an odd couple?"

Maddie shook her head. "They liked me. They thought I was smart—Frank showed them my book of poetry. They all thought the iambic pentameter was brilliant. And back then, I looked like you, kiddo. Gorgeous, I mean."

"So, why did you—what happened to make you—what happened?" Alecia asked, finally meeting Maddie's gaze. She was surprised to find that her mother's eyes were a purplish-gray. Why didn't she know that before?

"I got sick. And no one could deal with me. Including me."

"How many years were you drinking?"

"Well…I started when you were about six and got clean about two years ago. I had a little relapse again, when my partner broke up with me."

"Six?" Alecia repeated. "Was I really so terrible at the age of six?"

"Terrible?" Maddie's eyebrows went up. "You were never terrible, Allie. I didn't drink because of you. I drank because of me."

"So, why'd you stop?"

Maddie shrugged. "No real reason."

"I mean, did you drive drunk and run over a small child?

Was your license revoked? Did someone you love beg you to quit?"

Maddie shook her head. "I just got tired. After twenty-some years, I had to put down a lot of vodka in a day just to function. One day, I woke up, and didn't feel like doing it anymore. Kind of the way I felt about Frank, when I left. I just...didn't feel like being there anymore. And I drove the car until I didn't feel like driving anymore, which is how I ended up in Portland. It's a nice city. Rains too much, but nice."

Alecia thought of her job, of fighting for so long and waking up and not caring anymore. Maybe that was how Ben felt about her: that she was a battle that he didn't have the energy to fight anymore. "Are you alone out there in Portland?" she finally asked.

"I had a partner. Until recently." Maddie sighed. "I don't blame her, really. I probably shouldn't live with anyone."

"What about Aunt Roxanne?"

Maddie smiled wistfully. "She was really the only friend I ever had." She looked at Alecia. "I probably should've told Gabe where they went."

Alecia sputtered again and set down her cup. "You *knew*?"

Maddie nodded. "I wanted to protect her, the same way you wanted to protect Di." Maddie picked up her briefcase off the floor and placed a sheaf of papers inside. "It has been suggested to me that maybe I also wanted to get even with my big brother. For not protecting me." Alecia must've looked confused, because Maddie explained, "He was always putting me in the hospital, always acting like another one of the bad guys—one of the doctors." Maddie glanced at her watch. "I really should get going. Don't want to miss my plane."

Alecia reached for her purse. "Oh, let me just—"

"Please, Allie." Maddie put a hand on her arm. "I can afford a cup of tea."

Out in the lobby, Alecia waited for Maddie to retrieve her suitcase from the concierge. "Well, I guess this is it," she said, meeting her near the revolving door with a bellhop in tow.

"I'm sorry, Mom," Alecia said quietly, folding her arms across her chest.

"Sorry for what?"

She shrugged. "For not coming earlier."

"That's okay. It was nice to get out of Portland, though I can't say the weather here is any better!" Maddie laughed and then slapped herself on the head. "I forgot—I wrote something down for you." She fumbled in her leather satchel until she came up with an envelope.

"One of your poems?"

She shook her head. "They left along with my memory. It's W. D. Snodgrass—*Heart's Needle*." Then she grabbed Alecia in a hug, pinning her arms across her chest. This time, Alecia didn't even care that it was in front of the bellhop. "I'm glad I saw you again," Maddie said quietly. "I wanted to see if you turned out all right. And you did."

Outside the hotel, Alecia's breath hung in the air and for a moment, all she could do was stand and watch it. Even after her mother's cab had pulled away, Alecia didn't move, not to shiver and not to walk toward her car.

The envelope her mother gave her was still in her hand, and she took off her splint to rip it open. Inside, the half-smudged words on the page were written in Maddie's tremulous handwriting, but Alecia could still make them out.

> Love's wishbone, child, although I've gone
> As men must and let you be drawn
>   Off to appease another,
> It may help that a Chinese play

> Or Solomon himself might say
> I am your real mother.

She stared for a moment and then folded it back into the coat pocket. *Move on,* something said inside her, and she took the next step.

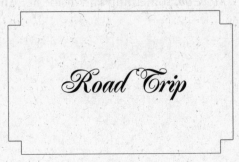

CHAPTER 30

Road Trip

An hour after our impromptu decision to leave, I'd managed to pack a diaper bag and a duffel, use Alecia's computer to confirm the Greyhound bus schedule, and even take a shower. If Dave was surprised that we were completely unprepared for our trip, he never showed it.

"Do you know how to get to the bus station?" I asked, watching him consult a map as we sat in his Chevy Impala at a red light. Max was in the backseat, happily calling out the myriad construction vehicles on the median strip.

"Sure. But Philadelphia..."

"You can't take us all the way there! You have to work!"

"I'm the boss, remember?" He tossed the map aside as the light turned green. "I can take off whenever I want. Besides, they'll be fine on their own for another day."

"But it's five hours each way. I can't—I don't..." I couldn't let him down, the same way I'd let Auggie down. I didn't want to take advantage of him. "The other day—at your house . . . ? I just got carried away."

"It's cool. Really." He grinned, sneaking a glance from the road. "Go with that."

"But what if . . . I'm not here for romantic purposes?"

Dave looked amused. "On earth or in my car?"

"Either. Both."

He laid a gentle hand on my knee and said, "Then I have ten hours to convince you otherwise."

WE WERE ON THE turnpike, hurtling down the road toward Harrisburg, when Dave asked, "Your dad's widow—she got any idea that you're coming?"

I shook my head.

"Well, you got a cell phone, right? Give the lady a call! Don't look so scared," he added with a laugh. "It's not going to be any easier, showing up in person. Besides, I'm not driving ten hours for someone who might be out of town." He jostled my leg again. "Even for you."

It wasn't just the idea of calling Christine making me anxious, it was the reminder that the cell phone in my pocket belonged to Auggie. What if he called to make sure I'd gone to the ER last night—or apologize? What if he called to ask if I was still planning to teach him how to cook? Gusty would only be at his mother's for the rest of the week, which meant that as soon as I returned from Philly, I had some nanny hunting to do.

Slowly, I opened the lid of my phone and dialed the number that I'd carried in my head for sixteen years, through fourteen countries. The one time I'd used it—at a phone booth in Eragny-Oise, France—my father had answered. That was the last time I'd heard his voice.

"Hello?" a deep voice said presently, and I blinked. It never occurred to me that in the two years since my father's death, Christine might have remarried, and I felt oddly let down.

My throat seemed to seize up, making me choke on the words: "Is—Christine—home?"

"Sophie?" the man asked, in a voice that suggested Little Miss Tongue Ring might have skipped curfew last night.

"Um, no. This is Di. Di Linzer." I waited.

"Oh, I'm sorry," he said, and he did sound sorry. "Christine isn't here right now."

"Will she be home"—I glanced at my watch and added five hours—"around five o'clock?"

There was a pause. "Who did you say this is?"

"Di Linzer."

More silence, until finally: "Oh, *wow*. Okay. Right." He sounded baffled. "She will be—yes. Can I…take your number?"

"Just ask her not to go out around five o'clock."

"So, how long has it been since you've seen your step-mom?" Dave asked, once I'd said goodbye and snapped the phone shut.

Stepmom. I'd only been introduced to my father's wife a couple of times and had certainly never considered her to be more than an interloper. Maybe I should've given her a chance, it occurred to me now.

"Since I got back to the States, I've been chasing this—dream of my father," I confessed. "But she's the one who knew him best. She has all the memories I'm looking for."

DAVE DROVE A LOT faster than a Greyhound bus. He drove a lot faster than anyone else on the road. It was two o'clock and we were already in Harrisburg, an hour and a half outside of the city. We stopped for milkshakes and chicken nuggets—our second bathroom break—and pressed on going ninety miles per hour.

"So, why aren't you dating anyone?" I asked, stealing one of his fries.

He smiled at me. "Good timing, I guess."

"More chicken?" Max asked from the backseat, and, forgetting to insist on the magic word, I handed him another nugget.

"When was your last girlfriend?"

"I dunno. Maybe...two months ago?"

I sat forward. "You mean, like, July?"

"Might've been August. End of August."

A week or two before he met me, or at least, saw me at a distance. "How long were you together?"

"'Bout a month. It wasn't anything serious." Dave shrugged. "I tend to end things quickly if I know it's going nowhere. I figure, 'Why waste the time?'" He stepped on the gas and passed a truck as if it were parked. "My mom thinks I'm too hard on people. She says no one gets a second chance."

"So, what was wrong with your last girlfriend?"

"Oh..." He hesitated. "She had these long, fake nails that would scratch up my back."

I looked at my own ugly, cracked nails and realized with some dismay that I didn't want to hear about anyone else touching Dave's back. *Now that we've kissed, is this a date?* I suddenly wondered. Out the windshield, cars approached and then slipped behind us as Dave zipped by.

"What about you—and 'Auggie'?" Dave asked. I turned and stared at him, but he kept looking at the road. "Your cousin—when I called up from the lobby—she asked if I was

Auggie. Kinda worried me for a second," he added. "Don't think I could go for a girl who'd want a guy like him."

I shook my head. "Nothing's going on. I . . . no longer work there."

Dave looked startled. "Since when?"

"This minute," I stammered, realizing this must be true. How could I go back?

"What happened—he find a cook cuter than you?"

I felt my cheeks flush. *So, it was a date.* "Something like that."

IT WAS FOUR O'CLOCK when Dave laid a hand on my shoulder. I opened my eyes, realizing we were on the outskirts of Philly, on Kelly Drive, which snaked alongside the Schuylkill River.

"Oh, my God. I fell asleep!"

"Relax. Max has been entertaining me. He's pointed out every dump truck for the last three hundred miles."

"Look, Mama, boats!" Max said, pointing at the crew teams in their floating shells.

"I see, Boo." I turned to Dave. "I can't believe I'm really here."

"That makes two of us." He laughed. "So, what's the plan?"

"Locust Street. Center City." I picked the map up off the floor to reorient myself.

"I mean, when we get there. You want Max and me to disappear for a while? Or just me?"

"I hadn't really thought that far ahead."

"Well, start thinking, lady."

As we navigated through town, I couldn't help thinking how strange it was that my father had lived in the city for fifteen years before his death. It was hard to imagine him being comfortable in a place without lawns and garages and trees, without more than a sliver of sky showing itself between the buildings. Where was the wood?

"Look, Max, a giant clothespin!" I said, tapping on the window when we passed it.

"Rutabaga stuffed with clothespins," Max said and then laughed hysterically.

"Here we go," Dave said, as we circled the block of Locust Street that contained my father's apartment. *Christine's apartment.*

"Get out now?" Max asked, kicking the back of my seat.

"In a minute, Boo." He'd been so good the whole way, and now, at the sight of the sidewalk, he was straining against his car seat, trying to eject himself. I, on the other hand, was suddenly ready to turn around and go home. Christine had convinced my father to move on—what could she possibly have to say to me that I didn't already know? Had I come all this way to put myself through more disappointment?

Dave put the car in park, leaned back in his seat, and stared at me. He had the kindest green eyes that took me back to the moment the other day, before I'd gone blind in Auggie's house, when Dave had patted the bed next to him and said, *Take a rest.* That's what I wanted to do right now. *Rest.*

"So, I guess if Max is going with you, I'm on my own, eh?" Dave asked.

I reached over and took his hand, the one that had given me no less than thirty reassuring pats this trip, and kissed it.

"No, really, it's cool. Get myself a cheesesteak."

I pressed his palm to my cheek and closed my eyes.

"I don't know how to break it to you," he said, "but I might not be here for romantic purposes."

I opened my eyes. He was grinning at me.

"Uppy!" Max yelled from the backseat.

"You're stalling, lady." At least he caressed my cheek when he said it.

"I'm kind of scared."

"I'm kind of sensing that. Or, at least, my wrist is."

I let go.

"Look, Mama!" Max held up his buckles, which he'd un-clipped. "I get out now?"

Dave shrugged. "Max is ready."

I sighed and then inhaled again. "Will you come?"

"Just waiting for you to ask."

THE MARBLE LOBBY, WITH its circular fountain and plush, green sofas, looked more like an ad agency or a law firm than an apartment building. Behind the security desk three uniformed men were standing guard, one of whom made me sign in and show my driver's license before he'd even call up to Christine's apartment to announce our presence. In the elevator, I let Max push the buttons, and then we rode the twenty-nine floors up to where my father used to live.

Christine, like the lobby, was equally modern. I had re-membered her as hopelessly ordinary compared to my mother; Roxanne was striking with her black hair and pale blue eyes. Christine, on the other hand, was short, had dirty-blond hair, a long face, and lifeless brown eyes that were only appealing when she smiled because then her cheeks hid most of them.

But when Christine opened the door, I was struck by what a beautiful middle-aged woman she'd become. Still petite, her hair was now highlighted, and the skin on her face glowed, as if she got regular chemical peels. There wasn't an age spot or a freckle to mar her complexion. Her smile, which in my memory had bordered on sickening, was warm and welcoming.

"Di? It's really you!" Christine said, pulling me into a hug. "Gosh, you're so tall! Last time I saw you, you were . . ."

"Tall," I finished.

Christine nodded and laughed and then held out a hand to Dave. "I'm Christine."

"Dave."

"Look at the planes!" Max stood over by the window, in the hall.

"That's my son, Max," I said, running to grab him. Of course, he had to embarrass me by screaming, making his legs go limp, and falling onto the floor.

"Max, the view is even better inside my apartment. You can see lots of planes, and helicopters and sailboats, too," Christine said, stooping down.

Max lifted his head and smiled. "Backhoes?"

"I bet we can even see some backhoes from up here," Christine said with a smile.

No wonder my father fell in love with you, I thought.

SHE GAVE US A tour of the place, which was far more elegant than our house in Highland Park had been. The living room had Persian rugs and Queen Anne furniture, the dining room had a chandelier, and the kitchen floors were marble. There was no sign of the man who'd answered the phone. I couldn't begin to imagine my father living here. Where would he have done his woodworking? Did she make him leave his Birkenstocks by the front door? "Gabe never wanted to move," Christine said, leading us into a glassed-in sitting room overlooking the city.

"With a view like this?" Dave said. "No wonder."

"It wasn't the view. He was waiting for Di to come back. Here, honey," Christine added, handing Max a Thomas the

Tank Engine piece. "It belongs to one of the women in my book club, who brings her baby when she comes. She left it here last time." She laughed when Max chucked it across the room, and it hit a plant. "Wow! Good arm!"

"Max, no throwing inside! You know better!"

"Come here, buddy. Let's see if we can find a crane from where we are," Dave said, picking him up and taking him to the window.

"I don't have much here in the way of food. Would anyone like tea or coffee or . . . ?"

"Coffee, if you've got it," Dave said, from the window.

"Let me help." I put my hands in my pockets and followed Christine through the living room toward the kitchen. *I would've grown up here. This would have been my kitchen. I would've gone to private school and college. I would've gotten a good job.*

"I wish I had known you were coming. Kurt said you might be calling at five o'clock. I never imagined that you were actually in Philadelphia." Christine put on a pot of tea and then moved to the coffee machine and filled the pitcher with water. "Believe me, this was not how either of us imagined your homecoming."

"Us," I repeated.

"Your father and I! He wanted a big party. Cake. Balloons. Lots of food." She sighed as she spooned coffee into the filter.

"I'm sorry about what happened to Dad."

Christine finished measuring out the coffee before she finally answered. "It was . . . horrific and devastating and so unnecessary. I'm only starting to feel like a human being again." She added, like a confession, "Kurt and I met at a bereavement group."

"He sounded nice on the phone." I glanced down at my

hands, folded on the table. "My mother died a year ago of cancer. Six months after Dad."

"Oh, dear. I hope she didn't suffer?" Christine asked, and I heard in her voice the unspoken *As much as we did when you left*. But no, I was imagining things: Christine's face was appropriately concerned.

Still, I answered carefully. "It wasn't easy."

"How did you hear about Gabe's death?" Christine asked.

"Alecia."

"But where were you all those years?" she asked, preparing a tray with teacups and cream and sugar.

"All over the place. England, mostly."

"How odd. We went to England for our ten-year anniversary trip. We were so close to you."

"Well, we moved sixteen times."

"It must've been hard for you, growing up that way."

I shrugged, not liking the pity on Christine's face. "I got used to it."

"Did you ever consider calling us?"

Us, again. Hadn't Dad ever told her about my one and only collect call? For as excited as he'd been about the new baby, he sounded equally relieved that I was alive. "I didn't want my mom to go to jail."

"It would've been up to the state to prosecute, not your father. He was a very forgiving man. I don't think you remember that side of him."

"My mother—she wasn't a very forgiving person. But, in the end, she forgave him." Christine stopped pouring the coffee and stared at me in confusion. "For falling in love with you."

Christine put the pot down on the counter, without even a hot plate. Her hand was shaking, I noticed, but when she replied, her voice didn't. "Your mother was the reason they broke up. It was her fault. Not Gabe's—and certainly not mine."

"She made a mistake," I said, my mother's words. "And Dad was going to make sure I couldn't see her again because of it."

"She made out with his sister. Big mistake."

I stared at her, shocked. "My mother—and Maddie?"

Her hand flew up to her mouth. "Did you not know?"

"I thought . . . there was the affair . . . with this British actor." *Clyde Johnson.* Or at least, I'd always suspected one, given how readily he took us in when we first ran away to England.

"There was that, too, the year before. Your father had forgiven her once for her infidelity. He'd pretty much had enough at that point. Had enough of both of them, for that matter . . ."

"Oh, my God," I whispered.

She sighed as she sank into the seat next to me. "I'm sorry it came out this way. I assumed you knew."

Dave appeared holding Max's hand. "We're in need of a potty."

WE SETTLED ONTO THE wicker furniture back in the sitting room, though I was having trouble tasting my cup of tea, much less enjoying the view. It seemed hard to focus on anything except the idea of my mother and Aunt Maddie. How many years had my mother minimized her role in the end of my parents' marriage? "It was just a kiss. Well, French!"

"You okay?" Dave whispered, and numbly, I nodded.

Down below, tugboats moved across the Schuylkill River, while overhead, airplanes circled for landing. Thankfully, Max had found a measuring tape in the pocket of Dave's down vest and was entertaining himself by pretending to measure everything in the room.

I looked over and caught Christine glancing at her watch. "Sorry," she said sheepishly. "I have to run off to give a lecture in a little while—educating doctors on the shingles vaccine. You could come, if you like."

"I—don't think so," I said quickly. "We have to—um . . ." I looked at Dave.

"Well, I work tomorrow," he said. "So, we need to get back to Pittsburgh tonight."

Christine smiled as she looked back and forth between us. "How long have you two been married?"

"Oh, we're—"

"Two days," Dave said.

"Not much of a honeymoon!" Christine said with a laugh.

"We're saving up for later," Dave said, looking at me.

"I almost forgot! Your presents!" she suddenly said, slapping her thigh.

"Presents?"

"For the first few years, Gabe bought you a gift every birthday," she explained, leading the way across the apartment. "After a while, he decided it was masochistic to go shopping for you, when it seemed you were never coming back. But he would never let me donate these to Goodwill." In the front hall, Christine stopped and opened a closet door, ignoring the plethora of objects that rained down around us: a tennis racket, a pile of hats, a walking stick . . .

"Except for one time, he just broke down and put them all in the trash. But I saved them," Christine went on, as she pushed aside some coats and stooped to the floor of the closet. "And after he died, I was cleaning out his things, and I almost gave them away, but I couldn't. I knew you'd be back someday."

The hall closet, filled with mismatched junk of every kind, was like a space capsule from our old house in Highland Park. It even smelled the same—something I couldn't quite identify. *Dad.*

"Let's hope you two have girls someday, because I think he set aside a Barbie doll for every year you were missing," Christine added, handing me a green garbage bag filled with gifts. I felt the heft of the bag and froze for just a second, realizing that this was it: I'd come all this way for something, and I was about to be sent on my way with the door prize.

"Presents!" Max said, lunging for the bag.

"Was Dad angry with me for leaving?" I blurted. "Is that why he never came after me?"

"Come here, Max. Let's go measure the kitchen," Dave said, scooping him up.

Christine's eyebrows furrowed as she looked at me. "Oh, Di, he tried. We sank loads of money into a private detective, who traveled around Europe—twice—and always came up empty."

"It wasn't like we were living in a cave in Afghanistan," I said.

"He had Sophie to care for, by then. They really had quite a strong relationship. I think, in some ways, she saved him after you disappeared."

"Well, that's good." Something was tugging at me, behind my eyes. Something much more insidious than pain. "Did he ever . . . wonder why I never called again?"

"I think he just assumed that you were okay. Because if you weren't, you'd have picked up the phone." Suddenly, Christine snapped her fingers. "I still have your composition book somewhere! Some word assignment you'd written for your teacher? The police confiscated it, but then returned it to your father. He hung on to it for years." She puckered her lips, squinted, and then, a moment later, snapped her fingers again. "Sophie's room! Of course. I moved Gabe's filing cabinet in there—I just—don't know what kind of state she left things in." Christine seemed relieved as we left the hall closet behind. "I've had to ground her a lot this year. Her grades were always so good. She wanted to be a doctor, like Gabe. Instead, she's found this boyfriend. And she hates Kurt, of course. Hates anyone who isn't her father." Christine sighed and opened the door. The room was a disaster: clothes piled on every surface, posters on the wall showing bands that I had never heard of. But it was the wardrobe that took my breath away. *My wardrobe.*

"He—Dad and I—we made this together. Back in Pittsburgh." My voice was a hoarse whisper. I held a hand up to my forehead. I felt so strange. Maybe I was going to faint. *Or throw up. Or sob.* Woozily, I reached out my fingers to touch the wood. I wished she would leave me alone so I could lay my head against the door, and run my hands across the grain and inhale the cedar inside. I hesitated and looked back. "Can I . . . ?"

"Oh, sure. Look around," Christine said, moving toward the filing cabinet in the corner of the room.

I opened the door to the wardrobe and found the inscription: *Di Linzer, May 5, 1986.* "Oh!" It was the day we'd left, carved into the wood, like a death date.

Christine's face was curious until she saw what I was looking at. "Yes, we . . . never noticed it when we gave the wardrobe to Sophie. She found the carving in the third grade and became convinced you were haunting her."

"She must've felt that way her whole life."

"Oh, no . . . well . . . maybe a little." Christine leaned against the cabinet with a small sigh. "We were all a little haunted by you, Di. A child disappears—even one that you never really knew—you just can't forget."

The feeling behind my eyes was getting stronger now,

making me squint. It was grief, trapped inside me, and if I could only cry, the pressure would go away. But not in front of Christine.

"Here we go." She pulled a composition book out of the file cabinet. "Your old journal. You might as well take it with you."

IN THE ELEVATOR, MAX pushed the buttons from the fifth floor to the lobby before Dave could stop him.

"Feelin' okay, lady?"

I rubbed my forehead as we started to descend. "Yeah, fine. Just this…feeling…in my head." I glanced at him. "I'm fine."

"You sure?"

I shook my head and stared at the floor counter as we dropped. "I'm fine."

CHAPTER 31

Emergency Room

It was a strange, little miracle, my cousin told me later: just a few hours after leaving Maddie behind, Alecia's nausea lifted, and the fog that had settled over her of late seemed profoundly absent. For the first time in the last six weeks, she felt alert—and hungry. Could forgiveness make you see clearly, she wondered, or was she just no longer pregnant? And had she really forgiven Maddie? *Maybe you've finally forgiven yourself,* Pastor Nate would say, an idea that puzzled Alecia as she navigated her car through the McDonald's parking lot. After all, Alecia had only lied to protect me, while I had practically admitted that I'd hoped Alecia's life would come crashing down. If she didn't already know how much Mazy Roberts loathed me, Alecia would've imagined we'd conspired together to make her fail.

She looked at the time on the dashboard: five-fifteen P.M., forty-five minutes before showtime. When she'd called Art to let him know that she was feeling better, he'd already heard from Carol, the cameraman's wife, that Alecia had never shown up at the salon for her private wig-fitting. "Why don't you take another few days to rest up?"

"I got a haircut, Art, not an appendectomy," she replied.

"You broke your arm, for God's sakes! Take time to heal."

A horn blasted, making her jump. Alecia adjusted her rearview mirror and saw a rotund man, red-faced and grimacing at her from the front seat of his SUV. "Easy, Big Mack. The food's not going anywhere," she muttered, turning back to study the drive-through menu. "I'll have a—a McDLT sandwich!" she blurted, resorting to the last advertising gimmick that she could recall. The menu was still silent. Behind her, Big Mack honked again. "A Big Mac and fries?" she tried. "And a Diet Coke—no! A vanilla milkshake!" This time the menu understood. Alecia was invited to pull around.

After paying at the first window and retrieving her bag at the second, Alecia slid into a parking space to eat her sandwich. She could just imagine Ben laughing at her. A *"McDLT—the hot stays hot and the cool stays cool"? That was 1985! When was the last time you've actually eaten a French fry?* The answer was somewhere in the ballpark of sixteen years before—before the Vera Wang wedding dress and certainly before her life on TV. It was strange how detached she felt from it all now, Alecia mused, as the salt from her first fry seeped into her tongue and made her salivate for more. She took a drag on her milkshake straw and groaned. *Orgasmic— no!—healing.* The milkshake was healing her. What did it matter if Heidi got her dream job when it wasn't even her own dream to begin with?

But it was, her father protested in her mind. *I encouraged you to have a career, and this was the one you picked. You are where you are as a result of the choices you've made, not me.*

Slowly, Alecia put down her cup and peered around the

parking lot. Could that be the truth? Was she entirely responsible for her own decisions? Could she be the only one who'd practiced sabotage—on herself? She thought of the last thing Art had said to her: "Heidi's got everything under control—she's handling the pressure just fine." As if Alecia had lost it: Ben, her father, her job, her best friend—"That would be you, Di!" she later snapped at my confusion—her lovely long hair, her mind.... Could she really step aside and let Big Head Heidi take everything?

Alecia looked at the clock again: too late to make the six o'clock news, but still enough time to make it to Carol's salon before it closed. Maybe she'd pick out something becoming, something blond and banged and even a little retro. Then she'd call Art to tell him she'd do the eleven o'clock. Better yet, she'd just show up.

As SOON AS SHE saw Mazy Roberts looming behind the news desk, bright lights capturing every nuance of her disgust, Alecia knew it was a risk to have come to work that night after all.

"What happened to the wig?" Mazy asked, watching Alecia limp across the room and into her seat. The clock on the far wall read ten-thirty.

"Carol wouldn't give me one—she loves my new look," Alecia lied, leaning her crutches against the desk. In actuality, she'd decided to forgo the salon stop altogether: Jeff had said she looked like Audrey Hepburn and that had to count for something. "Sorry I'm late, but I thought it was better than not showing up at all." She knew, suddenly, that this was not the case. Now that she'd marched in—well, lurched in—to Art's office and told him she was there to perform the job he'd promised her, now that she'd insisted Heidi be removed for the night and possibly forever, and now that she'd finally won the spot, it was suddenly clear that she'd claimed a position she didn't really want to be in: Becoming the Next Mazy Roberts. And while Alecia was pleased by how quickly Art had caved under her pressure—the words *legal action* seemed to soften him considerably—she was equally unsettled by the way Heidi's moon face collapsed as she grabbed her purse and left. What had Alecia hoped to prove? What had inspired her to come tonight but a French fry–induced fugue that she'd confused for a revelation?

"Oh, come on," Mazy snapped. "Heidi was doing a fine job." Then, as if Alecia had walked out to the stage pushing a bureau, Mazy called out, "We're gonna need some people down here to take away these crutches!"

"It's just the voice-over, Mazy. No one can see them on audio." Alecia put in her earpiece as Rich scurried out to the desk shuffling his script. Rich was never late unless there was a football game in progress.

"Whoa, Alecia!" he said, pulling out his chair. "Still not used to the new 'do. Reminds me of that chick from the movie, who blows all that shit up—"

"Natalie Portman," Jeff said in her earpiece.

"Can we get started, please?" Mazy asked, and Alecia listened as Jeff cued up the opening bars of the WTAE theme song. Just then, from somewhere on the floor, her cell phone rang.

"Oh, come on!" Mazy slammed her hand down on the desk. "Hold the music—Crutch here forgot to turn off her cell phone."

"I am so sorry!" Alecia scrabbled around in her purse, trying to silence the shrill noise. "Here we go. Let me just push…" *Holly,* the caller ID said. Which meant it was an emergency. "Oh, gosh—I have to take this."

"We're going on in ten!" Mazy snapped.

"Ten *minutes*. I need one second!" Alecia flipped open her cell phone. "Holly, I'm about to go on the air."

Mazy held up her hand to block the lights. *"Art?"*

"Oh! Sorry," Holly said. "Just—call me as soon as you're done." Alecia heard the worry in her voice.

"Is Ben okay?"

"He's fine. It's just . . . Di got back from Philadelphia—"

"Philadelphia?"

"Get Art in here, now!" Mazy shouted.

"And now she's being admitted to the hospital. They want to make sure she doesn't have a bleed in her brain."

ONCE AGAIN, THE BLINDNESS didn't last long. By the time we made it back to Pittsburgh and I was in the ER examining room, I could've read the eye chart on the bathroom door if they'd wanted me to, but luckily, no one asked. Instead, a nurse handed me a gown, told me to get undressed, and then left. I slipped it on over my sweater and brown cords. It was cold in the room and, besides, I didn't want Dave to leave just for the sake of my modesty. So far, he'd handled everything: made sure that Max's car seat was secured in his mother's car when she came to pick him up from the ER, that Holly was notified of where we were, and that the triage nurse understood this was the worst headache of my life. (For a little while, the Tylenol had seemed to help, and I was able to make it out of Philadelphia without more than a wince when we hit potholes. By Harrisburg, though, the streetlights were bothering my eyes, and by the time we passed Monroeville, I decided that if I was going to die, it wasn't happening fast enough.) Dave also made sure that the fluorescent lights were turned off, so I could lie in the dark examining room and massage my temples. If my left hand weren't still numb, I would've wanted him to hold it.

A half an hour passed before I heard the swipe of the curtain and footsteps. I opened my eyes just as the lights suddenly blazed on. A tall, blondish guy in a white coat stood beside the bed and stared at me for a moment like I was a problem on a math test—or a giant clothespin that someone had decided was art. He wore dog tags with his blue scrubs, which struck me as odd when, as far as I knew, this wasn't a MASH unit and he looked too young and preppy to have served in a war.

"Can you leave the lights off?" Dave asked.

"It says here you're having 'the worst headache of your life,'" the doctor said, ignoring Dave's request. "Is that true?"

"Well, I've never had one before. So, I'd have to say yes." My speech was slurred more from fatigue than impediment.

"And you've been going blind in the left eye?" I nodded. "Can you cover your right eye for me?" he asked, leaning in toward my face. He was one of those people who couldn't concentrate without looking pissed off. "How many fingers am I holding up?"

Somehow I managed to open my eyes wider. "One."

"Can you follow my finger?" he asked, and I blinked, staring at the name on his coat. *Catalano*.

"Can you follow my finger?" he tried again and then sighed. "You're not following my finger."

"You're Jason Catalano," I realized.

Jason squinted at me as if his glasses were fogging up. "Have we met?"

"At Children's Hospital. You stopped by to visit Gusty."

He snapped and pointed at me. "That's right. You're his nanny!"

"Not anymore," Dave said.

"Gusty doesn't know yet, and I really want to tell him myself. So please don't—ow!" I said, when Jason shined a light in my eyes.

"Don't worry, I never see Gusty," Jason said. I was glad when he tucked his penlight back in his coat pocket. "Look, I'm going to get you something for pain and nausea, hang some IV fluids, and then we'll run some tests."

"I don't have insurance," I blurted when he reached the threshold of the curtain.

Jason shrugged. "So what?"

"See?" Dave said, taking my hand.

ONCE THEY GAVE ME morphine and anti-nausea medication, I didn't care what they did to me or how much it cost. The pain was gone; now all I wanted to do was sleep. If they hadn't kept poking me awake to recheck my neurological exam, or take me to the CT machine, or stick needles into my back to tap my spinal fluid, I might've done just that.

When it was all over, I was finally allowed to sleep, which I did for one blissful hour, until Jason came back in again to tell us the news.

"Well, the preliminary results are looking good," he said, though I wouldn't have been able to tell by the grim expression on his face. "The CT scan was negative, as was the LP, but then I called your PCP, and she gave me a little more of the history."

"My what?" I asked. How many initials had he just used?

"Your primary care physician—Dr. Campbell?" Jason checked his clipboard. I forgot I'd listed Holly on the intake forms. "She told me that you went blind during intercourse last night, and we both agreed that we should keep you in the hospital to run some more tests. In a small percentage of cases, the CT scan is a false negative, and neurological symptoms with intercourse can be a warning sign of a sentinel bleed. You might have a leaking aneurysm."

"Who were you having intercourse with last night?" Dave asked. His voice sounded pleasantly curious, but his eyes looked shocked.

"It wasn't intercourse. She misunderstood."

"Who were you *not* having intercourse with last night?"

I opened my mouth, but before I could speak, Dave's face dropped. "Oh, no. Not *him*."

Jason looked back and forth between us. "I'm sorry, who're you?" he asked Dave.

"The driver," Dave said.

"Do you want him to go?" Jason asked me.

"No, I want him to stay!" I said, my voice cracking.

"Were you in bed with Catalano last night?" Dave asked.

"I was—*on* bed—Holly misunderstood!"

"Wh-hut?" Jason's laugh sounded nervous. He went and yanked the curtain closed again.

"We weren't having sex. I suppose there was some expectation there, but we never did more than kiss."

"Because you went blind?" Dave asked.

"Because I didn't want to!"

"I'm sorry, I'm just—trying to get my head around this." Jason flipped through his clipboard of papers again as if they might contain missing information. Finally, he looked up at me. "You . . . and my father . . . ?"

"Didn't have sex. It was considered and vetoed."

"My God." Jason cupped his palm to the top of his head, as if he were the one having an aneurysm. "He just—comes on to anything that moves! First his best friend's daughter— now the nanny!" He waved a hand toward me.

"Nothing happened."

"You oughta sue," Jason decided, nodding vigorously. "Sue him for sexual harassment!"

"Right, well…it wasn't exactly harassment. At least, it didn't feel that way…." I cringed, wishing the morphine would stop speaking for me, as Dave turned away, shaking his head. "But I really did go blind last night and today," I added. Jason looked at me blankly. "Which is why I'm here. Right now."

It was silent for a moment, until he finally let go of a breath of air. "Well, I'd still prefer we keep you. Just for the night." He sighed again and ran his fingers through his hair. "We should have neurology see you. Find out what's going on. Why you keep going blind." Jason nodded over and over, as if he was trying to convince himself of something.

Once he was gone, I looked at Dave, who was staring at the tile floor and scratching his head.

"Dave, I'm sorry."

He looked up. "I thought nothing was going on with you two."

"He said he wanted to have dinner. I'm the cook."

"So, you had no idea—"

"I had an idea."

That shut him up. His mouth closed, and his hand dropped from the side of his head.

"Hello, hello," sang a large nurse, before pulling back the curtain revealing a gurney and the rest of her behind. Dave turned and stared at the woman as she struggled to get the cart into the room, banging it into the wall and then into an IV pole. "Sir, I'm going to have to ask you to step outside," she finally said, frustrated. "We've got to transfer your wife from that bed to this one and get her upstairs."

"Right. Sure." Dave shook his head and stood up straighter. He looked back at me. "What about Max?"

"I'll send Holly to pick him up from your mom's tonight."

Dave's face wasn't happy. "Whatever you want."

"Sir, you don't have to leave the building, you just have to leave the room," the nurse ordered, practically running over his feet. "I need five minutes. So, step outside."

He nodded and walked away.

After I'd climbed onto the new gurney and watched the nurse gather my "personal effects" into a plastic bag, I pulled the scratchy hospital blanket up to my neck, and they wheeled me into the hallway. Dave, of course, was already gone.

CHAPTER 32

Long Night

It wasn't until Holly had come and gone—reassuring me that it was right to come to the hospital, and right to leave Max alone with her overnight—that I finally took out the composition book that Christine had given me and climbed back into my bed. I'd been too overwhelmed by my father's wardrobe—which had felt like encountering his coffin, if not my own—to even react to the fact that he'd apparently held on to it for over fifteen years. Here it was, one paragraph after another, artfully employing the Vocabulary Words of the Week to describe my daily sixth grade life. Plus, one more, stuffed into the back cover: a letter in my blue-smudged handwriting on a piece of lined paper that was so worn, it had the texture of cloth.

May 4, 1986

Dear Miss Otlin,

I'm very sad to have to write you this letter, but it seems I'll be going away for a while. My dad has sold his practice and is moving to Philadelphia. He wants us to be closer to Christine. He wants me to go, too, even though I'm happy living with Mom and the cats. Because of her mistake, I have to live in the city, and I have to go to Catholic school even though I'm not Catholic or Lutheran or Spiritualist, and I have to wear a uniform with knee-highs and a blazer. Because of her mistake, Mom gets to keep the house but not me. Mom says that she's going to appeal this, and that she doesn't care what anyone says, including the judge, and that no matter what, I belong to her.

You've been the greatest teacher ever.

Sincerely, Di Linzer

I read the last line again, thinking how curiously ominous it sounded, as if I knew I wouldn't see Miss Otlin again. Even stranger, one of the last memories I have of my teacher is combined with one of my father: Field Day at the middle school, just before the mile run. Miss Otlin looked like one of the gym teachers that spring afternoon, wearing shorts and a T-shirt and a whistle around her neck. Just before the race, my father appeared, walking across the grass in his hospital clothes and Birkenstocks—a complete surprise, since he'd told me he was working and couldn't come. When Miss Otlin came over for an introduction, I wished that, if my parents had to be in love with other people, Dad could want to marry my teacher. But, of course, the only person he noticed that day was me—right down to the hangnail on my left pinkie. As other kids stretched and sprinted before the race, my father took out the tiny scissors of his Swiss Army pocketknife and carefully cut the jagged nail of my smallest finger, taking time to blow off the edge and check the angle, the same way he sanded down a fine piece of wood. When he was finished, Dad looked up and smiled, saying, "Now you're ready."

As I clutched my old composition book and paced around my hospital room now, tears pricked my eyes. How could I have known as an eleven-year-old that no one else in the world would ever care about me the way my parents did? How could I have known that the Sixth Grade Mile Run Champion would end up like this—a complete and utter screwup, *alone, alone, alone*? My throat constricted around a sob, and I accidentally gasped.

"I guess I should ask—are you accepting visitors?" someone said from the doorway, and I looked up to see Alecia.

"Oh—hey," I said, somehow coughing instead of crying. I wiped my eye. "I mean, yes. Come in. How did you . . . ?"

"Holly called just as I was about to go on the air." She set her crutches against the wall. "Don't sue. I'm sure it killed her to break the HIPAA law."

"I don't mind." I blinked. "But what are you . . . ?"

"What the hell do you think, Di?" She laughed in disbelief. "You think I'm still mad at you? And even if I was, you think I wouldn't come?"

"No, it's just . . ." I pointed to the wall over her head, where a clock was mounted that read twenty past eleven. "Shouldn't you be on TV right now?"

She shrugged. "I got fired."

"How—*why*?"

"Art said if I left to come here ten minutes before going on the air, I was history."

"Oh, no!" I winced and held my head.

"Are you okay?" Alecia grabbed my shoulder.

"Oh, my God." The room grew blurry as my eyes filled with tears again. "It's all my fault!"

"No, it's not. Calm down. Lie down," Alecia added, leading me back to the bed with a limp.

"They said I still might have an aneurysm which is just leaking little microscopic amounts," I said hopefully, as she pulled back my covers. "If that's true, I still might have to have brain surgery—"

"Di, I don't want you to be dying! Even for my job! Okay?" Alecia snapped.

I nodded and rubbed my temples.

"Is it your head? Do you need something for pain?"

"My head is fine. I just feel terrible. I screwed everything up."

"Di, what's done is done! I left. I got fired. Get over it!"

"Not your job. My life!" I shook the composition book in my hand.

"I can't believe you actually went to Philadelphia," Alecia said. "I thought you were joking."

"I wanted to see Christine." I sniffed. It sounded so stupid now.

"Why?"

"I was looking for Dad," I said, my eyes filling up with tears again. "And he was gone. He's just…gone." Alecia nodded and gulped, then handed me a tissue from the night table. "What if he never forgave me?" I asked, realizing in that very moment that that was the reason I'd dragged Max and Dave all the way to Philadelphia—that was the truth I'd wanted from Christine.

She tilted her head to the side. "Your dad?"

"You said it yourself—I could've come back anytime, and I didn't. He must've hated me!"

"No, sweetie. Not you." Alecia shook her head. "Roxanne, maybe...but not you. There was nothing to forgive you for."

"I disappeared!" I threw my hands up in the air.

"You were caught in the middle. He missed you—but he didn't blame you."

"Yeah, well, I blew it," I said, wiping my nose. "I blew it with my father, with the Catalanos, with Dave ..."

"What did you do to him?" she asked, and I groaned again and told her everything, including my phone call to Holly the night before.

Alecia folded her arms across her chest. "I may not be a doctor, but I do know the difference between lying on a bed and having an orgasm."

"Holly never asked me for details." I sighed. "What do I do now? I can't go back to Auggie's house. And Gusty's going to be crushed."

"Di, the Catalanos aren't your family."

She reminded me of me, telling Gusty that the ICU wasn't his home.

"Christine isn't even your family," she added.

"Well, that was pretty clear." I shook my head and exhaled, wiping away another tear. "She told me that your mom and my mom kissed."

Alecia's eyebrows went up. "That's weird."

"Worse than weird." I reached for another tissue.

"Although..." She bit her lip, considering this. "Not entirely unexpected. I read my mother's diary. She seemed to think that Roxanne was the only one who cared about her." Alecia looked thoughtful, as she stared off behind me. "And

Roxanne always struck me as a little…bored with the whole suburban mom thing. And, of course, curious, adventurous…"

"I could've had a life!" I blurted.

"Yeah, and you wouldn't have Max."

It was true—but why? Why could you only have one beloved thing at the expense of another? Why was my strongest feeling that of missing someone else? It had been this way for too long.

"I am your family. And Max is your family. Shit, at least you've got us," Alecia added, when I started to weep.

"I just want my parents back. I want my life back."

"Yeah, well, this is your life. And at least they loved you."

I blew my nose. "It's not like Aunt Maddie and Uncle Frank don't love you."

"I wasn't saying that. It's just…your parents." She shook her head. "All that love couldn't have stopped when they died."

"But they were the ones who knew me back when I was…me!" I hiccuped.

"I remember you, silly," Alecia said, wrapping her arms around me, which was unfamiliar and unexpected. "I watched you learn to walk. Watched you throw your plastic cup of chocolate milk against the wall, when you were about two. God, I'll never forget the time when your mom handed you a cracker, and you ate it. I was just floored. The *baby* was big enough to eat a *cracker*?"

Chuckling, I wiped my face. Was this what I had needed as much as my father's memory—my own part of our family history? "Thanks," I said with a watery smile, accepting another tissue. She watched as I mopped up my face and blew my nose. "What about Dave?" I finally asked.

She shrugged again. "He'll get over it."

"He doesn't give people second chances."

"Yeah, well, life is about second chances. And *eternal* chances."

"I guess." I sighed and sat back on my pillows. "What about Ben?"

"We haven't talked. I—can't. Yet." Reflexively, Alecia touched her belly. "I don't even feel pregnant anymore."

"Since when?"

"This afternoon." She shook her head. "I have to find a doctor."

"You should still—no matter what..."

"I'll call him. I *will*," she added, meeting my worried eyes. "Look, Di..." Alecia shifted in her seat and glanced away. "I'm sorry. About... well, everything."

"Me, too." I opened my mouth to elaborate and then shut it again. Maybe we didn't need to rehash the worst parts of ourselves. "The good news is Christine gave me my inheritance." I watched as my cousin's eyes grew larger. "Yup. A whole bag of Barbie and Ken dolls, birthday and Christmas presents for every year that I was missing. There's got to be a man in there for Meg."

Alecia snickered. "Is it my fault Punk Rock Ken turned out to be the biggest dud of the century?"

"Yes, it is your fault. You gave him his personality."

"What was wrong with Dream Date Ken, again?" Alecia asked.

"The gymnastics instructor? Secret drug problem." I shook my head sadly.

A moment later, Alecia slapped herself on the forehead. "Hey, I know what you could do for money—sell the dolls on eBay!"

We looked at each other and laughed. Laughed so hard it was as if Alecia hadn't been fired, and Ben hadn't broken up with her, and Aunt Maddie had never left, and my parents weren't dead, and Gusty wasn't a diabetic, and Auggie's sons didn't hate him, and Dave didn't hate me. We laughed so hard that I wasn't in the hospital for potentially having a bleed in my brain. It was just like in Mary Poppins, when they could drink tea in the air, floating on chairs and tables, as long as they kept laughing. If only we never had to land.

CHAPTER 33

Waiting to Find Out

It wasn't just the hard hospital mattress making it difficult for me to sleep that night; it was the constant interruption: heart monitors that beeped out at the nurses' station, a code called on the fifth floor—which sent everyone into a frenzy—and a man down the hall who screamed "Help me!" over and over, and no one seemed to notice. There was one nurse who checked my vitals every six hours, another who performed a neurological exam every four hours, and a phlebotomist, who drew blood at six A.M. just as I felt myself dozing off. By the time the man from dietary (who introduced himself simply as "Dietary") brought me a tray of food, there was no time to eat it because "Transport" had arrived to cart me down to the MRI, where I was expected to lie perfectly still in the tunnel-shaped coffin. Afterwards, I met the echo technician, Lori, who did an ultrasound of my heart. Surprisingly, Lori was a different person than the technician who'd done the ultrasound of my neck last night, who was also different from the man who put tiny pieces of tape connected to wires all over my head for my EEG. By the time I made it back up to my room again for lunch, I'd met a total of ten new people, including the daylight shift of nurses. None of them were doctors, and none of them had any of my test results.

I'd just washed my face and was debating whether to change back into my regular clothes again—*One day,* Holly had promised, *and you'll be released*—when there was a soft knock on my open door. I looked up from the sweater in my hands to see Jason Catalano standing in the doorway.

"How're you feeling?" His voice was tentative and a little weary, but his eyes were surprisingly bright for working late. It must've been the cup of coffee in his hand that kept him going.

"Today? I feel great. Please come in," I added, yanking the back of my gown closed and hopping back into bed. "Tell me you have my test results! Tell me I'm going home."

"That's actually not up to me. And I'm sorry—I don't have any of your results. Once you leave the ER, you're out of my hands." He took a sip of coffee, glanced at the chair by my bed, but remained standing. "I, ah, I wanted you to know . . . I really can't tell my father that I saw you. And I won't."

"Thank you." A flicker of confusion crossed his face. "But I think he misses you," I added. "And so does Gusty."

Jason rolled his eyes. "The kid's going to die one of these times, and he doesn't even care."

"That's because he thinks no one else cares."

"Are you kidding? He's gotten every single thing he's ever wanted!"

"No, he hasn't. He has a lot of things he doesn't care much about. What he really wants is caring parents—maybe even a brother. A family."

"It's too late for that." He shook his head and swigged more coffee.

"The kid is thirteen years old! Don't blame him for your dad's mistakes."

When Jason looked at me again, I could just imagine the barrage of thoughts in his head. "My father makes me sick," he finally said. "It took my mom too long to divorce him. She left him three other times—*three times,* and she went back. Finally, she had the balls to go through with it."

"Do you wish Gusty hated him, too?"

"No. It's great if he and my dad are close. I'm happy for them." His jaw tightened. "I just wish Gusty could see what I see. That Dad takes what he wants from everyone around him no matter what the cost."

"But what did Gusty take from you besides your father?"

Jason stared at me for a second before he laughed bitterly. "I don't think it's that. Gusty just—Gusty's annoying."

"He's a kid. A desperate and lonely kid. And quite a sweet kid, when he's not acting out."

There was a knock at the door, and we both turned. "Dr. Catalano!" said a woman wearing a corduroy jumper, a white blouse, and black flats. She reminded me of a middle school teacher, of Miss Otlin.

"Oh, hey, Leslie." He turned back to me. "Leslie's our social worker here."

"So, you probably don't have my test results, either," I said to Leslie, who shook her head before glancing at Jason.

"I could come back later," she offered.

"Nah. I was just going." Jason stood up. "Good luck to you, Di. Leslie's going to help you get this hospitalization paid for."

"That's great! Oh, Jason—" I called after him. "Do you know anything about this"—I grabbed the notepad by my bed—"Dr. Winters who's coming in to see me?"

"Neurologist. Yeah. She's the best," he added with a smile.

Leslie pulled up a chair and glanced toward the empty

doorway where Jason had just been. "He has to say that," she said in a whisper. "She's his fiancée."

EVEN THOUGH I KEPT telling her that I wasn't disabled—that I couldn't possibly answer the question Explain Why You Can't Work with anything other than: *But I can!*—Leslie insisted I needed to sign up for short-term disability. "You couldn't work while you were here, could you? And we're talking about thousands of dollars in medical expenses. So, this is how you'll qualify for assistance," Leslie said. She asked me lots of questions—about my income and my savings and expenses, about my education or lack thereof. Leslie listened to my answers without judgment.

After she was gone, I thought about it some more, about taking my GED, about going to college and eventually getting a master's degree. But it was hard to imagine that, if Holly were to walk in right now and tell me nothing was wrong, if I suddenly had my whole life handed back to me (and Max), that I'd spend it sitting in a classroom. I would cook for a living, maybe open up my own restaurant someday.

After Dietary stopped in to collect my half-eaten lunch tray, I combed my hair and got dressed in my brown cords and wrinkled sweater from yesterday. It seemed an entire life had been lived in those clothes, and I had the urge never to put them on again.

Somewhere in my purse, my phone began to ring, and I rushed to fish it out.

"Don't you know cell phones are off-limits in the hospital?" It was Gusty, and the sound of his voice made me smile.

"Then why are you calling me on it?"

"I was just testing you." He laughed. "So, is it true? Are you really in the hospital?"

"Unfortunately, yes. How did you hear?"

"My mom told me at breakfast this morning. I guess your cousin left in the middle of the news and she had to do the broadcast by herself. What's wrong with you, anyway?"

"I'm waiting to find out."

"I would come and visit you, but I don't have a ride. Are they going to let you out by Sunday? That's when I get back to my dad's."

"Gusty . . ." I took a deep breath. "I can't—I don't—think I'm working for your father anymore."

There was a short silence. "What do you mean?"

"I won't be there when you get back on Sunday."

"What do you mean?" His voice grew louder. "Why?"

"I got another job." My throat felt tight. "A really great job that I just can't pass up."

"Does my dad know?"

"Not yet." It took all my effort to swallow without crying.

"You can't just leave us!"

"I have to, Gusty. It's a really great opportunity."

"Tell my dad to pay you more!"

"Gusty, I can't." My voice was a whisper. "I want to stay, but I just can't."

"Knock, knock," a voice said, and I looked up to see a petite woman wearing the whitest coat I had ever seen. *Valerie Winters, MD,* her pocket said. *Neurology.*

"I have to go," I said into the phone. "Are you okay?"

"No!"

"Are you going to go back to lunch now?"

"I'm in math class. We're having a pop quiz."

"Well . . . good luck on your quiz." I hung up to find Dr. Winters standing at attention, hands behind her back, chest puffed out. *Do I salute?* "Hi, Dr. Winters. That was Jason's brother," I added. Valerie blinked as if she'd never heard of Gusty or, for that matter, her fiancé.

She finally spoke, her voice flat. "You're dressed."

340 ~ MAGGIE LEFFLER

"Yes, I...am." *Excellent powers of observation,* Alecia
would say. *You must be a neurologist!* If only she were here
right now, cracking the jokes, so that even the bad news
might seem funny. "Is that okay? Am I not going home? Is
there something *wrong?*" My words seemed to tumble over
themselves.

"No, actually. Everything came back normal. You're fine."

"Everything? The MRI and MRA? The...ultrasound of
my neck—the one of my heart"—I snapped my fingers—
"the EEG!"

"All normal."

"So, what's wrong with me?"

"You have atypical migraines. I'm leaving two prescrip-
tions on the front of the chart. Follow up with my office in
two weeks." Valerie handed me a business card.

"But...don't you want to examine me?" I asked.

"Like I said, you're fine."

Fine. Nothing wrong. All normal. I thought of Alecia saying, "This is your life." Why did I feel so empty? "So, what do
I do now?" I asked instead.

Valerie craned her neck forward, as if she hadn't heard me
right. "Go home," she finally sounded out. If only she
could've provided me with an actual address to go along with
the order.

"But why—" *Why is this normal, when everything is all
wrong?* "Why didn't you want me to be wearing my regular
clothes?" I asked instead.

Valerie shrugged. "Usually we like to be the ones to tell
you when you can get dressed."

CHAPTER 34

Amazing Grace

t was three days later, Saturday afternoon—*The Day the Wedding Wasn't,* as Alecia had titled it—and she was making a collage. Max and I had gone out for bagels earlier that morning and came back with breakfast and all of the supplies: scissors, glue, magazines, and poster board. "It's going to make you feel better," I'd said, clearing a space among all the gifts at the dining room table. So far, Alecia had only cut out letters to write swearwords, as if she was planning on composing an obscene ransom note.

"I need to make Dave a pie," I called from the kitchen, as I rummaged through the cabinets looking for ingredients.

"Or you could just go see him," Alecia suggested. For the last seventy-two hours since my release from the hospital, most of our conversations had led back to Dave—how my calls kept getting shunted into voice mail after one ring, how he hadn't returned any of them—how he didn't have any right to be *that* angry. Alecia hadn't been shy about telling me that she was getting sick of it.

"I can't go empty-handed," I said, discovering that we were out of apples, butter, and flour. "We'll walk to Giant Eagle."

"You're stalling," Alecia called after me, as we finally walked out the door.

The truth was, while she was tired of hearing about "Dave this and Dave that," it was still better than having to listen to Alecia's own circular thoughts about Ben, considering what day this was—or wasn't. For as long as Alecia had been wishing I would move out, it was a relief to have me back—to have *us* back, she'd sheepishly confessed. Having a toddler around made it easier to distract herself from everything else that was still at stake—and all she'd lost.

Alecia blinked at her collage, noticing that the letters in the words *fuck, shit, damn, hate,* and *piss* could be rearranged to spell *Past Nate* with just a few leftover letters. If she added *mastorbation* to the list, she could even complete the word *pastor.* Unless it was *masterbation—mastur—*what the hell, she'd make the collage for him. It had to cheer him up.

Once she started paying attention to it, the magazines in front of her were filled with surprising displays of happiness: a white sand beach, two beach chairs, and a beer; a woman in a convertible, her hair flying in the wind; people laughing and jitterbugging, celebrating a pill for bladder control. Alecia was surprised to find her eyes filling up with tears at the image of a mother sponge-bathing her roly-poly baby, while a few pages later, the picture of a microphone in a spotlight on stage didn't move her at all. She cut out a full-page ad for an allergy pill: blue skies, green grass, and petals of dandelion floating around like wishes. Pastor Nate would like that.

It took two more hours to actually finish. She might've been done sooner if she hadn't set up a floor fan too close—

the heat in the building was perpetually set at Mercury temperatures—which whisked her poster board, along with the cutouts, right off the dining room table before anything was glued down. But finally, she secured her last word in the middle of the poster—*FEARLESS*—and then glanced at the clock on the wall. Quarter to two. Right now, she would've been swathed in Vera Wang and waiting with her father in the vestibule of the church, and Ben would've beamed at the sight of her.

ON THE THIRD FLOOR of Shadyside Hospital, she was disappointed to find that Pastor Nate's room was empty except for a janitor mopping the floor. The flowers were gone, the pictures of his grandchildren were taken down, and his bed was made up with fresh sheets. Outside the window, the sky seemed to be gathering itself up for a storm, as clouds scudded overhead like high-speed traffic.

"Did he go home, then?" Alecia asked the man, who slopped brown water all over the floor when he dunked his mop in a rolling bucket.

"You're asking the wrong guy."

Well, good for Pastor Nate, she thought. There was no reason to feel disappointed just because she'd missed him. It was actually better this way. She could drop off the collage at the church, maybe even frame it first, and wrap it up with a Get Well card. The idea made her feel better.

"Can I help you with anything?" someone asked from the doorway.

Alecia turned and flashed her fan-friendly grin to a nurse in purple scrubs. "Oh, probably not. I'm realizing he must've gone home. Pastor Nate?" The woman's eyebrows twitched. "Would you believe I don't even know his last name?"

"And who are you?"

"One of his parishioners."

"I'm so sorry. He"—The nurse glanced at the janitor who was busy sloshing more putrid water all over the floor— "died yesterday."

"*Died?*" Alecia stared. "I thought he was just diagnosed with cancer, like, two weeks ago! I think you must be confusing him with some other patient." The woman shook her head. "He was just here, less than a week ago! I sat in this room! This very room. What *happened?*"

"I'm so sorry," the nurse said.

I WAS SLICING UP Jonagold apples for the pie, and Max was coloring, when Alecia crutched back into the apartment.

"How was Pastor Nate?" I called. She'd left a note on the door.

"He wasn't there."

"Well, I have some bad news." I wiped my hands on a dish towel and came into the living room.

"*No.*" When I opened my mouth to finish, Alecia added, more forcefully, "No more bad news!"

"Car's gone," Max said from the floor, which I'd carpeted with newspaper so the markers wouldn't get everywhere.

She turned and stared—first at him, then at me. "Car's gone? You guys took my car? I thought you were walking!"

"It was too far for Max! I thought you said it was okay—"

"To visit Dave! He was the emergency—not the pie! Jesus, Di, when are you going to grow up?"

It was, unfortunately, a legitimate question. "Well, I left the car in the exit lane when I was unloading groceries. You know, where the curb is yellow?"

"I know what an exit lane is, Di. Why don't you?"

"I'm sorry. I'll . . . get it back." I waited, watching her move to pick up the phone. "Where's Pastor Nate?"

"He died!"

My hand flew up to my mouth.

Alecia picked up the phone and dialed. If anyone answered, it must've been a recording. I watched as her shoulders dropped and her head seemed to sag. She hung up. "The funeral is today." I watched her limp toward the bedroom. "It just seems like some terrible, awful mistake!" She threw her black skirt and sweater on her bed, then opened her dresser and rooted through a drawer of panty hose. Alecia pulled her jeans down, apparently forgetting about the brace covering them, because a moment later she tugged them up again and yanked on the Velcro supporting her knee. "Everyone's dying. Where the hell is God?"

Waiting for us to come around, I thought, leaning against the doorway and watching her change. Instead, I asked, "What are you planning on driving to the funeral?" since she'd just grabbed a set of keys off her dresser.

"Oh, my God." Alecia froze. "I can't go."

"Yes, you can." I led her over to the window and pointed to a glass structure on the side of the street where a few people sat huddled from the cold.

"What's that?" Alecia asked.

"The bus stop."

Alecia made a face. "They look so miserable. I wouldn't know what to do."

"You sit. You wait. Your bus will come." I smiled. "It's easy."

BY THE TIME SHE arrived, the funeral was almost over. The church itself, which should've been packed for her wedding, was standing-room-only for Pastor Nate, whose closed coffin sat at the front of the church, where Alecia and Ben should've been facing him, waiting for him to pronounce them man and wife. There weren't any hymnals, but she raised her voice with everyone else during the final song, "Amazing Grace," until she was overcome by a fit of giggles and had to stop, for fear that it would send her into crying.

Sometimes, as much as anything else, it was perfection that made her laugh at the wrong times. Like the afternoon when she was fifteen, and her tennis instructor told her she'd just hit a miraculous serve, and to duplicate that forevermore, which became impossible, since Alecia found herself laughing so hard that her arms became too weak to hold up a racket. Like the time she tracked Ben down to his apartment in the city, and there he was, run over by life, waiting for her to save him, and she, him. Because she knew they belonged together, from the moment he opened that door with his eyebrows sticking up in all the wrong directions. Like the time Christine openly howled at my father's funeral, when just seconds before, Alecia had been so close to actually screaming at the unfairness of it all—and finally, someone did. And now: the perfection of an entire congregation gathering to mourn and to sing. She closed her eyes and imagined she'd been falling from a burning building, and that the voices had woven themselves into a blanket to catch her. An entire community of strangers grabbed hold to make sure she didn't touch the ground. It was beautiful and miraculous and, like the tennis serve, couldn't be matched.

Outside, it was raining. Stepping aside from the throngs of people filing down the church steps, Alecia looked down at her soggy collage and folded it in half, then quarters, and then squashed it before looking around for a trash can. Someone held a black umbrella over her head, and she felt an arm slip around her back.

"I was wondering if I might find you here," Ben's voice said.

Alecia hesitated and then turned, amazement and relief rushing up to meet him. Considering all that had happened between them, he looked surprisingly normal—same blue eyes, same tousled red hair—surprisingly like himself. It occurred to her then that, just the other day, she'd had the same thought about Pastor Nate. She leaned into Ben. "I went to the hospital this morning, and they told me he'd died."

Ben's eyebrows went up. "You went to visit Pastor Nate at the hospital?"

"Well, yeah..." And then, finally, Alecia started to cry. "I'm sorry." She wiped her eyes. "It's just, I wanted to show him this...." She opened her hands so Ben could see the crumpled collage. "And to hear that he was...after everything that's happened...I feel so..."

"Sad?"

"Yeah, sad." She was glad when he let her bury her face in his black wool coat. It felt so good to smell him again.

Ben wiped her cheek. If he'd noticed her hair was black again or that her knee was in a brace and her wrists were bandaged and casted, he didn't show it. Instead, he seemed to be searching her face. "Can I walk you to your car?" he asked.

"Oh, actually, I took the bus."

"The *bus*?" Ben's eyebrows went up again. The rain was growing thicker, and they couldn't stand on the city sidewalk forever. "Let me drive you home," Ben said, pointing to his car down the block. It was only then that Alecia remembered her crutches she'd left behind in the vestibule of the church. She must not have needed them anymore; her knee was holding up just fine.

He shielded her with the umbrella, and kept his arm on the small of her back as they walked across four cracks in the sidewalk, past three parking meters, and through hundreds of droplets of rain. If only there was some way to keep the

spell of normalcy going—except that there was nothing normal about the fact that this was the day they'd planned to be
married, and Pastor Nate was dead.

When they reached the car, Ben unlocked the side door to
usher her into the passenger seat. She reached to unlock his
door and watched as he moved around the car. The rain was
streaming down the windows, nearly distorting the glass, and
she couldn't see the expression on his face.

"Hey, I think I figured out what that big slab of glass was,"
she said, as he climbed in the driver's side. "The mystery gift?
A cheese platter."

"So, that explains the knife," Ben said.

They sat and stared at each other. He hadn't done more
than put the key in the ignition and turn on the heat, which
fogged up the windshield. "You look good without makeup."

"I look like a ghost." She chuckled unhappily.

"You look like *you*." Reaching for her hand, he seemed
surprised to find it in a splint. "Alecia—"

"I know you know about—the pregnancy," she blurted.

"Yeah, Di's *boss* told me. That was quite the wake-up
call." He closed his eyes and winced. "I've been such an ass.
I'm so sorry."

"I was the one who forged your name on a legal document."

"Yeah, that was a mistake, but that's all it was—a mistake.
You were afraid of your father, and somehow I must've made
you afraid of me or you would've...confronted the situation." Ben's eyebrows furrowed, as he seemed to reconsider.
"Not that I...want you forging anything."

"I never told you that I didn't want children." She glanced
down at their hands, entwined over the emergency brake. "I
kept it from you on purpose, because I was afraid of what it
might mean."

"Yeah..." He sighed. "But I'm the one who needs to get a

career. Shit, I'm thirty-three. I don't know how you've put up with me. All my stupid ideas..."

Later, Ben would say that it had been the meeting with Augustus Catalano that had led him to this realization. For as much as Ben had disliked Auggie for dismissing his dream as naivete—while ostentatiously offering to contribute—Ben appreciated how he must've seemed to Auggie: That he was an immature boy, who'd never support a magazine, much less a family. That, rather than pursuing a higher power, he'd somehow hunted one down and killed it. And that he followed every impulse except the impulse of love.

"Your ideas aren't stupid. And you don't have to get a career. Just don't begrudge me mine."

When Ben looked at her again, really looked at her, she thought of the ease with which Pastor Nate had said, "Not at all," when she'd asked if he thought they were doomed. She remembered the way he'd encouraged her to visit the hospital chapel earlier in the week, how she'd been too afraid of feeling nothing in all the silence. But now, everything was different. The skies were opening up on their heads, and the music was still playing in her ears, and Ben was staring at her with eyes so hopeful and so afraid. "Do you love what you do?" he asked. "Because if the answer is yes, then I'll support you completely. I just never saw your career making you happy."

Maybe not lately, but there was a time when she'd felt exhilaration when they managed to put together a package by deadline that was good. "Well, I got fired, so it's kind of a moot point right now."

His eyes widened. "What'd you do?"

She pointed to her new hair. "That and I left early the night Di was in the hospital."

He nodded toward her leg. "What happened there?"

"I fell down a flight of stairs."

"Did you...is that how...?" He trailed off. "Is that how

you lost the baby, or did you have an abortion?" he finally asked, his voice hoarse.

"I'm still pregnant."

Ben looked up. "I thought—Di said she didn't know. And Holly said you must've . . . and when you didn't return any of my calls, I assumed—"

Alecia shook her head. "I thought about it. A lot. Every day. But at the back of my mind, I kept hearing: 'You *fell* down a flight of stairs, and this *stubborn kid* won't let go.'" Alecia shrugged. "She just kept hanging on."

"She?" He wiped his eyes, and his shoulders were shaking, even as he gave her a smile.

"Well, it's too early to know. But that's what I imagined. Oh, sweetie, don't . . ." she added, pulling his face to hers so she could kiss the tears right off his cheeks. As soon as she licked him, he started to laugh, sheepishly, and she joined in. They sat, arms wrapped around each other, rocking back and forth, as the rain pelted the car with all of its might. *I feel Something!* she wanted to shout, loud enough for Pastor Nate to hear. But somehow, she figured he already knew.

CHAPTER 35

The Burning Tree

n the end, I sent a letter:

> *Dear Auggie,*
>
> *As you may have heard from Gusty, I am unable to re-turn to work this week. ~~I wanted to thank you for making me feel so welcome~~*
> > *~~giving me the opportunity to become part of your family~~*
> > *~~making me your personal cook~~*
>
> *I wanted to thank you for the opportunity to work for you. Gusty is a real pleasure to know, and he's go-ing to be just fine. Enclosed you will find half of the finder's fee, and your cell phone. I'm sorry that I never found you a nanny. Thanks again, for everything.*
>
> *Sincerely,*
> *Di Linzer*

P.S. I will never forget the dinner and the dancing. It made my top five list of Incredible Moments.

P.P.S. Gusty was also hoping that I would mention that he really doesn't want to go to Choate after Shady Side Academy. Please ask him about cyber-school.

It was not an easy thing, sending a letter like that, nor was it easy giving Auggie back the one thousand dollars, when I happened to be thirteen in the hole. But I hadn't made good on anything—not the nanny for Gusty, not the cooking lessons, and not even a real warning of eternity, looming nearby. What had it all amounted to? Just me, leading them on: first Gusty, then Augustus, and finally Dave. That's why I couldn't face them.

MY MOTHER USED TO say that the longer it takes to tell someone you're sorry, the harder it becomes, which was certainly true of Dave and me. "You would think, if he wanted to see me again, he'd call me back," I said to Alecia Saturday evening, as she watched me sift through her wardrobe of sweaters. Thanks to Ben, we had just gotten back from the tow lot to pick up her car. I held up a sage green cashmere crewneck, and before I could ask, Alecia nodded and waved her hand. I slipped the sweater over my head.

"He's waiting for a sign," Alecia said.

I thought of the moment during the lumbar puncture, when Dave was sitting across from me as Jason fished around in my back with an incredibly long needle. "You're doing great, lady," Dave had coached me, squeezing my hands. He hadn't shied away from any of it: the needle, my fear and pain, or the fact that it was, by far, the weirdest first date ever.

I looked down at my brown corduroys and green top. "Do I look too much like a tree?"

Alecia raised her eyebrow. "Maybe you want to look like a tree."

IT WAS A GOOD thing *I* wasn't waiting for a sign, because the one outside of Dave's house said *For Rent,* and the apartment at the top of his stairs was empty.

"He's gone," a voice said as I was crossing the lawn to head back to Alecia's car. I glanced up from the pie in my hands to see Dave's mother, Nancy, sitting on her front stoop. "He took Lacey."

"Lacey," I repeated dumbly, wondering if she was the one with Lee Press-on Nails. Maybe he'd liked the way she scratched his back, after all.

"The dog." When she shook her head, blond curls flopped around her ears. "No one's gonna be around to feed her during the day or take her out for a walk. But he doesn't care. It's *his* dog." She exhaled a mouthful of gray smoke, which was when I noticed her cigarette. "How're *you*?" Nancy added pointedly, making me wonder how much she knew.

"Oh, fine, thanks." I shivered in my jean jacket. The air had finally gotten crisp; it was October, after all. "I, um, brought him this pie. And actually, there's something in the car for you, too." I went back and retrieved the loaf of pumpkin bread that I'd whipped up that afternoon, before Ben came back with Alecia and gave us a ride to the tow yard. "Just to say thanks for watching Max the night I was in the hospital."

Nancy waved the idea away. "He's easy. A good kid." She took another drag on her cigarette. "So do you know what the matter is?"

"Just a migraine, I guess."

"I mean with Dave. He's been a *bear*. I don't even know if he'll show up for brunch tomorrow. He always eats brunch at my daughter's, every Sunday."

"Could I maybe get directions to his new house?"

Nancy hesitated, so she must've known that I was the matter with Dave. But then she glanced down at the pumpkin bread in her lap. "Sure. Let me draw you a map."

NANCY WAS RIGHT. THE drive did take seventeen minutes, out past the winding lanes of Fox Chapel and onto the country roads of Shaler Township. At last, the trees were turning: there were golds, mixed with blood red, mixed with rust. After turning at a cluster of mailboxes marking the end of a gravel road, I followed it to the fork and then took another right onto a bumpy dirt driveway shrouded by trees. It wasn't until I saw the backhoe and the skid loader parked outside a rambling white Victorian house that I knew for sure I was in the right place.

Putting the car in park and switching off the ignition, I waited for my heart to stop turning over, along with the engine. "It'll be fine," Alecia had said earlier, as she shooed me out the door. A promise that I could almost believe, until it occurred to me that she was referring to Max, whom she'd vowed to feed, bathe, and see off to bed. Yes, Max would be fine, but what about Dave?

I gripped the steering wheel with sweaty palms and started my prayer: *Please, please, please*—I stopped, realizing that Dave was on the front porch. He was holding a nail gun and staring at me.

I exhaled and reached for my peace offering before getting out and stumbling my way across the grass toward him and then up the rickety steps of the porch. It was only six-thirty in the evening, but by the stony expression on Dave's unshaven face, I had the sensation that I was very, very late.

"I'm sorry," I blurted, instead of hi.

He nodded, unsmiling. Then, with a shrug: "You told me that you weren't looking for anything."

"But I am. I really am. I—made you this pie."

He looked at it and then up to me. "Thanks."

I opened my mouth, trying to figure out the right words. Instead, all that came out was: "I love your place. And your porch. And all the trees. What're those, hanging over the driveway?" I pointed behind us.

"Siberian elms."

"And—oh!" I gasped at the one in the side yard. It was short and squat with slender, twisting branches and a crown of red-orange leaves, like the one in my dream, except this one looked as if it was on fire. "What's that?"

"A hophornbeam."

"A hophornbeam." It even sounded like it belonged in Narnia. And when I blinked, for just a second, I could even see four children playing in that tree—Max and three others, hiding and seeking and just shrieking with glee. One of them had Ben's red hair and freckles and Alecia's devilish laugh: *Baby Meg.* I glanced back at Dave, who was watching me, but at least his face had softened a little, as if he didn't know what to think.

"Did they find out what was wrong with you?" he finally asked.

"Atypical migraines. Apparently, it's nothing to worry about."

"Well, that's reassuring," he said.

I looked down at my clogs for a moment. "Do you hate me?"

He shrugged again. "Kinda hard to."

"Do you want to put down the nail gun?"

"You gonna put down the pie?"

I set it down on the porch as he lowered the gun. "I'm so sorry."

Dave studied me for a second before nodding. "I know."

"I should've told you everything, but I was embarrassed and ashamed. And I didn't want you to think . . . less of me."

"Catalano's the one who should be ashamed. He knew exactly what he was doing."

"It was my fault for being there in the first place. And you were right—I shouldn't have gone for a guy like him." I stepped closer. "Can we . . . start over?"

Dave swallowed. "I don't want to start over. I want to start where we left off."

I raised my hand, the one that could crush men to bits, and put it over his heart. He picked it up and, for just a second, touched the tips of my fingers to his lips.

I stepped closer still, until we were close enough to rub noses. "Can I hug you?"

"I'm, uh, really dirty."

I wrapped my arms around him, rested my chin on his shoulder, and waited for him to let go of the breath he was holding. Finally, he exhaled, and we settled against each other like melting glaciers, his sweaty T-shirt soaking into my sweater.

"Ow," I said, tapping on the round container of Copenhagen in the pocket of his T-shirt.

"Sorry. I've been"—he shook his head, tossing the tobacco to the floor of the porch—"out of control. Chewing, like, a can a day. Normally one lasts me a week."

"Please. Quit."

He nodded. "Okay."

Dave drew me back to him, his arms clinging to my back, his breaths easing into sighs. Minutes passed, possibly hours, as we stood, holding each other, until something tickled the back of my leg, and I jumped, thinking it was an animal. A moment later, I screamed, realizing it was an animal, and she was eating my apple pie.

"Lacey, no!" Dave shouted, but it was too late, the dog had already licked the entire top layer of crust.

"It's okay; it's okay," I said, as he dragged her off the pie and scolded her back into the house. "We can still do dinner."

"All I've got is beer."

"I brought groceries. I'll cook for you. Is that—okay?"

"Yeah, I just . . . have no idea where my kitchen stuff went." He scratched his head. "Everything's in boxes."

"So, I'll start looking while you shower."

Dave grinned and nodded at my sweater, damp beneath my open jacket. "You might need one, too, after that hug."

I smiled and looked away, jerking my head toward the car, where the groceries were. "Help me carry?"

Lacey barked through the screen door as we ambled across the lawn, side by side, acorns crunching beneath our feet. "Out of curiosity," Dave said, hands in the pockets of his jeans. "Did they give you something to prevent those migraines?"

"Yeah."

He smiled. "Glad to hear it."

Epilogue

In early November, I called Leslie, the social worker, to ask what the status was on my short-term disability claim. I hadn't heard from the department of welfare—had she?

"But your bill has been paid," Leslie said, surprised. "Someone sent in the money through the hospital foundation. It was earmarked for you."

I blinked. "So . . . what do I owe?"

"Nothing."

"Nothing?"

"The hospital received a check for . . . twelve thousand, six hundred and sixty-five dollars and forty eight cents. Which means your bill is all taken care of."

I thought of Auggie, spinning me around in the marble foyer, as we laughed our heads off. "Who—"

"He did not wish to be named."

I prefer my random acts of kindness to be anonymous, Auggie had told me over our first cooking lesson. I thanked Leslie and hung up.

IT WAS APRIL, seven months later, the first sunny day that I had seen in a while, and it was warm—just fifty-five degrees, but after the winter, it felt like eighty. Walking up to the café in Shadyside, I felt light, the spring air in my nostrils and the breeze at my back. Signs of spring were everywhere: crocuses and even some daffodils pushing their way out of the ground, and a suicidal Rollerblader kamikaze-ing toward me on Ellsworth Avenue. He was wearing shorts but didn't have knee pads or a helmet. *In about one more pothole, he won't have a face, either,* Alecia would say. Someone waved from one of the tables outside of Café Zinho, and I held up my hand to shield my face from the sun. The pregnant ladies were already there.

"I'm telling Holly about Art," Alecia said when I pulled up a chair. She wore jeans and one of her sexier maternity shirts: black scooped neck, and form-fitting. Alecia had told me that this was the only time in her life she was going to have actual breasts so she might as well accentuate the positive. She was nine months along and absolutely radiant.

Holly, on the other hand, looked pale and nauseated, yet wore a new, sly smile, as if she were under a spell. (She had simply nodded *Yes,* when I'd asked if my hunch was true, as if voicing her secret would make it disappear: the IVF had worked. She was due in the fall.)

"So, I'm thinking he's heard through the grapevine that I was in talks with KDKA, right? And that he had some beef with my restrictive covenant?" Alecia was saying. "But no—he wants to offer me my job back. Evening anchor!"

"Alecia, that's great!" Holly said, swallowing a mouthful of bread or possibly—since I didn't see an actual loaf on the table—bile. "Or...isn't it?" she added, catching sight of Alecia's face.

"Well, I don't know. Five nights a week, smiling next to Mazy Roberts?"

"It's called acting," I said, reaching for one of the menus.

"That woman had me *fired*. Art said so himself."

"What happened to...?" Holly used her index finger to draw an imaginary circle around her own face.

"Heidi?" Alecia asked, apparently understanding sign language for Big Head. "Mazy got her an anchoring job at another station—in Kentucky!" She cackled. "And Vanessa's staying home with her baby."

"Good for her," Holly said, taking a small sip of water. "What'd you tell Art?"

"That I'd let him know by next week." Alecia shrugged as she closed her menu. "Ben's not crazy about the idea."

"Because of *The Burning Tree*?" I asked. For the last several months Alecia had made a job out of fund-raising for Ben's magazine—had managed to raise four grand, which still left them ninety-six thousand dollars away from the goal. For now, Ben kept his day job, teaching, and devoted his evenings to his website, "The Burning Tree Blog."

"Because of—everything. I mean, if I knew it would make me happy..." She trailed off, then glanced around. "Everyone else is eating bread. Where's our bread? What the hell happened to our waitress?"

"Over there," Holly said, nodding in the direction of another table. "Chatting with George Clooney. We can forget lunch."

I swiveled around in my seat. There was the server—blond ponytail, black T-shirt, little white apron—and there, looking fully engaged in her description of the specials, was Jason.

"Wait—isn't that...?" Holly realized, in nearly the same moment.

"Auggie's oldest son," I said with a nod.

"He looks different in contact lenses," she said.

"How is Auggie doing? Didn't Gusty say he was sick?" Alecia asked.

"He had a heart attack—on the golf course last fall," I whispered. "He's actually doing well now." So, I had been both right and wrong: his heart hadn't taken his life, though he had been on the verge of losing it. "And Gusty said his father and Jason have sort of . . . reconciled," I added.

"Well, stop staring, for Christ's sakes!" Alecia said. Holly obeyed, but I couldn't turn away. It wasn't because out of the hospital and out of the glasses Jason looked like his father. It was because of the gift. It was because I'd never thanked Auggie.

"Dr. Catalano took care of Di in the hospital," Holly whispered to Alecia. And then, to me, she added, "We can leave, if you feel uncomfortable."

"We're not leaving. I'm *starving*," Alecia said.

Ponytail was laughing her head off at something he'd said—a joke about polenta? Was that possible? Gusty had told me that Jason had called off his wedding to Dr. Valerie Winters, which may have accounted for his new look— leather jacket, jeans—and the honesty of his smile, which wasn't even for the waitress. I turned to follow his gaze. "And . . . there's . . . Auggie," I said, wishing I could hide. To get to Jason, he would have to pass our table. "I never thanked him for the money," I added, biting my lip.

"You never sent Auggie a thank-you letter?" Holly asked in a voice so horrified that I suddenly felt awful.

"It was an anonymous donation, remember? 'He did not wish to be named.' For all I knew it was Uncle Frank!"

"It wasn't." Alecia crunched on an ice cube. "I asked."

Holly shook her head dolefully and then glanced at Alecia. "She has to say something."

"Send the man some flowers. Don't accost him at a restaurant," Alecia replied, just as Auggie stopped walking two feet from our table and spun around.

"It's you," he said, bewildered. He looked thinner now, but still striking, in jeans and a white oxford shirt.

"It's me." I nodded sheepishly. "These are my friends," I added, gesturing to Alecia and Holly, who waved.

"Ladies," he said with a cursory nod, just like that day in the flower shop. "Have a wonderful lunch." He turned to resume his stride.

"Thank you!" I blurted, heaving my words at him like a medicine ball—or, given his openmouthed expression, a pie in the face.

"Oh, no..." Alecia muttered, accidentally kicking the table instead of me. There was a splash of ice water, a clink of silverware, and Auggie's blue eyes darted around, as if he might be embarrassed.

"Leslie, the social worker, said that someone paid off my hospital bill—all thirteen thousand dollars of it!"

He stared at me, as if debating whether to admit it, and the corner of his mouth turned up, just slightly, enough for me to know the truth. At last, he shook his head. "Di, I'm afraid that I have no idea what you're talking about. But I'm happy things worked out for you."

As he walked off to join his son, I felt elated, and I couldn't have immediately said why. Maybe it was because Jason had given his father another chance. Or maybe it was because if I couldn't accurately predict the future—and couldn't hope to change the past—it was time to let them both go. It felt good, too: the grace of right now.

"Are you happy now?" Alecia grumbled to Holly, who closed her eyes and laughed. A moment later, as our waitress finally approached, Alecia's face relaxed into a smile. "Bread!" she said with a squeal.

IT WAS ONLY A few days later that I was met with another surprise when I opened up Dave's front door and found Mazy Roberts standing on his porch. She wore a blue silk sweater underneath a taupe suit with a string of pearls. I wore a tank top beneath my overalls and a key—Dave's key—on a piece of yarn around my neck. "Oh! I—hi!" I stammered, staring at her through the screen door as if she were a Jehovah's Witness. It was my twenty-ninth birthday. I'd been waiting for Alecia to show up.

"Di. Congratulations." Mazy's nod was stiff and awkward: she might have been offering condolences. "Gusty tells me you're getting married."

"Eventually," I said. We had picked neither a date, nor a ring, but when Max and I moved in after Christmas, Dave began discussing it as if it were an assumption. "Please, come in!" I remembered, finally opening the door. "You must be looking for Gusty."

When she tentatively stepped inside the foyer, wooden floorboards creaked beneath her high heels. Then she followed me, as I led the way to the living room. I couldn't help thinking how odd this was—odd that she'd never been here before, and odd because she was here now. It was like the day we'd met, in reverse.

"As you can see, we've got a lot of work to do!" I said, ducking my head beneath a lightbulb that dangled on a wire. "Watch your step!" I added, before she could trip over a can of paint. Mazy's laugh was nervous, as if she were on a haunted mansion ride at Fun Land.

In the living room, the Pro Lawn Service team was busy painting the walls blue and debating the merits of each Star Wars movie. Gusty was voting for *Return of the Jedi* as the all-time best—for the Ewoks.

"Fuck the Ewoks," TJ was saying. "They have no penises. I mean, bears have dicks, right?"

"Well, they aren't bears!" Gusty said, waving his arm emphatically and splattering paint all over the tarp in the process. "They probably have a different way of mating!"

I coughed. "Um, Gusty?"

He turned, and, at the sight of Mazy, his eyes widened with surprise and, possibly, panic. "Mom!"

"Hello, Gusty. Gentlemen," she added, with a nod to TJ and Hobbes. "You have your class today, Gusty," Mazy said, tapping her watch. This was the spring his parents had decided to send him to PSAT prep. The kid was only finishing ninth grade, but they wanted to make sure he'd be a National Merit Scholar by junior year.

"I told you—Dave's gonna take me. Dad's gonna pick me up after."

"I thought maybe I would give you a ride today."

"But, Mom—"

"Aren't you going to introduce me to your friends?" she interrupted, her voice suddenly turning several shades brighter.

Gusty hesitated for just a second and looked between his buddies. "This is TJ," he finally said. "He can pick up railroad ties with his pinkie finger."

TJ grinned wickedly, and wiggled his pinkie.

"And this is Hobbes. He can...twirl pencils with one hand!"

Hobbes looked amused. "You calling me weak, Clarabell?"

If Mazy was perturbed by her son's stupid nickname or that he spent hours at our house after school and on the weekends, working for Dave and discussing Ewok anatomy, she never let on. After all, Gusty hadn't been in the hospital in five months. The woman had to be grateful.

"I was thinking that maybe you and I could grab some lunch," Mazy said presently, checking her watch again. It was just shortly after noon.

"Mom, I'm at work," Gusty said. "Dave's *paying* me to paint this room."

"Well, I just thought—"

"I want to stay, Mom!"

"Where's the birthday queen?" Alecia suddenly called, sticking her head into the doorway of the living room. Her cheerful expression seemed to stop short when she saw Mazy Roberts whirl around.

"Alecia—my goodness," Mazy said, her eyebrows shooting up. "You look different. When are you due?"

"Next week." Alecia had told me just the other day that when Ben had run his fingers through her short hair, she'd never felt more intriguing. Now, she began to fidget under Mazy's stare of disbelief. *For God's sakes,* she would probably say later. *I don't even have a belly button anymore!*

"What're you having?" Mazy asked.

"My husband thinks it's one of the few surprises we have left in life and refuses to let us find out." Alecia rolled her eyes.

"So, you did get married, after all," Mazy said.

"Just a small thing." They'd done it at Hartwood Acres, on a freakishly warm day in November, with Ben in his khaki suit and both of their fathers, Dave, and me as witnesses. Fran from the station even wept, possibly over the miracle that, after significant alterations, Alecia had managed to squeeze herself into the Vera Wang dress. Presently, she shot me a glance: *Let's go, already!*

"I just have to grab my purse," I said.

"No, you don't. It's your birthday."

"Then let me just say goodbye to Max. No paint fights, okay, guys?" I added, since it was just yesterday that I'd gotten home from work—making desserts at the Oakmont Bakery—and caught them pretending their brushes were light sabers.

"Okay, *Diotima*," Gusty said. I was already out the door, when I heard him say, "No, it's her *real* name. Something from Plato."

On the back porch, Dave and Max were brandishing power tools. Dave: an electric sander; Max: a tiny, handheld drill.

"Look, Mama!" he said, holding it steady. "I help fix!"

"What happened to Fisher-Price?" I asked Dave.

He looked sheepish. "The drill was just his size. And he's wearing goggles."

"No chain saws, okay? Or nail guns."

Dave grinned and kissed me. "He's fine. We're fine. Have fun."

Back inside, Mazy and Alecia were engaged in a quiet conference in the front hall. I hesitated just over the threshold. "You can take all the time you need," Mazy was saying.

"I don't need more time," Alecia said. "I've thought it through." Catching sight of me in the doorway, she smiled. "Ready?"

"Ready." I patted my sides where my purse should've been before remembering Alecia was treating. "Where's Gusty?" I asked Mazy, since she seemed to be moving toward the door with us.

"He wants to stay." Her voice was perplexed. "So..." She sighed. "I'm letting him stay."

"What was up with Mazy?" I asked Alecia, minutes later, once we were alone in the car.

"She wanted to welcome me back to the station." Her voice was dubious. "She said she'd only had me fired because she was going through an 'ugly divorce' at the time, and that you and I were somehow caught in the middle of it. She said she was sorry—or at least, I think she meant to..." Alecia glanced at me uncertainly.

"And you told her 'thanks, but no thanks'?"

"I told her yes. Actually." She kept her eyes on the exit

ramp. "But not to anchoring. I want to come back as a reporter sometime in the fall." Alecia smiled. "Art always said I was one of his best."

"Well, that's great!" I grinned, settling back in my seat. We were crossing over the Highland Park Bridge. "Where are you taking me, by the way?"

Beneath her movie star sunglasses, her grin was sly. "You'll see."

"Let me guess: Banana Republic for a new wardrobe? Or a salon for a makeover?"

"You don't need a makeover, Di."

"Really?" I said, flattered.

She just laughed and merged onto Washington Avenue, and we were off to Shadyside, I assumed until, not even a mile later, she took a left up a hill, so steep it was reminiscent of a roller-coaster ride. Behind us, the sky was still bright enough to make you squint, but just ahead, dark clouds were gathering at the peak. "Lincoln Lemington," she said, waving her hand in the general direction of the run-down houses out my window.

"Sounds familiar..." I said uneasily, both because of the impending rain and because I was pretty sure the neighborhood had been featured on the news for a recent shooting. The cluster of clouds looming over the summit was so mesmerizing, however, that it wasn't until we reached the top of the hill that I even noticed the little white church perched at the top.

"I think I've been here before!" I slowly realized, as Alecia turned off the main road and drove down the wooded lane toward the steeple. To the right of the church, and over the hill behind it, was the cemetery. Surrounded by stone fences, hundreds of tombstones were erected in grass that was so green, we could've been in Ireland. Alecia put the car in park and faced me again. "I thought we oughta visit the family."

"It was when Grampa died," I said, minutes later, as we walked around the myriad graves, looking for the ones marked with my last name: Linzer. "We'd just arrived at the Jersey shore when Dad got the phone call, and we had to go all the way back. It took us almost double the time—ten hours—because I left my doll, Katie, at that rest stop outside of Hoboken, and we went all the way back for her. Of course, she was never seen again." I shook my head.

If Alecia noticed that I'd been sadder about the loss of my Skipper doll than the loss of our grandfather, she didn't say. "Wasn't that the reason Uncle Gabe got you Jean, though?" Alecia remembered. "Because then Meg finally had a friend, rather than a little sister. It was like—you grew up."

It was—and not just because my new Barbie doll had breasts. I was ten years old, and it was the spring before my parents' divorce. I'd never been confronted with death, or its aftermath. It was the first time I'd ever seen an actual dead body—which looked more like a puppet wearing blush than an actual man—the first time I'd ever seen price tags on someone's personal things. Somehow, the estate sale had managed to shock me more than the open casket.

"The last time I was here, it was raining, too," I added, as the first drops began to fall. I would never forget how my father and I had wandered around and checked out the gravestones—the same way Alecia and I were doing right now. I was very aware of the grass, how it squished beneath my feet with every step. When I asked my father where the rest of the family plots were, he waved his arm in a big circle.

"Do you have any idea where they are?"

"Not at all," Alecia admitted with a laugh. She pointed at

a pair of tombstones leaning toward each other, like lovers. "Check it out. 'Harold and Maude.' " She glanced at me. "Wasn't that a movie?"

My foot caught on a nearby square stone engraved with the name *William Wojtzcak* and the dates *1903–1906*. "Look. He was only three," I said, crouching down to clear off some of the weeds growing over the gravestone.

Her hair was wet, but Alecia looked up at the clouds as if she'd just noticed the rain. Then she knelt down beside me and pulled up a fistful of dandelions covering the little boy's grave. "Why was your father so intent on being buried in Pittsburgh, anyway? He hadn't lived here for almost fifteen years."

"Probably because his mother made him promise. You don't know this story?" I told her how our grandfather, a door-to-door salesman, talked our grandmother into buying six funeral plots, even though she didn't even have six people in her family to bury. " 'For your children and their children,' he had said. And Hazel thought Jacob was so handsome, she bought them." Alecia snorted with laughter. "When Dad told me the story, I remember thinking, 'Even if I move to Tanzania someday, I am going to be buried in Pittsburgh, Pennsylvania.' "

"And here we are," Alecia said, her voice wry. She used my shoulder to push herself into standing.

I got up, too, and then we stood there not saying anything, just staring at the land, at the spaces that were left. It began to rain harder, but the air was humid enough that even in my tank top, it felt good. Neither one of us acknowledged that we couldn't seem to find the family. It seemed beside the point.

Finally, Alecia turned and gave me a smile. "You realize, don't you, that twenty-nine is the age you're going to be forever? This just happens to be the only time that you won't be lying."

I chuckled and then, a moment later, remembered that it was the same trip to the Jersey shore when my father had caught me lying to a waitress at Friendly's about my age. "I pretended to be nine when I was nearly eleven," I said to Alecia. "When Dad asked me why, I told him that I didn't want to be ten, that nine was the perfect age and the perfect odd number, and that I was sorry I couldn't stay nine forever. Dad asked what being older meant to me, and I said that you have to pay for groceries, and you have to write checks, and you have to be busy all the time, until you get cancer and then you die. He asked me why I was afraid of dying, and then I started to cry and said that I wouldn't be able to taste my food anymore."

Alecia tilted her head back and laughed.

My father had laughed, too, in the gentle way that he did, where very little sound came out, but the smile spreading all over his face was a big one. He told me he was laughing because he was thinking of something. Then his shoulders shook some more. I had to wait several minutes before I got to find out what he was thinking of, which turned out to be us. "I'm just so happy you're here with me right now," he'd said, reaching over to squeeze my hand.

At the memory, my own hand twitched closed. I glanced down, surprised for just a second. Then I reached out for Alecia's wrist and gave it a squeeze. "Thanks."

She looked at me and smiled. "Happy birthday."

Your family will find you, my mother used to say, and I'm starting to realize this is true. Maybe it turns out that when my parents got out of the car a few years ago I wasn't really alone after all. Or I was—but waited long enough to let the car fill up with other people who mattered. And maybe it turns out, when we get to the end, God just watches as the car unloads, and one by one we untangle ourselves and crawl out, and laugh, and shake off, and that's when I get to see that my parents were still in the car all along, and they already know who I've married, and they already know my children, and they already know that I am all right.

Acknowledgments

This book would not be a book if it weren't for my editor, Caitlin Alexander, who read draft after draft and made spot-on suggestions— thanks for your insight, encouragement, and goodwill. Thanks also to my agent, Jodie Rhodes, who found this manuscript a home before it even existed.

This book would not be a book if it weren't for my writers' group, "The Nomadic Scribes" (or, as Jen once called us, "CSI Fiction")— Cindy McKay, Scott Smith, Mike Murray, Eric Ruka, Joe Balaban, Irina Reyn, and Jen Bannan—thanks for your expert advice, great laughs, and bottles of wine.

This book would not be a book if it weren't for the help of my in-laws, Chris and Sue Martin, who enthusiastically watched my sons to give me time to write.

I am also grateful to Shannon Perrine, a wonderful friend, who took me to work with her for the sake of my research. (And thanks to the folks at WTAE, who even let me sit behind the news desk so that I could be further amazed by all that goes into creating a top-notch broadcast. Rest assured that these characters and all of their shenanigans are purely from my imagination.) Thanks to my sister, Katherine Brown, for brainstorming the arc of the novel, and to Elizabeth Finan, for being like another sister to me. Thanks to Many Ly, for her careful critique of an earlier draft, and to my old friend Dave Black, who gave me a job—and landscaping material—one summer. I hope things turned out happy for you. A special acknowledgment to my elementary school mate, Gusty Collangelo the IV, for having a great name, and all of my teachers along the way—what a difference you've made.

Thanks to my sons, Jacob and Owen—such little boys, such huge inspirations. Most of all, thank you to Tim Martin, my husband, my love, for more reasons than I can write.

About the Author

Maggie Leffler is a family practice physician who lives in Pittsburgh with her husband and sons.